SCHAUMBURG T
3 1257 01568 2767
W9-AVM-472

WITHDRAWN

Schaumburg Township District Library
130 South Roselle Road
Schaumburg, Illinois 60193

Schaumburg Township
District Library
schaumburglibrary.org
Renewals: (847) 923-3158

BEYOND COMPARE

Also by Candace Camp in Large Print:

Mesmerized
Secrets of the Heart

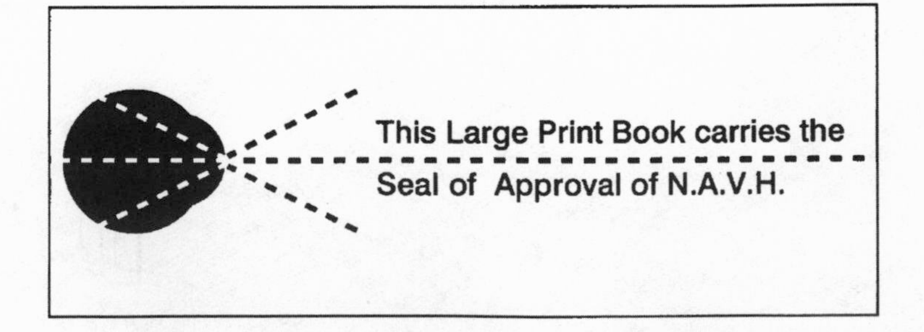

BEYOND COMPARE

WITHDRAWN

CANDACE CAMP

Thorndike Press • Waterville, Maine

SCHAUMBURG TOWNSHIP DISTRICT LIBRARY
130 SOUTH ROSELLE ROAD
SCHAUMBURG, ILLINOIS 60193

10/04
Gale
$30-
N

LARGE TYPE
F
CAMP, C

3 1257 01568 2767

Copyright © 2004 by Candace Camp.

All rights reserved.

All characters in this book have no existence outside the imagination of the author and have no relation whatsoever to anyone bearing the same name or names. They are not even distantly inspired by any individual known or unknown to the author, and all incidents are pure invention.

Published in 2004 by arrangement with Harlequin Books S.A.

Thorndike Press® Large Print Core.

The tree indicium is a trademark of Thorndike Press.

The text of this Large Print edition is unabridged.
Other aspects of the book may vary from the original edition.

Set in 16 pt. Plantin.

Printed in the United States on permanent paper.

Library of Congress Cataloging-in-Publication Data

Camp, Candace.
Beyond compare / Candace Camp.
p. cm.
ISBN 0-7862-6866-2 (lg. print : hc : alk. paper)
1. Americans — England — Fiction. 2. London (England) — Fiction. 3. Antiquities — Fiction. 4. Large type books. I. Title.
PS3553.A4374B49 2004
813′.54—dc22 2004053745

For STACY,
my favorite redhead.

National Association for Visually Handicapped
serving the partially seeing

As the Founder/CEO of NAVH, the only national health agency solely devoted to those who, although not totally blind, have an eye disease which could lead to serious visual impairment, I am pleased to recognize Thorndike Press* as one of the leading publishers in the large print field.

Founded in 1954 in San Francisco to prepare large print textbooks for partially seeing children, NAVH became the pioneer and standard setting agency in the preparation of large type.

Today, those publishers who meet our standards carry the prestigious "Seal of Approval" indicating high quality large print. We are delighted that Thorndike Press is one of the publishers whose titles meet these standards. We are also pleased to recognize the significant contribution Thorndike Press is making in this important and growing field.

Lorraine H. Marchi, L.H.D.
Founder/CEO
NAVH

* Thorndike Press encompasses the following imprints: Thorndike, Wheeler, Walker and Large Pr int Press.

1

Kyria was in the grand ballroom when she heard the shrieks. High and piercing, they sounded as if they came from some distance, or perhaps from the floor above. Kyria had been discussing with Smeggars, the butler, the placement of flower arrangements for the reception after Olivia's wedding. At the screams, she raised her head, listening, then cut her eyes toward Smeggars. He gazed back at her, his controlled face twitching just a fraction in a way that told Kyria he was thinking the same thing she was: the twins were at it again.

Sighing, Kyria turned away from her task and walked out into the hall, Smeggars following. She started down the hall toward the staircase, then broke into a trot when more screams and cries erupted. She hurried up the staircase, lifting her skirts to keep from tripping. On the second floor, she saw one of the upstairs maids at the far end of the hall, sitting on the floor with her hands to her head, having hysterics. Another maid stood over her, trying alternately to pull her up and soothe her. A footman and a parlor maid were rushing into the grand drawing room, the one they had been using the most this week because of the number of guests here for the wedding.

The arrangements for her sister's wedding had fallen, as most social things tended to do in this family, to Kyria's lot. Her father, the duke, appalled at the number of people invading his usually quiet domain, had retreated to his workshop out back, where he could putter about with his pots and shards to his heart's content. The duchess, who found most members of her social class empty-headed and unaware, had no interest in entertaining their guests, and domestic arrangements bored her. If she did from time to time decide to discuss menus or housing guests or other such things with the servants, she was apt to wander far afield into a discussion of the appalling conditions of the serving class in Britain and the efforts the servants should make to rebel against their lot. At the end of such discourses, the servants were generally left confused and the duchess irritated.

Thisbe, of course, being the eldest sister, might have been expected to be the one to take over such arrangements, but Thisbe was far more interested in her scientific experiments. And one would have been excused for assuming that in this particular instance, a wedding, it would have been the bride who'd be intimately involved in the planning and execution of the plans. However, Olivia had reacted with a horror greater than her father's at the prospect of the invasion of guests. So it was Kyria to whom the housekeeper and butler turned for orders, and it was she who had spent the past week arranging for food and lodging for a large number of guests, many of whom had brought along a servant or two. It was also she who was left the task of seeing that their guests were kept suitably entertained while at the same time she made arrangements for a wedding. Others might have been daunted by the task, but it was the sort of challenge Kyria thrived upon.

There were moments, of course, when she did wish that the twins had not seen fit to add to the challenge.

She hurried after the maid and footman into the drawing room. Inside the long, elegant room, pandemonium reigned. Lady Marcross had fainted dead away in one of the chairs, and the Countess St. Leger, the bridegroom's mother, was bending over Lady Marcross, chafing her wrists and fanning her with a handkerchief. Miss Wilhemina Hatcher, one of the many Moreland cousins, and another woman Kyria did not recognize had both jumped to their feet, overturning a stool and a spindly legged table, and were clutching each other and babbling hysterically. Lord Marcross was shaking his fist at the ceiling, while the maid and footman hurried around the room anxiously, hands and faces raised, calling, "Here, birdie! Here, Wellie!"

Old Lord Penhurst, deaf as a post, had his ear trumpet to his ear. His daughter was yelling into it, trying to explain to him what had happened, and periodically, over the hubbub, the old man's voice rose in a querulous cry of "What? Speak up, girl, dammit!"

Just past him Lady Rochester, almost Lord Penhurst's equal in years, thudded her cane down with authority, exclaiming, "Stop that noise this instant, Wilhemina!"

Kyria took in the scene in a glance. It was not immediately apparent what had caused the commotion, but she lifted her gaze, following the servants' and Lord Marcross's example, and there she saw the parrot, perched on the drapery rod above one of the west windows, a vivid orange-red bird, his blue wings tucked at his side, his head cocked as his bright eye took in the situation below him.

"Wellington!" Kyria grimaced. She raised her hands, gesturing for calm. "All right, everyone, there's no need to panic. It's nothing — just the twins' parrot." Lord Marcross harrumphed. "Damn fool pet, if you ask me."

"Well, don't just stand there, girl," Lady Rochester demanded of Kyria, bringing her cane down again for emphasis. "Do something!"

Lady Rochester, Kyria's great-aunt, was a fierce old woman who had dressed for the past thirty years in black, less because of her grief over her long-dead husband's demise than because she considered black a flattering color for her pale skin. From a portrait of the lady in her youth, Kyria knew she had once been a beauty, but little was left of that beauty now in her aged face, topped bizarrely by a wig colored as deep a black as her dress — not, of course, that anyone would have dared to call it a wig to her face. Lady Rochester was possessed of a razor-sharp tongue, which she never hesitated to use on those around her. She was one of the few people capable of making Kyria feel like a gauche young girl again.

Kyria put a pleasant smile on her face and said, “Yes, of course, I will.” She turned again toward the others, saying, “Now if everyone will just be quiet . . .”

She tilted her head up, saying, “Here, Wellie!” She patted her shoulder as she had seen Alex and Con do many times with the bird. “Come here and we’ll get you a treat.”

The parrot twisted his head first one way, then the other, observing her, Kyria thought, with a definite gleam of mischief. He let out a piercing squawk, followed by the words, “Treat! Wellie treat.”

“That’s right. Wellie treat,” Kyria said in a singsong voice, patting her shoulder again.

The parrot let out another squawk, then took off from his perch. Swooping down, he dug his claws into Lady Rochester’s hair and flew on, the intricate black wig dangling from his claws. Lady Rochester let out a squawk to rival the bird’s, clapping her hands to her head. The sight of Lady Rochester’s naked head was enough to send Cousin Wilhemina and her companion into hysterics again, and across the room old Lord Penhurst burst into a loud cackle of laughter.

Kyria clamped her lips shut over the

giggle that threatened to rise from her throat and ran after the bird, followed by the maid and the footman. Wellington led them along the corridor and down the front stairs. Kyria clattered down after them, the train of followers behind her growing as guests and servants joined the chase.

Cousin Albert walked through the front door at that moment and stood gaping at the sight of the crowd rushing down the stairs toward him.

"Close the door!" Kyria cried in consternation. "Close the —"

"What . . ." Albert began in confusion, then ducked as the flame-red parrot dived at him.

The bird flew out the door, and Kyria let out a groan of frustration. There was no telling where the thing would go now! She rushed past Albert, who had straightened up and was blinking rapidly. Shading her eyes, she looked up and spotted Wellington winging his way up into the branches of the old, spreading oak to the west of the house. She ran down the shallow steps that led to the formal front lawn and followed the parrot.

Beneath the oak tree, she stopped and looked up. Wellington was sitting high up on one of the bare limbs, shredding the wig with his claws. Kyria let out a groan. "Blast Theo and his presents!"

The maid reached her, and Kyria turned to her. "We've got to get that bird down. Fetch me some nuts, will you? And cut up an apple. I'll see if I can lure him down. And, Cooper —" she swung around to address the footman "— find Alex and Con and tell them to get down here right away if they don't want to lose Wellie."

The servants nodded and hurried off to do her bidding. The rest of the servants and the houseguests milled around, looking up at the parrot in the tree. Kyria glanced around at them, wishing futilely that there was someone here to help her. Reed, the most reliable of them all, had ridden out this morning with the estate manager to look into some problem at one of the farms, and Stephen and Olivia, along with her mother, were down at the vicarage discussing the upcoming wedding ceremony. Thisbe and her husband, of course, were deep in some experiment or other at their laboratory. The lab had been built a few years earlier to replace Thisbe's shed in town, which had accidentally been blown up in an experiment. It had set fire to her father's workshop and caused a general fright among the servants. This new lab stood at a safe distance from the main house and other outbuildings.

Clearly, Kyria thought, she was on her own. "Here, Wellington, come down," Kyria said in a coaxing voice. "I'll get you some treats. Much better than that old wig. Good Wellie. Here, Wellie." She patted her shoulder encouragingly.

The parrot paused in his industrious mangling of the wig and cocked his head, gazing down at her. Kyria smiled and continued to call to him. She wished she could whistle. It had been a skill she had envied in her brothers as a child, but try as she might, she had never been able to do it. It would have been of great use to her now, she thought, for Alex and Con, who often let the brightly colored bird out to fly around the large nursery, frequently called the parrot back with a whistle.

She turned to the crowd that had gathered behind her to watch interestedly. "Albert, can you whistle?"

He looked at her blankly. "Whistle?"

"Yes, whistle."

He shrugged. "I don't know. I haven't since I was a boy."

"Well, give it a try, will you?"

Albert did, but the little squeak he uttered

made the parrot do nothing more than cock his head in the other direction and let out a derisive-sounding squawk.

"Hello!" the parrot called. "Hello!"

"Yes, hello, Wellie," Kyria called back, and patted her shoulder yet again. "Here, Wellie. Good Wellie. Come to Kyria."

The parrot looked all around at the crowd, chattering and pointing, then let out a cry and flew to a higher branch, letting the wig fall to the ground, where it lay like a strange, lifeless animal. Kyria darted over to pick it up. It was ruined, she thought, wincing a little as she thought of the dressing-down she would doubtless get later from her great-aunt. She would, she thought with some bitterness, see to it that Alex and Con got to share her session with Lady Rochester.

The maid she had sent on her errand came puffing up beside Kyria now, holding a handful of cut-up apple and nuts. "Here, my lady. I got it as fast as I could."

"Thank you, Jenny," Kyria replied, taking a chunk of apple and holding it up so that the parrot could see it. "Look, Wellie, a treat!"

The parrot twisted his head this way and that and let out a few sharp noises, but stubbornly refused to budge from his high perch.

"I didn't see the twins on my way to the kitchen, my lady, but I sent Patterson to look for them."

"They must be out of the house," Kyria said. "They would never stay away from a commotion this big." Nothing drew either boy faster than the sounds of a disturbance. Of course, a great deal of the time, they were at the center of whatever disturbance was happening.

She continued to try enticing the bird with the bits of food, and he continued to ignore her pleas. The watching crowd of guests was growing louder around her, and when one of the women gave a titter of laughter, the parrot shifted on its perch. Kyria tried to hush the crowd, but she knew that though they might quiet for a moment, they would only grow louder and more restive, and the movement and noise were likely to make the bird flit farther away. The twins would be heartbroken if they lost the parrot. She had to act now.

The only thing to do, she thought, was to get closer to the bird, to move away from the noise and movement of the people, where Wellington could concentrate on her and the tasty treat she was offering him. She spared a fleeting wish for Alex, who was as nimble as a monkey and could climb — and had done so — almost anything around. Still, she had been rather good at climbing trees herself as a child, always tagging after her older siblings. Hopefully, one didn't forget such things.

She studied the tree — not a bad one to climb, with some low branches to get one started — then looked down at her attire. A fashionable dress with a bustle was scarcely the thing to go climbing in. But she could not take the time to change, so with a sigh she reached down and grabbed the back hem of her skirt and pulled it forward between her legs, bunching up the petticoats, and tucked the material into her waistband.

Her rearrangement of her clothes exposed a shocking amount of pantalet-clad leg, and Kyria heard more than one gasp behind her, as well as a little shriek from the ever-excitable Cousin Wilhemina. Even the maid, accustomed to the Moreland family's strange ways, was gaping at her with astonishment. Kyria knew that her behavior would give everyone fuel for gossip for several days to come, and it would doubtless become another in the long list of examples of her "oddities."

With a mental shrug, she stuck her lures of fruit and nuts into her pocket and strode over to the tree. Grabbing the trunk at the lowest limb, she pulled herself up, hooked a leg over the branch and climbed onto it. Standing, she began to climb, limb by limb, until she had reached as high as she could go and be sure the branch would support her weight. She looked down at the crowd below; everyone was staring up at her intently. It was, she realized with a little flutter of fear in her stomach, an exceedingly long way down. It occurred to her that she had been foolish to climb up here. She lifted her head and looked out into the spreading tracery of branches around her.

Wellington had moved during her climb and now unfortunately perched even farther up in the tree. Kyria sat down and scooted carefully out on her branch, then reached into her pocket and pulled out a piece of apple and extended it toward the bird.

"See? A treat, Wellie. Come here and I'll give it to you," she coaxed. "Good Wellie. Come here."

"Hello," the parrot responded, and let out a noise that sounded remarkably like a cackle of laughter.

"Yes. Hello." Kyria hid her exasperation and wiggled her hand a little toward the bird. "See? A treat for Wellie." She patted her shoulder. Carefully she edged out farther onto the limb, still coaxing the bird to come to her.

As she inched along the branch, she wondered how much farther she could go along the narrowing limb. She stopped, steadying herself with one hand on the branch and with the other holding out the piece of apple. "Here, Well—"

There was a loud crack, and suddenly, terrifyingly, Kyria was falling. She whacked into a branch below her and slid from it, turning, grasping frantically. Her hands caught and clung and suddenly she was no longer falling, but clinging to a branch. Below her, several of the women were screaming as they watched her. Kyria looked down at them, her stomach doing a sick flip-flop when she saw how far from the ground she dangled. She was going to die, she thought, and all from trying to save a silly parrot.

Then she looked out across the front lawn and beyond, and there she saw a horse, bay coat glinting in the sunlight, pounding along the driveway toward the tree. A man sat on the animal's back, bent low over the horse's neck, riding as one with his mount. His hat had fallen off and his wind-whipped hair glinted gold in the sunlight. A warmth started in Kyria's chest and she felt a sudden surge of hope.

She tightened her grip on the branch, watching him ride like a centaur toward her. The guests and servants scattered from his path as he leaped the low hedge separating the drive from the lawn and raced toward the tree. Kyria felt her hands slipping on the branch, and her stomach knotted with fear.

The rider reined to a halt beneath the tree, standing up in his stirrups and reaching up toward her. "Let go," he called. "I'll catch you."

For a moment longer Kyria clung, afraid to let go. Then, with a deep breath, she closed her eyes and opened her hands. She fell, and for an instant terror gripped her. Then she crashed into the stranger's chest and his arms went around her, as her momentum toppled them both off his horse and they hit the ground with a thud.

Kyria lay stunned. Slowly she opened her eyes. She was lying against the rider's hard chest, the cloth of his white shirt beneath her cheek; she could hear the pounding of his heart. She moved, carefully noting that everything seemed to be working properly. She had survived. She raised her head from the man's chest and found herself looking down into the bluest pair of eyes she had ever seen.

She felt as if she could not breathe, could not look away. He grinned up at her, a dimple popping into his tanned cheek in a way that made her heart stumble. It was a sensation Kyria had never felt before, and it startled and annoyed her.

"Well, hey, darlin'," he said, his eyes alight with amusement, his voice deep and softly accented. "If I had known you could just pluck a beautiful woman out of a tree in England, I'd have come over here sooner."

The timbre of his voice, the lazy, slow way his words slid out, sent a strange warmth twisting through Kyria's insides. She felt herself blush, and she realized that she wanted to giggle. The impulse irritated her even more; she had never, even in her first season, behaved like a simpering, giggling schoolgirl. The easy amusement on the handsome stranger's face told her that he was accustomed to foolish females acting this way when he smiled at them. Kyria scowled.

"I fail to find the amusement in this," she retorted, sounding annoyingly prissy even to her own ears.

"Do you?" His smile did not dim.

"Personally, I always enjoy rescuing pretty girls from trees."

Kyria looked at him repressively. The man was really quite irritating, she thought. He hadn't even the decency to pretend that she had not acted in a reckless and foolish way. A gentleman would have allowed everyone present to ignore what had just happened. Worse, he was actually trying to flirt with her!

"I didn't need rescuing," she told him haughtily.

His grin grew even wider. "Didn't you, now? My mistake."

Kyria grimaced and started to sit up. For an instant, the arm he still had looped around her waist stiffened, holding her against him in their far-too-intimate position. Her eyes flashed and she started to give him a blistering set-down, but before she could speak, he released her and rose lithely to his feet, the insufferable grin still in place.

He bent and offered Kyria a hand up. Pointedly she ignored his outstretched hand and stood, looking across to where the servants and guests were all gazing at them in astonishment, apparently rooted to the spot in shock. Her getting to her feet seemed to release the others from their paralysis, and they all started toward Kyria, a babble of words rising from them.

"Oh, my lady!" Smeggars was the first to reach them. "Are you hurt?"

"I am fine," Kyria assured the butler, shaking out her tangled skirts. It made her color all over again to think of how much leg she had exposed to her rescuer.

"Cousin Kyria!" Wilhemina seized the opportunity to burst into sobs, burying her face in her handkerchief.

"Damned watering pot!" Lord Penhurst commented in the trumpeting sort of voice he considered an undertone.

"Well, I never . . ." Cousin Wilhemina's companion began indignantly, but one stern glare from Lady Rochester stopped the woman's words.

Lady Rochester's maid had apparently come to her mistress's aid, for the indomitable old woman now had her head covered with an elegant, lace-trimmed black cap. She leaned on her cane, looking at Kyria, and let out a loud harrumph. "You'll break your neck one day, Kyria, the way you go at things. Mark my words."

"Yes, Aunt," Kyria replied meekly, too used to her great-aunt's strictures to bridle at them.

"Who the devil are you?" Lady Rochester

went on bluntly, pointing at Kyria's rescuer.

The stranger turned his charming smile on the old woman and swept her an elegant bow. "Rafe McIntyre, ma'am, at your service."

Lady Rochester did her best to look disapproving, but Kyria was sure she saw a glimmer of a smile flicker across her mouth.

"You're an American?" Cousin Wilhemina asked, tears forgotten as she stared at McIntyre.

"Yes, ma'am, I have to confess that I am. I'm a friend of the groom's."

"Oh!" Kyria whirled back to face the man, realizing now who he was. "You are Stephen St. Leger's partner." He was also Stephen's good friend and would act as his best man at the upcoming wedding. She had, she thought with another spurt of embarrassment, been rather rude to the man.

"Former partner," he corrected, and turned his brilliant blue gaze back to her.

He was, Kyria thought, undeniably handsome. The bright eyes and the bone-melting smile would have been enough for any man, she thought, but in addition, he had been blessed with a tall, wide-shouldered frame and well-modeled face framed by thick, light brown hair, just a trifle long and shaggy, and sun-kissed with streaks of gold. Kyria felt sure that half the women in the house would be swooning over him. Any hesitation they might have at his lack of aristocratic background would be more than offset by the fortune he had reputedly made in silver mining when he and Stephen were partners. For some reason, the thought made her feel even more annoyed.

"I must say," Lord Marcross put in, walking up to McIntyre and extending his hand. "Deuced good riding there."

"The credit belongs to the horse, I'm afraid," McIntyre said, easily turning the compliment aside, and looking for his mount.

The bay stood a few feet away, grazing unconcernedly. McIntyre grinned and walked over to take his reins and run a hand down the horse's neck. "Half the time he looks like he's about to fall asleep, but he can fly."

"Did you buy him in England?" Cousin Albert asked.

"Ireland," McIntyre answered, and in the next moment several of the men were clustered around him, talking horses.

"Oh!" Kyria remembered the parrot. "Wellie! Where is he? Did he fly away?"

She turned to look up into the tree. Sure enough, there was a flash of red and blue as the parrot flitted from one branch to another, somewhat lower down than previously, and let out a squawk, apparently peeved at being ignored.

Rafe looked up from his conversation. He glanced at Kyria. "Is that what you were trying to do up there? Catch the parrot?"

Kyria nodded.

Rafe put two fingers to his lips and let out a piercing whistle. To Kyria's vast irritation, the parrot rose from his perch and flew down in a wide circle to alight on McIntyre's shoulder.

"Good Wellie," the bird croaked.

Kyria glared at the pair of them. Rafe chuckled and ran his finger over the bird's head.

"Obnoxious bird," Lady Rochester said bitterly. "I always said it's ridiculous to keep a parrot in England. Belongs in Africa."

"The Solomon Islands, Aunt," Kyria corrected. "It is indigenous to the Solomons."

"Never heard of them," Lady Rochester sniffed, dismissing the place. "I can't think why your brother thought the creature was a proper gift."

"I have a cage, my lady," Jenny, the maidservant, said tentatively, holding up a small cage. "Cooper went up to the nursery and brought down one of the cages."

Rafe cast a questioning look toward Kyria, and she nodded. "Yes, please, put him in the thing. Then take him up to the nursery, Jenny, and transfer him to the big cage."

At Jenny's cringing look, she relented. "All right. Just leave him there for the moment. I will have the twins take him up. Where *are* those two, anyway?"

Jenny cast a glance behind her, and Kyria followed her gaze. The twins' tutor stood at the edge of the crowd, looking grim. Kyria motioned to him, and he came forward rather reluctantly.

"I don't know where they are, my lady," he began, forestalling Kyria's question. "I left them working on their geography and went back into my room to retrieve my Latin-grammar book. When I returned, they had vanished." He scowled. "I must tell you, my lady, young Master Alexander and Master Constantine exhibit a lack of decorum that I find unacceptable."

"Do you?" Kyria asked in a deceptively silky voice. "Well, Mr. Thorndike, I have to tell you that I find that *you* exhibit a certain lack of skill in keeping eager and inquisitive minds interested in their subjects. I believe that the duchess explained to you the methods by which she prefers her children to be taught. When I examined their study tablets last week, I —"

The man bridled. "I teach, my lady, as I was taught."

"By rote and repetition?" Kyria queried, one brow raised. "Geography can be a fascinating subject, an exploration of lands and people different from ourselves — rather than a memorization of the names of countries and their capitals. I think it might be wise for my mother to look over some of their recent work and perhaps explain to you again what she requires."

"That won't be necessary, my lady," the tutor replied icily. "For *I* am tendering my resignation." With that he turned on his heel and marched away, back ramrod straight.

Kyria let out a soft groan. "Oh, dear, that's the third one this year. Perhaps I spoke too hastily."

Beside her Rafe chuckled. "Well, speaking from experience, I imagine the boys will be quite happy to have lost a tutor." He paused, then added with a grin and a raised eyebrow, "Constantine and Alexander? The emperors?"

"Yes. They're twins, you see, and Papa is a classicist. And I am sure that they *will* be happy." She sighed.

At that moment, the butler, who had politely retreated from the guests, returned, one of the housemaids in tow. "My lady . . ."

"Yes, Smeggars?"

"Martha has some knowledge of your brothers' whereabouts, my lady." He turned a stern eye on the young maid, who was twisting her apron between her hands nervously. "Tell her, Martha."

"Um, well, I'm not for certain, my lady," the girl began shyly.

"That's all right. Tell me what you think."

"Well, um, I was cleaning out the grate in the nursery this morning, my lady, and I heard the twins talking to each other like, and, well, it sounded like they were going to the hunt."

"The hunt?" Kyria repeated blankly. "Are you sure?"

"No, miss. I mean, I heard them say something about the squire, and then one of them, Master Con, I think, said, well, they could intercede — no, intercept — them, I think. They were talking about where the hunt would run like."

"All right. Thank you, Martha." Kyria frowned, puzzled.

"Is there a hunt today?" Rafe asked.

"Yes. Our neighbor, Squire Winton, is the master of the hunt, and he was having one. Several of our guests went to it this morning, actually, but I cannot imagine why the twins would be talking about going to it. They are far too young. They aren't quite eleven, and anyway, they have always spoken of the hunt in terms of the greatest loathing. They love animals, you see, and —"

Kyria stopped short, looking up into the American's face with a gasp. "Oh, my heavens!"

"What? What is it?" He straightened at the look of alarm on Kyria's face.

"That's it. They have gone there to do something, I know it. They are going to try to stop the hunt!" Kyria groaned, raising her hands to her head. "The squire will be furious. And right before Olivia's wedding, too! I must do something. I have to stop them."

She turned and started toward the stables.

But Rafe was beside her in an instant, grabbing her wrist. "Wait. Let me help you."

The touch of his fingers, warm and callused, on her arm sent a strange sensation sizzling up Kyria's arm, and she blinked at him, momentarily distracted. "But I . . . I have to try to find them. I'm sorry, you must excuse me. But —"

"No, that's what I'm saying. I'll take you."

"Riding double? But he must be tired." Kyria glanced a little doubtfully at McIntyre's stallion.

"He barely broke a sweat. I promise you, he's strong. You needn't waste the time of having your horse saddled. Just tell me where to go." McIntyre took her arm unceremoniously and led her to his horse. He tossed her onto the horse's back, then mounted behind her.

"Where to?" he asked, his arms going around her as he took the reins firmly in his grip.

Wordlessly, Kyria pointed. Rafe dug in his heels, and they thundered off.

2

Kyria sat sidesaddle on the horse, her body against Rafe's chest, and his arms curved around her to hold the reins. She was encircled by his warmth, and she could not help but be aware of how her hip was nestled very intimately between his legs. She had never ridden this way before, and it was rather unnerving — not the least because it produced such strange sensations in her. There was an unaccustomed warmth in her loins, a kind of softening, a stirring that was undeniably exciting. She could not help but be aware of how very close he was to her or of the strength of his arm around her back.

"I should have taken my horse," she said, struggling to ignore the tumult within.

"Why is that?" he asked, his breath stirring her hair.

"Well, I . . ." She turned and found herself looking straight into Rafe's face, only inches away. She was suddenly very hot, her throat constricted. Kyria cleared her throat. "I, uh, I'm sure that in the long run, it probably would have been faster.

Your horse is bound to tire."

"I told you — he's strong. And you're light as a feather."

"Hardly," Kyria replied dryly. "I'm almost five foot ten."

"Yep, you're a tall one, all right." He grinned, his blue eyes looking at her with clear approval. "I noticed that right off. I like that. Still hardly weigh enough to tire this fella out." He reached down and patted his horse's neck. "You just tell me where to go."

"Cut across the meadow up there," Kyria said, pointing, doing her best to ignore the feel of Rafe's body against hers and finding it somewhat difficult to do. "I know where they set the dogs loose. The squire is very predictable. I am sure that is why Con and Alex thought they would be able to intercept them. If we go up Bedloe Hill, I think we'll be able to catch sight of them."

They galloped across the meadow and jumped the fence at the end, the stallion's hooves barely scraping the top. Kyria, held securely in the circle of Rafe's arms, the breeze of their passage ruffling her already-disordered hair, could not help but thrill to the excitement of the ride. Her pulse was up, her breath coming faster in her throat, as he urged the horse forward. Rafe's masculine scent teased her nostrils, mingling with the smell of horse and the crisp fall air.

She directed him toward a slope, and they started up it, necessarily slowing as the ground rose before them. As the climb became steeper, they dismounted and walked the rest of the way up the hill, Rafe leading his horse by the reins.

"I hope we can find them before they stop the hunt," Kyria said worriedly. "Squire Winton will be furious if they ruin it. He was so looking forward to our guests joining him. He is desperately hoping that Lord Badgerton will approve — he's a noted huntsman. And if Con and Alex ruin the hunt and make him look foolish . . ." She sighed. "He hasn't been happy with the twins, anyway, ever since their boa got out and —"

"Their *what?*" Rafe interrupted.

"Their boa constrictor. They love animals. They have a veritable menagerie up there in the nursery."

"Mmm." McIntyre looked at her in some fascination. "And what, ah, happened exactly when the boa constrictor got out?"

"Oh. He ate the squire's peacock." Rafe let out a choked noise, and Kyria glared at him.

"Oh, yes, laugh all you want, but I can tell you, Squire Winton found it less than amusing. The twins were lucky he was too agitated to put ammunition in his gun or that would have been the end of Augustus."

"Augustus would be the boa constrictor, I presume."

"Yes. It took all Reed's diplomacy — and a nice sum of money in compensation, too, I might add — to placate Squire Winton. He was inordinately proud of that bird. Personally, I thought it wasn't much of a loss. I have always found peacocks strutting across one's lawn rather too grandiose. Besides, they make a dreadful noise."

"I quite agree." Rafe's blue eyes danced with laughter.

Kyria cast him a quelling glance, repressing the smile that threatened to twitch up her lips. "It's all very well for you. You don't have to have the man as a neighbor."

"No, and thank heavens," Rafe put in earnestly, "what with peacocks crowing at all hours — or whatever it is peacocks do."

"They screech like someone is killing them," Kyria informed him disgustedly.

"I reckon, then, they didn't notice right off when Augustus got him."

Kyria gave a bark of laughter and clapped her hand over her mouth. "You dreadful man! That's not at all funny."

He grinned at her. "I know. That's why you didn't laugh."

"Well, I shouldn't have."

They reached the crest of the hill and gazed out at the vista spread below them. "There!" Kyria cried, pointing. "I can see a scarlet coat. Blast! They're stopped. Oh, dear, it must be the twins."

"Then let's go." Rafe swung her up into the saddle and followed suit, then started off down the hill.

They soon could no longer see the distant figures and had to rely on their memory as they moved quickly down the hill and cut through a stand of trees beyond. They emerged onto a narrow trail, and there Rafe gave the horse his head. Pounding along the track, they curved around another copse of trees and emerged on the other side onto a run of grass lying between the wooded areas.

And there, milling around, were a number of riders and horses. Rafe reined in the stallion and rode at a more sedate pace through the group to the front, where a straining, yapping brace of hounds was being held in check by the keepers. In front of them stood a portly man with wide, muttonchop whiskers who was dressed in the coat of the master of the hunt. He was almost as red in the face as his coat, and he flailed his arms around wildly as he shouted at the two boys before him.

Rafe saw immediately that these must be the twins in question. Slender as reeds and rather taller than most ten-year-old boys, they were black-haired and blue-eyed and as alike as two peas in a pod. They stood facing the large man, shoulders squared and arms at their sides. Behind them, cowering under a bush, was a small red fox.

Rafe had barely pulled his horse to a stop before Kyria was off and running toward her brothers. Rafe tethered his horse to the nearest bush and followed her.

"Squire Winton!" Kyria ran between the portly man and her brothers. "I am so sorry. I do apologize for them." She turned and glared at her brothers. "What do you think you are doing?"

The two boys crossed their arms almost in unison and stared back at her mulishly. "It is cruel and wrong, Kyria," one of them told her bluntly. "You said so yourself, and so did Mother."

"Yes, I know," Kyria said. "But you haven't any right to interfere with the squire's hunt."

"Well, what right do they have to slaughter some poor defenseless animal?" the other boy countered.

The squire let out a bellow at these words and shook his riding crop at them. "You young imps of Satan! Someone should take you over his knee!"

Kyria whipped back around and looked at the squire coolly. "May I remind you, sir, that the twins' discipline is entirely a matter for their mother and father and nothing to do with you."

"They are incorrigible!"

Kyria's eyes flashed. "They are not incorrigible! They are simply boys with good hearts who love animals and dislike seeing them killed purely for sport."

"You see?" The squire shook his forefinger at her. "That attitude is precisely why they are the way they are. You people encourage them to run wild and —"

Kyria set her fists on her hips pugnaciously. "We encourage them to think for themselves."

"They ought to be taken in hand!" The squire's eyes bulged, his face turning an alarming shade of red, and he took a step toward the twins.

Kyria took a quick step sideways, again interposing herself between the squire and her brothers. The squire remained in the same position, the crop raised menacingly, his face contorted with rage.

Rafe moved quickly between the squire and Kyria, sliding his hand beneath his coat as he said, "Now, hold on a minute here."

"Who the devil are you?" the squire demanded.

"Well," Rafe answered, pulling a short-barreled pistol out from beneath his jacket, "I'm the man with the gun."

All the others looked at him in amazement as Rafe continued, "I suggest you back away from the lady and these children and calm down a little. How does that sound?"

"What?" Squire Winton stared goggle-eyed at the pistol, then back at Rafe. "But . . . but . . ."

"I know what you're thinking," Rafe went on agreeably. "You're thinking this isn't much of a gun for a man to carry, and you'd be right. It's a sissy sort of thing. But I found the people in this country looked at me askance, you see, when I was out in the street with a Colt strapped to my side. So I figured this would be better, less alarming, you know, and I can just carry it in a pocket inside my coat. It doesn't even disturb the line."

"Criminy!" he heard one of the boys breathe behind him, and the squire took a quick step backward.

"Mr. McIntyre . . ." Kyria began uncertainly.

"Don't worry. I don't have plans to shoot anybody," Rafe assured her cheerfully. "Not yet, anyway. But I think we can have a calmer discussion of the facts now. Isn't that right, Mr. Winton?"

The squire nodded, casting another uneasy glance at Rafe's gun. Rafe stuck it back into his pocket and stepped aside, then leaned toward Kyria and murmured, "You might remember you were wanting to *stop* a big fight . . ."

Kyria grimaced at him, but then turned to the squire and said in a much more pleasant tone of voice, "Squire, please, accept my apologies for the boys. They will come home with me right now, and I will do my best to ensure that nothing like this happens again."

"But, Kyria . . ." one of the boys protested.

Kyria silenced him with one sharp glance and spoke again to the squire. "I wouldn't want any unpleasantness to spoil the friendship that our families have enjoyed for so long. The duke and duchess have always expressed gratitude for having such a good neighbor as you."

"But they stopped the hunt!" the squire exclaimed, unable to let go of his grievance.

"Yes, I know, and they acted quite unbecomingly in doing so," Kyria agreed soothingly. "I assure you that I will take the matter up with my mother and father."

"But what about the hunt?" The squire's voice was taking on something of a wail.

"Now, wait." Rafe spoke up again. "Sorry, I'm an American, so maybe I'm a little confused here. Let me get this straight. You're saying that all you folks are out here, with the dogs and everything, trying to chase down that one little fox?"

"Yes, of course. It's a hunt." Winton looked disdainfully at him.

"Oh, I see." Rafe nodded thoughtfully. "I was just . . . well, back home a fella usually just goes after a varmint like that himself, you know. He doesn't need a whole bunch of folks helping him."

The squire bridled a little at his words. "Well, of course, I don't need help. It's, well, that's the way it's done."

"Oh. Well, sure." Rafe glanced around. "Thing is . . . I think the other side got tired of waiting."

He turned and looked significantly at the bush in front of which the twins stood.

The boys turned to look, too, then stepped aside, grinning. The small red fox that had been hiding beneath the bush was gone.

"Bloody hell!" the squire exclaimed. He glared at Kyria. "Your father will hear from me."

"I am sure he will be happy to discuss the matter with you."

He shook his riding crop toward the twins one last time, saying, "They should have leashes on them!" He turned and stomped off back to his horse.

Kyria sighed, watching her neighbor stalk away. Rafe cast her a glance, one eyebrow raised.

"So," he said slowly, "tell me, is this what you'd call a typical day around here?"

Kyria had to chuckle. "Unfortunately, it is more often than not."

She swung around to face the twins, who hurried up to her and Rafe, agog with interest.

"What a cunning gun!" Alex exclaimed. "May I look at it? Please?"

Rafe held it out in the palm of his hand. "Yes, but you can't touch it. It's loaded. When we get back to the house, I'll unload and clean it and let you look at it."

"Will you?" Alex grinned. "That would be ever so good of you."

"It's so small!" Con said, peering at it. "I've never seen anything like it."

"It's called a derringer. The aim's no good. You can only use it close up, but it's handy to carry."

"I must say," Kyria interrupted crossly, "you two boys certainly have a ghoulish interest in guns for people who are so concerned about the squire hunting that miserable fox."

"It's not the same thing!" Con protested. "They are only killing that poor fox for sport. Theo says that a *gun* is a necessity."

"No doubt it is when you are in the wilds of Australia, as Theo was," Kyria said. "That's not the point, anyway. The point is — why did you have to do this? This week of all times?"

Con shrugged, but Alex replied seriously, "Actually, it seemed to me that this week would have the most impact. After all, it is the biggest and most important hunt the squire is likely to have, what with our guests being here, too."

"That is exactly what I mean. You embarrassed the man in front of some of the very people he would most like to impress. Now it will be doubly hard to placate him. And I imagine our guests were none too pleased about it, either."

"Mother says you cannot waver on what you think is right just because it isn't a popular opinion," Alex put in pedantically.

Kyria let out a low groan. "I'm sure she did. But she isn't the one trying to keep a large number of guests happy and bring Olivia's wedding off." She glanced around. "Now, where are your ponies? We're going home, and you can explain to Aunt Hermione why your parrot escaped from its cage —"

"No!" the boys cried out in unison, alarmed.

"Is Wellie all right?" Alex asked in concern.

"Yes, of course he's all right. Nothing could harm that wretched creature," Kyria said dryly. "But he flew all over the house and created an enormous flap, and then he snatched the wig off your great-aunt's head and shredded it."

The boys gaped at her.

"Did he really?" Con asked in an awe-struck voice, and Alex giggled.

"Oh, yes, very funny, I'm sure," Kyria told him, adding, "I doubt it will be quite as amusing when you have to face our great-aunt."

"No," Alex agreed. "But at least she just gives one a tongue-lashing and a few smacks with that cane, and I'd rather have that than a lecture from Papa. He looks at me in that way, and I know I've disappointed him."

Rafe glanced at Kyria, a half smile playing on his lips, and Kyria could not help but remember the moment when she had fallen into his arms and felt them wrap like iron around her. His body had been hard against hers, his heat surrounding her. She could remember, too, the way her own body had tingled in response. Thinking of the moment, she colored and turned her face away, unable to meet Rafe's gaze.

As the twins turned to Rafe, babbling their thanks, he held up a hand, saying, "Well, it was your sister here who risked life and limb to try to capture him, not to mention standing up for you with that tutor and the squire. So I reckon she's the one you ought to be thanking."

"We do!" Con assured him, and caught Kyria in a hug.

"You are the absolute best!" Alex agreed, wrapping his arms around her from the other side.

Kyria chuckled, planting a kiss on the head of each of her brothers. "Well, I'm glad you realize that," she said, "but that doesn't mean I am going to plead your case with Mother. You two are on your own there."

"But she's the one who told us we have to stand up for what we believe in," Con declared. "She can't get too mad, can she?"

"I don't think she intended for you to stand up for your beliefs by sneaking away from your studies and lying in wait for the squire. Nor will she like that your tutor quit."

"Old Thorny?" Alex exclaimed. "You're joking! He scarpered?"

Con jumped up in the air, letting out a cry of joy.

"Thank heavens! He was the worst tutor we ever had."

"No," Alex disagreed. "Spindleshanks was the worst."

"He was the meanest," Con conceded. "But he wasn't as boring as Old Thorny. All Mr. Thorndike has us do is copy Latin grammars and such, and it's deadly dull."

"That may be, but you two run through teachers faster than I do hairpins," Kyria pointed out, but she could not help but smile down at her two scapegrace brothers.

She was inordinately fond of them and resented any disparaging remarks anyone made about them. There were times when their tendency to get into trouble was exasperating, but she knew that whatever fuss was kicked up, Con and Alex had never gone into it with bad intentions. They were simply lively and intelligent boys whose curiosity and intrepidity sometimes led them onto paths that other children would not have taken. In Kyria's opinion, that fact indicated something lacking in the other children, not in Con and Alex.

They had reached the trees where the boys had tied their ponies, and after some discussion, they wound up with Kyria riding Alex's pony and the two boys doubling up on Con's — though both of them expressed preference for riding on Rafe's stallion. Rafe cupped his hands to give Kyria a leg up onto the pony's back. Then he mounted, and they started off.

Kyria glanced over at Rafe. She remembered the way it had felt riding with him on his horse, and a little shiver ran through her. She could not help but feel a tiny pang of regret that she was not riding back the same way, and the thought shocked her a little.

She was not the sort of woman to swoon over a man. She had never joined her friends in giggling and whispering about this man's broad shoulders or that one's fine eyes. There were men she acknowledged as being very handsome and others who were charming or intelligent — though rarely did she find all three. But though she might be aware of their good looks, they roused little excitement in her breast. She had realized long ago that she was simply not the sort of woman to be swept away by any man.

Her friends had long told her that she was entirely too prone to thinking and not enough to feeling, and the epithet given her by the eligible bachelors of London society — The Goddess — reflected not only her classic beauty but also her faintly aloof air. That she had gone for years without falling in love with any of the eligible men who sought her hand had cost her an ache or two. She would have liked to know the sort of love her parents obviously enjoyed. But, she reminded herself, it was just as well. Aside from a few notable exceptions, husbands were, in her estimation, dictatorial and overprotective, and marriage was a very unequal proposition. In her opinion a woman gave up her freedom, as well as her name, when she married. She had long ago resolved never to marry, and the years she had spent in society since her coming out had only confirmed that decision.

She cast another glance at Rafe, who was ambling alongside their ponies, his head bent to listen to the twins' chatter. He was, she thought with some irritation, precisely the sort of man over whom most women swooned. Kyria had little doubt that when she introduced him to the other guests at their house, all the women would be jockeying to talk to him. The carelessly tousled hair . . . the broad shoulders . . . the sky-blue eyes . . . the devastating smile . . . Kyria could well imagine how the ladies would be all atwitter about him.

He was a charmer, the sort of man who was interested in conquest. He would smile and flatter and woo one, hoping to add another lady to his collection. Kyria had been out for nine years now, and she was well acquainted with his type. She was also quite practiced at eluding such a man's advances. She set her mouth firmly. Mr. McIntyre would soon find out that she was one woman who would not fall into his clutches — well, figuratively speaking, she reminded herself, her lips twitching as her irrepressible humor rose, reminding her that literally speaking, that was precisely what she had already done.

The journey back to the house was slower than the ride out had been, and as they rode, the twins chattered away, demanding a recounting in detail of their parrot's flight, pondering the possible punishments that would be meted out to them for their escapade and pausing to pepper Rafe with questions about his horse, his gun, his accent and whatever else came to their agile minds.

Kyria would have stepped in to hush their questioning, but she quickly saw that Rafe was more than able to hold his own with the twins, answering some of their questions, deflecting others and turning the tables on them with questions of his own.

She was a little surprised, for she had found over the years as one of the reigning beauties of London society that most of her suitors were apt to wilt under an interrogation from the twins. Despite her father's high rank, hers was not a family given to formalities. Unlike other families of the nobility, where children were sequestered in a nursery and rarely ate with the family, interacting with their parents only at prescribed hours, in the Moreland household, the younger siblings were apt to be in and out of their elders' company at all hours during the day and usually took their meals with them, unless the duke and duchess were having one of their rare formal dinners.

Visitors to their home often found the twins' presence disconcerting, and one future earl who had been assiduously courting Kyria even went so far as to tell Kyria that he found the boys impertinent and could only wonder at the laxity with which they were raised. Kyria had responded by suggesting that he would be happier, then, if he no longer called on her.

But Mr. McIntyre seemed to have no such qualms in dealing with the boys. He talked and laughed with them in his slow, slurry way. He looked, she thought, to be accustomed to boys.

When she said as much a few minutes later, he turned that slow smile on her and said, "Oh, I'm afraid you'll find that I don't have much trouble talking to just about anybody. Whether that's a good trait or one that will drive you crazy just depends on you." He glanced over at Con and Alex and added, "I guess I wasn't much different from them — I had a tendency to get in trouble myself at that age."

"And has that changed?" Kyria asked, a little surprised at the teasing note in her voice. If she wasn't careful, she thought, the man would assume she was flirting with him — *which she absolutely was not.*

Rafe's smile broadened and he winked at her. "Well, now, I reckon a lot of people would say that I still manage to get in some trouble."

There was something about his voice, slow and rich like warm, golden honey, that stirred something inside her. She glanced away quickly, and it was a relief when Alex distracted Rafe's attention by asking another question.

When they got back to the great, solemn pile of gray stone that was Broughton Park, they were told by the footman who opened the door that the Moreland family was waiting for them in the formal drawing room. Alex and Con slipped off to run up the back stairs to the nursery, murmuring in suddenly quiet voices that they had best see if their parrot had survived his adventure unharmed.

Kyria and Rafe started up the grand front staircase, but as they climbed a man and woman appeared at the top of the stairs, smiling down at them.

"Kyria! Rafe!" The woman started down the stairs, followed by her companion. She was a small woman with large, expressive, brown eyes and deep brown hair, and her face was wreathed in smiles. She was dressed in a reddish brown velvet gown, and the paisley shawl flung around her shoulders had fallen from one arm, so that it floated out behind her as she walked. She was Kyria's sister Olivia, whose nuptials were to take place in two days.

"Smeggars told us what happened!" she went on worriedly as she reached them. "Are you all right? Thank you, dear." This last remark was addressed to Stephen St. Leger, who had picked up the trailing end of her shawl and tucked it solicitously around her shoulders.

"Yes, of course," Kyria assured her automatically. She had spent her childhood tagging along after her older brothers and sister, and she had grown accustomed long ago to downplaying any danger to herself. "I am sure Smeggars exaggerated."

"Rafe! I was beginning to wonder if you were going to come," Olivia's fiancé said, reaching out to shake his friend's hand. "I expected you days ago. I thought perhaps you'd decided to put down roots in Ireland."

"I got delayed purchasing a horse," Rafe explained, taking his friend's hand. "I have no timetables on this trip. I am completely committed to operating on my whims."

"I am well aware of how you operate," Stephen retorted, and the four of them continued up the stairs.

The formal drawing room was filled with Kyria and Olivia's large, rather noisy family, and when they first stepped into the room, it seemed a blur of noise and people to Rafe. Then a tall, statuesque woman stepped forward, assuming easy command of the situation.

"How do you do?" she said, smiling and extending her hand to Rafe. "You must be Mr. McIntyre. We have heard how you rescued my daughter this afternoon, for which I am very thankful."

"Ma'am." Rafe bowed over the duchess's hand. He had only to look at this woman, he thought, to see what Kyria would look like in thirty years. The Duchess of Broughton was as tall as her daughter, with equally red hair, save for a strand or two of white woven through it, and much of her former beauty still showed in the strong bones of her face.

"Yes, good show," a man said, coming up beside the duchess and reaching out to shake Rafe's hand. "Duke of Broughton. Pleased to meet you. Uncle Bellard speaks highly of you."

"Thank you, sir. I think very highly of him, too." Rafe had met the duke's uncle two months earlier, when he and the scholarly old gentleman had helped Stephen and Olivia find the source of several bizarre incidents that had plagued Stephen's ancestral home, Blackhope Hall.

"He wants very much to see you," the duke went on, "but you know Uncle Bellard — he doesn't much like these large gatherings."

Rafe could well imagine that the diminutive scholar, a very shy and bookish man, did not feel at ease in a crowd.

Broughton cast a distracted glance around the room and gave a small sigh. "Can't say as I much like them, either."

"I know, Papa." Kyria linked her arm affectionately through her father's. "You would much rather be outside in your workshop."

The duke smiled a little, getting a distant look in his eye. "Got a new shipment of potsherds today. You must come down and see them, Kyria. You, too, um . . ."

"Mr. McIntyre, Papa," Kyria put in.

"Yes, of course. Mr. McIntyre." He nodded pleasantly and strolled away, his hands clasped behind his back, his head turned down.

"Please don't be offended," Kyria said. "Papa knows who you are. It's just that trivial things like names tend to slip his mind, especially when there are antiquities to be considered. I'm sure he is thinking about his shipment. Mother will be lucky if she can keep him here until supper."

Kyria cast a sideways glance at him, saying, "If you are brave enough, I can introduce you to the rest of our family."

"Lead on," Rafe responded lightly. "I dare anything."

She walked with him over to where a black-haired woman sat deep in conversation with an older man. When Kyria said her name, the woman glanced up vaguely. Then her face cleared. "Ah. Kyria. Oh!" She stood up. "Are you all right? Smeggars said —"

"Smeggars fusses too much," Kyria said firmly. "I am fine. Thisbe, allow me to introduce you to Mr. McIntyre. He is Lord St. Leger's best man."

"His what . . . Oh, yes, of course, the wedding. I had forgotten. Dr. Sommerville and I were having such an interesting discussion concerning the allotropes of carbon. Did you know —"

"I'm certain I do not," Kyria interjected hastily. She turned toward Rafe and said in explanation, "Thisbe is a scientist."

"Pleased to meet you," Thisbe said, reaching out to shake Rafe's hand. She was tall, like Kyria, but her hair was as black as night and pulled back in a no-nonsense fashion, and her clothes were plain rather than elegant. Not as beautiful in the face as Kyria, there was nevertheless a certain arresting handsomeness in her strong-boned features, and her blue eyes shone with intelligence.

"You are the silver magnate, aren't you?" she went on in the disconcertingly blunt way that Rafe was beginning to expect from the members of the Moreland family. He had thought Stephen's Olivia unusual, but he was beginning to see that the entire brood was decidedly different.

"Yes, I suppose I am," he replied. "Or, rather, I was. We sold our mine."

"And what are you doing now?"

"I decided to take a tour of Europe, and I started by going to visit St. Leger. Of course, when he told me he was getting married, I had to stay on."

Thisbe nodded. "I hope it was no problem to delay your travel."

"None whatsoever. My plans are very flexible," Rafe said agreeably. "I intend to spend a month or two in France, then go on to Italy."

"You will be going to the museums?" Thisbe asked, looking interested.

Kyria was somewhat surprised when Rafe smiled and said that he would, going on to ask Thisbe what she would recommend. Kyria would not have thought him the type to visit museums — but then, she reminded herself cynically, no doubt he simply recognized the best way to charm her sister.

"Thisbe is the twin of our eldest brother, Theo," Kyria told Rafe. "Unfortunately, it doesn't seem as if he is going to be able to make it back for the wedding."

"He was in Australia when we wrote him," Thisbe explained. "He's an explorer, you see."

"Really? Where has he gone?"

"All over, really — Africa, the Amazon, India, Burma, Ceylon, Arabia," Kyria replied. "He has been doing it for years."

She looked at Rafe, waiting for the sort of comments that usually followed when Theo's peripatetic ways were discussed. Some were intrigued, others baffled, but nearly everyone agreed that it was, in the words of Lord Marcross, "a deuced peculiar thing for the heir to a dukedom to be hanging about in deserts and jungles and such."

"I'm sorry he's not here," Rafe said. "I would like to meet him."

"He is an extremely interesting man," Thisbe agreed warmly.

"There are those who would say that seeking adventure all around the globe is scarcely a fitting thing for a future duke," Kyria pointed out.

Rafe shrugged. "Why not?"

"Why not, indeed?" Thisbe smiled at him. "You are exactly right, Mr. McIntyre."

"I think I am missing something here. What is a future duke *supposed* to do?" Rafe asked.

"Be stuffy," Thisbe interjected, and Kyria could not suppress a giggle.

"I don't think that's exactly how they would phrase it."

"No, but it's what they mean," Thisbe retorted. "People don't like it that Theo comes back home brown as a nut and full of the most interesting tales to tell, instead of spending his time in some boring old men's club or out shooting grouse."

"I think they would say he should be getting to know the estate he will inherit," Kyria said in the interests of fairness.

"Yes, but Reed handles all that. He enjoys that sort of thing." Thisbe's voice expressed her obvious puzzlement at her other brother's peculiar interests. "Numbers and farming and the Exchange and all that. Why should poor Theo have to worry about those things when he hates all that and Reed loves it?"

"Reed loves what?" asked a deep, masculine voice, and Kyria turned to see her other brother, who had come up behind them as they talked.

"Handling all the family business for the rest of us," Kyria said, smiling fondly at Reed.

He was a quiet man two years older than Kyria, not as tall or as devastatingly handsome as Theo was, but attractive in his own, more subdued way. His hair was dark brown, cut tidily, and his gray eyes under straight black brows were direct and clear. He was, Kyria knew, considered the most normal of all the Moreland clan, for he had not been drawn to any of the interests, deemed peculiar by the rest of the British nobility, that had attracted the other Morelands. Though learned, he was not the scholar that his father and great-uncle were, and he preferred to spend his time managing the business of his father's estate rather than exploring or engaging in scientific research or championing a political cause.

His was a practical nature, and in the

midst of his more flamboyant, even eccentric, relatives, this fact made him something of an oddity. It also made him the person to whom most of the family turned whenever they had a problem.

Kyria introduced Rafe to Reed, and Reed shook his hand warmly. "Ah, I understand I owe you my gratitude for —"

"If another person says 'rescuing Kyria,' I think I shall scream," Kyria put in warningly.

Reed shot her an amused glance and went on mildly, "I was going to say for helping the twins out of their *contretemps*."

"Everyone knows about that, too?" Kyria asked.

Reed shrugged. "The squire sent a servant over with a blistering note about the twins' conduct. Father gave it to me, of course, as he never reads the squire's notes."

"What are you going to do?" Kyria asked.

"Why do anything?" Thisbe inquired. "Fox hunting is barbaric."

"I'd rather avoid a feud with our neighbor, actually," Reed said. "I fear I'll have to send him some of that shipment of cognac I received the other day. Good liquor usually serves to soothe

the squire's anger."

Olivia and Stephen rejoined them at that point, and Stephen suggested that he show Rafe to his room.

As they strolled out, Stephen murmured, "Head spinning yet?"

Rafe chuckled. "It has been an interesting afternoon."

He paused at the door to the drawing room and looked back, his gaze going to Kyria. Stephen followed Rafe's gaze.

"Ah," he said. "Is that the way the wind blows?"

"She is the most beautiful woman I've ever met."

Stephen nodded. "Her nickname among the fashionable blades is The Goddess. She's been pursued by earls and dukes — and even one prince. She's turned them all down."

"Is that right?" A faint smile began on Rafe's lips.

"Olivia says she is determined never to marry."

The smile grew broader. "I always like a woman who knows her own mind."

Stephen cast a narrow glance at his friend. "Rafe, she is going to be my sister-in-law. I know you like a challenge, but this is one woman you cannot —"

"Honestly, Stephen, I am not quite such a cad," Rafe retorted.

"I know you are not," Stephen replied. "It is just that I . . . well, I am a little protective of Olivia — and of her family, I find. I know you're not the marrying kind."

"You're right about that," Rafe replied easily. The war had taught him how easily and permanently the ties of love could be snapped. The only way to get through life heartwhole was to keep one's heart to oneself. "Just a little flirtation to pass the time, my friend." He smiled. "I think your new sister-in-law is probably well acquainted with the art of flirtation."

Stephen chuckled. "Yes, I imagine she is. You may have just found your match there. Better watch it, or you may end up the one whose heart is in danger."

Rafe did not dignify his friend's comment with a reply. His heart had been out of danger for more than ten years. He was, he told himself, quite safe.

But as he and Stephen left the room, he could not resist casting a last glance at Kyria over his shoulder.

3

The next two days were filled with preparations for Olivia's wedding, and Kyria was so busy that she could almost say she did not notice Rafe McIntyre. It was a trifle annoying, she thought, that had he been any of her many suitors, she would not have even thought about him. Unlike some of the other men there, he did not hang about or try to set up a flirtation, yet she was always aware of where he was and what he was doing.

Kyria spent most of the day on the move, arranging the masses of flowers brought in by the gardener from the estate's greenhouse, solving household crises with the housekeeper or butler, soothing this guest or the other's ruffled feathers over some imagined slight and trying to see that all the guests were kept entertained in one way or another. She blessed Lady St. Leger, Stephen's mother, who was tactful, pleasant and willing to be bored for the sake of harmony in the house. Kyria could count on her to keep the shyest or most longwinded guest occupied.

To her surprise, she found that the other person on whom she could rely was Rafe McIntyre. He did not hover, yet it seemed that he was always there when she needed someone to keep the male guests busy playing billiards and cards during a rainy afternoon or to say a few words to a shy spinster or to charm Lady Rochester out of a black mood. Kyria was thankful for his being there, and yet she found it somehow irritating, too, that he was able to so easily charm everyone, man or woman, into doing what he wanted. It confirmed her opinion that he was an inveterate flirt.

The day of the wedding dawned crisp and clear, without any of the rain that she had feared would spoil the ceremony. Kyria and her maid, Joan, helped Olivia dress. They were joined by Thisbe and the duchess, and much to everyone's surprise, the duchess, usually not a sentimental person, began to cry as Kyria and Joan settled the white dress around Olivia.

"Oh, dear," she said, dabbing at her eyes with her handkerchief. "I vowed I would not do this." The duchess leaned over and gave her youngest daughter a kiss on the cheek. "Dearest Olivia, you are such a beautiful bride. I have never believed that any of my daughters must get married in order to have a happy and fulfilled life. You know my views on marriage and a woman's place in society."

"Yes, Mother, I know," Olivia said with a smile.

"We all do," Kyria added.

"Don't be impertinent," the duchess said, though she could not keep a smile from flitting across her face. "Olivia, I am simply filled with happiness to see you today. I think your young man loves you very much. I cannot tell you how proud I am that both you and Thisbe married so well. I think a mother cannot help but feel great happiness, knowing that you will be happy, and yet great sorrow to see her daughter leave her home . . ." She paused and blinked away her tears again. "Well, I will leave you to your sisters now. I must go or I fear I will be embarrassingly red-eyed at the wedding ceremony."

She cast a smile around at her three daughters and left the room. Thisbe watched for a few moments as Kyria fastened the long line of tiny pearl buttons that marched up the back of the white-satin wedding dress. Then Thisbe stood up and began to move restlessly about the room, going over to look out the window into the side yard.

"I wonder how Desmond is doing with

the twins," she mused. Her husband, in the absence of their tutor, had taken on the task of keeping an eye on Constantine and Alexander throughout the wedding day.

"They promised Mother that they would behave today," Kyria said, glancing back to where Joan was occupied laying out the long train of Olivia's dress. "She threatened them with taking away their menagerie if they did not. And Mr. McIntyre promised to give them boxing lessons if they were good. Of course, the problem with the twins is that they don't really mean to misbehave. It just sort of happens."

"Boxing lessons," Thisbe said in disgust. "They are so bloodthirsty sometimes. Yesterday they were telling me all about shooting a gun. It seems your Mr. McIntyre gave them a lesson in physics, using a gun as an example."

"All boys are bloodthirsty," Kyria replied offhandedly. "And he's not *my* Mr. McIntyre."

"He always seems to be where you are," Thisbe replied a little archly. "I think you have made a conquest of St. Leger's American friend."

"He would have one think so," Kyria said coolly. "But I think he is just an inveterate flirt."

"Kyria! You wrong him," Olivia protested, twisting around to look at her sister.

Kyria put her hands on Olivia's shoulders and firmly turned her back around, then finished doing up her buttons. "Do I?"

"Yes. I think he is quite smitten with you. So does Stephen." Olivia smiled, her large brown eyes lighting up. "I was hoping you might like him, too. I thought the moment I met him that perhaps you would. He is so different from other men."

"He has that peculiar accent," Kyria admitted.

"Oh, Kyria! It is more than that. He has done things, seen things that the men we know have not. He fought in a war. His home was burned down. He traveled west to seek his fortune and found it. From what he and Stephen have told me about their mining adventure, it was a great deal of work — and danger, as well."

"Danger?" Kyria asked. "How was it a danger? You mean, going down into the mine?"

"I don't think that so much as that the land is so wild. Stephen told me that they were once attacked by a grizzly bear."

"A what?"

"A huge sort of bear, quite fierce. And they had to defend their claim from men who would have taken it from them. He 'rode shotgun,' Stephen told me, when they transported their silver, to fight off any thieves."

Kyria shrugged, feigning indifference. "I can well imagine that he has been where there is danger. I cannot see that that makes him a particularly attractive candidate as a husband."

"Husband?" Olivia exchanged a significant look with Thisbe. "Then you have thought about it."

Kyria flushed. "Well, isn't that what you meant? I have not considered Mr. McIntyre as a husband. I have not considered him at all."

"He is a terribly attractive man not to consider at all," Thisbe mused. " 'Methinks she doth protest too much.' "

Kyria grimaced at her sisters and stepped back from Olivia, saying crossly, "Just because you two found husbands, that is no reason for you to be scheming to get me married, as well."

"As if you were not always scheming to find me a mate," Olivia protested as she sat down at the vanity and let her maid start to work on her hair.

"That was different," Kyria told her. "I knew that you would be happy married to the right man, just as Thisbe is. But there are some of us who simply are not destined for marriage."

"And you are saying that you are one of those?"

Thisbe asked. "How did you arrive at that decision?"

"It is obvious, isn't it?" Kyria retorted. "I have been out for nine years, meeting the most eligible bachelors, and I have not yet found a single one whom I would wish to marry."

"That doesn't mean you won't," Thisbe argued.

"It seems to me an indication of it," Kyria replied.

"You've only met all the eligible bachelors in England," Olivia reminded her. "That is why you should take a closer look at an American."

"American, English, what difference does it make? Once you marry, your life is no longer your own. Marriage is a completely inequitable institution. You lose control of your money, you promise to 'obey' some man, and you even give up your name."

"Well, yes, of course, and the laws

should be changed," Thisbe agreed. "But people can scarcely stop marrying until that happens."

"It sounds like an excellent idea to me."

"Besides, that isn't what is keeping you from marriage," Olivia said. "You just told me it is because you haven't found the right man. And when you do, all the other things won't matter."

"Dear, sweet Olivia." Kyria went to her sister and leaned down to kiss her lightly on the cheek. "You are happy, and rightfully so. You are marrying a wonderful man who loves you very much. And you have such a sweet, loving nature that I am sure nothing will make you as happy as marriage and children. But as you well know, I am not possessed of your sweet nature. I am willful and headstrong, completely used to having my own way. The prospect of sitting around a fire every evening while my husband snores in his chair and a baby bounces on my knee does not fill me with pleasure. I love to go to parties and flirt. My life is laid out exactly the way I like it. I do what I wish when I wish, and I have no one to answer to. It is the perfect situation for me."

"But what about love?" Olivia asked, her eyes shadowed with concern as she looked at her sister in the mirror. "How can you be happy without love?"

"I have done well enough without a man's love for several years. I suspect I shall be able to continue." She smiled reassuringly at her sister. "Besides, it isn't as if I have no love in my life. I have you and Thisbe and Reed and the twins and Mother and Papa. I have a busy life. And I am quite happy without a man."

"So was I, until I met Stephen," Olivia responded. "Then I realized that there was actually a huge hole in my life. I just didn't know about it."

"I will happily remain in ignorance," Kyria said lightly.

"You are quite sure that you have no interest in Mr. McIntyre?" Olivia pressed her, frowning in concern.

"Quite sure. He is, I will admit, attractive and even charming in an obvious sort of way."

Across the room, Thisbe made a choked noise, but when Kyria turned toward her inquiringly, she merely smiled and gave a little cough.

"However," Kyria went on firmly, "I am not in need of rescuing by any man, and I have had enough experience with hardened flirts not to be taken in by one of them."

"Hardened flirt?" Olivia objected. "Why, Kyria, you scarcely know the man. How can you —"

"I have seen enough of him," Kyria said. "I have found that there are only a few types of men. One of them is the grave sort who spouts off his admiration of you and his love of your wit, your beauty, your spirit. That sort wants to marry you and spend the rest of his life smothering you with all his care and protection. Then there is the adventurer, who wants to marry you for your money and spend the rest of his life spending it. There is also the flirt who simply wants to have fun and dance and charm you and has no desire to ever marry at all. And lastly, there is the man who sees every woman as a challenge and a conquest, and his ambition is to win your heart — and your body — and when he has accomplished that, he is content and leaves. I am not sure which of the last two categories Mr. McIntyre fits into."

"Kyria!" Olivia cried, shocked. "What a cynical view of life!"

"Not of life," Kyria protested. "Only of men." She smiled. "Don't look so appalled, love. I have learned to steer clear of those who want to marry me and simply have fun with the flirts. Even one who wants a conquest can be entertaining to match wits with."

"Then I would think that Mr. McIntyre is just your sort," Thisbe interjected.

Kyria looked momentarily nonplussed. Then she shrugged and said lightly, "Well, there are some that are too dangerous."

"What do you mean?" Olivia asked.

"She means," Thisbe put in astutely, "that there are some men whom even a cynic cannot resist."

"I knew it!" Olivia crowed. "You do feel an attraction for him."

"Certainly not." Kyria lifted her chin obstinately. "And why, may I ask, are we sitting here discussing that American when it is *you*, my dear, and your love that we should be talking about?"

Olivia smiled, quite willing to be led into a discussion of the manifest superiority of Stephen St. Leger to all other men, and for the next few minutes, she and her sisters indulged in discussing Olivia's fiancé and the upcoming honeymoon.

Joan put the last pin in Olivia's hair and stood back, and Kyria exclaimed in delight, "Oh! You look beautiful."

Kyria and Joan pinned the veil into her hair, and Olivia stood up, letting the others smooth and shake her skirts and train until everything was exactly right. She gazed at herself in the mirror with some amazement. Even Olivia would have to agree that this afternoon, at least, she was beautiful, Kyria thought.

Tears welled up in Kyria's eyes, and she felt a cold clutch of pain in her chest. She was filled with pride and happiness for her younger sister, as well as a fervent hope that her married life would be wonderful. Yet she could not help but realize that she was losing her sister, as well. Kyria had not felt the pain of parting when Thisbe had married, for Thisbe and her new husband had returned from their honeymoon to live in the massive Broughton House in London with the rest of the family. But Olivia would return from her honeymoon to Blackhope Hall, the St. Legers' family seat, and from now on, Kyria would see her only on visits.

Kyria thought of the years of late-night sisterly gossip sessions, curled up on one or the other's bed, of the countless times that they had turned to each other with a problem or a fear or a joy, and suddenly it was all she could do not to cry.

"Oh, Olivia!" Kyria threw her arms around her sister and hugged her hard. "I'm so happy for you."

"Thank you," Olivia replied, her own voice raspy with tears. "I'm going to miss you so. Thisbe . . ." She turned, and Thisbe joined them, putting an arm around each of her sisters.

"It will never be the same," Olivia said.

"It will be better," Thisbe told her stoutly.

"Yes. Don't cry. Stephen will be most displeased with me if I send you down to the wedding all red-eyed," Kyria teased.

"Promise me you will come to visit me when we return."

"Of course," Thisbe replied. "You will soon be sick of us, we shall visit so often."

"Now," Kyria said, smiling and firmly pushing all sad thoughts to the back of her mind, "it's time we started for the church."

Kyria's hard work was rewarded by the fact that the wedding went off without a hitch. Standing beside her sister and watching Olivia's lovely, glowing face beneath her wedding veil, Kyria knew that every minute of work had been worth it.

She watched Olivia, her face turned up to Stephen's, her eyes shining with love, and for an instant, she felt a flash of envy. What, she wondered, would it be like to feel such love for a man? Kyria glanced out into the audience, her eyes seeking her own parents. Theirs had been a love match, too. Her mother, while genteel, was certainly not of a birth equal to the duke's, but he had been smitten with love for her the instant she had burst into his office, demanding better conditions for the workers in one of his factories. They had married despite all his family's protests and despite her mother's disdain for the members of the nobility.

Thoroughly unalike, the gentle, vague, studious Broughton and his fiery, determined, social-reformer duchess had remained happily in love for almost thirty-three years now. Theirs had been the example of love with which Kyria had grown up, and she could not imagine marrying without that overwhelming emotion. And, Kyria reflected wryly, with all the blessings she had been given in life, love seemed to be the one thing that she lacked.

Her gaze went back to Stephen and Olivia, then beyond the couple to Rafe McIntyre. He smiled at her and winked, and Kyria quickly glanced away, a flush rising in her cheeks.

It was absurd, she thought, what Olivia had said about Mr. McIntyre. Utterly absurd. She had no interest in the man, and she was sure that he had no interest in her, other than as a mild flirtation, perhaps, to pass the time until his friend was married and he returned to the United States. It was only Olivia's naiveté that interpreted McIntyre's smooth, flirtatious manner of speaking as some sort of real interest in Kyria.

Besides, she added mentally, she had no interest in him, anyway. There was something a little too smug about the look in his eyes, which were, by the way, just too blue for a normal man, and the way the skin around his eyes crinkled when he smiled was, really, nothing that should have made her heart give a little lurch. Rafe McIntyre was all too aware of his effect on women, Kyria thought, and she was determined to show him that she was not the typical woman.

Even if she was attracted a little bit — nothing more than that, certainly! — she felt certain that he was not the sort of man she could possibly come to care about. There was a great deal more to a man than charm and good looks and being able to ride like a centaur, after all. She felt certain that his character was not such as she could admire. He was a Southerner, someone who had fought to keep the institution of slavery, someone who had owned other human beings. Kyria was not as given to political reforms as the duchess, but she held the same sort of humanitarian ideals as the others in her family. She could not imagine loving someone who had had so little regard for the lives of others.

No. Whatever little lurch her heart might give at the sight of him, Kyria was certain that Rafe McIntyre was not the man for her.

Stephen lifted Olivia's veil and kissed her, and Kyria realized, with that same odd mixture of joy and loss, that the ceremony was over. The newlyweds led the way up the aisle, and Rafe gave his arm to Kyria to escort her out after them. She tucked her hand in the crook of his elbow, feeling suddenly as self-conscious as a schoolgirl. She did not look at him as they followed Stephen and Olivia, and when they reached the foyer of the church, she started to turn away, pulling her hand from his arm.

Rafe put his hand over hers, holding it there for a moment, and Kyria looked up at him, eyes flashing. "I beg your pardon, Mr. McIntyre, but you seem to have an annoying habit of not releasing a woman when she wishes it."

White teeth flashed in his tanned face. "I beg *your* pardon, ma'am. My mama always said I was lamentably lacking in manners. I just wanted to say something to you, and every time I see you, you take off like a rabbit."

Kyria's back stiffened at his words, and she raised her eyebrows in her haughtiest manner. "I have had a great deal to do the past few days, Mr. McIntyre. I am sorry if I was unable to attend to you. However, I feel sure that you found other companions."

He chuckled. "Others, true. But none who could compare to you."

"You are adept at flattery."

"Not flattery. The truth."

"Mr. McIntyre —" Kyria pulled her hand from his arm and folded her hands together "— you said that you wished to say something to me."

"Yes. I understand that there will be dancing this evening."

"After the reception and wedding supper, there will be a ball."

"I wanted to request the honor of a waltz with you," Rafe went on, "that's all. I just wanted to make sure I got my bid in before your dance card was all filled up." He grinned. "I promise you, I do know how to waltz, despite my being an American."

Kyria looked at him, a little puzzled, and he explained, "Lady Rochester asked me the other day if I had ever read Shakespeare. She seemed to think I grew up in a log cabin in the wilderness."

"Oh, dear." Kyria suppressed a smile. "My great-aunt has a secret fondness for the novels of your James Fennimore Cooper, I'm afraid. I apologize."

He shrugged. "It's all right. Actually, I did live in a log cabin in Colorado when I was mining for silver. But when I was younger, I lived in a place somewhat more civilized, and I had to learn all the social graces, including dancing. So I think I can promise not to step on your toes." He paused, his eyes looking into hers, and again, Kyria felt the same strange little lurch of her heart. "Will you honor me with a dance?"

"Of course." Kyria smiled, hoping that he had not seen anything in her face to betray the odd sensation she had felt, and turned away to join her parents.

The newly married couple received guests in one of the formal state rooms off the rotunda in Broughton Park, and afterward, the guests streamed into another of the large, elegant rooms, built almost two hundred years earlier for a family of high consequence and rarely used in the present by their easygoing descendants. There, an extensive wedding supper had been laid out, the result of hours of work and planning by Kyria and the Broughton House staff. The festivities were capped by an evening of dancing in the grand ballroom, sometime during which the newlyweds would leave for the beginning of their honeymoon.

Kyria, keeping an eye out for any problems and consulting with the butler, as well as making sure that no guest was left untended or without conversation, had little time to enjoy the proceedings. Even after Olivia and Stephen led the party out onto the floor for the first waltz, Kyria spent most of her time starting conversations wherever silence or boredom lurked and making sure that there were no wallflowers left stranded. To that end, she enlisted the services of her brother Reed and Rafe McIntyre, for she soon saw that, as he had promised, Rafe was able to waltz, was indeed quite adept at it, and whenever he returned his partner from the dance floor, she was always smiling and rosy with pleasure.

"You obviously have the magic touch," Kyria told Rafe when he returned to her after escorting a chattering Lady Marcross off the floor. "Lady Marcross is usually more given to tears than to smiles."

He grinned, raising his eyebrows. "Jealous?"

"Hardly," Kyria retorted. "I simply wish I had had you at some other balls I have given."

"No more than I wish it," he retorted, and held out his hand to her. "Now . . . you owe me something for all the pleasantries I've had to dispense for the past hour."

"I do?"

"Yes. That dance you promised me this afternoon?"

"Oh, but . . ." Kyria stopped, then smiled and gave in, reaching out to take his hand and let him lead her onto the floor. "All right. I suppose I should find out for myself what magic you work."

"Hardly magic," he told her, putting his hand to her waist. They stood, waiting for the music to begin. "You know what my secret is?"

Kyria shook her head.

"I listen to what a lady has to say."

Kyria made a face. "It has to be more than that."

"You'd be surprised. *You* are accustomed to attentive men. Look at you — of course your dance partner or any other man listens to you, looks at you, responds to you. But if you take Lady Marcross, whose husband probably falls asleep while she is talking, or her children, who are so accustomed to her tales of her ailments and woes that they nod and murmur 'mmm' without hearing a word . . . well, a woman like that blossoms when someone actually listens to her and answers."

"I am sure that it has nothing to do with that face," Kyria said dryly.

"What face?"

"*Your* face," Kyria retorted. "Don't be coy, Mr. McIntyre. I am sure that you are used to women swooning over you."

He let out a chuckle. "Why, darlin', what a bold thing to say."

The music began at last, and Rafe swung Kyria out onto the dance floor. He moved easily and gracefully, his hand at her waist, guiding her with a gentle confidence. There was no awkward pushing or pulling, no uncertainty of step, only a wonderful sensation of floating, secure in his arms. He gazed into her face, his intense blue eyes locked with hers, and it seemed for the moment as if there was no one else on the floor but the two of them.

Kyria breathed in a little shakily, understanding now exactly what brought that flush of pleasure to his dance partners' cheeks. She could feel the warmth spreading through her, too, an almost giddy excitement, and she wondered how even Lady Marcross could think of anything to say as she danced with this man. Kyria felt as if every thought had flown from her head.

Something flared in Rafe's eyes, and his hand tightened fractionally on her waist, and Kyria knew that it was a response to her own emotion. For the strangest moment, it was as though she felt what he felt, that she knew him, not in words or any sort of coherent thought, but as if they were somehow connected.

The music ended, and they stopped dancing. Kyria was suddenly disoriented, the moment of connection gone, leaving her feeling faintly empty and bereft. They stood for a moment, gazing at each other. Then Kyria whirled and moved quickly away.

Rafe stepped out onto the terrace and took a deep breath. The air was chilly, but it felt good on his skin after the heat of the ballroom. He was still strangely shaken from his dance with Kyria. He had felt something as they danced, something he had never experienced before, and he wasn't sure what it was, only that it was exciting and disturbing at the same time.

He strolled along the terrace and down the steps, reaching inside his jacket and pulling out a cheroot. Biting off the end, he struck a sulfur match on the sole of his shoe and lit the small cigar.

He ambled along one of the garden paths, smoking and gazing around at the garden, lit by torches placed along the paths. The walkway led around the corner of the house to the side lawn, where he had first seen Kyria. He smiled a little to himself as he looked over at the large oak tree. He turned, gazing out across the wide, well-kept driveway and onto the expanse of lawn beyond.

A flicker of movement caught his eye, and he peered into the darkness. Someone was walking up the driveway, the dark figure barely picked out by the torches that lined the drive on both sides.

It seemed odd to Rafe that someone would be trudging up the drive at this hour, particularly with a wedding celebration in full swing in the house, and he watched the man curiously. He wore a hat and greatcoat, and he walked quickly, his arms wrapped around himself, as if to wrap the warmth of his coat more closely to him.

Suddenly another figure bolted from the trees and launched himself at the man walking up the driveway.

"Hey!" Rafe shouted, and started toward them.

The two men grappled, moving in a strange, awkward dance. Rafe tossed aside his cheroot and started running, wishing that his guns were not lying in a drawer in his bedroom upstairs. Metal flashed in the darkness between the men, then was gone, leaving one of the men crumpled on the ground.

4

Rafe called out again. The attacker looked back and saw Rafe running full tilt toward him, hesitated for a moment, then bent down, tugging something from the man he had attacked. The man on the ground rolled over, huddling protectively in on himself. The attacker glanced up again at Rafe, then turned and ran into the shelter of the trees.

Rafe skidded to a halt beside the man on the ground. "Are you all right?"

He bent over the man, speaking in what he hoped was a reassuring tone. "Can you talk? What happened?"

The man groaned, and Rafe gently rolled him onto his back. His coat fell open, revealing a dark stain spreading across his white shirt. Rafe whipped his handkerchief out of his pocket and folded it, pressing it to the man's wound.

The stranger opened his eyes and looked at Rafe, his gaze panic-stricken.

"It's all right," Rafe said quickly. "I won't hurt you. Let's get you into the house and see what we can do about that wound."

The man stretched out one hand to Rafe, his fingers clutching Rafe's lapel. "Please . . . Kyri . . ." he whispered.

"What?" Startled, Rafe stared at him. "Kyria?"

The man's hand dropped away from Rafe, falling to a small bag that was tied to his belt. His hand closed protectively over the bag as he said, "Give . . . please."

"You want to give this to Kyria?" Rafe asked. "Well, you can do that yourself, just as soon as I get you inside."

The man spoke again, this time a jumble of words in a language that Rafe did not understand. Carefully, Rafe slid his hands beneath the man and began to lift him. He was a slight man, not as tall as Kyria, and Rafe picked him up easily, rising to his feet. The man let out another groan.

"Sorry," Rafe murmured. He started toward the house, calling for help.

A moment later, the front door opened, silhouetting one of the footmen. He stood stock-still for a moment, then after calling back into the house, started down the steps on a run. Seconds later, two more footmen came hurrying out.

The men helped carry the stranger around the side of the house and in through the kitchen door. They were met with a stifled shriek from a housemaid.

"Get the butler," Rafe ordered, and the girl nodded and hurried away.

They laid the man down on the long wooden table in the servants' dining hall. Rafe's handkerchief was soaked with blood, and he replaced it with a napkin, trying to stanch the blood.

"Get me bandages. Medical supplies," Rafe told the footmen, who were still standing at the table staring down in amazement at the man they had carried in. "Now!"

One of the footmen hustled out, and shortly afterward, Smeggars hurried into the room. He stopped at the sight of the man on the table.

"My God. I thought the girl was hysterical." He looked up at Rafe. "What happened, sir?"

"Someone attacked him," Rafe explained. "I was outside having a smoke and I saw him walking up to the house." He described the assailant rushing out of the trees at the man and the tussle that ensued. "I think he stabbed him."

"Good Lord!" Smeggars exclaimed. "I will get bandages."

"I sent the man after some medical supplies," Rafe told him. "If you will get me some scissors, I'll cut away his shirt."

"Of course, sir." Smeggars stepped out of the room and was back in a moment, scissors in hand. He was followed by the footman, with a wad of bandages in one hand and a small tin box in the other.

Rafe set to work cutting the blood-soaked shirt away from the wound and carefully peeling it off. Despite his efforts to be gentle, the man cried out in pain. The wound was not wide, but it was deep. Rafe folded up one of the bandages and pressed it again to the wound.

"He needs to be stitched up," Rafe said. "I can do it, but he really should have a doctor."

"I have sent one of the footmen to find the doctor. He and his wife are here tonight," Smeggars replied.

"Good. We'll wait, then." Rafe leaned closer to the man, listening to his breathing. There was an ominous gurgling noise as he breathed. "That doesn't sound good. I think he may have a punctured lung."

Rafe turned to Smeggars. "Do you know him?"

Smeggars shook his head. "I have never seen him before tonight, sir. He . . . he looks foreign."

Rafe nodded. Even given the underlying pallor from shock and loss of blood, the man looked much too dark-skinned to hail from England. His hair was thick, black and short, curling slightly on his forehead.

"He asked for Lady Kyria," Rafe said.

"What?" Smeggars turned to Rafe in astonishment. "Are you certain, sir?"

Rafe nodded. "I guess you'd better send for her, too."

"But, sir . . ." The butler glanced askance at the wounded man on the table.

"I know. Not a sight for a lady," Rafe agreed. "But it may be that she can identify him. And he seemed to want to talk to her, to give her that thing on his belt." Rafe looked at Smeggars. "I reckon if Lady Kyria knows him, she would want us to send for her."

"You're right, of course." Smeggars released a little sigh and turned to go in search of Kyria.

The doctor appeared soon after Smeggars left. He stopped, staring at the man on the table in some shock. "My God! I thought the footman was drunk!"

He went over to the table, lamenting, "I don't even have my bag. I never thought . . ."

Rafe showed him the bandages and supplies that the footman had brought and stepped back to give the doctor room enough to examine the man.

"I think his lung has been punctured," the doctor finally said. "And he has lost a great deal of blood."

"I know." Rafe looked at the doctor. "It doesn't look good, does it."

"I fear not."

The patient moaned and opened his eyes. A stream of words poured from him, and the doctor looked at Rafe. "Do you know what he said?"

Rafe shook his head. "Not a clue. I don't even recognize the language."

"Please . . . Ky . . . Ky . . ."

"Kyria?" Rafe asked, stepping closer to the man. "We've sent for her. Hold on, and she will be here in a minute."

The doctor turned away to send one of the servants for needle and thread, then stood over the man again and traded the bloody bandage for a fresh one.

The man gasped with pain, and he coughed. Blood trickled from the corner of his mouth, and he drew another painful breath. Rafe had seen enough death to read it in the man's face. He glanced at the doctor and saw there a confirmation of what he already knew. The man was near death, and neither bandages nor a needle and thread were likely to do him much good.

"Please . . ." The man's hand moved a little, reaching toward his waist. Then he turned his face to the side, and a little sigh escaped him. He went still.

"He's gone," the doctor said quietly.

There was the click of a woman's heels on the stone floor of the hall, and Kyria hurried into the room, her face creased in a frown. "Rafe! What happened? Smeggars told me . . ."

Rafe moved quickly toward her, but not before her gaze went to the table. She gasped, her hand flying to her mouth. Her face paled. "Is he . . ."

Rafe's arm went around her shoulders, supporting her. "He's dead."

Kyria let out a little cry of dismay, and she turned instinctively, burying her face in Rafe's shirt. Rafe's other hand came up to stroke her back soothingly.

"I'm sorry. I couldn't get to him in time."

Kyria's hands curled into Rafe's jacket, and she hung on for a moment longer, too shocked by the sight of the body on the table to speak or even summon up a coherent thought.

Gradually the shock began to subside,

and she realized that she was clinging to Rafe. Even as she thought how good and comforting it felt to lean against him thusly, she knew that she should not be doing it. It was, in fact, a little frightening to realize how good it felt.

She raised her head and stepped back, doing her best to hide the fact that it took some effort to let go of him. "I'm sorry," she said a little shakily. "I have never seen —"

"Of course not. I'm sorry you had to see him," Rafe said. "It was just that he asked for you. I thought you might know him."

"What?" Kyria looked at Rafe, then with a visible effort, turned around and looked again at the man lying motionless on the table. She swallowed, feeling a little sick and faint, but she forced herself to take a step closer and gaze more closely into the man's face.

She turned back to Rafe, saying, "I have never seen this man before. What happened? Are you sure he asked for me?"

"The first time he said, 'Kyri . . .' and then a moment ago it sounded as if he was trying to say your name again."

"Yes, my lady," the doctor agreed. "He definitely seemed to be trying to say your name. And he said, 'Please.' That's all we could understand. He spoke in a foreign language."

"I don't understand." Kyria forced herself to look at the man on the table again, then shook her head. "He is a complete stranger to me. I cannot imagine why he would have asked for me. What happened?"

"Someone attacked him," Rafe explained. "I was outside smoking a cigar, and I walked around to the front of the house. I saw him coming up the driveway. I thought it was odd, so I kept watching him, and then all of a sudden, this other fellow ran out of the trees at him, and they started to fight. I ran over, but I couldn't get there in time. The other man stabbed him and took off."

"I can't believe it!" Kyria drew in a shaky breath. "You're saying someone attacked a man right in front of our house! But why? And who could he be? Why did he say my name?"

"I have no idea. But I got the impression he wanted to give you something. He had a small bag tied to his waist. When I got there, he said your name, and then he put his hand on the bag and said, 'Please, give . . .' All I can think is that he wanted to give you whatever was in that bag. I assume that was why he was coming here."

"But why? I don't even know him!"

Rafe shrugged. "I don't know. But

maybe you ought to look inside the bag."

Kyria drew in a sharp breath and took an involuntary step away from the body, shaking her head.

"Don't worry. I'll get it for you. Here." Rafe took Kyria's arm and propelled her from the room and to a bench in the hall outside. "You sit here. Smeggars will get you a glass of water."

"Yes, of course, my lady." Smeggars moved off quickly, obviously relieved to have something useful to do.

"You just rest here for a minute," Rafe told her. "I'll get the bag."

Kyria nodded and leaned her head back against the wall, closing her eyes. It didn't help much, since she could still see the dead man's face in her mind's eye — the open, staring eyes, the unnatural pallor of his dark skin. She pressed her hand against her stomach, which was still roiling. She had never seen a dead person — or, at least, not one who was not prepared for burial and in a casket — and the experience unnerved her.

She thought about the way she had clung to Rafe, letting him hold her in the protection of his arms. It had been a decidedly weak thing to do, she knew, not the sort of thing that Thisbe or her mother or even Olivia would have done. But she could not help but recall how wonderfully warm and safe it had felt for that moment, to be enclosed in his heat, to smell the masculine scent, mingled with the faint, lingering smell of tobacco and cologne, to feel the hard strength of his arms around her and hear the reassuring thud of his heart beneath her head. Something stirred deep inside her as she thought of his holding her, and she realized with a guilty start how far her thoughts were wandering from the scene of death she had just witnessed. It was another sign, she supposed, of how shallow she was.

"My lady." Kyria looked up to see Smeggars holding a small tray with a glass of water on it. She took the glass and sipped from it, grateful for the distraction.

"Smeggars, don't tell anyone else about this."

"Of course, my lady. What would you have me do with, um . . ."

"Send for the constable, of course. But tell the servants who know about it to keep quiet. I don't want my family or the guests to hear of it. I am terribly sorry for that poor man, but I refuse to let this sad news disturb my sister's wedding day."

Smeggars nodded in understanding. "I

shall make sure that not a word is uttered."

"Thank you." Kyria took another sip of water, feeling somewhat more in control of herself.

She glanced over to see Rafe standing in the doorway, a small, canvas, drawstring bag in his hand. "Here it is."

Kyria stood, looking doubtfully at the bag. "And you are sure he meant it for me?"

Rafe shrugged. "All I know is, he said your name and something like 'give' or 'please give,' and then he started babbling in some foreign tongue."

"Really? What language?"

"Not one I recognized. So I would say with some certainty not French or Spanish or German." He glanced around. "Shall we open this?"

"Yes. Let's . . . go somewhere else." Kyria did not like to think about lingering here.

She started down the hall, Rafe beside her, and emerged from the servants' area into a wide hall. Turning away from the direction of the ballroom, she went into one of the smaller drawing rooms.

Rafe set the bag down on a table near the door, and Kyria opened the drawstring and reached in, pulling out a hard, squarish object wrapped in velvet. Carefully, she unwrapped the velvet to reveal a small box. She could not help but let out a small cry of delight.

The box was ivory, with a curved lid rather like a very small trunk. All around the box were intricately carved patterns and what looked like some sort of figures. Its crowning glory, however, was a huge dark gem, crudely cut and unfaceted, that was set into the center of one side of the box.

"It's beautiful!" Kyria exclaimed, picking up the box and looking at it closely. She ran a fingertip over the carvings, then over the almost-black gem, peering closely at it. There was something compelling about the box, a beauty that drew her.

Rafe moved nearer to see it, coming up so close behind Kyria that he was almost touching her. Kyria swallowed, very aware of his presence. She could smell again the scent of him, feel the warmth of his body, and it seemed as if all her nerve endings were suddenly alive and tingling, as if they could reach across the inch that separated them and touch Rafe.

"What is that?" he asked. "Is it glass?"

"No, I don't think so," Kyria replied, smoothing her fingertip over the jewel. "I think it is a black diamond. It's very rare."

"A diamond?" Rafe asked in amazement. "They come in colors?"

Kyria nodded. "There are yellow diamonds and brown ones, blue ones, even pink. Black diamonds are unusual, though, and they are often found in areas where one doesn't normally find diamonds. Primarily they come from Brazil and parts of Africa. This one is huge, which is, of course, extremely rare."

Rafe looked at her, intrigued. "You certainly seem to know a lot about diamonds."

Kyria gave a self-conscious laugh. "Well, jewelry is an interest of mine. It is a little frivolous, but . . ." She shrugged. "I love the beauty of gems and precious metals."

"Beauty isn't frivolous," Rafe replied, his gaze resting on her face. "Beauty is what humans have always strived for. In art, in music, architecture — and jewelry."

Kyria smiled faintly. "Yes, but jewels and dresses are not exactly serious. Not like science, say, or the treatment of workers or the vote for women."

"Ah, I see. Like the things that some of your family are involved in."

Kyria nodded. "I fear my mother sometimes finds me rather shallow. Thisbe looks for great discoveries. Theo explores uncharted territories." She shrugged. "I design necklaces and earrings."

"Do you really?"

Kyria nodded. "I designed the pearl necklace Olivia wore today. It was made from an old necklace that had been in the family for generations, but it was much too old-fashioned to wear. So I had the pearls reset."

"I noticed it," Rafe said. "I thought it was beautiful. You are very talented."

Kyria smiled, a blush staining her cheeks. "I'm not really. It's just something I dabble in. There is a jeweler in London who does all the work for me."

"But the design was lovely to begin with. He could not have done the work without your idea."

Kyria had received compliments before on her jewelry, but rarely had she admitted to anyone outside her family that she had designed a piece. Society, she knew, would have found it another oddity in her, no matter how attractive they thought the jewelry was. Jewelry-making was not a suitable occupation for a member of the nobility. In fact, society found no occupation suitable for a noblewoman. And while her family always praised the pieces she had made, she felt sure, deep down, that they considered it pretty, but not important in the way that the matters that occupied other members of her family were important.

She was faintly surprised that she had told Rafe about her hobby, and she suspected that she probably would not have if her nerves had not been shaken by what had happened. She was also a little surprised that it pleased her so that Rafe liked her work. She was accustomed to men complimenting her looks, but not something she had done.

"I designed the necklace for myself originally," she went on. "But then I realized that it would suit Olivia much better. The pearls have such a soft luster, and they are, of course, perfect for a wedding."

Rafe smiled, and his eyes drifted over Kyria's face. "You are right. Pearls would not suit you. Not brilliant enough. You are a woman for diamonds." He reached out and brushed his knuckles across her cheek. "Or maybe emeralds to match your eyes."

A shiver ran through Kyria at the touch of his skin on hers. She looked up at him, her face only inches from his. She gazed into his eyes, unable to look away, aware of her breath coming faster in her throat. She could feel the heat of his body. She remembered the feel of his shirt beneath her cheek, the warmth and comfort as his arms enfolded her. But the warmth she was feeling now had little to do with comfort.

He wanted to kiss her now, she knew. Kyria had dealt with men trying to steal kisses from her before. She was adept at stepping back or turning her cheek, making a light remark that changed the moment. But she made no move to do any of those things, simply stood gazing up at Rafe, feeling her blood move with sudden heat through her veins. She wanted to kiss him, wanted to feel his lips on hers with an excitement that fizzed along her nerves like champagne.

His hands went to her arms, first wrapping lightly around her wrists, then sliding slowly up her arms. She shivered again at the feel of his hands, faintly roughened, gliding over her soft flesh. His hands reached her shoulders and tightened, pulling her into him as he bent toward her. Kyria knew she should have protested, should have drawn back, but she did not. She let him draw her to him, turning her face up to his.

His mouth settled on hers, slow and soft, his lips moving against hers with an increasing urgency. Kyria's heart slammed in her chest. She had been kissed a few times by eager suitors, but never before had it felt like this. Never before had she wanted to press against him as she did now, nor had her hands slid up to his chest and dug into his lapels, holding on under the onslaught of pleasure.

He made a noise deep in his throat as she leaned into him, and his arms slipped around her, pulling her tightly against his rock-hard body. She felt the strength of his muscles through their clothes, their bodies locked together all the way up and down. She slid her arms up and around his neck, holding on tightly as his mouth took hers.

"Kyria!" Her father's voice sounded down the hall, calling her.

Kyria stiffened and stepped abruptly back. Rafe's arms opened, letting her go, and for an instant they simply stood staring at each other, shocked by the intensity of what they had just experienced. Kyria drew a shaky breath and turned away, her hands going to her burning cheeks.

"Kyria? Are you down this way?" The duke's voice came again as his footsteps rang down the hall.

Kyria cleared her throat and said, "Yes, Papa. I'm in here."

She reached up to pat her hair, hoping

that she did not look as stunned and flushed as she felt. She started toward the door just as her father stopped at the door and peered into the room.

"Ah, there you are, my dear," he said, smiling benignly and stepping into the room. "Smeggars said he thought you went this way. Your mother sent me. She said to tell you to come help Olivia. She's gone up to change into her traveling clothes. What are you — Oh!"

He stopped, his eye caught by the small white box on the table. He approached it, intrigued, and picked it up carefully. "I say — what a beautiful artifact! Where did you get it? Byzantine, isn't it?"

"Is it?" Kyria asked, as she and Rafe moved to where the duke stood admiring the ivory box.

"Oh, yes, I think so. Not my specialty, of course." He turned toward Rafe, saying in explanation, "I am much fonder of the earlier Roman Empire, you know, and even earlier — the Greek, Etruscan, Cretan. I don't really know a great deal about the later empire. But I would definitely say that it looks like Byzantine work."

He ran his finger over the rounded top, easily distracted from his mission, as he always was by any ancient object. "This style, like a humpbacked trunk, is typical of the Byzantines, as is the carved ivory. Not as beautiful as their cloisonné work, in my opinion, which was really quite phenomenal, given the times. I would hazard a guess that this was done before the height of their art. This glass is unusual, though. Typically, they used carnelian and turquoise."

"I don't think it is glass, Papa. I believe it is a black diamond, just unfaceted."

"Really?" He looked up from the box, surprised. "Black diamond, eh? Never seen one."

"Neither have I," Rafe told him. "But your daughter seems to know her jewels."

"Oh, my, yes." Broughton chuckled and cast a glance of affection at his daughter. "That's my Kyria. Well, well, my dear, this is very interesting. I would say it is quite a special piece, given the intricacy of the carving and the rarity of the jewel. Of course, they wouldn't have been able to facet it back then." He pushed at the top of the box. "That's odd."

"What is?" Kyria asked.

"I thought it would open," her father replied. "It certainly looks like a box, but it doesn't seem to have a lid, or at least, one that will open."

"Really?" Kyria took the box and examined it closely. "I can't see any line of separation, but with all this carving, it could easily be hidden."

"Surely it's not solid," Rafe put in. "It doesn't seem heavy enough."

"I wouldn't think so," the duke agreed. "It must open. There must be some hidden catch or something."

"Is that typical of Byzantine artifacts?" Rafe asked.

Broughton shrugged. "Frankly, dear chap, I don't know. You would need an expert in the field. Someone like Dr. Jennings or . . . who else? Dr. Atkinson. Early Eastern religious art is one of his specialties, if I remember correctly. Perhaps Uncle Bellard knows someone else."

"How old are we talking about here?" Rafe asked. "If I remember my history correctly, the Byzantine Empire was during the time of Constantine and Justinian. Am I right?"

The duke nodded. "Yes, I would say sometime after A.D. 500 and before the Turks, say, 1400 or so. I'd lean toward the earlier time rather than the later, say, before A.D. 1000. Of course, you would have to talk to an expert in the field. How did you come by it, Kyria? I had no idea you had an interest in artifacts."

"I don't. I mean, I think it's beautiful, but I don't know anything about it. I had no idea how old it was or where it came from until you told me just now," Kyria replied. "I don't know where it came from. A man came to the house tonight. Papa, it was awful. He was attacked as he approached the house, and he was killed."

"Killed!" Broughton exclaimed, staring at Kyria, then turning toward Rafe.

"I saw it happen," Rafe told him. "I chased the attacker off and brought the man inside, but he died soon thereafter."

"Sweet heaven! What a shocking thing!"

"I told Smeggars not to tell anyone about it," Kyria explained. "I don't want Olivia and Stephen to know. I don't want anything to spoil Olivia's wedding day."

"No, of course not. You're quite right, my dear." The duke set the box on the table, then sat on the nearest chair. "This is terrible. Who was he? And what does he have to do with this box?"

"The man had it on him," Rafe explained. "He was carrying it in a bag that he had tied around his waist. Obviously, it was very important to him. And apparently he was bringing it to Lady Kyria."

"Kyria! But why?"

"I don't know." Rafe told him the man's dying words. "I assume that he must have been coming here to deliver that box to her."

"But who would send you something like that, Kyria? Why?"

"I don't know," she admitted. "The only thing I can think is that it is from Theo."

"Theo! Well, I suppose that would make some sense," her father agreed.

Kyria turned to Rafe. "Theo is my oldest brother, Thisbe's twin. He travels all over the world, and he often sends presents home, particularly for Con and Alex. With them, it's usually exotic animals, but he has sent other things that caught his eye — some piece of native art or a gem or something. He sent Mother a lovely paisley shawl from India, and he sent Reed that abacus, you remember, Papa?"

The duke nodded vaguely. "Yes. Although I wouldn't have thought that he would have sent something so ancient. He and I had rather an argument about that the last time he was here, you know. He had become quite adamant about a country's ancient treasures remaining in that country rather than being taken abroad for study. Of course, I am against the practice of destroying ancient sites to remove the treasures to sell. But on the other hand, one cannot simply stand by and watch those artifacts turn into rubble, can one? Inattention, lack of care, lack of money . . ." The duke frowned, his face reddening as he recalled the argument.

"I am sure Theo agrees with that," Kyria said soothingly. "He would not want to see anything bad happen to an ancient treasure. Perhaps that was the case with this one. Maybe that is why he sent it here."

"Sir, I don't want to interfere here," Rafe began, "but I can't help remembering how that box got here. That the fellow carrying it was attacked and killed. His attacker bent over him after he stabbed him, and he didn't run away until he saw me running at him. I can't help but wonder if he wasn't after that box. If maybe that box is the reason he killed him."

Kyria nodded worriedly. Broughton stared at Rafe, horrified. Clearly his interest in the ancient object had pushed other considerations out of his head.

"Are you saying . . . do you think there is a danger of him trying to *steal* it?"

"I think there could be a danger, sir, to whomever has possession of that box," Rafe replied flatly, and his eyes went to Kyria.

5

The duke drew in his breath in a sharp gasp. "To Kyria? You think that this puts Kyria in danger?"

Kyria shot Rafe an irritated look and turned to her father. "No, Papa, I am sure that I'm not in any danger. Mr. McIntyre is just raising a possibility. We have no way of knowing that that was why that man was stabbed. It could have been a private argument between them. Or he could have just been a robber in general, not after that box in particular. Perhaps he simply saw the man walking and thought he would be a vulnerable target. Isn't that right, Mr. McIntyre?"

Kyria turned back to Rafe with a significant look. Rafe looked back at her blandly.

"No point in taking any chances," he replied. "I'm just suggesting that we ought to take precautions. We don't know exactly what that box is or how much it's worth, or even for sure why that man was bringing it to you. But given how old you say it is and given that whopper of a diamond on it, I would say it's something somebody might want to steal. And whoever killed the man who delivered it could have knowledge of the box, and that could have been the reason he attacked him. If so, then he knows that that thing is now inside this house. I'm not saying that he knows that Kyria has it or that he would try to harm her to get it, but I can't help but think that this thing would be a lot safer if you locked it up in a secure place."

"Yes, yes, you're absolutely right," her father said. "You mustn't take it to your room, Kyria. Perhaps I could lock it in my collections room. The cases all have locks, and the room itself has a very stout lock on the door."

"And there are bars on the windows," Kyria added. "It gives the house a certain prisonlike appearance."

Rafe grinned. "I saw that the other day from the garden. I wondered if you had some mad relative locked up there."

"No. Only Papa," Kyria said, linking her arm affectionately through her father's. "I agree with you, Papa. I think it would be safest to put the box in your collections room. The diamond alone is valuable, let alone the value of the box."

The duke patted her arm. "Very well, my

dear." He picked up the box, saying, "I shall take this right to the collections room, and then we must join the others."

"And we aren't going to say anything about all this to the others tonight," Kyria reminded him.

"Oh, no, you're right. Well, I must tell your mother, of course, but I will wait until after Olivia and Stephen leave. And Reed. I am sure he will want to deal with the constable." He frowned. "Perhaps we had better have a family meeting about the matter tomorrow. It really is most distressing."

Olivia was standing in the middle of her room with Thisbe and the duchess when Kyria hurried in. She was already dressed for her honeymoon in a brown traveling dress, rather plain — which was how she liked her clothes — but trimmed with elegant gold buttons down the front of the jacket and cut to show off her excellent figure. She turned when Kyria entered the room. Her cheeks were high with color and her eyes sparkling with excitement. She looked lovelier and happier than Kyria had ever seen her, reinforcing Kyria's determination not to let anything spoil Olivia's day.

"Kyria!" Olivia cried, holding out her

arms. "Where have you been? I'm almost ready."

"Dearest, I'm sorry." Putting on her brightest smile, Kyria hurried across the room to hug her sister and kiss her cheek. "I was talking to Smeggars about the food."

Kyria knew that the best way to stop any curious questions from either of her sisters or mother was to bring up domestic arrangements.

"Oh." Olivia waved away Kyria's explanation. "Well, you are here now." She stepped back and executed a little pirouette for Kyria's inspection. "You were right about the traveling dress. It's perfect."

"It is," Kyria agreed, forbearing to mention the struggle involved in getting her sister to agree that the large buttons and tight-waisted jacket were not too outlandish.

"You look beautiful," their mother declared, coming over to kiss Olivia on the cheek. "*All* my daughters are beautiful. Inside and out," she added, with a smile for Kyria and Thisbe. "Come now. We must let Olivia leave."

Kyria, glancing at her mother, was astonished to see the glint of tears in her eyes before the duchess turned away. Thisbe, on the other hand, was unashamedly wiping tears from her cheeks. Kyria felt a lump rising in her own throat and swallowed hard. Picking up Olivia's matching reticule, she handed the little bag to her sister and swept her out of the room.

Outside, Stephen and his bride stepped into the ducal carriage, their well-wishers pouring out of the house to send them on their way. Kyria, smiling and waving to her sister as the carriage pulled away, could not help but steal a glance down the driveway and wonder where exactly the dark stranger had been when he was attacked. She shivered, imagining the scene.

"Cold?" a man asked softly behind her, and she turned to see Rafe McIntyre standing close to her. He shrugged out of his jacket and wrapped it around her shoulders, bare in her elegant evening gown.

"Thank you." Kyria wrapped the jacket tightly around her, immediately warmed. "Where . . . where was it?"

"Down yonder." He pointed to where the line of trees ended, just as the drive started to curve as it drew in front of the house.

Kyria watched as the carriage moved toward the place where Rafe had pointed and could not help a little sigh of relief when it passed safely. She had not really expected a crazed attacker to leap out of the trees at the newlyweds, but she could not keep from being a trifle edgy.

"It's so sad," she said with a sigh. "I cannot help but think of that poor man."

All around them people were going back into the house to continue the party. It seemed terribly macabre to think of them dancing and laughing, having fun, when a man had died downstairs.

"It doesn't seem kind to tell them," Rafe said, as if he had read her thoughts. "It had nothing to do with them."

"I know. You're right. Better to let them enjoy the evening." Kyria turned to him. "However, I find it a little hard to pretend that there is nothing wrong. I believe I will plead a headache and retire early this evening."

He nodded, and as she turned to walk away, he said quietly, "Perhaps you should lock your door tonight. Just to be safe."

"Now I think you're trying to scare me," Kyria told him.

But later, upstairs in her bedroom, after her maid had left, Kyria found herself turning the key in the lock.

Kyria did not sleep well that night. Her thoughts kept returning to the man who had died — the awful pallor of his face, the pitiful way his hand had lain on the table, the palm turned up. *Who was he? Did Theo send him here with that package? And why?* She had no answers, only more questions.

She thought, too, of the box. She was tempted to rise and go down to her father's collections room to look at it again, but she found herself reluctant, after what had happened tonight, to go wandering about the dark halls.

The box was elegant in its simplicity, and the diamond was stunning. Because of her father's hobby, she was accustomed to pieces of astonishing rarity and beauty, but it still amazed her to think of the depth of artistry in the carving and the skill it had taken to hide the latch of the box — for surely it must open somehow. And to think that a gem of such magnificence had been mined so long ago . . .

She remembered how it had looked, how smooth the ivory had felt beneath her hands . . . the weight of it . . . the cold, dark depths of the diamond. And thinking this way, she could not help but remember, too, the way Rafe had held the box, his hands dark against the creamy ivory, his fingers gentle as they glided over the carving.

Warmth blossomed deep in her abdomen and the flesh of her arms prickled, as she thought of those same hands sliding up her arms. No one had ever kissed her as he had; she knew that she would not have allowed it. She could scarcely believe that she had allowed him. She told herself that it was because she was upset by the death of the stranger, that she was more vulnerable than usual. But she knew that such reasoning was merely excuse-making. The fact was that Rafe's kiss had stirred something in her that was more powerful than anything she had ever felt. It was exciting and frightening and it left her feeling unsure of herself — a feeling that also was quite new to her.

It irritated her that she had felt such a rush of passion — she was far too honest and pragmatic to term it anything else — for a man who was so obviously a charmer and a flirt. She was not the sort to fall for a man's honeyed words, and she hated to think that she could be easily swayed by a handsome countenance.

But even as she thought this, she knew that she could not dismiss Rafe McIntyre so easily. She had sensed that there was far more to him than the practiced flirt. There had been, for instance, his quick, cool handling of the attack on the stranger, his easy assumption of command. Smeggars had told her of how deftly he had bandaged the stranger's wound before the doctor arrived. However light his words, however easy his smile, there was, too, a hint of darkness that lurked behind his eyes, a certain watchfulness that never went entirely away.

It occurred to her that she knew nothing of his life, what events had shaped him, beyond the fact that he had been Stephen St. Leger's partner, and she found herself wanting to know. Perhaps now that the bustle of the wedding was over, she could take him for a ride around the estate. She could show him her favorite spots and they could talk . . .

Kyria sat up with a grunt of displeasure and busied herself for a moment with punching her pillow into a more pleasing shape. It annoyed her that she was letting her thoughts stray this way. One would think she was a silly schoolgirl!

And so it went throughout much of the night, her mind jumping from one thought to another as she tossed and turned in her bed. She did not fall asleep until almost dawn, and then she was dragged from her slumber a few hours later by the sound of people in the hall.

Kyria yawned and threw her arm across her eyes, wishing that she could simply turn over and go back to sleep. But she knew that many of their guests would be leaving this morning, and she must do everything she could to get their departures out of the way so that she and her family could sit down to discuss the strange events of the night before.

So she rose and rang for her maid to help her dress, then spent the rest of the morning overseeing the myriad tasks that had to be accomplished to get a large number of people off in their carriages or driven to the train station in the village.

By two in the afternoon, all the guests who would be departing that day were gone, leaving an unfortunately good-size number who would remain for at least a day or two longer. Kyria reflected gloomily that this number contained many of their most troublesome guests, most of whom were in one way or another relatives and considered it their privilege to spend long periods of time at the family seat. But at least she did not have to rack her brain for ways to entertain them; her mother had told her, "For pity's sake, Kyria, don't provide them with too much fun, or we shall have the whole lot with us through

Christmas." In any case, old Lord Penhurst needed no entertainment, only a comfortable chair in which to nap most of the day, and Lady Rochester required much the same thing, along with a younger relative or two at whom to snipe during the times she was awake.

Therefore, Kyria was able to slip away with a clear conscience to her father's collections room, where her family had decided to gather in midafternoon. She found she was the last to arrive — a not-entirely-unusual circumstance, as Reed was quick to point out with a smile.

They were grouped around the long central table, which was cluttered, as usual, with various objects that her father was in the process of arranging. Except for Theo and Olivia, all Kyria's siblings were there, along with Thisbe's husband, Desmond, her mother and father and their great-uncle Bellard. A small man with rather rounded, hunched shoulders from years of poring over books, Uncle Bellard was a retiring sort who had stayed largely to his rooms over the past few days, avoiding the guests, especially his sister Hermione, the quarrelsome Lady Rochester. However, Kyria was not surprised that the prospect of seeing an ancient box had lured him from his private rooms. He was not the antiquarian that her father was, but his bright, inquisitive mind and love of history doubtless made him interested. Nor was he the kind of man who could easily resist a mystery in any form.

She was also not surprised that Con and Alex were there. Most families would have deemed children who were not quite eleven as too young to participate in any sort of important discussion. It was one of the many Moreland "oddities" to treat children as equal members of the family, who, though young and in need of guidance, were intelligent creatures with thoughts and opinions of value.

However, when she saw Rafe McIntyre sitting at the table among her family, she felt a curious blend of surprise and excitement. Her pulse grew faster, and she found herself wishing that she had checked her image in the mirror before she entered the room. She was reminded all over again of her sleepless night and the irritation she had felt both toward him and at her own behavior. Annoyed, she blurted, "What are *you* doing here?"

"Manners, Kyria," her mother admonished.

"Sorry, Mother," Kyria said, looking with displeasure at Rafe. "But Mr.

McIntyre is not a member of the family."

"No, but he is the one who found the body," Reed reminded her. "Or rather, found the man who would shortly become the body. He has just finished telling everyone exactly what happened last night."

Kyria could hardly dispute the logic of Reed's words, so she merely sat down in the empty chair beside her sister, relieved that at least she did not have to sit next to Rafe. She glanced across the table, and Rafe winked at her. She could not keep a smile from touching her lips — and that in itself was annoying.

"Now, then," Reed went on, "I assume, Kyria, that you already know the details of our visitor's death and the discovery of the box, since you were there. So unless anyone has any further questions for Mr. McIntyre, I would like to move on to what I've found out about our mysterious visitor."

"You know something?" Kyria asked, surprised.

"Not much," Reed admitted. "I talked to the constable last night and this morning, but he was able to find out nothing more than that a dark-complexioned man reportedly got off the train in the village yesterday afternoon and asked directions to Broughton Park. Presumably he walked here. However, Mr. McIntyre and I went through the man's pockets last night, and we came up with a few things."

Reed opened an envelope and shook out some items onto the table. "We found a ticket stub for the train trip from London, as well as a receipt for a room at an inn in London and a ticket on a ship from Istanbul arriving three days ago in Southampton. Both the name on the ticket and the receipt match the name written on the calling cards in this card case."

"You mean you know who he is?" Desmond asked, leaning forward with interest and adjusting his wire-rimmed spectacles.

"I am assuming that the name on the card and the ticket is in all likelihood that of the man who was carrying them, although, of course, I cannot be certain," Reed said carefully.

"Oh, Reed, you sound just like a solicitor," Kyria said impatiently. "Just tell us who he was."

"The card says 'Leonides Kousoulous,' " Reed said.

"He was Greek, then?" Thisbe asked.

"It would certainly fit with his coloring," Reed admitted, and looked toward Rafe questioningly.

"It could have been Greek he spoke," Rafe agreed. "I studied ancient Greek in school, but I understand that the modern language is somewhat different, and I have never heard a native speak it, certainly."

Reed opened the gold card case and took out one of the calling cards, which he handed to his father. "It also says something underneath the name, as well as what looks like an address. I am afraid my Greek is a little rusty, too, but I thought you would be able to read it."

The duke nodded as he perused the card. "Yes. It identifies him as a dealer in antiquities. But the address is in Constantinople."

"Yes, and the departure point of the ship he took to England is Istanbul," Reed reminded them. "Among the English-pound notes in his pockets were several coins which I believe to be Turkish."

"Hmm. Interesting," Broughton said, nodding thoughtfully. "Well, no surprise, I suppose, that an antiquities dealer was in possession of such a thing. Uncle Bellard believes, as I do, that it is of Byzantine origin."

"Oh, yes." Uncle Bellard bobbed his head happily, looking more than ever like a bird. He patted the two heavy tomes sitting on the table in front of him. "That rounded top is typical, as are the biblical engravings. I'm not an expert, but I do happen to have a few books about the later empire. I looked through them this morning after Broughton showed me the box, and I found a drawing or two."

He opened the two books to the appropriate pages and began to pass them around the table. "They're both from the period A.D. 500 to A.D. 1000, and you can see that they are very similar to this box. One of them is ivory, with carnelian and turquoise set in, and the other is cloisonné."

Everyone examined the drawings closely as they came around the table. Thisbe looked up after examining the page. "Yes, but what does our box look like? We haven't seen it, or at least *I* haven't."

"Oh, yes, quite right. Terribly sorry." Broughton rose to his feet and crossed to one of the glass-faced cases against the wall. He unlocked the case and took out the ivory box. He brought it back and set it on the table, and everyone leaned closer to get a better look.

"It's beautiful," the duchess said, rather awed. "What are those carvings on it? And that stone! It's magnificent."

"It's a black diamond, Mother," Kyria

explained, as entranced as the others with the box, even though she had seen it before. "Or at least, I'm almost sure it is. Isn't it beautiful?"

"The carvings are biblical scenes," Uncle Bellard put in. "One, I am fairly certain, is the story of the loaves and fishes, and another is of the betrayal in the garden of Gethsemane. I'm not entirely sure about the two smaller ones on the ends."

"What's inside it?" Alex asked, ever the curious one.

"We don't know," Kyria replied. "We haven't been able to open it."

"What?"

"I have looked it over and over," Broughton said. "I can't find a seam, a hinge, a latch. Nothing! I am sure it must open, but there's obviously some secret to it."

"Wizard!" Con exclaimed, thoroughly interested now, and came around the table to stand between his great-uncle and father and lean so close to the box that he was practically lying on the table. There was nothing Con loved as much as a puzzle.

"The Byzantines were excellent craftsmen," his father went on. "It was probably a clever bit of extra safety for whatever was inside the box."

"No doubt the relic was very important to them," Uncle Bellard added, nodding.

"Relic?" Kyria asked. "What relic? What are you talking about?"

"Uncle Bellard and I agree that it is probably a reliquary," Broughton explained. At the blank looks of most of those around the table, he explained, "That is something, usually some sort of box, which contained a sacred relic — a splinter of the 'true cross,' say, or a saint's finger bone or something."

"A finger bone!" Kyria exclaimed, and everyone looked askance at the box.

"Do you think there's a finger still in it?" Alex asked, obviously pleased at the thought, and came around to join his twin and peer at the reliquary.

"I doubt very seriously that there is anything in it," Reed said flatly. "The thing is hundreds of years old, after all. And it wasn't necessarily a finger, anyway. A relic could be any number of things, although obviously, it couldn't have been very large." He looked at the box, which was no longer than six inches and a little more than half that wide and deep.

"Well, it would make sense that the stranger came from Istanbul," Thisbe commented, "given that the box is Byzantine in origin. But what I wonder is, why did he bring it here? Why did he ask for Kyria?"

Reed shrugged. "No one knows. That is all Mr. McIntyre understood of what he said. My assumption is that it is something from Theo."

"It seems awfully peculiar," Desmond said.

"Theo's gifts are often peculiar," Reed pointed out. "However, the last we heard from him, I thought he was in Australia or someplace like that."

"One never knows with him," Thisbe said. As Theo's twin, she was the closest to her brother, even though Theo's adventuring had kept them apart for the past several years. "He goes wherever his whim takes him. And if he was in Australia, where we sent him the letter about Olivia's wedding, he could have decided to come home, in which case, he would probably have taken a ship that would come through the Suez Canal, wouldn't he?"

"Yes, you're right. And he would have been right there, close to Turkey."

"But if he was coming for Olivia's wedding, where is he?" the duchess asked pragmatically.

"Yes, and why wouldn't he have brought the thing with him?" Kyria added.

Reed answered with a shrug. "I have no idea. Perhaps he was struck by another of his whims and decided to stay in Istanbul and just send this box on."

"You think it's a wedding present?" Kyria asked doubtfully. "It seems a little odd."

"Why didn't he send a note explaining it?" the duchess added. "Theo, at least, scribbles a note, usually."

"That's true," Kyria said.

Rafe McIntyre spoke up. "I don't know your son, ma'am. But maybe he told this fellow who brought the box whatever it was he wanted to say to you. We just don't know what it is."

The duchess nodded. "Yes, that makes sense, I suppose. Theo was never as comfortable with a pen and paper as the rest of my children."

Reed let out a snort. "You mean he'd rather face a charging elephant than write a letter."

"Still, I agree with Kyria," Thisbe commented. "An ancient reliquary seems an unlikely wedding gift. Especially for Olivia. It's more something Papa would like."

"Not really my period," the duke pointed out. "Besides, the chap said, 'Kyria.' "

"Perhaps he was saying, 'Kyrie,' " Desmond suggested quietly, and everyone turned to look at him. "It is Greek for lord, isn't it? *Kyrie eleison?* Perhaps he was trying to say Lord Broughton?"

"But I'm not called that," the duke said.

"Yes, but a Greek isn't going to necessarily know the intricacies of British titles," Thisbe put in. She turned toward Rafe. "Could he have been saying, 'Kyrie'?"

Rafe shrugged. "I suppose it's possible. Once he said only the first syllable, and the first time . . . I don't know. I'm not sure what the ending of the word was. It sounded like Kyria, but of course the two words are very similar."

"But why would Theo send that to Papa?" Kyria asked. "Theo would know that that wasn't the era that Papa studies."

Reed nodded. "It makes more sense that he sent it to Kyria because of the diamond. We all know that she loves gems. Although I have to say it seems extravagant, even for Theo."

All around the table, heads nodded in agreement. They were all silent for a moment, looking at the reliquary. Then the duke said, "You know, Kyria, that chap I mentioned last night — Jennings? Actually, he lives not that far from here. Only a few hours' ride. It wouldn't be too difficult to take this over and show it to him, get his opinion. I am sure he could tell us a lot more about this reliquary than Uncle Bellard and I can. He has studied the Byzantine Empire for years and years. I could write him, telling him why you want to see him."

Kyria sat up straighter, smiling. "That would be wonderful. I would like that. Perhaps he would even know something about how it should open."

"I have to go to London tomorrow," Reed put in. "I'm sorry, Kyria, but it's important business. I won't be back for at least a few weeks, but I could escort you then."

Kyria bridled. "I don't need an escort, Reed. I am quite capable of going to see Mr. Jennings by myself."

"Kyria —" her older brother frowned "— I don't think that would be wise."

"Because she is a female?" the duchess asked, leaning forward, her eyes flashing.

"No," Reed answered automatically. "Well, yes . . ." He squirmed a little under his mother's fiery gaze, then burst out, "Blast it, Mother, this isn't an equality-of-the-sexes issue. It could be dangerous! Look at what happened to the last person who was in possession of that box. I have no idea why someone attacked Mr. Kousoulous, but I cannot dismiss the possibility that it was because he wanted that box. It is obviously quite valuable. Surely you cannot want to have Kyria running about the countryside carrying that box."

"No, of course not." The duchess leaned back, frowning.

"No one will know I have the box," Kyria protested. "I will be fine by myself."

"Oh, no, dear," the duke put in worriedly. "I am sure that would not do. If there is even the slightest possibility that that man's attacker might go after you . . ."

Everyone began to talk at once, but Rafe's voice cut through the noise, "I will escort her."

All heads at the table swung toward him.

"I had planned to go to London and then on to the Continent, but I had no set day of departure. I can easily delay the trip to ride with Kyria to this fellow's place," Rafe explained.

"Are you sure?" the duchess asked politely. "That would, of course, relieve my mind."

"It's no problem," Rafe assured her. "My intention when I set out to visit Europe was to take a leisurely trip, to move from place to place as the mood struck me. A few more days here will scarcely make a difference. And I will take my guns, just in case we run into something nasty."

"He's terribly good with his pistols," Alex declared. "He showed us the other day when he gave us that lesson in physics. He was pukka."

"Oh, Alex, I wish you would not use that dreadful military slang." His mother sighed.

The duke looked delighted. "There you go, Kyria. Mr. McIntyre can escort you, and that will take care of it nicely."

"I don't need an escort," Kyria said stubbornly, shooting Rafe a glare.

"Let's hope not," Rafe replied, smiling back at her blandly. "But better safe than sorry, my mother always said."

"Good." Broughton smiled, pleased to have disposed of the matter. "That's settled, then. I shall send Jennings a note."

The family meeting broke up not long after that, and the duke returned the ivory reliquary to its place in the locked case. Kyria started out of the room, feeling thoroughly disgruntled. The last thing she had intended today was to commit herself to a day spent in the company of Rafe McIntyre.

Before she reached the door, Rafe stepped forward and stopped her, saying with a grin, "It won't be so terrible, ma'am. You'll hardly know I'm there."

That, Kyria thought, was most definitely not true; that was precisely the problem with this man — she was always much too aware of his presence. However, she could not help but feel she was being a trifle unreasonable. Rafe was doing her a favor by escorting her safely, and she had been churlish about it.

"I'm sorry, Mr. McIntyre. You must not take it the wrong way. I am simply a little sensitive about people trying to protect me. Swaddling one in silk still leaves one unable to move."

"Your family is just concerned about the danger. They have every reason to be."

Kyria sighed. "I know. And it really isn't my family that is the problem. They are generally quite willing to allow any of us our freedom. It is the main reason we are considered so peculiar."

"Who was it, then, that got you all-fired determined to do everything on your own?" He held up a hand, saying, "No, wait, let me guess. Your suitors?"

"I have grown so tired of hearing what a delicate flower I am, how in need of protection. Really, Mr. McIntyre, look at me. Do I look delicate? I am taller than a good number of them. It is ludicrous."

He shook his head. "Now, me, I like a sturdy female."

Kyria arched one well-tended eyebrow at him, murmuring, "Sturdy?"

Rafe's blue eyes danced. "That doesn't sit too well, either, huh?" He leaned in closer, and Kyria's pulse began to race. "I have an advantage over those other fellows, though. It's hard to think of a person as a delicate flower when I first saw you clambering around in a tree like a monkey."

Kyria had to smile back, a dimple popping into her cheek. "Belatedly, thank you for coming to my rescue then." She hesitated, then added, "And thank you for offering to escort me. Papa would have insisted on doing it otherwise, and he would have hated taking off time from his pots. I apologize for being rude."

"Apology accepted," Rafe said, adding, "provided, of course, that we take a little trial run."

"A what?"

"You know — go out for a ride tomorrow, while your father is waiting to hear from his Mr. Jennings, just to see if anyone pops out to knock us over the head."

Kyria looked at him, realizing that he had neatly maneuvered her into doing precisely what she had not wanted — and twice, at that! He smiled at her, his arms crossed, leaning negligently against the doorjamb, and there was something so appealing about him that Kyria could not keep from chuckling.

"All right," she agreed. "Tomorrow I'll take you on a tour of the countryside."

6

Kyria and Rafe rode out the next morning on their tour of the estate. Kyria had thought about circumventing any degree of intimacy on their ride by bringing along the twins, who were still somewhat at loose ends without a tutor. However, she could well imagine the smile that Rafe would send her if she did, the knowing twinkle in his eye. It would be as good as acknowledging that she could not handle being alone with him, she decided, and she immediately discarded the idea.

So, after breakfast the next morning, when Reed had departed for his trip to London, she ordered their horses brought round, and the two of them set off. Kyria could not help but feel a certain lift of her spirits as they rode along. She had worn her newest riding habit, a royal-blue skirt and bodice cut in a military style, with black frogging down the front. She had had it made right before she and her family left London at the end of the season, and she had not yet worn it. This morning seemed the perfect time for it, crisp, but dry, with an autumn sun casting its golden light over the landscape.

She led him on a tour of the estate farms, calling greetings to the workers who stopped their work to hail her and occasionally pausing to talk to one or two of the farmers. Then, with a mischievous smile, she asked him if he cared to see the local haunted spot.

"Of course," he agreed, the dimple in his cheek deepening. "A visit wouldn't be complete without a haunted place."

They cut through a copse of trees and came out in a small clearing. Backed by a graceful laurel tree stood six stones of varying height, some no more than four feet and one as tall as six. They were rather narrow stones, standing on end in a jumbled little group, not a circle, yet not a line, either. They were pitted and weatherbeaten, decorated with lichen, some leaning a little to one side.

Surrounded on three sides by trees, the spot was hushed, except for the faint rustle of the bare branches in the breeze. They dismounted, tethered their horses to a tree and approached the stones.

"Why is it haunted?" Rafe asked. "It seems a very pleasant place to me."

"Does it?" Kyria looked at him, faintly surprised. "A number of people dislike it. They find it eerie."

"Why?"

She shrugged. "I don't know. Perhaps the quiet. Or maybe it's the local legend."

"And what is that?"

"Oh, one with a wicked lord, of course, who lusted after a beautiful maiden. She used to come to this spot, you see, late at night, to dance with her sisters. He followed her and saw them dancing, and he was so filled with lust that he grabbed her and began to ravish her, but the sisters were witches, you see. That is why they danced in the clearing beneath the laurel tree, and when he tried to harm their sister, they were so filled with fury that they called down revenge on the lord right then and there. But in their haste and their fury, they missaid the spell, and all of them were turned to stone on the spot."

"Ah, I see. So the tallest one must be the wicked lord."

"Of course. And the smaller one beside him, leaning away, that is the object of his desire, trying to pull away from him. And the others are the sisters."

"One of them was very short," he commented, pointing to the smallest stone.

Kyria chuckled. "She is kneeling as she wails out her grief and anger."

"Ah, I see." Rafe nodded. "It seems too beautiful a spot for such a tale."

"I know. It is one of my favorite places. It seems to me . . . well, as if it is a magical place." She cast a sideways glance at him, faintly embarrassed. "Of course, Olivia tells me that it wasn't magic at all, but probably one of the ancient places — a burial ground, perhaps, or maybe the remains of a pre-Roman fort that was later torn down. But Theo maintains that it is really one of the rings, like at Stonehenge, a place of ancient Druid worship, and that the rest of the circle was torn down during the Middle Ages by zealous Christians — that was done, you know." She smiled. "Theo prefers a little magic, too, I think."

"It's a special place," Rafe said, turning around and looking at the whole clearing, "whatever it was. I'm glad you brought me here."

They strolled among the stones, and Kyria stopped to brush her hand across one or two of them. She was a little surprised that she had wanted to show Rafe the stones. She rarely came here with anyone else, even her sisters and brothers. It was a place where she liked to sit alone and daydream, letting the rest of the world drift away.

They sat down for a time beneath a large oak tree, leaning back against the trunk, not saying much, simply enjoying the quiet. As they sat, Rafe slipped his hand into hers, interlacing their fingers. Kyria glanced at him, aware that she should say something, make some protestation. But she said nothing. It felt good to have his hand in hers, his warm, rough flesh against her softer skin; it felt somehow right.

"What is it like where you lived?" she asked. "Is it very different?" She had always loved to hear Theo's stories of the places he had been, and there had been times when she had been rather envious of his life. There was something in her that yearned, too, to see other places, to have great adventures. Though she was in most ways very satisfied with her life, enjoying the parties, the clothes, the designs she drew, even the task of keeping her large, off-kilter family running along more or less smoothly, she also found herself longing for something more.

Rafe smiled. "England is very beautiful and green — and small. Where I lived — in the Rockies — the mountains were towering and majestic. It is the sort of place that makes you realize how very minor you are in the scheme of things. In the winter, you have snow several feet deep and you get snowed in so long you get cabin fever and think you're going to go insane from all the white and the alone. The West is huge — great, sweeping plains of grasses, enormous herds of buffalo." He shrugged. "Of course, that is entirely different from where I grew up. Virginia is much more civilized. Even the mountains are a more normal size."

"What was it like there, where you grew up?"

"Wide, lazy rivers, fields and fields of tobacco. Hot as Hades in the summer." He smiled faintly, remembering. "Our house was redbrick, neat and square, with a fireplace on either end."

"Why did you leave?" Kyria asked.

He glanced at her, then away, and shrugged. "It was after the war. Times were . . . hard." Rafe gazed out across the clearing, his face hardening. "Everything was different. I was different. It was time to move on."

He released her hand and stood up in one fluid motion, reaching down to Kyria to help her up. "Just like it is now," he said, his tone light as it usually was, but his face remote, unreadable.

Kyria took his hand and stood up. When he would have released her hand, she held on to it for a moment longer, looking at him intently. There was something that had lingered in her mind from the moment she met him, a question that, raised as she had been in her mother's humanitarian beliefs, had worried at her every moment she was with Rafe, but which, for politeness' sake, she had refrained from asking. But now, surprising even herself a little, she blurted it out. "How could you have . . . have done what you did? How could you have owned a slave?"

His eyebrows sailed up, though his eyes remained as unreadable as before, but he said only, "I'm afraid you have been misinformed. I have never owned a slave."

Kyria looked at him blankly. "I wasn't misinformed, exactly. No one told me. I just assumed . . ."

He gave her a twisted sort of smile, almost a grimace. "A large number of people in the South didn't own slaves, you know. My mother and I were among them. We were the poor relations. My mother married badly, according to her family — and to her, actually, after my father died, leaving her penniless. He was a schoolmaster, very handsome, they say, but utterly lacking in worldly goods, I'm afraid. After his death, we had to depend on my uncle."

"Oh. I . . . I'm sorry." Kyria blushed, further embarrassed that her uncustomary rudeness had pushed him into a subject that was obviously uncomfortable for him.

Rafe shrugged. "There is no need." He smiled, a little more genuinely now, and went on, "It wasn't the terrible life of an orphan you might imagine. My uncle was a very kind man. He gave my mother a cottage on his plantation, and I was educated with his own children. I even had a horse to ride. And when I was older, he sent me to college. I was going to read for the bar after that." He stopped. "But then the war came along, and that was the end of that."

He started to turn away, but Kyria reached out and placed her hand on his arm, halting him. She knew that he wanted to end the subject, but she could not leave it. It seemed to her suddenly very important that she know.

"Then why," she asked, "did you fight?"

He looked at her levelly for a moment, then said, "I said I am a Southerner, ma'am. I did not say I fought for the South."

Kyria's hand fell away, and she looked at

him in astonishment, which mingled with a strange swelling of relief. "You mean . . ."

He gave a curt nod. "Yes. I fought for the Union — for abolition, I should say, for I didn't really give a damn about the Union." Kyria barely heard his last words, for he turned away as he said them, "And I was a traitor to my home."

Rafe strode quickly away to the horses, and Kyria had to break into a trot to catch up with him. "But, wait!" she cried, amazed by his words. "That was a wonderful thing you did. A courageous —"

He swung around, his face hard and closed. "I don't talk about the war," he said flatly.

"But I only meant that —"

Rafe took a quick step forward, startling her, and grasped her by the shoulders. Before she could even gasp, he jerked her forward and planted his lips on hers.

His mouth was hard, even bruising, and the suddenness of the kiss took Kyria's breath away. She went limp for a moment, her senses whirling, before a saving anger swept through her and she stepped back, pushing against his chest.

"What was that?" she blazed, her green eyes glittering like emeralds. "Do you think that you can kiss me into submission?"

"I kissed you to shut you up," he snapped back. A twinge of humor tugged at the corner of his mouth as he went on, "Obviously I didn't succeed."

"You certainly did not, and you *will* not, either," Kyria warned. "I am not some tavern wench that you can —"

The rest of her speech was lost as he gave a half laugh and pulled her into his arms again, his mouth stopping hers. This kiss was gentler and more lingering, his lips moving over hers in a way that made her forget her ire and sink into him, her arms going up around his neck. Her mouth opened under his and she let out a little moan of pleasure. His arms closed around her tightly, pressing her into him. Her breasts flattened against his solid chest, and she could feel the hard lines of his legs against hers through the cloth of her habit.

He raised his head for a moment only to change the slant of their mouths and kissed her again. Kyria's heart slammed against her rib cage, and she found herself wanting to press so tightly to him that she blended into him. It was the strangest feeling she had ever had — hot and peculiar and exciting — and she wanted the moment to go on forever.

His hands slid down her back and curved over her hips, digging into her buttocks and lifting her up into him. Kyria gasped as she felt the hard length of him against her, and an answering fire leaped to life deep within her loins. Desire rushed through her, stunning in its intensity, and she trembled, holding on tightly to him.

Rafe raised his head, his arms loosening slightly around her, and for a long moment he stared down into her eyes. Kyria gazed back up at him, flushed and momentarily speechless. He started to speak, but the words seemed to stick, and he stopped and cleared his throat. "I think it's time we went back," he said finally.

It was another long moment before his arms went slack around her and he stepped back. Kyria turned away, straightening her jacket and skirt, struggling to regain control of her wayward senses.

"Yes." Her voice came out small and shaky, and she stopped, drawing in a breath, then saying more firmly, "Yes, no doubt you are right."

The ride back to Broughton Park was made largely in silence, while Kyria struggled with her thoughts. When they arrived at the house, a groom hurried to take their horses, and a footman eagerly opened the door to them.

"My lady," he said with obvious relief, reaching out to take Kyria's hat and riding crop.

"What is the matter, John?"

"There is a man here, a foreign man."

Kyria's interest was instantly aroused. She noticed that the footman had not called their visitor a "gentleman." She glanced over at Rafe and saw that his attention, too, had been caught by the word *foreign*.

"He is in the blue parlor," John went on. "He wanted to see His Grace, but your father left strict instructions not to be disturbed."

Kyria could well imagine that her father, after the events of the past few days, had probably locked himself in his workshop and would not come out until supper, if then.

"Her Grace said that you would deal with the matter when you came home. I told the visitor that it would be some time before you returned, but he insisted on waiting for you. So I placed him in the blue parlor."

His placement was another indication of the footman's evaluation of their visitor; he had put the visitor in the smallest, least-formal parlor. Something about the footman's tone told Kyria that the footman had doubtless kept a careful eye on the room ever since and would also subject the visitor to a thorough scrutiny as he left.

"Very well, I will see him. Thank you, John." She started down the hall, unsurprised to find that Rafe accompanied her.

The man she found sitting on the green-velvet love seat waiting for her was short and olive-skinned, with large doe eyes set in a round face. His black hair was slicked back from his face, somewhat offsetting the babyish effect of his large eyes and full cheeks. The air was filled with the musky scent of his cologne.

He rose as Kyria and Rafe entered the room and beamed at them. Kyria noticed that his practiced smile did not reach his eyes, which remained shrewd and assessing. He was well dressed in a brown, European-style suit, and beside the sofa on which he had been sitting stood a black, gold-topped cane. Gold rings sparkled on three of his fingers, one of them centered by a blood-red ruby. It matched the ruby that twinkled in the midst of his golden brown silk ascot.

"Ah, Lady Moreland, please forgive my

intrusion," he said in good, if rather heavily accented English and bowed toward her. "I am Youssef Habib."

"How do you do?" Kyria responded politely.

He cast a curious glance at Rafe, who, in his American way, stuck out his hand and introduced himself.

"I beg your pardon for not writing for an appointment," Habib went on. "But I had urgent business with your father."

"I am sorry, but the duke is not seeing anyone today," Kyria replied. "So I am afraid that you have wasted your time."

"It is a matter of the utmost importance," the man told her earnestly.

"Perhaps you would like to explain the matter to me," Kyria said. "I will see that my father receives your message."

"I am a dealer in precious objects, my lady," Habib told her. "Ornaments and vases, pottery of all sorts, statues, boxes — all of great antiquity. Word has reached me of an object in your father's possession, an ivory box, inscribed with scenes."

One of Kyria's eyebrows shot up. "Word has reached you? How, may I ask?"

"When one has been a dealer for as long as I have, my lady, one hears things," he said, making a vague gesture. "It is said that not long ago, a box such as this turned up in a shop in an Istanbul bazaar. Later, this box disappeared from the shop — at the same time the owner of the shop was murdered."

Kyria stiffened and the freezing look she turned on the antiquities dealer would have done her great-aunt Lady Rochester proud. "You are suggesting that my family has something to do with theft and murder?"

"No, no, my lady," the man hastened to assure her. "Of course, your father would have had no notion, I am sure, of what happened. But there are others who are not so scrupulous. Certain dealers in antiquities do not question where an item comes from."

"And what does this have to do with my father? Or with you, Mr. Habib?"

"As I mentioned, my lady," the man continued in an obsequious manner guaranteed to raise Kyria's hackles, "I learned that your esteemed father now has this box. I would be very interested in acquiring it from him. You see, I have a client who collects such things, and he has expressed a desire for this box. So you see, if I could just speak with your father and look at —"

"I am sorry, Mr. Habib, but I am afraid that you have wasted your time," Kyria said. "My father has no interest in selling any of his possessions."

"If I could just speak to the duke . . ." Habib tried again, but Kyria cut him off quickly.

"The duke is not receiving visitors," Kyria said flatly, standing up and going over to ring for the footman.

"My client would be willing to pay top price for the item, I assure you," the man continued, following Kyria.

Rafe stepped in front of Mr. Habib. "The lady said no."

"Ah, John," Kyria said as the footman entered the room. "Mr. Habib's business is finished here. If you will see him to the door . . ."

"Certainly, my lady." John stepped forward, looking happy to comply with her order.

"Of course, my lady. Thank you for your time," Mr. Habib said, with another smile that did not quite ring true. "But please, in case your father might change his mind . . ." He whipped a card out of his pocket and scribbled something on the back of it. "Here is my card, and on it, I have taken the liberty of writing my address while I am in London. I shall be here a few more weeks, and I would very much like to hear from your father."

Kyria took the card, and Habib left the room, followed by John. Kyria turned to Rafe, her brows lifting. "That was interesting."

"Wasn't it?" Rafe agreed. "What does his card say?"

" 'Y. Habib, Beirut and Istanbul,' " Kyria read, then handed it to Rafe. "At least I can read this one — it's in French. He wrote the name of an inn in London on the back."

"Wonder how he knew so quickly where that box is," Rafe commented, glancing at the card and giving it back to her.

"I would say the easiest way would be if he was the man who killed Mr. Kousoulous." A shiver ran down Kyria's spine as she expressed the thought. Had she been conversing with a killer?

"Could be. Of course, I guess he could have followed Kousoulous — or the man who killed him — and the path led here."

"One thing I know is that Theo would never have had anything to do with a stolen artifact," Kyria said firmly.

"I wonder how much Habib really knows about the box," Rafe mused. "He didn't give a terribly detailed description of it."

"Yes, and he assumed it was sent to Papa, not me. Nor did he mention Theo or the man who brought it here."

"I suppose it's possible that he was fishing for information, maybe even hoping to get a look at the thing."

"Well," Kyria said, her eyes determined, "it makes me even more eager to talk to this expert of Papa's."

Kyria and Rafe started out for Dr. Jennings's home two days later. Her father had sent a messenger to his colleague, asking him to see them on Wednesday, and Jennings had scribbled back a very brief reply on the same notepaper the duke had used, saying that they could come.

The night before they left, Kyria had had trouble sleeping. She had tossed and turned, and it had seemed that the more she ordered herself to go to sleep, the wider awake she grew.

Finally, she had climbed out of bed and put on a dressing gown and slippers and gone down to the library to find a book. On the way, she passed her father's study, and as she did so, she paused, then changed her mind and went into the study. What she really wanted, she knew, was to look at the ivory box again.

Since the late Mr. Kousoulous had brought the reliquary to her, she had gone every day to her father's collections room to look at the ivory box. There was something so compelling about its beauty that she kept coming back to it. She had found herself sitting with it for several minutes at a time, just staring at it. She felt, frankly, a little foolish, and she wondered if this was the way her father felt about his acquisitions.

She went to the top drawer of her father's desk and pulled out the small key that lay inside, hidden beneath a sheaf of writing paper. Though her father kept the collections room locked against the unlikely possibility of a burglary, he did not mind anyone in the family going in to look at his artifacts, and his wife and children were all well aware of where he kept the keys. She picked up the small key and unlocked the middle drawer, then took out the ring of keys inside it.

She walked down the hall to the collections room, unlocked the door and went inside, turning on the gas lamp on the wall. She made her way around the various statues and over to the far wall, where her father had locked away the ivory box.

Kyria unlocked the door of the display

case and opened it, taking out the artifact. The ivory felt cool in her hands, and she rubbed her hand over it caressingly, her fingertips seeking out the engravings.

She sat down in a chair and put the box on the table, leaned her chin on her hand, elbow braced on the table, and studied the box. What lay inside it? She could not help but imagine some sort of treasure kept hidden from the world inside the beautiful container. She wondered if the years had destroyed what had lain within or if thieves had removed it or if it lay there still, waiting for someone to open the box and reveal it.

She bent down close to the box, examining the black diamond. It was dark and fathomless, astounding in its sheer size, yet it was not the size of it alone that evoked wonder. Even crudely cut as it was, it held the lure of diamonds, the power and beauty that had attracted humans for centuries.

Kyria traced the diamond with her fingertips, laying her head down on her arm on the table. She blinked, her eyelids drooping as she watched the reflection of the gas lamp behind her dance in the gem.

Light flickered in the dark stone, alive and twisting, reflecting from the small fire in the brazier. Smoke twisted in a thin plume upward. It was dim and cool, the thick walls warding off the blazing heat.

She knelt, waiting. Dusk was falling and the time would soon be upon her. She could hear the chanting outside as the crowds grew in number and strength.

The light of the torches played over the walls, casting eerie shadows. Her heart thudded, part fear and part anticipation. It would be soon now. Soon . . .

Kyria jerked awake. She sat up abruptly, looking around in confusion. Her heart was racing, and her breath came fast. It took her a moment to realize that she was sitting in her father's collections room. The ivory box sat on the table in front of her.

She drew in a shaky breath. What a strange dream! She had no idea where she had been in the dream or what had been happening. There had been such an eerie quality to it that it left her feeling frightened. Even as she tried to recall it, the details were already slipping away from her.

Kyria pushed back from the table and picked up the reliquary. She stood looking down at it for a moment, rubbing her thumb thoughtfully over the black diamond. Then she shook her head, pulling her wandering thoughts back together and returned the box to the case, locking it behind her.

It was not far to Jennings's home, a ride of no more than two or three hours. Normally, Kyria would have taken the family carriage, but Rafe preferred to ride, saying that he wanted to be outside where he could see an enemy approaching, not caught in a box on wheels, slow and blind. It was a trifle unusual, Kyria knew, to call on someone wearing her riding habit, but then, given that this man was a scholar like Papa, he probably would not even notice.

The pleasant October weather held, the sun shining palely upon them as they rode. Kyria felt a trifle awkward around Rafe at first. She could not help but think about the kiss they had shared the other day. This was the first time they had been alone since that time, and they were in much the same situation. She glanced at Rafe, her heart beating a little more rapidly in her chest, and wondered if he, too, was thinking of their kiss. He looked over, as if he could feel her gaze on him, and their eyes locked. The very air between them seemed to thrum with tension.

Then Rafe glanced away and the moment was broken. They rode in silence. Kyria kept her eyes turned away from him, too, letting her heart calm to its normal rate and her cheeks lose their flush. It was some minutes before she looked at him again.

She noticed that Rafe's eyes were constantly scanning their surroundings. It had been the same the other morning when they had ridden out. His watchfulness kept her mindful of the small bag that hung from her saddle. Inside, wrapped in velvet, was the reliquary, just as the stranger had brought it to her. Was it really so valuable that someone had killed Kousoulous for it? she wondered. And was the murder the work of the man who had visited two days ago? She imagined him waiting, hanging about the area, even watching the house, waiting for them to leave . . .

Kyria gave herself a firm mental shake. She was working herself up into fear for no reason. Even if the dealer who had tried to buy the box from her was the man who had killed Kousoulous or had ordered his death, it was unlikely that he was still lurking around the estate, watching them.

Gradually her nerves quieted down, and Kyria was able to enjoy the ride. The initial awkwardness between Rafe and her eased, and they rode along in easy silence for the most part, now and then chatting about Rafe's visit to England and Ireland or about Stephen and Olivia and the peculiar events that had brought them together.

It seemed a surprisingly short time before they reached the village of Upper Lapham, where Dr. Jennings resided. They left their horses at the inn's stable and asked directions to Jennings's place.

A narrow, two-story cottage, Jennings's home was almost completely covered in ivy, so that the brown brick was visible in only a few places. A tiny, neglected yard separated it from the street.

Rafe stepped to the door and rapped the knocker. The sound met with silence from within. Rafe knocked again, louder this time. They waited, but again there was no answer. Rafe looked over at Kyria, then reached up and banged once again on the door.

Above them on the second floor, a window was flung up, and a man's voice shouted, "Stop that! Go away!"

Startled, Rafe and Kyria looked up to see a man sticking his head out of the window just to the right of the door. He had a head of bushy black hair, into which a pair of wire-rimmed spectacles had been shoved back, and the lower part of his face was hidden by a beard equally bushy and black. He scowled down at them.

"Dr. Jennings?" Rafe began pleasantly.

"Go away!" the man repeated, then pulled his head back inside the window and slammed it shut.

Kyria and Rafe looked at each other.

"Well," Rafe said, "not exactly a friendly soul, is he?"

"Papa said Dr. Jennings replied to his note. He should be expecting us," Kyria said, then added, "Papa did say he was a trifle odd."

"If by odd, he means disagreeable, then I'd say this is our fellow."

Rafe turned back to the door and reapplied himself to the brass knocker. After a few moments, the window above them crashed open again.

"Stop that infernal racket! I'm trying to work!" The same man appeared above them, leaning out the window. "I told you to go away."

"But you are expecting us!" Rafe said quickly, before the man drew back into the room again.

"Dr. Jennings? My father sent you a letter," Kyria explained. "The Duke of Broughton. I am Lady Kyria Moreland."

"Broughton!" The man glowered at them. "Impossible. He said you were coming on the twenty-sixth." He started to pull back in.

"Today *is* the twenty-sixth," Kyria said.

"Nonsense!" Dr. Jennings looked at her darkly. "Today is the twenty-fifth. It says right here on my calendar . . ." He pulled back into the room. A moment later, his head reappeared. "Are you saying that today is Tuesday?"

"Yes, sir," Kyria responded.

"Damn!" Jennings grimaced, then said, "Begging your pardon, my lady."

"Then you will see us?" Kyria asked, giving him the sort of smile that she knew few men could resist.

Dr. Jennings seemed immune to the force of her smile, for he continued to frown. Finally, he sighed and said, "All right. All right. For Broughton's sake. Good chap, excellent scholar," he went on, apparently giving his highest encomium, adding dampeningly, "even if he is a duke."

He disappeared again, closing the window, and after a few moments they heard the lock turning in the door, and Dr. Jennings opened it. Although it was afternoon, he was wearing what was clearly a nightgown with a dressing gown belted over it and velvet house slippers on his feet. His hair, on closer inspection, contained not only a pair of spectacles shoved up from his nose, but also a pencil, which was thrust into the bushy mass over one ear.

"Come in, come in," he said gruffly. "You're letting in the cold." He led them back through the small house, passing two rooms, both with books and papers piled high on every surface. There was no fire lit in either of the rooms, and the house was chilly.

He led them into his study, and here was the warmth that the remainder of the cottage was missing, for a fire burned merrily in the grate. The scholar picked up a pile of books from two chairs and moved them closer to his desk.

"Here. Here. Sit down. Tea? Damned housekeeper took off. Beg your pardon, my lady. But I could see about getting us a pot of tea." He glanced about vaguely, as if a teapot might appear somewhere in the room.

"No, thank you, we're fine," Kyria assured him. "We don't want to take up any more of your time than we have to."

"Right in the middle of research,"

Jennings said by way of agreement, nodding. "What was it Broughton said? Now where is that letter?" He began to paw through the papers on his desk. "A Byzantine reliquary, wasn't it?"

"Yes." Kyria opened the drawstring bag and reached inside, pulling out the ivory box and unwrapping it. "Or at least, that is what Papa thinks it is. He was hoping that you could tell us more about it."

Dr. Jennings reached over and took the box she offered, his eyes lighting with interest. "Oh, yes, this is a lovely example of Byzantine craftsmanship. Yes, indeed."

His touch was light and delicate as his hands smoothed over the box. He reached up and fumbled for his glasses, finally locating them, pulled them down to study the details of the box. "Mmm-hmm. Biblical scenes. Of course, it's hard to be exact without knowing its origins. Where did you get this?"

"Someone brought it to us. We have no idea where it came from."

The man shook his head, tsk-tsking over the lack of knowledge. "Much better to know where it was found. But I think I can safely say that Broughton's right. It's from the period after, oh, say A.D. 600, probably no later than 1000."

"Can you tell us any more about it?" Rafe asked. "With a diamond that big, I would think it was probably a pretty rare piece back then, wouldn't you say?"

"Diamond?" Jennings glanced at him, startled, and turned the box around in his hands to look at the jewel on the front again. "Is that what it is? I thought it was an ordinary stone."

He peered at it more closely. "No, no, of course, I see the translucence." Jennings blinked rapidly, then set the reliquary down quickly on the desk in front of him. He turned back to them, an odd look on his face.

"What is it?" Rafe moved forward a little in his chair, intrigued by the scholar's expression. "Did you recognize the box?"

"No . . . I . . . ah, well, it couldn't be." He paused, his face troubled. "It simply couldn't be . . ."

7

"What couldn't it be?" Kyria asked, excitement stirring in her. She glanced at Rafe and saw that he, too, looked hopeful. "Do you know something about this box?"

"It's only a legend," Jennings said quickly, but there was doubt in his face as he looked back at the reliquary on the desk.

"What is only a legend?" Rafe asked. "Please tell us what you're thinking."

Instead of answering, the scholar picked up the box again and turned it around carefully in his hands, his fingers moving searchingly over it. "Do you know how it opens?"

"No. We haven't been able to find any way to open it," Kyria answered. "Do you know how?"

"No. It wouldn't be easy. The Byzantines were clever craftsmen."

"Have you ever encountered one before?" Rafe asked, watching the scholar's face carefully.

"No, not personally."

"But you have heard something, haven't you?" Rafe prodded shrewdly.

"Yes," the older man admitted. "I have heard of a box such as this. I have heard . . . but it is only a legend, a myth. I know of no one who has ever actually seen . . ."

Jennings took a last, lingering look at the box and sighed. "There is a legend that Byzantine priests made a special reliquary for a very important relic. It is said that this box was carved from ivory and was made so that it could not be opened except by those entrusted with the box. This reliquary was set with an enormous black stone with unknowable depths. The stone, the entire reliquary, was revered as an object of great mystical power, suitable to hold the relic inside."

"What was the relic?"

"A piece of the *labarum*." He looked at the other two's blank faces and said, "What do you know of Constantine?"

"The emperor?" Kyria asked. "I . . . didn't he . . . Well, he really established the Byzantine Empire, didn't he?"

"They changed the name of Byzantium to Constantinople," Rafe offered.

"Yes. Well, first I must explain a little history," Jennings said, and began on what was obviously a favorite subject of his.

"Constantine came to power in the fourth century. At this time, you have to understand, the Roman Empire was ruled as a tetrarchy." He paused and looked at his audience questioningly.

"Four rulers?" Rafe suggested.

Jennings nodded in satisfaction. "Exactly. It was a four-headed Empire. There was a struggle for power among the four rulers. One of the rulers, Maxentius, claimed to be sole emperor. There was a great deal of turmoil, and eventually Constantine had to face Maxentius on the field of battle. Constantine's troops were greatly outnumbered, approximately twenty thousand men to Maxentius's one hundred thousand men."

Rafe and Kyria nodded their understanding, and Dr. Jennings went on, "Now you have to understand, during this time, Christians were persecuted by the Romans. They were outlawed, and tortured and killed because of their religion. But Constantine, who was not Christian, had a vision before he went into battle. In this vision, he said, he learned that he would conquer under the sign of Christ. Because of this vision, he had a new battle standard made, and his soldiers carried it into the battle with Maxentius. This battle standard, which was known as the *labarum,* consisted of a long spear overlaid with gold, with a bar across it so that it formed the shape of a cross. On the top of this spear was a wreath made of gold and jewels and inside the wreath were the initials of Christ, the Greek letters *Chi* and *Rho* laid over one another. To us they look like a *P* and an *X,* with the *X* intersecting the *P* in the center."

"I've seen the symbol," Kyria said, nodding.

"It is called Chi-Rho or, sometimes, the monogram of Christ. It was a popular symbol of Christianity. Hanging down from the cross bar was a purple banner, interlaced with gold and embroidered with gold thread and jewels, and on this banner was written in Greek *'Touto Nika,'* which is usually translated into the Latin *'In hoc signo vinces,'* which means 'In this sign you shall conquer.' "

"And I'm guessing," Rafe put in when Jennings paused and looked at them, "that under this banner Constantine's much smaller army defeated the other fellow's huge army."

"Exactly." Jennings nodded with satisfaction. "In gratitude for his victory, Constantine then passed the Edict of

Milan in 313, which stated that thereafter Christianity was to be tolerated throughout the Roman Empire and the persecution of Christians was to cease."

Jennings leaned back in his chair, linking his hands across his stomach, and continued in his professorial mode. "Eventually, there were just two Roman rulers, Constantine in Rome, ruling the western part of the empire, and Licinius in Byzantium, ruling the eastern part. To make a long story short . . ."

Kyria thought that he was well past that opportunity, but she refrained from saying so, merely nodding and listening.

"Constantine later had to fight Licinius, who had a larger army than Constantine and a much larger fleet of ships. Now, Constantine had to lay siege to Byzantium, but the way was blocked by his enemy's fleet. This much larger fleet pursued Constantine's ships, but they were waylaid by a storm, which destroyed 130 of his enemy's ships and killed five thousand of his men. After that, Constantine was able to defeat Licinius and become the sole ruler of the Roman Empire. So you can see that he had two miraculous victories under this sacred *labarum*, and that battle standard came to be regarded as a religious relic."

Jennings paused somewhat dramatically, then said, "It is a scrap of this sacred *labarum* that is said to be inside an ivory reliquary of great beauty and decorated with a jewel as dark as midnight. The Reliquary of the Holy Standard."

"Our reliquary?" Kyria asked, looking in amazement at the ivory box.

Jennings shrugged. "As I said, it is only a legend. And even if it did exist, it was doubtless lost or destroyed during the sack of Constantinople."

The look he turned toward the reliquary, however, was a great deal less than certain. "All of that business about the monks protecting it is merely a story, that's all. No one has ever had any proof of it."

"What monks?" Kyria asked. "What story?"

"It is part of the legend," Jennings replied. "It is a strange, sad truth that during the Fourth Crusade, the knights who had supposedly sailed to preserve Christianity in Egypt wound up sacking Constantinople, the premier Christian city of the eastern empire. The Byzantine church was enormously wealthy and possessed of great works of art — reliquaries such as this, chalices, altars, statues, icons. A great deal of it was stolen and carried back to European cities, especially Venice."

"You're joking!" Rafe exclaimed.

Jennings shook his head. "Unfortunately, I'm not. It was a disgraceful episode in the history of Christianity." He gave them a wry look, adding, "By remarkable coincidence, Constantinople was Venice's chief rival as the gateway to the trade route to the Orient." He shrugged. "Anyway, the legend is that seeing what was about to happen, some church officials were determined to save the Reliquary of the Holy Standard, and they entrusted it to a group of monks, who secretly left the city and took it to a remote area where they have cared for it and kept it safe ever since."

"Where?" Rafe asked pragmatically.

The scholar shrugged. "Who knows? Somewhere in the wilds of Turkey? There is no evidence of it. It is merely legend, gossip given import simply by the passage of time."

"And yet here is this reliquary that matches the description," Kyria said.

Dr. Jennings looked back at the box. "Yes," he agreed. "Here it is."

For a moment, they sat in silence. Finally, Rafe stirred and said, "Dr. Jennings, is there some way we could find out more about this reliquary? Anyone who could tell us anything more?"

Dr. Jennings squirmed a little in his seat and finally blurted, "Well, there is Nelson Ashcombe."

"Who is that?"

"He's a preeminent archaeologist," Jennings replied, then sighed. "At least, he was. The last few years . . ."

"I have heard of him," Kyria said. "My father has spoken of him."

Jennings nodded. "He was quite well-known, one of the best in the field. His digs were funded by Lord Walford."

"Lord Walford was one of my father's friends," Kyria said. "He died a couple of years ago."

"Yes," Jennings concurred. "Since then, I believe the younger Lord Walford has continued as Ashcombe's patron. But Ashcombe's reputation has declined. He has spent the last few years looking for that da— er, dashed reliquary."

"What?" Rafe glanced at Kyria, then back at the other man. "You mean he believes in it?"

Again, Jennings nodded, looking pained. "He has destroyed his credibility — or close to it."

"I reckon it would cause something of a stir, then, if it turned out he was right,"

Rafe suggested. "If that box really is the reliquary he's been looking for."

"It cannot be," Jennings said stubbornly. "Just because it is made out of ivory and cannot be opened does not mean that it contains a scrap of the *labarum*. It is far more likely that it is simply a reliquary box from the Byzantine period — or even a replica of the Reliquary of the Holy Standard. A fake." He sighed. "I am sure you are going to take it to Ashcombe, but I wish you would not. He will be so ecstatic at the thought of justifying his mad theory that he will be certain it is *his* reliquary. I don't think the man has any objectivity left. If he goes around trying to foist this box off as the Reliquary of the Holy Standard, he will ruin himself in the historical community. Frankly I am surprised the present Lord Walford hasn't let him go already."

"Perhaps he has some loyalty to the man," Kyria suggested.

"And you think I do not," Jennings responded. "The truth is, I admire Ashcombe. He is a brilliant excavator. But I am first and foremost an historian, and history is based on facts, not myths and legends."

"I guess someone should have told Herr Schliemann that, then, when he went looking for Troy, based on Homer's stories," Kyria shot back.

Dr. Jennings had the grace to look abashed. "Yes, yes, I know. But at least there was some written evidence there, not just wild stories passed down through the ages. And you have no proof that this is the reliquary." He looked at them challengingly. "Where has it been all these years? Why has it surfaced now?"

"All very good questions," Rafe commented a few minutes later as they left the professor's house and started toward the inn where they had stabled their horses. "I certainly wish we knew some of the answers."

The day, which had started out so clear, had turned gray while they were in Jennings's cottage. They walked quickly, keeping an eye on the lowering clouds.

"I do, too," Kyria agreed, wincing as she felt a drop of water hit her hand. "Was that rain?"

"Yes," Rafe replied an instant later when the skies opened up.

Kyria let out a small shriek and, picking up the long skirts of her riding habit, began to run. They raced down the main street to the inn, but they could not escape a soaking. They rushed inside, where they were met by the innkeeper, who exclaimed over their state and the weather and offered them the comfort of a private dining room with a roaring fire.

They accepted with alacrity, and he bustled them into the cozy room, followed a moment later by his friendly wife, carrying several towels.

"There, now, miss," the woman said, giving Kyria a towel and quickly unbuttoning her wet jacket and pulling it from her shoulders. "I'll just hang this on the chair here by the fire, and it'll dry well enough. You sit down right here, and that fire'll soon take the chill off you, as well."

She directed Kyria onto a stool, then turned to manage the maid who had brought in a tea tray. She finally left, promising to return with a warm repast.

Kyria shivered and nudged the stool closer to the fire, spreading her skirts out to aid in their drying. The shirtwaist beneath her jacket was only slightly damp and would dry soon enough, but her hair was thoroughly wet and straggling down from its moorings. She took the pins from her hair and set them aside, letting her hair fall down, and began to dry it with a towel. Rafe, who had shrugged out of his jacket, stopped, caught by the sight of her. He watched her squeeze the water from her long, thick hair and blot it with the towel, then run her fingers through it, straightening out the tangles and spreading it to dry. Something clenched in his gut, and he thought of the rooms upstairs in the inn. His mouth was dry as he watched the firelight play over Kyria's white skin, touching it with gold, and warm her flame-red hair.

He cleared his throat and turned away, searching for something to say. "Well, ah . . . perhaps I should hire a carriage to return to Broughton Park. The weather seems to have betrayed us."

"Perhaps it will stop by the time we have eaten," Kyria replied, and he was pleased to see that she seemed not to have noticed his gawking at her like a schoolboy a moment before. "Here, come sit by the fire with me. It will warm you."

Rafe hesitated for a moment, then crossed to the other chair. He busied himself with arranging his jacket across the arm of the chair to dry, then sat down. Kyria, occupied with fanning out her hair in front of the fire, did not look at him.

He relaxed into the chair, watching her work her fingers through her hair, and his fingers itched to reach out and replace her hands with his. His eyes drifted over her figure, the crisp, white shirtwaist dampened and clinging to her breasts. What he wanted to do more than anything else, he knew, was pull her into his lap and kiss her until they were both blazing with heat. But realizing that he had probably already been much too bold the other day in the grove, he forced himself to think of something else.

"Do you plan to seek out this Ashcombe fellow?" he asked.

"Who? Oh. I don't know." Kyria sighed and turned to him. "What do you think?"

"I'm not sure." Rafe reached down and picked up the drawstring bag, which Kyria had set on the floor beside her stool, and pulled the ivory box from it. He held it in his hands, leaning closer to the fire. The firelight played over the white box, picking up the depths of the dark gem. Rafe rubbed his thumb caressingly over it.

"Perhaps it's only a legend, as Jennings said. Still . . . I cannot help but feel that this is a very special object, indeed. What if Ashcombe is right?"

"I know." Kyria reached out and traced the stone with her forefinger. Her finger brushed his thumb, and the touch echoed through her. She pulled back her hand hastily, her nerves jumping. She realized that what she really wanted to do was smooth her fingers over his, tracing the bones of his hand, and the thought unnerved her.

There was a knock on the door, and the innkeeper's wife entered, behind her two maids carrying trays. They laid out a sumptuous meal on the table, then left Rafe and Kyria to enjoy it.

Rafe found he had little appetite. All he could think about was Kyria and how he would like to stroke her bare white skin . . . lose himself in her luscious mouth.

He shifted restlessly in his seat, trying to force his attention to the food. The last thing he should be thinking about was Kyria. It was far too tempting, given their situation here, alone in an inn, away from everyone who knew them.

He had thought that he could safely flirt with her, that it would be an amusing diversion with a sophisticated woman who could play the game as readily as he could. But the other day when they went out riding, he had learned how very wrong he was. He had been unprepared for the kind of raw hunger that had swept through him, the fierce urge to crush her to him and devour her. He had wanted to fall to the ground with her and take her right there, heedless of everything.

That, of course, was unthinkable. It would be the act of a cad to make love to Kyria, even if she were as willing and passionate as she had seemed when he kissed her the other day. She was a well-brought-up young lady, and even though she was past the age when most women married, he felt sure she was still a virgin. He knew well how sheltered young women were in the society where he had grown up; he was certain that here in the more rigid society of England, they were probably even more watched and protected. Moreover, her response when he had kissed her the other day had been enough to tell him that she was untouched. She had been passionate, but untutored, clearly surprised at the sensations that had swept through her.

A man of honor would not seduce such a woman; marriage was the only option. Even less could he consider it with Kyria. He was a guest in her home; to play fast and loose with her would be doubly an insult. Besides that, she was the sister-in-law of his best friend, a man who had saved his life and for whom Rafe would risk his own. And even if he had been low enough to ignore all those things, Rafe knew that his feelings for Kyria were enough to compel him to stay away from her.

He liked and respected Kyria far too

much to do anything to hurt her. Hers was a passionate and loving nature, and he had little doubt that where Kyria was concerned, one meant the other. Where she gave her body, she gave her heart, as well.

And he was no one to whom she should give either.

Rafe knew that others might think him an eligible bachelor. He had fortune and education and was old enough to settle down. Some might think that a family like the Morelands would not consider a common American good enough for one of their daughters, but he had seen enough of the family to suspect that such considerations would not weigh with them.

But the truth was that he was anything but an acceptable prospect for marriage, he thought bitterly. He was an outcast from his home and family, a man whose past lay in ruins. His life had been broken on the shoals of war. Four years of bloody battle had taken away not only his youth, but much of his heart. The aftermath had removed the rest of it.

He was a restless man, the sort who would probably never settle down. He had nothing to give any woman. And Kyria, of all people, deserved much more than a man whose life was built on wreckage.

The only rational course, therefore, was to keep his hands — and his thoughts — off Kyria. Unfortunately, as he was finding out, that was something that was far more easily said than done. No matter how he tried, he could not seem to tear his eyes away from her, could not keep his thoughts from returning again and again to how it had felt to kiss her . . .

Kyria was as sharply aware of Rafe as she sensed he was of her. The dining arrangement was most intimate, she realized. No man outside her family had ever seen her like this, hair tumbling wildly down around her shoulders. Rafe's shirt was open at the collar, exposing his tanned, corded throat, and he had undone the cuffs and rolled them up, baring the lower part of his arms. She supposed that this must be how it was for a couple on their honeymoon, and just the thought made her unable to meet Rafe's gaze. She wondered what he was thinking, if he, too, had considered how near they were to the anonymous beds of the inn's rooms, private and secluded.

Kyria could not keep her eyes from going to his hands, strong and brown, with the lightest dusting of hair on the back. There was something about his hands that set up a curious trembling in her stomach. Kyria was filled with an inexpressible yearning, a longing that she had never felt before.

She tried to keep her attention on her food, cutting it up and chewing it with determination. It tasted like sawdust. Finally, she set her fork and knife down with a clatter. Reaching for her glass, she took a gulp of wine. She could not stand to sit here this way, thinking . . . feeling . . .

Abruptly, she set her glass aside and stood up. Her eyes went to his face. Rafe stood, as well, his eyes going to her face, his initial expression of questioning and concern falling away as he looked at her. He knew, she thought. He knew what she was feeling — the coiling heat and the pulsing urgency — and the realization both embarrassed and aroused her. He was looking back at her in a way that left little doubt that the same sensations were surging through him.

Kyria's breath caught in her throat and she started to turn away, her heart hammering against her rib cage. Rafe reached out and caught her by the wrist. She looked back at him. She told herself she should pull away from him, but instead, she found herself taking a step forward. Her eyes locked with his, and in another instant she was in his arms.

8

Rafe's mouth came down on hers, eager and searching as Kyria's arms twined around his neck as she clung to him. The taste and texture of him was a delight to her. His skin flamed into heat against her, separated only by the thin cloth of their shirts. His arms tightened around her, and his fists clenched in the material of her shirtwaist and skirt. They were so close, so tightly pressed together that Kyria could feel the heavy thud of his heart through her own body, and the very life force of him heightened her arousal.

Hunger twisted through her sharply, multiplying with every movement of his lips, every touch of his fingers. The quick intake of his breath, the low moan deep in his throat, the enveloping scent of his skin — all vibrated through her like a caress, sending the heat inside her spiraling.

Rafe's hands stroked down her back and curved over her hips, his fingers digging into her buttocks and lifting her up into him. Kyria could feel the heat and the hard desire of him, and she was filled with a wild urge to wrap her legs around him. An ache blossomed between her legs, bitter-sweet and longing, so that she wanted to weep and laugh at the same time.

His hand stole between their bodies, coming up to curve around her breast. Kyria quivered at the intimate touch, her breasts seeming to swell in response. His fingers were gentle and skillful, caressing her through the thin cotton of her shirt-waist, skimming over her nipple and cupping her fullness. His thumb circled the hard button of her nipple, lazily teasing it to life. Kyria moaned softly, adrift in a haze of pleasure.

Nimbly he unbuttoned her shirtwaist and let it fall open, his hand sliding down into the opened neck and underneath the soft lace of her chemise. A shudder of pleasure ran through her as his fingertips skimmed over her bare flesh, caressing the soft orb of her breast and teasing the nipple into even greater hardness.

His mouth left hers and began a trail of fire down her throat and chest. Kyria's breath rasped harshly in her throat, tension tightening in her abdomen, increasing with every touch of his lips to her skin, until she felt as if she might explode.

His lips found the soft flesh of her

breast, and Kyria jerked, desire skyrocketing inside her. Heat flooded between her legs, her blood pulsing within her like thunder, and she dug her fingers into his hair. His tongue made lazy circles over the top of her breast and down to the fleshy nub of her nipple.

Kyria gasped, shocked at the things his mouth was doing to her — and even more shocked at the desire that pulsed harder and harder within her at each new intimacy. He drew her nipple into his mouth, tugging gently, and Kyria sagged against him, scarcely able to stand under the onslaught of pleasure.

Her senses whirled. She had never imagined such pleasure. She had never dreamed that she could want the things she wanted now — the fierce, instinctive hunger that wanted to feel him, know him . . . *have* him.

With a groan, Rafe lifted his head. For a long moment he stared down into her face, his blue eyes glittering, his face stamped with hunger. "Kyria . . . sweet heaven, I want you." He groaned then, releasing her. "We cannot. It would be —"

He muttered a curse and pulled up her chemise to cover her breasts, letting the sides of her shirtwaist fall back together. "I am sorry. I should not have . . . done what I did."

He glanced toward the open door. Kyria followed his gaze, and she flushed with embarrassment, realizing that the innkeeper or his wife or anyone else could have just walked in on them. They had been blind to everything except their desire. Whatever was the matter with her?

Hastily she began to button up her shirtwaist with fingers that trembled. She hardly dared glance at Rafe. What would he think of her? She had always been so calm and collected, so much in control. It was a little frightening to realize just how much she had been out of control a few moments before. Had Rafe not had the good sense to stop, she had no idea what she might have done, where their kisses and caresses might have led. Kyria pressed trembling fingers to her mouth and walked over to the fire.

"I cannot say that I regret what I did," Rafe went on. "I am not that much of a gentleman. But it was wrong of me. I should have . . . exercised more control."

Kyria spun around to face him, a saving irritation spurting up. "You were not the only one involved, I would remind you! It is not entirely your responsibility. I believe that I had something to say about the matter."

Rafe looked at her, nonplussed. He had expected her to be weeping in distress or even perhaps frightened by his forceful passion. It seemed that Kyria would never cease to surprise him.

"I am not a child," Kyria said angrily. "You do not have to protect me from my own weakness! You do not have to accept responsibility for actions that were at least half my fault."

It was especially galling, she thought, to know that, in fact, he *had* protected her, that he had been the one who had thought of the consequences and had stopped, not she. Even now, she suspected, if he pulled her back into his arms, she would go willingly — and that was a decidedly lowering thought.

"I did not mean that!" Rafe snapped, his own irritation rising at her rejection of his apology. It had been damned difficult to stop, with lust thrumming through him, and here she was, throwing it back in his face as if it were nothing. "Of course you don't have to be protected from yourself. But, dammit, I am older and more experienced than you, and —"

"How do you know?" Kyria asked, lifting

her chin defiantly. “How do you know that you are more experienced? Maybe I have kissed dozens of men. Or more than kissed them!”

She looked so beautiful, standing there with her eyes blazing and her color up, her hair tumbling wildly around her shoulders and her shirtwaist buttoned up wrong, that Rafe wasn’t sure whether he would most like to kiss her or shake her.

Instead, he gave a low growl of frustration and jerked his jacket off the chair, shoving it on as he strode toward the door. “I’ll have the horses saddled.”

He marched out the door, closing it sharply behind him, leaving Kyria glaring impotently at the door. She would have liked very much to have heaved something after him, but years of breeding would not allow her to break any of the inn’s crockery. So she simply seethed to herself as she twisted her still-damp hair into a knot atop her head and pinned it as best she could.

She didn’t know who she was more furious with, herself or Rafe. The man had not even suggested as an excuse that he had been so swept away by her beauty that he had lost all control! And how could she have behaved so unlike herself?

Kyria pulled on her jacket and buttoned it up to the top, then schooled her countenance into some semblance of composure, so that when Rafe came back into the room she was able to meet him with a polite and calm, if somewhat chilly, greeting.

The rain had stopped, although the sky was still gray, and he asked her if she would prefer to ride or to hire a carriage and tie their horses behind it. Kyria quickly opted for riding. She could not imagine being cooped up inside a carriage with Rafe all the way home. She would prefer being exposed to the possible rain.

They said little on the way back to Broughton Park, the silence between them chillier than the October air. They kept up a good pace, which had the advantage not only of expending some of their pent-up feelings, but of shortening the ride and making the lack of conversation less awkward.

Rafe cursed himself silently all the way home. He had messed the whole thing up royally, and he wasn't sure whether he could make it right. The truth was, he knew that he should not even try. He should simply take his leave of the Morelands and go on with his tour of Europe.

It was obvious that he could not control himself around Kyria. If he stayed, he would be putting himself into exactly the sort of situation he should avoid. And yet, even as he thought the words, he knew that leaving was the last thing he wanted to do.

Kyria's emotions were just as turbulent and perhaps even more confused. What had happened between Rafe and her had been electric. She had never been in such a situation, and she didn't know what to think. She was stunned and amazed and more than a little unsure of herself.

She had acted in a way that was completely unlike her, and that bothered her. She was usually so calm and in command of herself. No man had ever disturbed her senses or shattered her control. That Rafe had — and might do so again — was frightening. And yet she could not help wanting to feel once more that wild, explosive pleasure, more intense than anything she had ever known.

What had it been like for him? What had *Rafe* felt? She could not help but remember his words: he was more experienced than she. Had he found her lacking? It had seemed to her that Rafe had been as filled with passion as she had been; she remembered the surge of heat in his body as they kissed, the tightening of his arms, his labored breathing.

Kyria swallowed, realizing that passion was welling up in her again, just remembering what they had done. She flushed with embarrassment and glanced over at Rafe, relieved to see that he was not looking at her.

The rain held off until they reached Broughton Park. Kyria took the reliquary straight to her father, and Rafe excused himself and went up to his room. Kyria was a little surprised that he did not go with her to the duke, but she was relieved to be out of his presence for the moment. Yet she could not but feel a sharp twist of hurt that he seemed as though he could hardly wait to get away from her.

The duke was eager to hear all the details of Jennings's assessment, and before they were through, several other members of the family, including the twins, had heard of her arrival and slipped in to learn the outcome. It was quite late before they finished talking and her father locked the reliquary away in his collections room. Yet despite the late hour, Kyria felt not tired, but curiously on edge.

She had difficulty falling asleep. She kept remembering what had happened between her and Rafe at the inn. The very thought of it sent heat curling through her, and she wondered how she would be able to face Rafe tomorrow, how she could talk to him as if nothing had happened. She was afraid that as soon as he looked at her, she would turn red and go weak in the knees, and everyone around would know that there was something wrong.

As it turned out, there was nothing to worry about. She came down to breakfast the next morning, having spent a great deal of time on her grooming and several minutes more schooling her face into just the right expression of calm beauty, only to find out from Thisbe that Rafe had ridden out this morning with Cousin Albert.

"A nice young man," the duchess commented. "He has been quite helpful, hasn't he, Kyria?"

"What? Yes, I suppose he has."

"The twins adore him," Thisbe put in.

"Too bad he's an American," Lady Rochester said. She had finished breakfast long ago, but it was her habit to remain at the breakfast table for ages every morning, thereby managing to put a damper on the good spirits of as many people as she could.

Thisbe cast a sardonic look at Kyria,

then said, "I can't imagine what that has to do with anything, Aunt Hermione."

Lady Rochester turned her gimlet eye on Thisbe. "Can't you? Humph." She pointed her spoon at Thisbe and went on, "Then you haven't been seeing the way he looks at Kyria."

"Aunt Hermione!" Kyria gasped.

"You think I don't see things?" the old lady asked contentiously, her face ablaze with triumph. There was nothing she liked better than stirring things up. "That jumped-up Yankee's interested in you, mark my words."

"He's not a Yankee. He's a Southerner," the duchess told her. "He explained the difference to me the other day. I rather like him — he's a young man who stood up for his beliefs. And," she added on a note of relief, "he has helped keep Alex and Con occupied since their tutor left. It will take me weeks to find them another tutor."

"He even took Cousin Albert off our hands," Thisbe said with a grin. "That is the work of a saint."

"Don't be facetious, Thisbe," Lady Rochester told her, and plowed ahead. "But one has no way of knowing what his family is. They could be anything."

"Actually, I think his father was a

schoolteacher," Kyria offered.

"You see? That is what I mean."

"I see nothing wrong with his father being a schoolteacher," Kyria's mother said, stiffening.

"He is well educated," Kyria went on. "He was studying for the law before the war."

"At an American college," Lady Rochester retorted, her tone leaving little doubt of her opinion of the value of such an education. "Besides, what difference does that make? It isn't as if one would welcome a barrister into the family."

The duchess stared at her husband's aunt blankly. "Who said anything about welcoming him into the family?"

"Really, Emmeline, it would do you well to pay a little attention to what is happening right under your nose. I just told you that he has been looking at Kyria in a way that —"

"Oh, for heaven's sake," the duchess snapped. "Half the bachelors in London look at Kyria that way — and far too great a number of married men, as well, I'm sorry to say. Men are always falling in love with her."

"Yes, but does she usually look back?" Lady Rochester parried.

The duchess's fork clattered to her plate and she looked at the older woman with narrowed eyes. "Exactly what are you implying?"

"Aunt Hermione. Mother. Please," Kyria said, a flush rising in her cheeks. She cast a significant glance toward the footmen standing at either end of the sideboard, doubtless listening avidly to their conversation. "I assure you that you are mistaken, Aunt Hermione. Mr. McIntyre and I are mere acquaintances."

Lady Rochester cocked an eyebrow and proclaimed, "Hardly looks that way when you go jauntering off about the countryside with him."

"Mr. McIntyre was a perfect gentleman," Kyria said flatly, returning the old woman's steely gaze.

"Doesn't matter what happened. What matters is how it looked," her great-aunt retorted.

One look at the duchess's flushed cheeks and bright eyes told Kyria that her mother was about to let loose with her opinion of Lady Rochester's statement, so she quickly said, "I am sure that no one could find any exception to it, Aunt. You must be getting tired," she went on, turning a significant look on Lady Rochester's daughter and put-upon companion. "Cousin Rosalind, don't you think it's time for Aunt Hermione's morning nap?"

"What? Oh! Oh, yes." Rosalind jumped up and immediately began fussing over her mother, getting her shawl and handing the old woman her cane, calling for a footman to help them.

By the time the two women had left the room, the duchess's color had died down, and she said with a rueful smile, "Thank you, Kyria, dear. I am sure that in another moment I would have said something I would have regretted. I think that Lady Rochester positively enjoys making me lose my temper."

"She enjoys making everyone lose their temper," Thisbe assured her. "Whenever I think of the things she said about Desmond when we got engaged, I get absolutely furious all over again."

The duchess turned her piercing blue gaze on Kyria. "My dear, is there any truth to what she was saying? Are you interested in Mr. McIntyre?"

"Of course not, Mother," Kyria responded. "I mean, well, we scarcely know each other and, anyway, well, you know I have no intention of marrying anyone."

"What? What's this about marrying?" Kyria's father walked into the room and glanced around vaguely.

"Nothing, Papa," Thisbe told him with a smile, and popped up to give him a kiss on the cheek. "We were simply having a few words with Aunt Hermione."

"She's not here, is she?" the duke asked anxiously and cast a wary look around the room.

"No, Henry, she just left," the duchess assured him, and her husband let out a sigh of relief.

"Good. She's usually gone by this hour."

Kyria chuckled. "I wondered why you had started working early in the morning before you had breakfast."

"The woman's a terror," the duke said, sitting down and taking a quick swig of the coffee the footman brought him. "Do you know she asked me yesterday why I kept so much old *junk* around? I ask you . . ."

"I know. Poor Uncle Bellard is absolutely trapped in his rooms," Kyria said.

"Since Uncle Bellard's rooms consist of a bedroom, sitting room and a large workroom, an area larger, I might add, than many people's homes, one can scarcely feel too sorry for him," the duchess pointed out. "Besides, it's his own fault. She is only his sister; she has no power over him. He should stand up to her."

"You know how conflict distresses Uncle Bellard," Thisbe put in. "You can tell how interested he was in your reliquary, Kyria, by the fact that he ventured downstairs, despite the fact that Aunt Hermione is still roaming the halls. But tell us, what was Dr. Jennings able to tell you about the box?"

Thisbe had been one of the few family members who had not joined them the evening before when Kyria had come in, as she and Desmond had already retired. Kyria told her about what Dr. Jennings had said, and Thisbe responded with appropriate astonishment.

"What are you going to do now?" she asked when Kyria finished. "How can you find out if this is really the Reliquary of the Holy Standard, or whatever he called it?"

"I'm not sure what to do. I don't know that I will ever be able to learn whether it's the real thing. I wish we could open it, but even if we could, no doubt it is empty after all this time."

"Nelson Ashcombe has quite a reputation," the duke said. "I had not heard that it had fallen off in recent years because of this obsession. His patron, you know, was Lord Walford, who was a friend of mine. I could write you a letter of introduction. I have heard he's a terrible recluse."

"I would like to hear what he has to say," Kyria admitted. "I suppose I could go to this dealer who visited us, too, and see if he can tell me any more about it. I am reluctant, though, to show him the box. There was just something I didn't like about the man, and I cannot help but wonder if he was connected to what happened to poor Mr. Kousoulous."

"On the other hand, even if Mr. Ashcombe thinks that it is the reliquary that Dr. Jennings was talking about, you still would not *know*," Thisbe pointed out. "I mean, Dr. Jennings was right. Without any idea where it came from, it is rather difficult to tell if it is the real thing or just some other reliquary or maybe even a fake."

"I know. I wish Theo had sent some sort of explanation!"

The duchess frowned. "It doesn't seem like Theo to send something to us that carried that sort of danger."

"I am sure he didn't realize it," Thisbe said, sticking up for her twin. "Either that, or Mr. Kousoulous's death had nothing to do with the box. I mean, we have no proof that it was not entirely unrelated to the reliquary. I know that Theo would never put Kyria or any of us at risk."

"I wonder if he is going to return anytime soon," Kyria said.

"If he does not come home soon, we will get a note from him," Kyria's mother said firmly. "He always lets us know where he is eventually. I think it might be best to wait until we hear from Theo before you go haring off to London, Kyria. I don't like the idea of your traveling, carrying that box."

"Perhaps Mr. McIntyre could accompany her again," Broughton offered. Kyria could see from the glitter in his eyes that her father was as eager as she to learn more about the reliquary.

"I doubt that Mr. McIntyre wants to continue to escort me about," Kyria said quickly. The last thing she wanted was for her father to ask Rafe to accompany her, thus putting him in a position where he could scarcely refuse. "Mother is probably right. We should wait to hear from Theo. Later, when we return to London, I can always pay a call on Mr. Ashcombe."

The duke looked disappointed, but he subsided. Kyria could feel her sister's curious eyes on her, but did not meet her gaze. She felt sure that Thisbe wondered about her quick dismissal of Rafe's possible escort to London, but she did not want to talk about what had happened yesterday, even to her sister.

Kyria did not have to face Rafe again until that evening at supper, for by the time he returned from his ride, she had managed to busy herself with various household duties and did not see him. When she walked into the anteroom where they gathered before dining, Kyria felt Rafe's eyes on her immediately, and she could not keep from turning toward him.

He was looking at her intently, and his bright blue gaze, as always, set up a dance of butterflies in her stomach. Unconsciously, she pressed one hand to her stomach, and for an instant looked unaccustomedly vulnerable. Rafe smiled at her then, his expression warming, and she could not help but smile back.

Gradually he made his way around the room to her and leaned down to murmur in her ear, "Am I forgiven?"

Kyria looked up at him, her eyes searching his. "I don't know that you are any more at fault than I," she replied softly.

"Do you want me to leave?" he asked. "I, doubtless, should go on to London. Your parents will begin to think that I am never leaving."

Kyria chuckled. "Believe me, there are

several others in their own family that they would rather be rid of first. Do not leave on my account." However odd and unsettled she felt right now, she knew that she did not want it to end. "Of course, if you wish to go, that is quite another thing . . ."

He shook his head slightly. "No. I do not wish to go."

"And I don't want you to." Kyria glanced up at him, and Rafe smiled.

"Then it's settled."

The remainder of the evening, Kyria found, went much more smoothly.

Kyria was sitting in her mother's informal sitting room the next morning, trying to concentrate on a piece of embroidery while Thisbe worked on her notes and their mother sat at her small, mahogany secretary, catching up on her correspondence, when she heard the heavy thud of footsteps out in the hall. She glanced up in surprise, for the servants were normally quiet in whatever they did and the steps sounded much heavier than either of the twins produced.

Her face fell slack with surprise as two men strode into the room. One was short and heavyset, with wide shoulders and chest thrust into an ill-fitting serge jacket. His companion was taller and slimmer, with a long, lantern jaw. Kyria had never seen either of them before, and she could not imagine what they were doing coming into her mother's sitting room unannounced. She drew in her breath sharply, fear suddenly blossoming in her stomach.

At the sound, Thisbe glanced up from the notebook in which she had been jotting down numbers, and her mother turned from her desk. The pen fell from her hand, dribbling ink across the letter she had been writing, as she started to rise, indignation on her face.

"Who are . . ." the duchess began, then stopped as the lantern-jawed man pulled a pistol out of the pocket of his jacket and pointed it at her.

"Never yer mind that," the man said roughly, his voice tinged with the London East End. "Just give me the box an' everythin' will be all right."

"The box?" The duchess's voice was as cool and collected as if she had been receiving a neighbor for tea, not rough-looking armed men. "I am afraid I don't know what you are talking about."

Kyria felt a swelling of admiration for her mother.

The stranger, however, was irritated. He shook the gun at the duchess, saying, "Yer know, all right. Don't go tryin' to pull the wool over me eyes. I want the box — the fancy box — and I'm not leaving till yer give it to me."

"She doesn't have it," Kyria announced, standing up. "She doesn't know anything about it."

"Oh, is that right?" The man turned his attention to Kyria. "Well, now, maybe yer can tell me where it is, then, seein' as how you know so much."

As he spoke, the larger of the two men moved over to stand beside Kyria, his face grim and threatening.

"It is locked away," Kyria said, ignoring the heavyset man. "For safekeeping. None of us can get to it."

"Somebody's got the key," the lantern-jawed intruder growled.

"Well, it isn't one of us," Kyria replied levelly. She didn't know what to do. Obviously she and her mother and sister had little hope of overcoming two men, especially with one wielding a gun. But if they could just delay them, keep them talking, surely someone — a servant or a guest — would notice and get help. Someone would tell Rafe. She did not question her certainty that Rafe would rescue them.

"It isn't here," Thisbe added, arranging

her face in a vapid expression that Kyria would never have believed possible. "We are just the women of the household."

Kyria glanced at her mother and saw on her face such a look of horror as she gazed at her eldest daughter that Kyria had to press her lips together to hold back an inappropriate giggle.

"That's right," Kyria said. "Surely you cannot think that we know the whereabouts of something so valuable."

"That may be," the gunman agreed, then strode quickly across the room and grabbed the duchess's arm, pulling her to him and holding the pistol to her head. "But I'm thinkin' yer know who does, and yer goin' to take me to him 'less yer want to see yer mother's brains splattered all over the room."

"No!" Thisbe and Kyria cried in unison, stepping forward, and the large man reached out and wrapped his hand around Kyria's arm, jerking her to a halt.

"Take your hands off me, you fool," the duchess said crisply. "Unless you wish to find yourself in worse trouble than you already are. If you think that I am going to give in to such threats . . ."

The man let out a snort of laughter. "Yer don't have to, Yer Highness. They'll do it for yer." He nodded his head toward her daughters, both standing across the room watching them, eyes huge in their pale faces.

"Only my father can enter the room . . ." Kyria began.

"Kyria!" the duchess exclaimed.

". . . and he is not here," Kyria finished. "I am terribly sorry, but the keys are kept locked in his study. So you can see that it's impossible."

"Not if you want your mother to live, it ain't," the man retorted, giving a nod to his silent companion. He wiggled the gun provocatively against the duchess's temple. "Now take me to that study."

9

The large man, still gripping Kyria's arm, pulled her toward the door. Such a bizarre procession down the hall surely would not go unnoticed, Kyria thought. She and Thisbe exchanged glances, and she knew that her sister's thoughts ran along lines similar to her own. Kyria hoped that her father would prove to be anywhere else but his study.

"I cannot imagine why you are so interested in that old box, anyway," Thisbe remarked, continuing her pretense of empty-headedness. "Personally I would much prefer to have something new, wouldn't you, Kyria?"

"Of course," Kyria replied, glad that Thisbe was trying to distract the men. The more they kept the men's attention on the three of them, the better chance they had of someone, perhaps down one of the halls or in a side room, being able to help them.

"Shut yer yap," the man holding the duchess growled. "What do I care what yer think of the box?"

"Well, I should think that the opinion of a woman of taste and breeding would be invaluable concerning an object of art," Kyria replied. "I am simply saying that you would likely get more money for something newer and more attractive — a jeweled necklace, for instance."

"It's the box. I got me orders," he told her shortly.

"Yes, I am sure you do," Kyria said. "I hope your master instructed you —"

" 'Ere!" the man exclaimed. " 'E ain't no master of mine. I'm me own man, see."

"You mean *you* are the one interested in the box?" Thisbe asked.

"No! 'Course not. But I work only for meself, see. He has a job, and I takes it. We're equal, like."

Kyria let out a little laugh. "I doubt that. How much did he pay you? Did he tell you that in certain circles, this box is worth thousands and thousands of guineas? Maybe more?" She hoped that the man wouldn't notice that she was contradicting what she and Thisbe had just said. But she wanted to seize on the weakness she had spotted in the gunman — his pride in being his own man. "I suspect that he is paying you a mere pittance, whereas he intends to sell the box to a client for a hundred times, nay, a thousand times what he is offering you. And you are the one who is doing all the dangerous work."

Her words were met with a blank silence as the intruder appeared to digest what she had said. Kyria had little hope of talking the man out of what he was doing, but she did hope that the new thoughts she had planted in his mind would distract him. As best she could tell, the other man, the one gripping her own arm tightly, had no thoughts whatsoever.

Just at that point, they crossed an intersecting hallway, one that ran back through the house. Kyria automatically glanced down it, and to her horror, she saw Con coming around the corner, a smile on his face and a cricket bat in his hand. He stopped abruptly when he saw them, his mouth dropping open. Kyria shot him a fierce look, silently begging him to understand and run away for help.

Con apparently got the mental message, for he spun on his heel and ran back around the corner, disappearing from sight. But beside her, the intruder holding her arm let out a roar, and Kyria knew with a sinking heart that he had spotted her brother.

"There's a boy!" he shouted, pointing.

He dropped her arm and started to go after Con, but his companion stopped him with a gesture.

"Boy!" Lantern Jaw yelled. "Come back 'ere." He paused and the seconds ticked by. "If yer don't, I'm pulling this trigger, and it's the last yer'll see of yer mother!"

"Constantine! I forbid you!" the duchess called out.

"Shut up!" The man reached up with his free hand and slapped the duchess.

With something like a snarl, Kyria started toward him, her hands coming up like claws. The large man grabbed her arms, pulling her back. The other man dug his fingers into the duchess's hair, jerking her closer to him and pushing the pistol hard against her temple.

"Oh, yer a feisty one, eh?" Lantern Jaw said, leering at Kyria. "Go ahead, come at me, girlie, and *she'll* be the first to go." Then he raised his voice. "Yer 'ear that, lad? If yer want to see your mum alive, yer come to me."

To control herself, Kyria curled her fingernails into her palms so tightly they drew blood. The large man was too strong for her to break free of him, anyway, but it took all her self-control not to scream with rage.

For a long moment, they remained in their silent tableau. Then there was the sound of footsteps, and they all turned to see Con walking toward them slowly, the cricket bat still dangling loosely from his hand. His eyes were huge in his pale face, and he looked somehow smaller than usual.

Con looked up at the intruder as he drew near, and tears swam in his blue-gray eyes. "You aren't going to hurt me, are you, mister?"

Kyria, who had never heard her brother express even one concern over getting hurt, felt a spurt of hope. She knew one thing their tormenters did not — that wherever Con was, Alex was never far away. With any luck, he had been behind Con, out of sight, but had heard everything and was even now on his way for help.

"There, there, Con," Kyria said in sugary tones, taking a handkerchief out of her pocket and bending to wipe away her brother's tears and thereby block the boy from their captors' view for a moment. "I am sure the man will not hurt a little boy."

Con, looking up into her face, gave her a conspiratorial grin before he drew his face back into lines of terror and said in a quivering voice, "Are you sure? He looks so fierce."

"Yes, I'm sure. Just do what he says and everything will be all right."

She put her hand on Con's shoulder, pulling him to her side, so that the cricket bat was more or less hidden in her skirts. Even though the men had already seen the bat, she thought it best to keep it out of sight, in case they might begin to think about it and realize what an admirable weapon it would make. The large man took her arm in one hand and Thisbe's in the other, and they started once again down the hall. Con continued to snivel and whine as they walked along, contriving to stumble and fall once, slowing their progress even further. Thisbe and Kyria kept the pace as slow as they dared, and their mother stalked along in icy contempt for the man who matched her pace and held a gun to her head.

However, they could not keep from finally reaching the study. Kyria's heart sank when she opened the door and found her father sitting behind his desk, sorting through a stack of papers. Even worse, old Lord Penhurst was in the room, too, snoring in one of the wing chairs, his handkerchief over his face.

The duke looked up vaguely from his work at the sound of their entry, then gaped at them. He started to speak, but the only sound that emerged from his throat was a croak.

Penhurst snorted and awoke, saying, "What's that you say, Broughton?" He pulled the handkerchief from his face and looked at the group by the door. "I say!" The old man sat up straighter and leaned forward, rapping his cane on the floor. "What the devil is the meaning of this?" He turned toward the duke. "Deuced queer start, I must say, Broughton."

"What . . . why . . . who are you?" Broughton stuttered out, rising to his feet, his face the color of his pressed white shirt. "Emmeline, are you all right?"

"Perfectly," his wife replied crisply, even though the bright red mark staining her cheek gave lie to her words.

"I want the box." The intruder with the gun came quickly to the point, motioning his captives forward into the room and pulling the duchess with him toward her husband. "Yer give me the box, or your missus 'ere'll pay for it."

"Good Lord," Broughton breathed, his usually pleasantly vague face drawing up wrathfully. He started around his desk toward the man. "You dare to put a hand on my wife?"

"Stop right there!" The gunman made a show of pressing the weapon to the duchess's temple. "I'll dare more'n that, 'less I get somethin' from yer," he went on, looking rather smug. "Ain't so grand now, are yer, Duke?"

"Damned impudence!" Lord Penhurst exclaimed, punctuating his comment with a sharp rap of his cane. "Throw the rascal out, Broughton."

Lantern Jaw shot an angry look at the old man, then turned to the duke. "What'll it be? Yer goin' to give me that box, or am I goin' to 'ave to use this on yer missus?"

"Henry, don't give in to him!" the duchess ordered. "You know I cannot abide bullies."

Her husband gave her an anguished look. "Emmeline . . . I cannot let him hurt you."

"It is a pointless threat," the duchess responded, turning to look at her captor. "If you carry it out, then you have lost your advantage. The only way you retain the threat is to not shoot me, which means that it really is rather useless."

"If yer don't shut yer gob, I'm goin' to shoot yer, anyway!" the man exclaimed. "And don't think I won't. I got three other people right 'ere I can use to get the duke to give me the box. 'Ow many of yer do yer think 'e'll let me kill 'fore 'e gives it to me?"

"Stop it!" Broughton ordered. "I will give you the box. But it is in another room."

He turned and went back to his desk, pulling open a drawer.

"Stop!" the gunman said.

"I have to get out my keys," Broughton explained reasonably, reaching into the drawer.

"Dixon." The gunman looked at his companion and nodded toward the drawer.

Dixon released his hold on Kyria and Thisbe, and moved quickly to the duke's side. The duke's left hand emerged from the drawer, holding a ring of keys, but as he started to draw out his other hand, Dixon clamped his large hand around Broughton's wrist and gave it a sharp, downward tug. A letter opener fell out of the duke's hand and clattered into the open drawer.

The duke sighed and looked toward his wife, his eyes eloquently sending his regret. Kyria, glancing at her mother, saw the duchess smile at him lovingly, tears gathering in her eyes.

"Henry . . ."

Broughton straightened and started toward her, but Dixon came up quickly beside him and now clamped his hand around the duke's upper arm.

"All right now, Duke," the gunman said. "That was yer only chance. The next time you pull a trick like that, I'm firing this pistol. After that, it'll be one of these young ladies — or maybe that little boy."

At those words, Con let out a cry and went running to his mother, grabbing her skirts and leaning against her. "Mother! Please don't let him hurt me!"

Kyria noticed that he still carried his cricket bat in his hand, despite his apparent distress. She had the strong suspicion that he was up to something, and she hoped that he would not act precipitately, but would wait for help to arrive.

Their father strode out the door first, followed by the duchess, Con by her side and Lantern Jaw at her other elbow, his gun pointed unrelentingly at her head. He paused in the doorway and glanced back at the others, who were following. He started to speak, then stopped and cast an annoyed look over at Lord Penhurst, who had risen to his feet and was pounding his cane pugnaciously on the floor.

"You young ruffian!" Penhurst shouted,

and waved his cane threateningly in his direction. "I'll see you in gaol!"

Lantern Jaw looked as though he would have liked to leave the rest of them behind, but he apparently realized that he could not afford to leave anyone who might go for help, for he gave an irritated twitch of his head and said, "Bring 'em all."

Dixon looked at Thisbe and Kyria, then back at Lord Penhurst, his mind obviously taxed at the predicament of keeping hold of all three. He wound up letting go of the women and shooing them and Lord Penhurst out the door in front of him, rather like a farmwife with a brood of chickens.

There was little Kyria could do to delay their progress, for the duke's collections room lay right next door to his study. However, Lord Penhurst made an excellent job of it, toddling along with his cane and releasing a steady stream of invectives at their captors.

"Young people have no respect today," he ranted. "Why, in my day, there would have been no mollycoddling. You would be transported for this. Hanged, more likely. Which is exactly what you deserve. Broughton, you ought to be more careful who you let in the house."

"I say, Penhurst, that's hardly fair," the duke protested, stopping and turning back to address the old man at the rear of the group. "I didn't ask them to break in."

"Humph! It wouldn't have happened when your father was alive, that's all I have to say," Penhurst retorted. "We knew how to deal with rascals then. You're too lenient, always have been. Always helping out the workers, always giving in to their demands —"

"Lord Penhurst," the duchess broke in, "this is scarcely a result of paying a decent wage for a decent day's work. If anything, it goes to argue my point — that when people are treated unfairly and paid a mere pittance for backbreaking work, it is no wonder that there is crime. Perhaps if this man, loathsome as he is, had had the chance to earn an honest living and support his family —"

" 'E ain't got no family," Dixon seemed to feel obliged to point out.

"And I ain't no mug!" the gunman exclaimed, looking offended. "I never done a honest day's work in me life!"

"You see?" Lord Penhurst waved his cane wildly. "That's what I mean. Worthless, the whole lot of them. Ought to ship them to Australia."

Kyria tried to glance unobtrusively around. She thought she glimpsed a bit of movement at a doorway down the hall, but she dared not look in that direction. The duke stopped in front of the door to his collections room and bent over his key ring, searching slowly through the keys. Kyria and Thisbe stopped behind their mother and her captor. Kyria noticed that beads of sweat were dribbling down the side of the gunman's face. As it was scarcely warm weather, she could only assume that he was feeling more nervous than his obnoxious behavior let on.

The duke finally found the right key and fitted it into the lock. Opening the door, he moved inside, the others streaming in after him.

" 'Cor!" the gunman exclaimed, glancing around him at the cases filled with ancient objects and the vases and statues and various pieces of pottery that littered the tables of the room.

Kyria noticed that her little brother fell away from his mother's side as they walked, moving behind her and her captor and around to the other side of the gunman, the cricket bat still dangling from his hand. The gunman, still a little stunned by the profusion of objects in the room, seemed not to notice Con's movements.

Broughton moved across the room to the center case, key in hand to open it. He stopped abruptly and stared into the case. "Good Lord!"

"What?" The duchess's guard looked at him.

"Why, it's gone," Broughton said, stunned. He pointed toward the glass-fronted case, at a vacant spot between a necklace on a stand and a small vase. "The box is gone!"

"What!" their captor exploded, releasing the duchess's arm and stepping forward in his agitation. "What are yer saying? Don't try to pull the wool over me eyes —" He waved his pistol at the duke.

"I'm not!" There was nothing false about the panic and distress in her father's voice. "The reliquary has been stolen!"

The gunman's hand dropped as he stared, slackjawed, at the empty spot in the cabinet, and in that moment Con seized the advantage and struck, swinging his bat upward with all his strength and cracking it smartly into the man's gun arm. The man let out a howl of pain as the gun went flying out of his hand. A shot went off, shattering one of the gas lamps across the room. The ruffian turned and grabbed

Con with a shriek of rage and shook him, then flung him aside.

The duchess cried out, "Con!" and ran to her son.

Kyria flew at the man, kicking and hitting, and he struggled to hold her off. Thisbe started toward her sister to help, but Dixon managed to grab her and hold on. Lord Penhurst brought his cane down smartly across the big man's knuckles, and Dixon cried out, releasing Thisbe and turning toward the old man with a growl.

At that moment Rafe burst through the doorway, a gun in each hand, followed by Alex, wielding a fireplace poker. Quickly assessing the situation, Rafe shoved one pistol into his belt and brought the other one down smartly, butt first, on Dixon's head. He kicked the thick-set man's knees out from under him, sending him crashing to the floor, and finished the job with another crack of the pistol butt. He started then toward Kyria, struggling in the other attacker's grasp. But before he could reach her, the duchess whirled from her son's side and bent down to pick up the cricket bat he had dropped, then came up like an avenging angel, her eyes lit with fire and a wild, almost inhuman cry issuing from her lips. She swung the cricket bat, striking the gunman's head with a loud *thwack*. He toppled like a felled tree.

The duchess stood over him, glaring down at him. "How dare you touch my child!"

"Emmeline!" Broughton rushed to his wife and pulled her into his arms. "Oh, thank God. I was afraid I had lost you!" He looked over her shoulder and caught sight of his eldest daughter, who had snatched up the nearest object to use as a weapon. "Thisbe! No! Not the Etruscan vase!"

There were a few moments of confusion as everyone turned to everyone else to make sure they were all right. Rafe crossed the room to Kyria in two quick strides and pulled her into his arms. Instinctively, her arms went around his waist and she leaned against his chest, her eyes closing in relief.

"I knew you would come," she breathed.

"Of course," he replied, and his lips brushed her hair. "Thank God for Alex. Are you all right?"

Kyria nodded. "Yes, I'm fine." However, she made no move to leave the shelter of his arms. "It was Mother who was in danger. And Con. Con!"

She gasped as she recalled what had happened to her younger brother, and she whirled around to see where her younger brother lay on the floor, still dazed. The other members of her family were all huddled around him, the duchess kneeling on the floor beside him.

"You are a hero," the duchess was telling Con, reaching down to wipe the hair from his forehead. She twisted to put an arm around Alex and pull him close. "Both of you are heroes."

"You are the one who has been hurt," Broughton said, reaching down and tugging his wife to her feet. He turned to cast a burning glance at the unconscious villains on the floor. "When I think that that fellow hit you!"

"I survived," the duchess reassured him, smiling at her husband and reaching up to pat his cheek.

They were interrupted by the sound of pounding footsteps outside, and in the next moment, a crowd of servants came streaming in, all drawn by the crack of the pistol shot, followed a moment later by the few guests who were still in residence. Kyria realized that she was still standing very close to Rafe, his hand resting lightly on her back, and she took a self-conscious step away.

"I say," Cousin Albert remarked mildly,

looking the scene over. "Why are those men on the floor?"

"Deuced peculiar household," Lord Penhurst declared. "Always has been. How is a fellow to take a nap around here?"

With those words, he turned and shuffled off, leaning on his cane. There were exclamations and explanations all around, and the butler sent a footman for rope to tie up the miscreants.

It took some minutes to get rid of their curious guests, and by the time they had done so and closed the door, their uninvited guests were beginning to wake up. Dixon let out a groan and made a move to touch his head, only to discover that he was tied up. He let out another groan and laid his head back on the floor.

"Blimey, Sid," he whined, "why'd I let you talk me into this? No good ever comes outta leavin' the City. I told you."

"Shurrup," the lantern-jawed man replied in a slurred voice. "Yer took the money well enough, din't yer?"

"Not really enough, though, was it?" Rafe asked pleasantly, striding across the room and squatting down beside the men.

None too gently, he grasped the gunman, Sid, by the arms, jerked him to a sitting position and leaned him against the wall. He looked straight into the man's eyes, and his voice was flat and hard as he asked, "All right, who hired you?"

Sid sneered back at him. "I ain't tellin' yer nothin'."

"You aren't talking to an English gentleman now, Sid. I don't believe in fair play. I believe in taking care of my own, and you have gotten in the way of that. Do you understand what I'm saying? Now, you can talk right here and now, where you have a well-mannered, upright duke watching the proceedings, or you can talk later to me — when we're alone." He paused, then added, with a faint smile, "Trust me, you'll end up telling me."

Something in his eyes must have convinced Sid of the truth of his words, for the man squirmed, looking away from Rafe, and said, "I can't tell yer nothin'. I don't know nothin'."

"You were hired by someone. What was his name?"

"I don't know." Sid shrugged. "These ropes are too tight."

"You'll wish they were as *loose* as this later if you don't start answering my questions."

"I don't know nothin'." Sid's voice took on a whine similar to that of his companion's. " 'E didn't tell me no names. 'E just said as ’ow ’e wanted the job done, and I agreed. ’E paid me ’alf and said I’d get the rest when I brought him the box.”

“What did he tell you about the box?”

“Just that it was small and white, made of ivory, like, and it ’ad a giant black stone on the side of it.”

“What did he look like?”

“I don’t know. Just a gent, you know. A foreign gent.”

“A foreigner?”

“Talked funny.” He paused, then added, “Not like you. More like a Frenchie or summat.”

“Was he French?”

“ ’Ow should I know? ’E was just foreign, like.”

“Was he dark? Fair?”

“Dark, I guess. I din’t pay much attention.”

Rafe grimaced. “You certainly are an unobservant fellow. It’s a wonder how you would have managed to hand the box over to the right man.” He turned to the heavyset man. “What about you, Dixon? Can you give me any better description of the man who hired you?”

Dixon looked at him blankly. “I didn’t see nobody, mister. It were Sid ’ere as ’ired me. I told ’im it would come to a bad end.

It's no good leavin' the City."

Rafe studied him for a moment, then turned back to Sid. "All right. How did he find you?"

"I don't know wot yer mean."

"The man who hired you could scarcely have put an ad in the newspaper for a thief. How did he know that you would do the job?"

"Oh. 'E asked the barkeep, Tommy, and Tom said as 'ow I was good for nickin' a few things."

"What barkeep?"

"Down at the tavern. The Blue Bull."

"Where is that?"

"London, 'course." Sid looked at Rafe as if he were daft. "Where else?"

"What part of London?"

"Cheapside. Down by the docks."

"And did you meet your employer there?"

Sid nodded, then winced at the pain the movement brought. "Yeah. Tommy told me to come by, and this bloke was waitin' fer me."

The Morelands had all been watching the interrogation with interest, and Kyria moved forward now, saying, "Where are you supposed to meet him? You must have set up some way of meeting him after you got the box."

Sid's gaze flickered over to Kyria for a moment, and his lip started to curl into a sneer, but then his eyes went to Rafe, who was watching him steadily, one hand tightening into a fist, and Sid dropped the sneer.

"I'm supposed to meet 'im tomorrow night, after I get back into the City. At the Blue Bull."

Kyria turned to Rafe. "We could go there. We could intercept him and find out who it is."

Rafe nodded and stood up. "I'm afraid that's all we're getting out of him at the moment." He flicked a glance at the man on the floor and added, "I may have another little talk with our friend later, but for now I reckon Smeggars can lock him up. Do you have any handy dungeons?"

Sid and his companion paled a little at his words. Kyria smiled. "Just the cellars, but I imagine they will do nicely."

Broughton rang for the servants, and Smeggars returned with several of the footmen to carry the miscreants away to the root cellars. As soon as they had left the room, Kyria turned excitedly to Rafe.

"We can catch the train to London tomorrow. Then we can go to this Blue Bull tomorrow evening and —"

"Now, hold on a minute," Rafe interjected. "You can't go to a place like that."

"Why not?" Kyria flashed back, bridling.

"You'd stick out like a sore thumb, for one thing," Rafe retorted. "Women who look like you don't frequent places like the Blue Bull."

"I'll wear a disguise," Kyria said blithely.

"But wait. Just a minute," the duke put in. "Aren't you forgetting, my dear, that we have a more immediate problem?"

"What?" Kyria turned to him, puzzled.

"The fact that the reliquary is missing," Broughton said.

"What!" Rafe's eyebrows flew up, and he stared at the man.

"Oh." Kyria's excitement deflated. "That's right. The box is gone."

As one, they all turned toward the open cabinet where the reliquary box had sat and where now there was only a blank space between the vase and the necklace.

"How could it be gone?" Rafe asked, striding over to the case to peer inside.

"I don't know. I was flabbergasted when I went to open the case for that chap and the box was not there. I cannot imagine what happened to it. I had the case locked and the door to the room locked."

"You mean you don't know where it is?"

the duchess asked her husband in surprise. "I thought you were pretending — just to fool that man. I thought you must have put it somewhere else."

Broughton shook his head sorrowfully. "No. It's disappeared."

They all stood looking at one another in consternation.

Con raised his hand tentatively. "No, sir," he began in a small voice, "it isn't missing. I know where it is."

"You do?" the duchess cried, and everyone swung to look at Con.

"Well, where is it?" Kyria asked when Con supplied no further information.

Looking rather abashed, Con said, "In the nursery."

His revelation was met with a stunned silence. Quickly he added, "I didn't know you were going to be looking for it!"

"But how . . . why?" Kyria asked finally, a shudder running through her at the thought of the valuable artifact lying about in the boys' rooms, amidst their balls and bats and animal cages.

"It was a puzzle," Con said simply.

"Oh," Kyria said, and the members of his family nodded in understanding. Con's attraction to puzzles was well-known. There was nothing he liked better than figuring out some sort of puzzle, whether it was a riddle or a jigsaw or a lock.

"I thought there must be some way to open it if I only looked hard enough." He paused and cast a look around at the others.

Thisbe straightened, something about his tone alerting her. "And did you?"

He nodded. "I did."

His announcement was met with a babble of voices from his family. It was Rafe's voice that finally rose above the others, "Well, go get it, boy, and show us."

Con took off, with Alex on his heels, and returned a few moments later, carrying the ivory box. His father took it from him and checked it anxiously.

"I didn't hurt it," Con protested.

"All right," the duke said, putting the box on the table. "Now show us what you did."

"I looked and looked all over the box," Con began, enjoying having an audience. "I thought that the secret to opening it must be in the carvings somewhere, because it would be easy to hide a crack in all those lines. So I got out my magnifying glass and looked it over, and sure enough, I found something. Only it wasn't a line, it was a hole — two holes, to be exact." He pointed with a stubby forefinger to a carving just above the diamond. "What you have to do is take a wire and put it into these holes."

He pulled out two short, thin wires from his shirt pocket and carefully inserted each one into a small hole in one of the engravings. Gently, he wiggled and twisted the wires until at last there was a barely audible click.

"That unlocks it. And now it opens right up."

He put his thumbs on either side of the holes and lifted, and the domed lid went up. Everyone leaned forward to see what lay inside. Kyria drew in a sharp breath.

Inside the box was a piece of faded purple cloth, frayed and weatherbeaten. Gold threads glinted from the depths of the purple, and there were several small gems sewn onto it, as well as a few more gems lying loose in the bottom of the box. On one edge of the cloth was a curve of gold leaf, rather like a small part of a letter.

"Sweet Lord," Rafe breathed. "Constantine's battle standard."

10

“Is it?” Alex asked. “That’s what Con and I thought when he opened it this morning, but I wasn’t sure.”

“It certainly fits the description,” Kyria said. “I don’t suppose we can know for sure, but it seems very likely to me.”

“It’s amazing that the cloth could survive this long, isn’t it?” the duchess asked, leaning over to study the cloth, carefully linking her hands behind her back like a child to avoid the temptation to touch it.

“Some might say it qualifies as a miracle,” Rafe said.

“It does seem unusual, but of course, there are the mummies excavated in Egypt.”

“But surely they were specially treated.”

“True, but the arid climate helped, as well. And this was sealed in a box — obviously one that was quite difficult to open, so very little air got at it,” Broughton said. “And we don’t know where it was kept all these years. It could very easily have been in a very dry climate.”

"However it was preserved, I think it's quite likely that this is the holy standard Dr. Jennings told us about," Kyria said. "Either that, or it's a very clever fake. I think it would be incumbent on us to find out more about it, don't you?"

"Yes, my dear, I am sure you are right," her father agreed. "I think a trip to London is in order. You should show this to Ashcombe. You should probably talk to someone at the British Museum, too."

"I think it's also clear that this box is dangerous," Rafe said. "After what happened this afternoon, it would be foolhardy not to assume that Mr. Kousoulous was killed because someone was after the box. They are obviously still after it. The constable can lock up those two who invaded this house, but that won't stop whoever hired them. He will just find someone else to do his dirty work, or do it himself."

"That is why we need to find out who that someone is and stop him," Kyria said.

"But how are you going to do that?" Thisbe asked. "You have no idea who hired those men."

"No, but there is that tavern where they were to meet him. We can go there and see who shows up. And there is Mr. Habib, who was so eager to buy the reliquary from me. I think it's very likely that he had something to do with it. I mean, he knew the box was here."

"But, Kyria, my dear, I don't like the thought of you investigating this," the duchess said, frowning. "That could put you into even more danger."

"That is why I am going with her to London." Rafe's voice was firm.

This time Kyria did not make a fuss about Rafe's going along with her. After this afternoon's events, she was quite willing to have the added protection. "Once we get to London, Reed will be there, as well. And we shall warn the servants to be on guard against anyone trying to get into the house." She paused, then added, "Besides, these people, whoever they are, will think that the box is still here, at least for a while. If anyone is in danger, it will be everyone here at Broughton Park, not us traveling to London."

"Con and I can come, too!" Alex offered eagerly. "We'll help you."

"You most certainly will not," their mother said sternly.

"But why not?" Con argued. "We haven't a tutor, so —"

"You will have before long," the duchess countered. "I have already written the agency and told them to find me new applicants. I am sure that I will be interviewing them shortly, and in the meantime, you can keep to your studies with Thisbe and Desmond."

"But Mr. McIntyre taught us a lot of bang-up things, and —"

"It was very nice of Mr. McIntyre to do so, but it is not his job. And I have no intention of exposing the two of you to danger, as well. It is bad enough that Kyria will be there."

"But we can help!" Alex protested. "We helped today, didn't we? And Con is the one who figured out the secret to that box. We could probably help a lot."

"Besides —" Con took a different tack "— Kyria just said they'll think the box is here at Broughton Park, so we would actually be in more danger if we stayed here than if we go to London with Kyria."

The twins continued to plead their case, but their mother was adamant, and finally they subsided. The duke returned the reliquary to its spot in the display case and locked it, and everyone began to file out of the room.

Kyria started toward her room to find her maid and start her packing for the imminent trip, but Rafe reached out and put his hand on her arm, stopping her.

"I want to talk to you," he said, his expression serious. "Whatever you said to your mother, I think it will be dangerous. Once we start poking our noses into this, they will know we're in London and they're likely to figure that the box is there, too."

Kyria sighed, sure that Rafe was going to try to stop her from going, or at least from participating in any investigation. He would assure her that he would take care of it all and that she needn't worry. She had heard similar sorts of things from her admirers many times before, when she wanted to go somewhere or do something that wasn't considered proper for a lady. She could have said the words for him: "A gently reared lady like yourself doesn't know and, indeed —" this was usually said with a deprecatory smile "— it is better that you don't know the things that could happen to a woman."

She crossed her arms and waited for his words, wishing that she had not exhibited such relief when he had come tearing into the room to help them. It had been a mistake to admit that she had wanted him to come rescue them; men tended to take that sort of thing as a sign that women were not equipped to handle a situation.

"So I thought that it would be best if you carried a gun," Rafe went on.

His words were so far from what she had expected that Kyria simply stared at him for a moment, speechless.

"Have you ever shot a gun?"

"No," Kyria admitted, still somewhat stunned.

"I can give you lessons this afternoon, if you'd like. I think it would be best if you carried the derringer as we travel. It's not much use at a distance, but it's light and easy to carry in your pocket or your reticule. And there's not really much question of aiming. Just point it at their middle and shoot. But inside the house, I think it would be best if you had a .45 close at hand, in case of intruders. We can practice on that this afternoon." He stopped and looked at her, puzzled. "Why are you smiling?"

Kyria shook her head. "Nothing. It's just . . . that wasn't what I expected you to say. I have never had a man offer to arm me before."

He grinned. "Well, it's probably not a necessity at a London soiree."

"No. But I have found in the past that a man's usual response is that it would be much better if I simply stayed at home."

He chuckled. "Oh, but that wouldn't do at all. Then how would I get to travel to London with you?"

"So you aren't going to try to persuade me not to go to that tavern tomorrow night?" Kyria asked.

"Oh — as to that, I don't know. The tavern could be tricky."

"I can carry my gun," Kyria pointed out.

"I'm not sure that would be enough. I have a suspicion that that fellow's tavern is probably filled with cutthroats and thieves. I don't relish the prospect of our having to shoot our way out of there. But that isn't the worst problem with you being there. A woman like you in a place like that would be a sure sign that something's wrong. If I were meeting someone there for nefarious purposes, I'd light out of there as soon as I spotted you."

Kyria rolled her eyes at him. "As if *you* would not be just as out of place there as I."

He shrugged. "I might have to dirty myself up a bit, find some rough clothes." He grinned. "I can look pretty despicable."

"I can disguise myself, too," Kyria shot back.

"Women don't go to that kind of place."

"I'll go as a lady of the night."

An image of Kyria in a gaudy, low-cut dress, her breasts almost spilling out of the top, flashed into Rafe's mind, and lust surged through him. He looked away quickly lest she read in his face what he was thinking.

"I would prefer not to have to fend off your customers, if you don't mind," he said shortly.

"And I don't want to be left out of it," Kyria replied stubbornly. "I have just as much reason for wanting to find out who this man is as you have — more, really, since the reliquary was sent to me."

She sighed. For a moment, when Rafe had offered to teach her to shoot to protect herself, instead of demanding that she stay out of the way, she had felt a spurt of hope that he was different from other men, that he would not demand to wrap her around with cotton batting and protect her from life. But now, it seemed as if he was going to be just the same, doing his best to prevent her from participating in the investigation. No doubt he and Reed would cook up some scheme to sneak out of the house without her and go to the tavern alone.

She was pondering just how she could thwart such a plan when Rafe sighed and said, "I guess we'll have to figure out some other way to do it, then. Maybe we can hire an anonymous hack and simply sit in it outside the tavern and watch who goes in and out. Of course, the light wouldn't be good, but perhaps we could see someone who looks foreign. The problem will be how narrow the street is, of course."

Kyria smiled to herself. *Perhaps he isn't like other men, after all.* "I could dress like a boy," she offered.

He groaned. "You couldn't pass for a boy."

"I could, too. A young man. I'm quite tall enough, and I can borrow some of Theo's clothes from when he was young. A tweed jacket covers up a great deal."

"Not the way you walk," Rafe pointed out.

They continued to bicker companionably as they walked to Rafe's room to retrieve a set of pistols and some ammunition. They went back out through the garden and down to the meadow where Rafe had taken the twins to explain physics by way of a rifle.

Rafe set up the tin cans he had used days earlier, which were lying beside a large rock. He explained how to load the revolver and had Kyria practice it, then took her through the steps of aiming, cocking and firing the pistol. He demonstrated for her, sending the cans flying from the rock in four quick shots.

Kyria's eyes widened, but she said only, "Show-off."

He grinned. "Well, now, darlin', I had to show you my qualifications as a teacher, didn't I?"

He set up the tin cans again and handed her the pistol, butt first. He stood beside her. "All right, now raise it and aim. Better hold it with both hands. It's got a little kick to it."

He moved closer as he spoke, one hand going beneath Kyria's arm to steady it, his other hand resting lightly on her back at her waist. Kyria was intensely aware of where his hand touched her arm. She could smell his scent, feel his warm breath on her cheek as he leaned closer, looking down the barrel of the gun. It was that, she knew, more than any weight of the gun, that made her arm tremble. She wondered if he was thinking, as she was, of that afternoon at the inn, if being this close to her had the same effect on him that it had on her.

"Okay, now, you want to just squeeze the

trigger," he said. "Don't jerk it."

Kyria swallowed, forced herself to concentrate and pulled the trigger. Her hand went up under the force of the gun, surprising her. She looked at the targets. Her bullet had not hit any of them.

Rafe chuckled a little at her disappointed look. "Don't worry. Pretty soon you'll be knocking them all down. Now, did you feel that kick? You've got to be ready for that. That's why it's good to steady your arm with your other hand. Now, take in a breath and let it out and then squeeze the trigger . . ."

Before much longer, Kyria sent one of the cans flying, and she let out a shriek of triumph. They stayed at it for some time longer, until Rafe was satisfied with her progress, then started back to the house. It seemed a trifle unreal, she thought, to be walking back to her house with this man on this crisp autumn day, carrying the revolvers they had been shooting. It was at once so normal and accustomed, so comfortable, yet at the same time strange and exciting.

She wondered what would happen when this was all over. Would he return to America? Kyria felt a sharp pang at the thought of never seeing him again. She looked up at him. It seemed impossible, she thought, that he might disappear from her life.

He turned, apparently feeling her eyes on him, and grinned at her, his mouth quirking up in that devastating way it had, making Kyria blush and look away.

They parted at her bedroom door. He pressed the small derringer on her and told her to carry it when they left the next day.

Kyria spent the rest of the day packing. Late that evening, before she undressed and got into bed, she went down to her father's study and got the key to his collections room. It was silly, she supposed, to check on the reliquary again, but she knew that she would not be able to sleep until she had ascertained that it was still safe and in place.

She unlocked the door and crossed the room to the case where the reliquary sat. She stood looking into the case for a moment. Obviously, the box was safe and sound, just where it should be. There was no need to take it out. But Kyria realized that she wanted very much, indeed, to take the box out and hold it. It was an odd feeling and one that seemed to grow stronger every time she looked at the box.

Opening the door, she picked up the reliquary and held it for a few minutes, tracing the carving and the diamond in a caressing way. There was something about the stone that soothed her, attracted her, and she felt strangely reluctant to set it down. Finally, however, she put the reliquary back into the case and locked it, then turned and left the room, carefully closing and locking the door behind her.

Later, upstairs in her room, she let Joan help her undress and brush out her hair. Then, belting her dressing gown around her, she took out a sketch pad and pencil from one of her drawers and sat down in the comfortable chair by the window.

All the time her maid had been brushing out her hair, a design had been teasing at the back of her mind, and she wanted to get it down on paper before she forgot it. She drew a long upward curve, turning it down at the end and curling it in upon itself like a seashell. A quick line up the middle split it into two strands, and she finished it with some crosshatching. She studied the design for a moment, then began to draw a necklace. It would be in gold, she thought, a series of these symbols, each linked to the next. Perhaps earrings with the same figure engraved on them — a small block of gold. Her fingers nimbly added little drops dangling from the bottom edge of the block.

There was a classical look to it, she thought; it rather reminded her of the ancient jewelry her father collected, although she could not recall any with that particular design. She tilted her head to the side, thinking. Only a certain sort of gown would look right with this jewelry . . .

She flipped over to a new page and began to sketch a gown, her fingers moving quickly over the page. Kyria smiled as she drew. She could well imagine what her mother would say about her frivolous nature, drawing dress designs after everything that had happened today. But the drawing soothed her nerves, and she was pleased with the result.

As she drew, her mind wandered to Rafe, and her smile deepened. She would have been surprised if she had been able to see the way her face softened and her eyes took on a certain glow. He was different from what she had supposed him to be when she first met him. She was excited to be going to London with him to investigate the reliquary box — and she knew that only a part of that excitement, maybe not even the larger part, had to do with the investigation.

She stood up, a faint smile lingering on

her face, and tucked the sketch away in one of her bags. Whatever happened, she thought, as she slipped out of her dressing gown and laid it across the foot of her bed, this trip promised to be interesting.

Torches lined the walls, casting a flickering golden glow against the sand-colored blocks of stone and partially illuminating the men in front of her. They walked with measured tread, and she followed woodenly behind them. She could not see their faces, only their backs, covered in the white ceremonial robes. Wide, golden bracelets wrapped her arms, weighing her down, and her head beneath the headdress felt heavy, too. She could smell the cloying scent of the incense, making her eyes burn.

She had not been able to sleep the night before because she had been so excited, so scared . . . Now the moment was upon her, and fear clutched icily at her stomach, creeping up through her chest.

The time was almost upon her . . .

Kyria's eyes flew open, and she lay for a moment, her breath rasping in her throat, panic gripping her. It took a few seconds for her brain to clear. *What a bizarre dream! And yet so strangely familiar.* She had dreamed it before, or something very like it, although she could not quite recall the details of that other dream. *There was that heavy scent and the flickering lights and . . . fear.*

She shivered a little and pulled her covers, which she had partially kicked off, more tightly around her. The cause of the strange dream was nerves, she supposed, an excess of fear and fury left over from the day's events. Still, it was unsettling. It made no sense. She had no idea where she was in the dream or even who she was, let alone who the faceless men were. Burrowing deeper into her bed, she tried to push the dream out of her mind. But it was a long time before she finally fell asleep.

Kyria and Rafe boarded the train for London the next morning. The twins had persuaded their mother to allow them to ride into the village with Kyria and Rafe, and they came aboard to check out the compartment before Kyria finally shooed them out and sent them back to the coachman, waiting on the platform below.

Kyria was very conscious of the small derringer in her reticule, as well as of the valise Rafe carried, inside of which lay the precious reliquary. She herself had put it in the valise this morning and had opened the valise to check it during the carriage ride to the village. She was tempted to open it again, but she resisted. It would be foolish, she knew, to appear too interested in the valise. She would have to be content with the knowledge that the case was tucked safely between Rafe's legs and the wall of the train and that Rafe was carrying the pistol she had used for target practice the day before inside his coat.

She glanced out the window as the train began to chug away from the station. The coachman and the twins had already gone. She settled back into her seat.

"I have been thinking about tonight," Kyria began. "The best way for me to dress to go into the tavern is as an ale-guzzling, old woman."

"Is that right?" Rafe looked at her with interest. "I thought you were going to go as a boy."

"I saw that there would be problems with that. Even with dirt on my face and such, I would still look too young and, well, dandified, don't you think? I mean, I think I could pass as a lad, but not the sort who would frequent that sort of drinking establishment."

"You're right there," Rafe agreed.

"And, as you pointed out, if I went as a

woman of the night, that would present an entirely different set of complications. But who ever notices an old rummy?" Kyria asked triumphantly. "I'll wear some old clothes out of the ragbag, and I'll roll them in the dirt. I'll put dirt in my hair and on my face, and wear a cap. And I can black out several of my teeth. Alex did that one time to play a joke on Olivia, so I know how."

"I think it would be better if we waited in the carriage and watched the tavern."

"But then you would see only who went in and out. What if our man was inside when we arrived? And wouldn't it look suspicious to have a carriage, even a hack, hanging about outside? I'll wager it isn't the sort of establishment where people arrive or leave in a hansom."

"Perhaps, but it's far better than taking you inside there and someone seeing through your disguise."

"No one will," Kyria argued. "I'll make myself look so that even you won't recognize me. I'll just come up to your table and beg for a drink, and then in a little while I'll pretend to fall into unconsciousness from the drink."

Rafe's mouth twitched. "You have quite a performance planned."

They continued to debate the merits of

her suggestion for the next few minutes, and after that they fell into a silence. Lulled by the rhythmic sound and motion of the train, Kyria began to feel sleepy.

She had not slept well the night before. Even after her peculiar dream, she had kept thinking about the dream and what it meant. And when she finally *had* gone to sleep, she had tossed and turned.

And now on the train, Kyria's eyes had just fluttered closed when she was startled awake by the door to the car slamming shut and a conductor rushing through. Just before he reached the door at the end of the car, it opened, and another man in uniform burst in, and the two of them began to talk excitedly.

Kyria looked questioningly at Rafe, and he shrugged, then stood and crossed to the open door of their compartment and looked out. A strange look crossed his face, and he turned back to Kyria.

"He was talking pretty fast, but I think the gist of what he said is that they've caught a couple of boys without tickets in the horse car, pretending to be stable lads."

"The twins!" Kyria jumped to her feet. "I *knew* I shouldn't have let them accompany us to the train station!"

Picking up their valise, Kyria and Rafe followed the conductor to the horse car, where a group of stable lads were gathered interestedly around a skinny man in a train attendant's uniform who had his hands curled into the collars of two youths. The boys were dressed in rough trousers and shirts, with a few artistic streaks of dirt on their faces, and they were talking earnestly and at great length to the attendant.

The boys were, in fact, the twins, and after a few minutes of explanation to the conductor and payment for the two boys' fare, as well as an apology from the twins for the trouble they had caused, Kyria and Rafe returned to their compartment with the twins in tow.

"It would serve you right if we got off at the next station and took the first train back to Broughton Park," Kyria told her brothers tartly.

"You need to be in London tonight," Con pointed out, obviously unperturbed by her threat. "Taking us back would mean you would miss your chance of catching the man who hired the men who invaded Broughton Park."

"Besides, we can help," Alex added. "Look at how we got on board the train without anyone noticing us."

"You two are a sneaky pair, all right," Rafe admitted, grinning. "What I don't know is whether you're training to be investigators or criminals."

Kyria sighed. "It's a wonder I haven't turned prematurely gray, given the way you two act." She sighed and sat down. "Now change back into your own clothes and wash your hands and faces. I'll send the family a cable at the next station and let them know you're with us."

The twins grinned and made their way down the corridor to the water closet to clean up. Kyria looked at Rafe and shook her head. "I wish I could ship them back immediately. But I'm afraid none of the servants except the head groom can really keep the two of them in line. We'll have to keep them with us until Mother can send Jenkins to fetch them back. I am sure they know that, the little wretches." She grimaced at Rafe. "Oh, stop grinning. You are as bad as Theo. You positively encourage them."

"You have to admire their ingenuity."

Kyria pressed her lips together, trying to look severe, but finally she had to chuckle. "Be that as it may, I am putting the largest, fastest footman in charge of them until Jenkins arrives."

* * *

The rest of the trip passed without incident, although they did lose Con for a few minutes in Paddington station when he caught sight of an organ grinder with his monkey.

They were met at the station by the assistant coachman, who had been left behind with the skeleton staff that resided in their London house when the family was in residence at Broughton Park. Kyria was surprised that Reed was not there to greet them, and the coachman explained that he had been called away to Liverpool on business for a few days.

The news took Kyria somewhat aback, but she quickly recovered. She was sure that she and Rafe could handle the matter of the reliquary on their own. For the sake of propriety, Rafe offered to seek a room at a hotel, but Kyria waved off the notion, pointing out that a houseful of servants and the lively twins' presence should be chaperon enough. In truth, though she would not have admitted it, she did not like the thought of being at Broughton House without Rafe there.

When they arrived at the town house, a solid redbrick Georgian mansion, Kyria made it her first task to carry the reliquary into her father's study and lock it away in the large wall safe. After that, she spoke to Phipps, their London butler, regarding the foreign man who had brought her the reliquary.

Her hunch that he had visited their London house first was correct, for both Phipps and the footman who had opened the door to the man remembered his visit well. He had spoken in broken English and they had understood little of what he said, but they agreed that he had asked specifically for Kyria.

"Bit of cheek, that," the footman added. "Not even a 'Miss' or 'Lady' in front of your name."

"Impertinent," Phipps agreed. "I told him to seek you at Broughton Park, my lady. I hope that was all right."

"Yes, of course. That was fine." Kyria could not help but think that if only she had been here, the poor fellow might not have died.

Kyria selected a footman named Denby to keep watch on the twins. He seemed young and fit enough to chase about after the boys, and his thick arms looked as if he could lift a twin in each hand. His only fault, as best she could see, was a placid nature, which she feared might make him too likely to overlook many of the twins' transgressions.

Reminding the boys that they would be returning to Broughton Park as soon as Jenkins, the head groom, arrived to fetch them and that they would not be helping her and Rafe in their inquiry, she turned them over to Denby. The boys, naturally, protested, although they gave in finally after Kyria told them that they could help her with her costume for the visit to the waterfront tavern this evening.

Whether her look was due to their help or Kyria's own expertise, Rafe was not sure, but he was taken aback when she came down the stairs that evening, outfitted for their adventure.

While Kyria had been preparing for her role, Rafe had spent most of his time trying to think up some reason to leave her behind this evening. The last thing he wanted was to see Kyria exposed to any danger, and going into the sort of place he expected the Blue Bull was seemed to be jumping into the most dangerous situation one could find. As if the risk of drunken brawls or men pawing her was not enough, he could not imagine Kyria, with her tall, striking, flame-haired beauty, blending in with the tavern's patrons. Taking her with him was risking discovery for both of them, not only among the tavern's rough clientele, but also with the very man they were hoping to catch.

But when Kyria walked into the informal drawing room, he came involuntarily to his feet, his jaw dropping open in astonishment. In Kyria's place stood a bent, dirty crone several inches shorter than she, as well as a lifetime older.

A scarf, stained and smudged, covered her head, and below it a tangle of brown hair, streaked with white, tumbled out, matted and dirty. The same scarf covered part of her forehead, and below it Kyria's milk-white skin was several shades darker and caked here and there with dirt. Her nose looked somehow wider and her eyes smaller, and her lips were thin and colorless. She walked with a stoop, as if her back hurt, and her lithe body was covered in bulky rags of an indeterminate color that gave her a lumpish shape. Shoes with holes in the toes completed the picture.

When Rafe said nothing, merely stared in astonishment, Kyria broke into a grin, displaying the pièce de résistance: four of her teeth appeared to be missing, and the remainder were an appalling yellowish color.

"Good Lord!" Rafe exclaimed, recoiling. Kyria burst into laughter, followed by the twins, who had come downstairs to view the results of their handiwork.

"Isn't it wizard?" Alex cried, coming around to look at Kyria again. "You look horrible," he told her happily.

"Wizard," Rafe agreed dryly, adding, "well, at least I won't have to worry about fighting off your admirers."

"I told you I could blend in," Kyria reminded him. "Oh! The last thing — we need to splash a bit of liquor on me. Gin would be best, but I doubt Papa or Reed have any here."

They went to the smoking room, accompanied by the twins, and rooted through the liquor cabinet, and though they could find no plebeian gin, they shook a bit of whiskey over her ragged clothing to add a realistic smell.

Kyria slipped the heavy revolver Rafe had given her into a pocket amidst the folds of her clothing and stuck the small derringer up her sleeve. Rafe, with a pair of Colts and a knife in a scabbard strapped to his arm beneath his sleeve, was even more heavily armed.

"Did you expect to be attacked in Europe?" Kyria asked, watching him check his pistols and thrust them into his belt, one at his side and one at the back.

He grinned at her. "When you transport silver ore, you get accustomed to arming yourself. A useful habit, as it turns out."

"Mmm."

They took one of the family carriages, an old-fashioned one that did not bear the ducal crest on the side, and though the coachman looked dubious about their destination, he drove them to Cheapside without a murmur. As they neared the tavern, the streets grew increasingly narrow, until there was barely room enough for the carriage to move between the dark and dingy buildings. There were few street lamps to light the way.

They found the Blue Bull, a narrow brick building, its color unrecognizable beneath the years of grime. A sign hung above the door, sporting a blue bull — or at least half of one, for much of the figure's lower body had weathered away. Rafe had instructed the driver to drive past the tavern when he found it and let them out a block away so that no one at the tavern would see them emerging from a conveyance so at odds with the neighborhood. The carriage rolled on past the next narrow cross street before it stopped.

Rafe stepped down from the carriage and glanced carefully around, then reached up to help Kyria out of the vehicle. She looked around her. The street was so dark she could see little, but she was well able to smell the place. The stench of rotting refuse assailed her nostrils.

Rafe sent the carriage into a side street to await them. He would have taken a hack, since it would have been less-conspicuous a vehicle, but he suspected that they just might need a quick getaway, so it would be better to have a carriage waiting for them.

"Are you ready?" he asked Kyria in a low voice.

"Yes, go on — it won't do for anyone to see us out here chatting," Kyria said.

Rafe looked around sharply once more. It went against his grain to turn and walk away from Kyria, leaving her to follow, but given the roles they had adopted, it would not do for them to be seen entering together. He tugged his cap lower on his head and began walking toward the tavern, using all his discipline not to turn around to look at Kyria following him.

She let him get several steps in front of her. Her heart raced as his figure walked away from her, soon swallowed up by the darkness of the poorly lit street. She was all alone in the wretched street with who knew what sort of criminals lurking about. Fear twisted through her, but Kyria shoved it down.

Taking a deep breath, she started forward into the darkness.

11

Rafe strode along, his ears stretched to hear Kyria's artfully shuffling and stumbling progress behind him. When he reached the door of the tavern, he paused and sneaked a careful look to his right. Kyria was leaning against the side of a building and coughing as if her lungs might come up. That, he supposed, would do as much as anything to keep everyone away from her.

Rafe opened the door and went inside. The tavern consisted of a single, low-ceilinged, dimly lit room, with a pockmarked bar against one wall. A loutish-looking barkeep stood behind it, glowering around the room, and several disreputable types leaned against the bar, drinking their ales. The remainder of the area was littered with tables and chairs in various stages of dilapidation, and more than half of them were filled with men, each more criminal in appearance than the one before.

Rafe, adopting the hard countenance and steely gaze he had employed in more than one Western saloon, made his way to an empty table against the left-hand wall. It was not far from the door and afforded a good view of the rest of the room, especially the doorway. It was the barkeep himself who ambled over a moment later and loomed above him.

Rafe looked up and locked gazes with him challengingly. The barkeep was the first to give in, finally barking out a belligerent, "What yer want?"

"Pint of ale," was Rafe's equally terse reply.

They stared at each other again for a time, then the barkeep shuffled away. At that moment the door opened, and Kyria stumbled in. She reeled across the room, stopping at one table, then another, trying to cadge a drink and being brusquely repelled in each instance. Rafe watched her, his whole body tensed, waiting for the moment that he might have to come to her defense.

But no one did more than snarl at her, and after a few moments, the bent and twisted old crone stopped in front of him. "Buy a poor gel a drink, mister?" she asked, her voice roughened and tinged with the East End.

He scowled at her, but Kyria sank down into the other chair at his table, continuing to plead. Finally, with an irritated jerk of his head, Rafe raised his hand to the barkeep and signaled for a drink.

"Thankee, kind sir, thankee," Kyria said, scrabbling for his hand and trying to pat it.

"Behave," Rafe muttered, and jerked his hand away, schooling himself not to smile into her laughing eyes.

"Awr, now, don't spoil all a gel's fun," Kyria retorted in her gravelly voice, adding in a murmur, "Have you seen anything?"

"Nothing's jumped out at me. Just looks like a room full of shady types."

"We're here before him," Kyria said with satisfaction.

The barkeep brought two glasses and slapped them down on the table, casting a glare at Kyria. After he left, Kyria lifted a glass and stared down at it.

"This smells dreadful," she whispered. "And I'm positive this glass has not been washed."

"Pour a little on your dress," Rafe suggested. "It will add to your aroma." He took a drink and repressed a shudder. "I think we'll be pouring a few of these on the floor tonight."

They made a show of drinking and surreptitiously poured part of their drinks on the floor.

"What shall we do?" Kyria murmured, picking up her glass as if in a toast, sloshing a good bit more of it out.

"Wait," Rafe suggested, "and see who comes in."

With a nod, Kyria settled in, her eyes turned toward the door, and their vigil began.

Time crept by. They watched as the patrons of the tavern got progressively drunker. Each person was given a careful scrutiny, but there was nothing to any of them that seemed out of the ordinary for a place like this.

After managing to pour the contents of two glasses on the floor, Kyria laid her head down on her arm and pretended to pass out in order to avoid having to deal with any more liquor.

Rafe watched as two fights developed and took their course, deftly snatching away their drinks as two of the men reeled into their table and careened off. People entered and a few exited, but none appeared to be looking for anyone.

Rafe was beginning to wonder if their intruder had lied to them about meeting his employer at the Blue Bull when the door opened and a man entered who caught Rafe's interest. The new customer was wrapped warmly in a dark-blue pea coat, a luxuriant beard and mustache covering the lower half of his face. He walked slightly hunched over, his hands shoved into his pockets, and as he walked, his eyes roved over the crowd.

Rafe's pulse quickened, and he nudged Kyria with his elbow. She opened her eyes and watched with a narrowed gaze as the stranger crossed the room and sank into a chair. He turned toward the bar and lifted a hand, and there seemed to Rafe that there was an unconscious arrogance in his gesture that did not fit with the man's humble attire.

The barkeep ambled over, and when he reached the table, Rafe saw a subtle shift in his attitude. He bent down in a way that for that brusque man indicated a certain subservience, and he returned in a few minutes with a bottle of whiskey and a glass.

A mistake, Rafe thought, pleased. The man had dressed to blend in, but he had given away his affluence with his attitude and a full bottle of good whiskey. No one who could afford that would normally be frequenting a place like the Blue Bull. There was also the fact that even though he glanced around the room now and then, he also kept looking at the front door of the tavern.

"I think we have him," Rafe muttered to Kyria, and went up to the bar to order another drink, strolling past the new customer as closely as he could without drawing attention.

When he returned to the table, Kyria groaned and made a show of waking and rubbing her face, looking around, then returned her head to the table, facing in Rafe's direction.

"Did you see him?"

"As well as I could," Rafe murmured, propping his chin on his hand to help cover the slight movement of his mouth. "This place is damned dim, and he's got his cap practically down to his eyes. The rest of his face is hidden by the beard."

"False?" Kyria asked.

"I'll wager." Rafe sighed. "And with the way he walked and those bulky clothes, it's hard to get a good guess as to even his height and shape."

"Is he foreign?"

"He's dark for an Englishman," Rafe said. "I'm not sure if that means he's foreign. He isn't the dealer who visited us, that I'm relatively certain of. There's a scar near his eye, and it draws his lid down in an odd way."

"A disguise, do you think?"

"I don't know. It could be real — or as real as your salt-and-pepper hair."

He took a drag of his drink and firmly refrained from wincing. Kyria stirred restlessly in her chair.

"Shouldn't we go talk to him?"

"Wait till he leaves and we'll brace him outside. This isn't the best place to be if he starts to fight."

Rafe kept a surreptitious eye on the stranger, who began, after a few more minutes, to grow somewhat fidgety. The man looked around the room more carefully, then returned his gaze more noticeably to the door. Finally, after thirty minutes or so, with a disgusted twitch of his mouth, he stood up and began to walk toward the door.

Rafe tapped Kyria on the arm, and she once more went through a performance of raising her head and looking blankly around, although this time, she ended it by draping herself over Rafe's arm. Their quarry was almost to the door by this time, and Rafe stood, Kyria rising quickly beside him. They started toward the door, and Kyria abandoned her drunken shuffle in the excitement of the moment.

As the stranger stepped outside, he suddenly grasped a man who was entering the tavern. With a twist of his body, he deliberately propelled the newcomer through the doorway and into the group nearest the door, resulting in a commotion of spilled beer, raised voices and flying fists.

"Blast!" Rafe swore.

He and Kyria sprinted to the door, but they wasted precious seconds while Rafe shoved a couple of the combatants aside. They stumbled out the door and looked up and down the street, seeing, a good half block away, their fleeing suspect. Rafe tore off after him, with Kyria in hot pursuit. The man skidded around the corner of a building, and the next thing they knew there was a loud pop, and the sound of something small striking the brick behind them.

Rafe swore again and, grabbing Kyria, ducked into the nearest doorway, the stench of which was enough to make her gag.

"Was that a gunshot?" Kyria asked, covering her nose and mouth in an attempt to breathe without smelling the odor. She tried not to think about what they might be standing in.

"Yes. He's firing at us," Rafe replied.

"Damn! He knows who we are. How?"

"My guess is he realized it when we stood up and started for the door after him. We may have been less than subtle." Rafe paused, then went on, "He may not know *exactly* who we are. For all I know, there may be any number of people who are interested in his activities. But he knew that we were following him."

Rafe paused, listening. There was a clatter of horses hooves and carriage wheels on the cobblestone street. Rafe peered around the doorway to see a carriage disappearing at a good clip down the dark street.

"I think he's gone." Rafe stepped cautiously out. He glanced down the street in the direction the carriage had gone, then back up to where it must have come from, when something caught his eye.

A figure stood in the opening of a nearby alleyway, cowled and robed all in white. Rafe sucked in his breath, and in that instant the figure disappeared.

"What the hell!" Rafe started forward, and Kyria followed him.

"What? What's the matter?"

"There was the strangest-looking . . ." Rafe hurried over to the alleyway where he had seen the figure and peered into it. It was pitch-black inside, and he could see nothing beyond a few feet. He wished he had a lantern. Frowning, he turned. "Nothing. It's gone now."

They started toward the side street where their own carriage waited.

"We should have left first," Kyria opined. "Then we could have waited outside for him to emerge and talked to him then."

"It would have been wiser," Rafe agreed. He glanced at her and smiled. "Next time we lie in wait for someone, we'll have to remember that."

"Who do you suppose he was?"

Rafe shrugged. "The man who wants your reliquary — or someone who is acting as an agent for that man."

Kyria sighed. "We're no better off than we were."

"Well, we did get a look at the man."

"Yes, in disguise," Kyria retorted. "Could you even tell how tall he was?"

"He wasn't short. Exactly how tall . . ." Rafe shrugged.

"He wasn't Mr. Habib," Kyria said. "At least we know that. Which would seem to indicate that there is more than one person after the reliquary."

"Yes. Although I suppose he could be an associate of Habib's."

"Sid did say he was foreign," Kyria conceded. “On the other hand, it could be that there are two people working separately.”

“Yes.”

“I don’t see how this is helping us much.”

“We still have the barkeep,” Rafe said. “Sid told us that it was he who arranged the meeting, right?”

“True.”

“So I can question the barkeep and see if he can tell us who our man was.”

“He obviously seemed to know him.” Kyria’s face brightened.

They reached the carriage and climbed into it. Rafe looked at Kyria and said, “I don’t suppose I could persuade you to go home now and leave me to question the man.”

“You certainly could not,” Kyria said cheerfully.

“It won’t be pretty.”

“No. It wasn’t pretty being threatened by Sid and Dixon, either,” Kyria retorted. “And you might need help. I can’t in good conscience leave you here by yourself to face the barkeep.”

The two of them sat in the carriage, waiting for the minutes to pass, having agreed that it would serve their purposes better to confront the barkeep after all the customers had left.

It was some time before that occurred, and Kyria had dozed off once or twice, then jerked awake to find Rafe, irritatingly enough, sitting there wide-awake, one corner of the window curtain pulled aside, gazing out at the tavern door.

"How can you do that?" Kyria asked, squirming in her seat and blinking to keep her eyes open.

"Habit I picked up in the war. Reconnaissance. Never lost it — comes in handy sometimes." He stiffened slightly and leaned forward. "I think it may be closing. There's a stream of them coming out." He pulled a watch out of his pocket and glanced at it. He looked at her. "You ready?"

Kyria nodded, and they slipped out of the carriage and moved quickly down the street. As they approached, the door opened, and a final two customers staggered out. Behind them in the doorway stood the barkeep. He started to close the door, but Rafe was there before he could do so and braced his arm against the door, shoving it back.

" 'Ere, now," the barkeep said gruffly. "We're closed. Go 'ome."

"I don't want a drink," Rafe told him, stepping into the tavern. Kyria slipped in after him. "I want information."

The man looked at them with narrowed eyes, his gaze going from Rafe to Kyria and back. " 'Ere. Weren't you in 'ere before?"

"Yes, we were. But now I have a few questions."

"Get out. I ain't answerin' no questions." He jerked his head toward the open door, but Rafe reached into his coat and pulled out one of his long-barreled Colts.

"How about now?" Rafe asked.

The barkeep simply stared at him, his hands falling to his sides. Kyria moved around Rafe and pushed the door to, then shot the lock home. Rafe gestured toward one of the tables.

"Why don't we sit down?"

The barkeep glowered, but did as he suggested.

"I got nothin' to say."

"Don't you want to hear the questions first?"

"I'm not a gabster," the other man said flatly.

"Let's try a little persuasion first." Rafe reached into his coat again and came out with a wallet this time. "Kyria . . ."

She took the wallet and opened it, peeling off a ten-pound note and laying it on the table before the barkeep. The man sneered. "I told yer, I'm no gabster."

Kyria put down three more of the notes before the barkeep's expression became less stony. At the fifth note, he said warily, "Wot yer wantin' to know?"

"A pair of men — one named Sid and the other Dixon . . ." Rafe began.

"Yeah, I know 'em," the barkeep answered. "Sid comes in often enough."

"You set him up with a man — a foreign man, perhaps?"

"Yeah, so?"

"Who was that man?"

The barkeep shrugged. "Din't give me no name. Just said as 'ow he wanted a partic'lar kind of man for a partic'lar job. Sounded like Sid to me."

"And was he the same man who was in your tavern tonight? The one to whom you gave a full bottle of whiskey."

"I don't know nothin' 'bout 'im," the barkeep said, sweeping up the notes on the table and leaning back in his chair, crossing his arms with finality.

"Would fifty guineas loosen your tongue?" Kyria asked.

He frowned, cupidity warring with fear on his face.

"Not even a hundred guineas." He hesitated for a moment, then added, "I don't know the gent's name. I don't want to know it, and that's a fact. You look in his eyes, and they're cold as death. So I don't ask and 'e don't tell. It's better that way."

"You think he's telling the truth?" Kyria asked as they walked back to the carriage, having left the barkeep sitting there with the stack of notes clutched in his hand.

"I suspect so. Either he doesn't know his name, as he said, or he's too scared to tell it. Whichever it is, we won't get any more out of him."

She sighed as he handed her up into the carriage. "What will we do now?"

"There is still the antiquities dealer to watch," Rafe replied. He stepped up into the carriage and closed the door, and they set off down the street. "We don't know but he may be involved in this, too. The man we saw tonight could be someone Habib hired to strongarm you once he found out that an offer to buy the reliquary wasn't going to work."

"Or, I suppose, the man at the tavern could be someone who was using Habib as an intermediary, trying first to buy the reliquary before stealing it," Kyria said.

"And we can talk to Dr. Jennings's expert," Rafe continued.

"Nelson Ashcombe? I'd like him to see it, just to confirm that it is indeed the reliquary and that the remnant inside is authentic," Kyria admitted. "But I don't imagine he can help us much with identifying our thief."

"Ashcombe has been after the reliquary for years. I wouldn't be surprised if he knew the names of some other men who would be interested in getting it. He might even know which ones would not hesitate to steal it."

"That could be." Kyria brightened a little as she thought of the avenues still left open to them.

They rode home, discussing the events of the evening and pondering whether their quarry had known who they were when he ran from the tavern.

Kyria, pulling the scarf from her head, took out the pins that held the false, dirty-and-graying locks to her own hair beneath, and also unwrapped the dirty shawl from around her shoulders and arms. She itched in several places, and she could not help but wonder if it was simply from the rough cloth of the things she wore, or if her old, dirt-smeared clothes had provided a home for various unsavory insects that might have lurked in the floors of the tavern.

The house was hushed when they entered, the twins and most of the servants long since asleep. Kyria knew, however, that in her room Joan would be waiting up for her as she always did. Tonight, for once, Kyria intended to take full advantage of her presence. Joan was welcome to sleep late the next morning, but there was no way Kyria could go to bed tonight until she had washed away all her dirt.

Together she and Rafe walked up the stairs to the second floor and along the hall toward their respective rooms. There was something very intimate about their situation, Kyria thought. The lights in the hallways were turned low, and with Reed gone and the twins upstairs in the nursery, Kyria and Rafe were the only ones on this floor. Kyria could not help but think about the fact that Rafe would be sleeping in his bed only a few doors down from her. She remembered how it had felt to be in his embrace, his arms hard as iron around her. She remembered his kiss, hot and hungry, and his hands on her skin, making her tremble with desire. She tried not to look at Rafe, afraid her thoughts would show on her face.

As they reached her room, the door opened and her maid popped out. "I thought I heard you, my lady," she said, bobbing a curtsy. "I have a bath all ready for you. I was just waiting to bring up a kettle of hot water to warm it for you."

"Joan, you are a lifesaver," Kyria said, smiling. "There is nothing I want more."

The maid nodded and hurried away down the stairs to the kitchen to get a steaming kettle. Rafe paused at Kyria's door and bowed over her hand. He could not keep from smiling at the comical aspect she presented, part Kyria and part the old drunken hag she had played tonight — her bright red hair, luxuriant and beautiful as ever, straggling down from its pins, and below it, her refined features, smeared with dirt and drawn with lines at her forehead, eyes, and mouth, the bright green eyes shining out of the mask with all their vivid beauty.

"You are a woman in a million, my lady," he said softly.

Kyria grinned, showing the full glory of her painted teeth. "Ow, give us a kiss, luv."

He chuckled. "Be careful; I might just take you up on it."

Kyria cocked an eyebrow. "I think I'm safe."

She turned and went into her bedroom, and he stood for a moment, looking down at the floor. In truth, despite her present disguise, the image his mind conjured of her taking a bath was a powerful one, and it stirred his loins. He could well imagine her long, lithe white body sinking down into an elegant slipper tub, the water rising up to cover the glory of her breasts.

Rafe turned away abruptly and headed down the hall toward his room. It was far better, he knew, not to think about such things. The problem, of course, was that he could not seem to gain control over his runaway imagination — which was greatly aided by the memory of how Kyria had felt in his arms and the taste of her in his mouth. Though much had happened since then, it had been only a few short days since they had kissed in the private room of the inn, and his senses remembered every instant of it — the silken softness of her skin beneath his fingers, the faint scent of lavender that clung to her hair, the sweet sounds of surrender that had issued from her lips.

He let out a low growl of frustration and closed the door to his room harder than was absolutely necessary. The more he got to know Kyria, the more he wanted her — and the more he knew that he could not take her lightly. She was enough to make a man almost forget the hard lessons he had learned, to make him wonder if his heart and soul were not really as dead as he had believed.

He prowled about his bedroom for a few minutes, idly moving things about on his dresser, then going to the window and staring out blindly, finally coming back and throwing himself down in the chair beside the bed. Rafe tried to think about the events of this evening or the identity of the man who had come to the tavern — indeed, anything except the image of Kyria relaxing in her bath — but he found that little else could stick in his mind.

Grimacing, he rose and began stripping off his rough clothes and throwing them on the floor. It looked as if it was going to be a very long night. He could only hope that a nice cold wash-up at the basin would help.

In her room, Kyria found that getting rid of all traces of her "drunken hag" was a good deal more time-consuming than donning the persona had been, especially when it came to returning her teeth to their usual state of sparkling whiteness. Finally, scrubbed clean, she pulled on a nightgown and crawled into bed, but once there, she found sleep hard to come by.

She thought about Rafe lying in his bed

only a few doors down the hallway. No one would see her if she slipped down to his room. Even in the dark, Kyria blushed at her wayward thoughts. She could not remember any other man who had affected her this way. She thought of the kisses they had shared the other evening, and her blood heated, her loins going warm and soft. She pressed her legs together, for it seemed to help ease the growing ache there, as she remembered Rafe's hands on her body, his fingers caressing her breast and teasing the nipple to life.

Restlessly, Kyria turned over and tried to move her thoughts in another direction. She thought of the box downstairs in the safe, and she wanted to go down there to make sure that it was all right. It was foolish and unnecessary, she reminded herself, but she could not deny the urge to get it out and look it over again. It was very strange, she knew, that she so often wanted to check on the reliquary. It wasn't just a desire to make sure it was safe, or even a desire to look at its beauty again. She simply felt unaccountably drawn to it, almost compelled to look at it.

She was exasperated with herself. Why was she suddenly so subject to her urges and desires? She had lived her whole life in control of herself, and now she seemed at the mercy of this whim or that, unsure of what was happening and why, no longer even sure of what she wanted. It disturbed her, this loss of command — and yet, she had to admit, there was something exciting about it, as well. There was a certain thrill in knowing that when she awoke the next morning, she would not know exactly what was going to happen that day, or even how she was going to feel.

Kyria smiled to herself and rolled over, looking up at the heavy, green-velvet tester above her bed. Life had not been dull since Rafe McIntyre had ridden into it. And she was quite certain that she did not want to go back to the way it had been before him.

She closed her eyes and, smiling, at last slipped into sleep.

Shadows danced on the walls, grotesque and unnerving. The waiting was so hard. A shiver ran through her, though she was not certain whether it was from the coolness of the thick stone walls or from the thought of what faced her.

It was the duty of all who served the Mother. Her blessed favor would be laid upon her like a mantle after this night. And the whispers of blood and pain would not matter.

She stiffened, listening. There was a growing murmur, as faint as the rustling of leaves. Now she was more certain, the sound swelling into the familiar sounds of chanting and the shuffle of feet, the tinkling of bells and the beat of tambors. They were coming. He *was coming.*

She rose, taking an involuntary step backward until she felt the hard, cold stone at her back. Her breath caught in her throat.

The time was upon her. . . .

12

Kyria's eyes flew open. She lay still for a moment, unsure of where she was or what was happening. Her heart pounded in her chest, and there was a sheen of moisture on her face.

She turned her head. Light was seeping in around the edges of the draperies. It must be morning. And she was here at Broughton House. She wet her lips and wiped a hand across her face, brushing away the stray hairs.

What had awakened her? She had been dreaming, she thought. Gradually, wisps of the dream drifted into her mind. It had been so odd, so different from most of her dreams. She had dreamed this same thing or something very like it before — more than once — and she found it disturbing.

She could not help but wonder if the dream was somehow connected to the reliquary. She had not had this dream before the box came into their house, and twice she had had this dream right after she had been looking at the box. Last night, she remembered, although she had not gone down to look at the reliquary, it had been very much on her mind. On the other hand, the box had not actually appeared in the dream, nor had Habib or Kousoulous or anyone else connected to the box. Indeed, there had been no one even *in* the dreams except herself — and the unrecognizable backs of a few men.

She sat up slowly. Her eyelids were heavy, and she would have liked to have lain down and gone back to sleep, but she knew that she would not be able to now. With a sigh, she got up and washed her face and rang for Joan. She might as well get dressed and start the day.

The twins were downstairs in the breakfast room when she entered it, alive with curiosity about what had happened to her and Rafe the night before. Kyria glanced at Denby and saw that he was already looking a trifle tired. She hoped that he would last until the head groom arrived to take Con and Alex home. Perhaps she ought to put a second footman on them, as well, so that they could work in shifts.

The boys were disappointed in her recounting of the events of the night before; Kyria felt sure that they thought her lacking in spirit for not having chased the villain to ground. However, they soon recovered and were full of other plans to catch the man. Rafe joined them about then and was regaled with all the twins' new ideas, most of which featured themselves in hot pursuit of the thief.

"Somehow I don't think the duchess would be too pleased if we let you two run all over London checking out dens of thieves," Rafe commented.

"You'll be with us," Alex said. "Kyria, too, if she wants," he added magnanimously.

"Why, thank you for allowing me to participate," Kyria told him. "However, I don't think we will be together, as you will be home here with Denby. Mr. McIntyre is right — Mother would be most displeased if I allowed the two of you to run about doing whatever you pleased when you disobeyed her and sneaked off to London with us."

"She's already displeased," Con reasoned. "She'll punish us, anyway. So it seems to me that we might at least get to do something fun first."

Kyria could not suppress a smile. "You are a complete hand — both of you. All right, you can come along with us this afternoon when we go to find the dealer. How is that?"

"Wizard!" Alex exclaimed, jumping up from his chair and grinning at his brother in a way that told Kyria the boys had gotten more out of her than they had expected.

"What are we going to do with Mr. Habib?" Con asked, settling down to business at once.

"*You* are going to do absolutely nothing," Kyria told him sternly. "We are not going there to stir up a fuss."

"Well, perhaps only a little one," Rafe stuck in.

"What do you mean?" Kyria glanced at him. "I thought we were going to observe Mr. Habib and follow him if he went anywhere."

"Yes, but I've been thinking. We can scarcely just sit there in the carriage for hours on end, waiting for Habib to decide to leave his room. What if he doesn't? Or what if he has already left?"

"Well, we shall ascertain whether he is there," Kyria said, then added with a frown, "I suppose it would look a trifle peculiar for a carriage to remain at the inn for ages."

Con nodded. "If you are in the courtyard, the ostlers will come out and want to do something with your horses."

"Better to stay out of the courtyard,"

Alex said. "But then, what if Mr. Habib comes out and gets in a carriage and drives away from the inn? You won't know it's him."

"That's true," Kyria agreed. "Well, I suppose one of us will just have to stay inside the inn somewhere to watch him and then . . ." She sighed. "It will be a great waste of time and effort, won't it? Clearly we should have thought it through better."

"I did," Rafe said with a grin. "That is what I was about to say. I was thinking about it last night when I couldn't sleep." He thought it prudent not to mention the reason for his sleeplessness. "And it occurred to me that it would be much better if there was someone hanging about the inn who would not seem out of place — especially if we slipped a few coins to the ostlers so that he could simply blend in among them."

"But who . . ." Kyria stopped as understanding dawned on her. "Tom Quick!"

Rafe nodded. "Exactly."

Tom Quick worked for Olivia, helping her in her investigations. He was a lively and engaging young man, sixteen or seventeen years old — no one, including himself, was sure of his age. He had been raised on the streets, with a few brief stops in orphanages, and his last name came not from his father, whom he had never known, but was given to him by his companions because of the speed of both his hands and mind. His career as a pickpocket had ended one day when he had tried to rob Reed Moreland. Reed had quickly realized the lad's intelligence and potential, so instead of handing him over to one of the "peelers," he had taken the boy in and seen to it that he was fed, clothed and educated.

As a result, Tom was devoted to Reed, and when Reed had asked him to work in his sister's office, as much to watch over her and make sure nothing happened to her as to actually help her, Tom had readily agreed. He had spent the past couple of years in Olivia's employ and had grown as devoted to her as he was to her brother. On their most recent job, Tom had gone with Olivia to the St. Leger estate, masquerading as Olivia's servant to help her expose the medium who had been bilking Stephen St. Leger's mother out of money. It was on that occasion that Rafe had met both Olivia and Tom Quick.

"With Stephen and Olivia off on their honeymoon, I reckon that Tom has little enough to do and would be happy to get a chance to spy on our friend Habib."

"I am sure you are right. I'll send a note around to him immediately," Kyria said.

The addition of Tom Quick to their adventure met with the approval of the twins, who recognized in him a kindred spirit.

"Can we stay with Tom?" Con asked. "We can help him."

"No." Kyria cut off that avenue of discourse immediately. "Absolutely not."

"It would hinder Tom, you see," Rafe offered. "He would have to worry about keeping you safe, and that would interfere with his following Habib."

Con grimaced, but shrugged and fell silent, recognizing the truth of his words.

"If Tom will meet us at the inn," Rafe went on, "we'll set him up there to watch for Habib. Kyria and I can go in and talk to Mr. Habib, so that Tom can see who he is. Whether Habib is working with the mysterious man from last night or not, I figure if we question him a little, it might spur him to take some action, and then Tom can follow him. Plus —" he gave a small smile that did not bode well for his quarry "— I'd just like to have a little chat with our friend Habib."

"Can we talk to him, too?" Alex asked hopefully.

Kyria shot him a warning look. "Alex . . ."

"Oh, all right," he agreed. "It was worth a try."

"And this morning, while Mr. McIntyre and I are at the archaeologist's, you have to apply yourself to your studies," Kyria continued.

"But our books are at home," Con stated.

"I am sure that there are adequate books here for one morning's lesson," Kyria said. "I will come upstairs and look through them right after breakfast. Now, I suggest the two of you get set up in the schoolroom before I change my mind."

The twins beat a hasty retreat, and Kyria and Rafe were left to eat the remainder of their breakfast in peace.

When their lingering breakfast was over, Kyria went upstairs to the schoolroom as she had promised and looked over the books the twins had already selected. As she had suspected they would, Con and Alex, faced with the prospect of her setting them a lesson they didn't want, had looked through what was at hand and had chosen a project that interested them and that would, therefore, keep them busy and out of trouble most of the morning.

She left them working and went downstairs, where both Rafe and the carriage were waiting. She opened the safe and removed the reliquary, putting it back into the same concealing valise that they had carried on the train.

As Rafe stepped up into the carriage a few minutes later, he caught a flash of something white at the corner of the house. He paused, turning to look. There was nothing there.

"What is it?" Kyria asked. "What are you doing?"

Rafe frowned. "Just . . . I thought I caught a glimpse of something. Never mind."

Their first stop was the home of Nelson Ashcombe, the late Lord Walford's archaeologist. The duke had, as promised, given them a letter for Ashcombe introducing them and asking him to meet with them. It came as something of a shock, therefore, when Kyria handed the missive to a rather slovenly looking maid who then left and returned a few moments later with a refusal.

"What?" Kyria asked, for a moment thinking that she had misunderstood the maid.

The girl blinked, then said, more slowly and loudly, "I said as 'ow the master don't want to see you."

"That is what he said?"

"No. It were more highfalutin and had a lot of words that a proper girl like meself wouldn't repeat. Mostly it was about 'ow he was busy and couldn't be bothered by dilly somethin' or others and society misses."

"Dilettantes?" Kyria raised a brow and started to form a scathing retort, but then she closed her lips tightly together. She had been raised not to blame servants for their employer's faults.

After a moment, she said calmly, "Pray tell Mr. Ashcombe that I have with me a certain object which I think he will find interesting. An object which he has been seeking for some time."

The maid looked uncertain, but turned and disappeared up the stairs again. It wasn't long before she came back.

"Mr. Ashcombe's indisposed," she said shortly. "He said . . ." She appeared to struggle with how to phrase it, then finally gave up and went on, "He said to tell you to go away."

"Very well. Thank you." Kyria turned and left, waiting until she and Rafe were outside to vent her irritation. "Ohhh! What a perfectly rude man!"

"I reckon not too many people ignore a

duke's wishes," Rafe guessed.

"No, they don't. It's not that I expect everyone to fawn over me because my father is a duke — in fact, I quite dislike it." She paused, then added honestly, "However, you are right — it rarely happens that I am ignored, and arrogant as it may be on my part, it is really most annoying. Especially when it is important. And Papa was his benefactor's friend!"

"Since the benefactor is now dead, maybe he doesn't feel he has to pay any attention to the man's friends."

"Obviously not." Kyria sighed as Rafe handed her up into the carriage. "You would think he would at least have some curiosity about the reliquary, since he has been trying to find it for some time."

"Dr. Jennings said he had lost credibility for doing so," Rafe said. "Maybe he thought we were playing some sort of joke on him. Or maybe other people have tried to get in to see him, saying the same thing."

Kyria sat, drumming her fingers on the valise for a moment. "Didn't Dr. Jennings say something about his lordship's son now supporting Ashcombe?"

"I'm not sure. He may have. Do you know him?"

"No. I think he lived abroad until his father died and he had to return to take over the estate. I may have seen him sometime, I suppose, but I can't remember what he looks like." She smiled. "That, however can be remedied."

Kyria opened the window and called up to her coachman, "Lady Esterby's, please."

"What are we doing?" Rafe asked.

"Going to pay a call. It is a trifle early, but Lady Esterby won't mind once she lays eyes on you."

His brows rose lazily. "And why is that?"

"Well, at the risk of inflating your head —" Kyria prefaced her remark teasingly "— it is because Lady Esterby is never averse to meeting a handsome new man. One with buckets of money is even more intriguing, as she has five daughters to marry off. She is also one of the biggest gossips in town — which is precisely why we are going to see her — but it also means that she will be so eager to spread the news that I came to call on her with a stranger, an American, no less, in tow that she would probably welcome us in her dressing gown."

"And what do we hope to gain from this visit — other than, of course, saddling me with a mother of five marriageable daughters?"

Kyria's lips curved up. "I am sure you

will be able to manage her quite easily. And the result, we hope, is that we will discover exactly where we might be able to meet the present Lord Walford."

This was, in fact, what they did, though not before they had had to wade through a great deal of social niceties. Lady Esterby received Kyria looking somewhat surprised, but her expression quickly changed to delight when Kyria introduced her to Rafe, adding that he was the American partner of Lord St. Leger. Lady Esterby was then sure that Kyria must be eager to see her eldest daughters and sent the butler to bring them down to the drawing room.

After the giggling girls entered, looking somewhat sleepy-eyed and puzzled, Kyria sent Rafe a significant look, from which he assumed that it was his job to entertain the girls. It did not take much to set them talking, only a compliment or two and a question about their latest party. With them taken care of, Kyria and their mother settled in for a gossip fest. It took several minutes of general rumors and scandals before Kyria managed to direct the other woman's conversation toward the late Lord Walford.

"Didn't his son come back to take over

the estate?" Kyria asked at this point.

"Oh, yes." Lady Esterby nodded her head. "Such a handsome man. And quite eligible."

Kyria nodded encouragingly. She had been sure that if the man was unmarried or only recently so, Lady Esterby would know everything about him.

"Esterby's nephew assures me that he is a bang-up fellow, as he calls it. I have tried to get George to bring Lord Walford to dine with us, but of course, he won't make the slightest push to help my girls, even though he is Esterby's heir. You know how young men are."

Kyria knew how George Esterby was, at least. When Lady Esterby's nephew had first come to town, he had spent a few weeks dangling after her so persistently, taking none of her hints or snubs and annoying everyone in her family with his frequent calls, that finally Reed had taken him aside and told him to stop making a cake of himself or Reed would have to chuck him into the Thames.

"I had not realized Walford was your nephew's age," was Kyria's only comment.

"Oh, he's not. George has rather a case of hero worship, I imagine," Lady Esterby said in a rare moment of acuity. "Lord

Walford must be several years older than you. That's why you wouldn't have met him. He left England some years before your coming-out."

"Yes, I thought he had been abroad."

"I believe there was something of a scandal, but I cannot remember what it was," Lady Esterby went on regretfully. "That was when my daughters were quite little, you know, and I was not so much in the thick of things, you might say. Of course, he is quite respectable now. Young men so often fall into wild ways, don't they, and then come about later? I believe he was in the Levant — or was it Egypt? I get all those places confused," Lady Esterby admitted with a giggle. "I'm afraid I never had the head for studies that you and your sisters do. But I believe he was quite involved in all those ancient things, the way his father was — and, of course, the duke."

"I see. Perhaps that is why I have not seen him at parties."

"No, he is not very sociable," Lady Esterby concurred with a sigh. "I think George knows him more from some club or other. He will doubtless be at Editha Tarkey's rout tonight, though — they are some sort of cousins, I believe." She cast a frowning look over at her daughters, sitting like three dolls in a row on the sofa and tittering at some comment Rafe had made. "I do hope Sally doesn't have a cold. She sneezed twice at dinner last night. It would be simply ghastly if she showed up tonight at the Tarkeys' with a red nose. There are so few parties this time of year."

Having obtained the information she was seeking, Kyria let Lady Esterby ramble on for a few more minutes about her daughters and their various possibilities of beaux, then deftly brought her call to an end.

"I hope you got what you needed," Rafe grumbled as their carriage turned once again toward Broughton House. "My eardrums will never be the same."

"It's your own fault for making them giggle so," Kyria responded unsympathetically. "But, yes, I did find out where Lord Walford is likely to be tonight. It's no wonder I have never met him if he only shows up for Lady Tarkey's parties. They are always such crushes one can scarcely move about. It is her goal to have as many guests as she possibly can, so that she can toss names about later — which is largely the same reason that people come to them."

"Then there will be no problem with your being invited."

"Oh, no. I am sure there is an invitation to it on the receiving table. I shall just have to look."

"Will there be dancing?" Rafe gave her a lazy smile. "You know, I never did get a second waltz with you."

Kyria could not keep from smiling playfully back. "I will promise you a waltz — provided, of course, that there is any room to dance."

They returned to Broughton House, and after a light luncheon, set out again in the carriage, this time with Con and Alex in the seat across from them. When they arrived at the inn, the name of which Habib had written across the back of his calling card, they found Tom Quick loitering in the courtyard, arms crossed and leaning back against a brick wall, his blond hair gleaming in the sunlight, as he watched the passage of people in and out of the yard.

At the sight of the Moreland carriage, he grinned and sprang forward to open the door as soon as it rolled to a stop. He swept a bow to Kyria. "Welcome, my lady. Mr. McIntyre. Looks like this is my lucky day. I was that bored sittin' there in the office this morning." He leaned in, grinning at the twins, and went on, "Well, and what bit of bribery did you two use to get taken along on this caper?"

"We never did!" Con retorted indignantly.

"We did our schoolwork," Alex offered. "And we have no tutor."

"Chased off another one, eh?"

"I am afraid I had a hand in this one," Kyria admitted. "The tutor and I had a disagreement concerning his methods of teaching, among other things."

Quick's grin grew broader as his gaze shifted to Kyria. "Well, if it comes to a disagreement, my lady, my money'd be on you."

"You're right about that," Rafe said.

Tom reached down and lowered the steps, then offered a hand to Kyria. Rafe followed her. The twins would have followed, but Kyria stopped them.

"You are staying with the carriage."

"Aw, but, Kyria . . . why can't we just go with Tom?" Con asked. "We ought to get a look at Mr. Habib, too, don't you think? What if we see him again somewhere? We should know what he looks like."

Kyria sighed and cast a glance at Tom.

"I'll look after 'em, don't you worry," he

told her. "We'll just walk along real quiet like and get a look at this chappie when you meet him. Then we'll come back out here, and I'll keep an eye on them."

Somewhat reassured, Kyria went with Rafe into the inn, careful not to glance back to see what Tom and the boys were doing. The inn was a clean and respectable place with a large public room, gleaming with polished mahogany and brass. The host, seeing them, hurried to meet them and inquire of their needs. When Rafe mentioned Mr. Habib's name, a measuring look came into the innkeeper's eyes, but he merely bowed and offered to show them to the private room where Habib was just finishing up his lunch.

With a knock on the door, the innkeeper opened it and ushered Kyria and Rafe inside. Habib was standing at the window looking out into the back garden, the remains of his lunch on the table in the middle of the room. He turned at their entrance, and his eyes widened with surprise.

"Lady Moreland, I am so pleased to see you," he began in his heavily accented voice. He started forward, bowing, his hands clasped together at his chest. "And Mr. . . ."

"McIntyre," Rafe told him.

Habib gestured at the innkeeper impatiently. "Please go." He followed the man to the door and closed it behind him, then turned, offering Kyria a wide smile. "You have thought over my offer, yes? You will sell me the Byzantine box?"

"No, I'm not here to sell you the box, Mr. Habib," Kyria told him firmly.

"We are here to ask you what you know about the men who broke into the Morelands' house," Rafe said bluntly.

"Broke into? I don't understand."

"They came to steal a box — the box you wanted. I find that rather odd," Rafe continued.

"But I would buy it! Why should I steal it?" Habib shrugged, looking innocently from Kyria to Rafe and back.

"Perhaps because I refused to sell it to you," Kyria suggested. "And perhaps you aren't particular about how you get your hands on it."

"My lady, you hurt me," Habib said with a wounded expression, placing his hand to his heart. "I am a famous dealer. I have a reputation."

"And just what is that reputation?" Rafe asked, his voice as steely as his gaze. "Are you well-known for your ability to get what your clients want, no questions asked?"

"I don't understand," Habib repeated. "What are you saying?"

Kyria glanced toward the window and saw Con's face appear on the other side, peering in. He turned away, gesturing excitedly. Kyria's eyes widened, and she quickly looked over at Habib. Fortunately, Habib was staring at Rafe and did not see the boy.

"We caught the men who tried to steal the box," Rafe said. "They are sitting in jail right now. And they were pretty quick to implicate you."

"Me!" Habib stared at Rafe, his mouth falling open. "They say I have something to do with this? They lie!"

Kyria sneaked a look back at the window, where Alex was now beside Con, both of them peering into the window, cupping their hands around their eyes to see better. Behind them Tom was also gazing interestedly into the room. Kyria scowled at them. Con gave her a cheerful wave. Kyria glared and jerked her head at them to leave, then whipped back around to see if Habib was watching.

He was still looking at Rafe, but Kyria had lost the thread of the conversation. Rafe was saying, ". . . about the man they met at the Blue Bull in Cheapside. Do you know this tavern?"

"No! I have never been there!" Drops of sweat had broken out on the man's brow.

"They described the payment they were promised," Rafe continued, lying freely.

"They lie! I do not . . . I have not —"

"Who are you buying this box for? Who is your client?" Rafe pressed, looming over the man.

"I cannot tell you!" Habib backed away nervously and cast an imploring look at Kyria. "Please, my lady, I swear to you. I sent no one. I had nothing to do with this."

Kyria slid over closer to Rafe so that Habib, looking at her, could not see the window out of the corner of his eye. "I find that hard to believe," she told the dealer. "Who else knew about the box? You knew where it was — that is very damning, Mr. Habib. How did you know unless you had Kousoulous followed and murdered? How did the ruffians who broke into our house know unless you told them?"

"Others know!" Habib protested, reaching up to wipe the sweat from his brow. "I did nothing. I swear to you."

"How do they know?" Rafe pressed.

Habib shrugged, making vague sweeping gestures with his hands. "Everyone knows."

He swung away toward the window, and

Kyria let out a noise of protest, quickly muffled. Her brothers and Tom were no longer framed in the window, and she sighed with relief.

"Who is everyone?" Rafe continued.

"Istanbul," Habib answered. "Many people in Istanbul know. It is common gossip. Rumor. You see? Everyone whispers that Kousoulous has it and he takes it to England. To the Morelands."

"Let me tell you something, Habib," Rafe said, moving again toward Habib in that slow, deliberate, dangerous way he had. His voice was low and hard as he stared down into the other man's face. "I don't take kindly to threats. In fact, they make me real mad. Almost as mad as people trying to steal from me or mine. It happens again, I'm going to come after who did it. Am I making myself clear?"

Habib bobbed his head rapidly. "Yes, clear, very clear. But I do not . . . I have not —"

"Then you better keep on *not*," Rafe countered. He gave the man one last, long look, then spun on his heel. "Kyria? You got anything to add?"

"No," Kyria said. "I think you covered everything."

Rafe crossed to the door and opened it

for her, then followed her out of the room.

"Now," he said, taking Kyria's arm as they strode out of the inn, "if we are lucky, our friend back there will go scurrying off to his client or partner or whoever with news of our visit. Do you know if Tom got a look at him?"

Kyria grinned. "Yes. I believe he did."

13

Lady Tarkey's rout was the crush that Kyria had predicted. They had to first wait in their carriage as the line of vehicles inched forward, and then at last when they were able to disembark, there was another line snaking up the steps and into the house. At least, Kyria thought, if she had to endure the wait, it was some consolation that she was doing it with Rafe. Aside from being the most handsome man in the crowd, he also enlivened their time with sotto voce questions and comments about their surroundings, from the explosion of plasterwork cherubs and nymphs on the ceiling to the small man sporting orange-colored mustaches so waxed and intricately curled that whenever he moved his head, he seemed in imminent danger of putting out his female companion's eye.

Kyria smiled and nodded at various acquaintances, noticing that her arrival with a handsome stranger caused a ripple effect of heads turning all up the staircase.

After she and Rafe greeted their hostess

and her daughter at the top of the stairs, they strolled into the main ballroom, barely making it past the doorway because of the crush of people.

"Lady Kyria!" They turned to see an eager young man making his way through the crowd toward them. As he was large and somewhat clumsy, his progress was not easy and left more than a few people glaring in his wake. "Excuse me. Beg your pardon. Lady Kyria! I'm so dreadfully sorry. Was that your toe? My sincerest apologies. Excuse me . . ."

He arrived at last at Kyria's side and bowed extravagantly over her hand. As he bumped into the man behind him, his greeting was less the elegant gesture he had envisioned than a bit of buffoonery.

"My dearest lady, you are more beautiful than ever," he told Kyria, beaming down at her. "It seems a year since I have seen you."

"It is something more like a month."

"London is dreadfully dull without you." His gaze slid to Rafe, standing at Kyria's side, and he frowned.

"Oh, Lord Crandon," Kyria said, following his gaze, "please allow me to introduce Mr. McIntyre. He is visiting us from America."

"How do you do?" the young man replied politely, but Rafe could see the jealousy in his eyes.

As they made a rather limping attempt at small talk, another gentleman joined them, this one older and suaver, but as patently suspicious of Rafe. Within five minutes, they were surrounded by no fewer than six bachelors, all of them jockeying for Kyria's attention.

"You must give me your first waltz," said one who was dressed in a resplendent uniform and regarded the world with a face permanently frozen into an aristocratic sneer.

"Must I?" Kyria replied coolly. "I am afraid, Captain, that I have promised the first waltz to Mr. McIntyre." She slipped her hand through Rafe's arm.

"Yes," Rafe confirmed, closing his other hand possessively over Kyria's where it lay on his arm, his gaze remaining on the captain's for a long, challenging moment. Then he turned toward Kyria, smiling. "And I believe I hear them striking up now. If you will excuse us, gentlemen . . ."

He bowed toward the others and Kyria gave them a smile as she allowed Rafe to lead her toward the dance floor.

"We will be lucky if we can make it

through this crowd before the dance is over," Kyria commented as they wound in and out through the throng.

Rafe grinned. "As long as we get away from your platoon of admirers, it's all right."

"They are just bored. The season is over, and a great many people are gone."

He cocked a brow at her. "Do you expect me to believe that those men flock to you only when the other belles are gone?"

Kyria chuckled. "No, I am not that humble."

They reached the dance floor at last, and Rafe smoothly pulled her into his arms and out into the flow of dancers. For the moment, Kyria abandoned all thought of the purpose of their evening and just enjoyed whirling about the room, secure in Rafe's arms.

All too soon, however, the waltz ended, and Kyria returned to reality with a little sigh. She glanced around, finally spotting two of London's premier hostesses. If anyone could introduce her to Lord Walford tonight, she was sure that one of these two women could.

As she and Rafe made their way toward them, the women's faces brightened, their eyes sliding curiously over Rafe. One of them opened her fan and brought it up to her face in a coquettish gesture at odds with her age.

"Lady Kyria," the other, older one greeted her. "Surprised to see you here tonight."

"Yes, I have returned to London unexpectedly," Kyria told her, smiling, and continued, "Lady Colcaughten. Mrs. Marbury. Pray allow me to introduce you to Lord St. Leger's American partner, Mr. McIntyre."

"Mr. McIntyre, how delightful," Lady Colcaughten twittered, laying her hand on his arm and subtly turning him a little away from the group. "I have heard so much about you."

"You have?"

"Oh, my, yes. Why, the St. Leger wedding was quite the talk of London — so small, so quiet, so fast, one might say."

"Might one," Rafe replied enigmatically.

"Everyone who was privileged to attend was full of news about it, which is only to be expected." She edged away, tugging a little at his arm. "Please let me introduce you around."

Rafe cast a glance back at Kyria, who nodded encouragingly. With a resigned look, he turned and allowed himself to be steered away.

Mrs. Marbury appeared chagrined at being cut out by her companion and started to go after them, but Kyria stopped her with a hand on her arm. "Mrs. Marbury, you are just the person I was hoping to see."

"Really, dear?" The woman perked up at Kyria's compliment. It certainly never hurt one's standing in society to win Kyria Moreland's approval. "I'm so glad."

"There is someone here tonight that I have been hoping to meet," Kyria went on.

Mrs. Marbury's eyes lit up at the prospect of learning a bit of gossip. "Really? Who?"

"Lord Walford. His father, you know, was a great friend of my father's."

"Yes, the dear duke. How is he?"

"Quite well." Kyria knew that "the dear duke," if asked, would not have the slightest idea who Mrs. Marbury was. "The thing is, my father is interested in corresponding with Lord Walford, as he did with his father. Lord Walford is, I understand, also interested in antiquities. But I, alas, have never been introduced to Lord Walford. I was hoping that you might know him . . ."

"Oh, my, yes, I met him at the Featherstone ball in April. Such a lavish affair — I am sure you remember."

"Of course," Kyria lied without compunction.

"An elegant gentleman. Quite distinguished — and handsome!" She laid a hand on her breast, closing her eyes in a sort of mock swoon. "If I were not a married woman . . ." She let out a merry little laugh. "Well, I would be happy to introduce you, if you'd like. I hadn't realized he was here this evening."

The woman quickly began to scan the room for their quarry. "I don't see him around here. Let's try looking this way."

She started off through the crowd, and Kyria followed her. It was clear that Mrs. Marbury was an expert at hunting the elusive party goer, for it took her little time to tour the ballroom and hallway beyond, glancing into the various nooks and corners where someone might be conversing. At last spotting their quarry near the stairs chatting apparently desultorily, with another couple of men, she straightened and swept toward the group like a battleship under full sail.

"Ah, Lord Walford," she caroled gaily. "And here I was telling Lady Kyria that you were not at this rout."

One of the gentlemen turned to look at

her, then bowed slightly and offered up a faint smile. "Mrs. Marbury, how nice to see you again." His voice, while polite, conveyed a distinct lack of enthusiasm. His eyes went past her, however, to Kyria, and his face brightened a little.

He took Mrs. Marbury's hand and kissed it in an old-fashioned, courtly way that brought out a little giggle from Mrs. Marbury. "I knew you would be pleased to see me," she teased, wagging her fan flirtatiously at the man. "I've come to introduce you to Lady Kyria Moreland."

Lord Walford turned to Kyria, giving her a polite nod. "My lady. I believe our fathers were great friends. 'Tis a pity that we have never met before." He looked at Mrs. Marbury. "I must thank you for correcting that unfortunate situation."

Kyria studied Lord Walford as Mrs. Marbury continued to gush at him. He was a tall, lean man with thick, black hair, marked by matching waves of silver at each temple. His skin, like Rafe's, had obviously been tanned by years in the hot sun, and his eyes were an odd color somewhere between green and hazel. Razor-thin cheekbones pushed against the skin of his face, giving him an almost fierce demeanor.

It took some more minutes of polite conversation with Mrs. Marbury before the woman spotted someone who offered better grist for gossip and left Kyria alone with Lord Walford.

"I am sorry to interrupt your conversation," Kyria told him, nodding toward the two men with whom Walford had been talking.

He smiled. "You needn't worry. I was merely putting in my time until I could politely leave. I am not one who enjoys parties overmuch, I am afraid." He paused, then went on, "Now, is there something I can help you with?"

Kyria glanced at him, a little startled, and blushed. "I am sorry. I must seem most ill-bred to you, forcing an introduction on you this way."

"One can scarcely consider it forced when one is introduced to a young woman as beautiful and charming as yourself. However, it is also obvious that you have no need of male companionship. I feel sure that you are accustomed to being surrounded by a flock of eager suitors. Therefore, I must think that there is some reason you wished to make my acquaintance."

"There is," Kyria admitted. "I want to talk to Mr. Ashcombe. Mr. Nelson Ashcombe."

"My father's archaeologist?" Walford asked, his eyebrows going up in surprise. "I must say, I never would have guessed that that was your request."

"Does he not work for you, as well?" Kyria asked.

Walford gave an elegant shrug. "I am not sure if anyone can really claim that Nelson Ashcombe works *for* him. I think it is more that he works for himself and allows someone else to pay the bills for it."

Kyria smiled. "That hardly seems like a good proposition for you."

"Ah, but he also allows you to hang around his dig and poke about among the things he unearths. And I am afraid that I inherited my father's fervor for such things. I got into a spot of trouble when I was young . . ." He gave her a wry smile. "I was a little wild, you see, and my father shipped me off to one of his digs to keep me out of trouble. I was supposed to learn the error of my ways, I think, but in reality, what I learned was that I loved the dig just as much as he did. I loved the area, too — Turkey, Persia, Mesopotamia — the 'cradle of civilization.' There's no place else quite like it. Once I had been there a few months, I never wanted to leave it. Of course, when my father died, I had to come home — one's duty and all that, but I miss it sorely."

"And do you, like Mr. Ashcombe, believe in a reliquary containing Constantine's banner?" Kyria asked curiously.

"The Holy Standard?" Walford gave her a quizzical smile. "I have to admit that I think that it is probably just a legend. Ashcombe is a little mad on the subject. It has rather hurt his reputation, you know, which is too bad. He is a tremendous scholar, a giant in his field. I have supported him, of course — I mean, I could scarcely not do so, after the years he worked with my father." He paused, then asked, "What about you? Do you believe in the reliquary?"

"I am rather beginning to," Kyria replied cautiously. "I went to Mr. Ashcombe's this morning to talk to him about it, but he refused to see me."

"Really?" Walford looked surprised. "Ashcombe is usually quite happy to discourse on it. You must have caught him on a bad day. Or perhaps he thought you were there to ridicule him in some way. Ashcombe is a proud man. I will send him a note tomorrow morning and request that he speak to you. How is that?"

"That would be wonderful," Kyria said,

smiling. “I can’t tell you how grateful I am to you.”

“It’s no trouble, I assure you.” He gave her a small, deprecating smile. “The least I could do for Theo’s sister.”

“Theo?” Kyria glanced up at him, surprised. “Do you know Theo?”

He nodded. “We are well acquainted. We got to know each other when we were in Turkey at the same time. Fellow Englishmen in a foreign land, that sort of thing. But it turned out that we had more than that in common. We had many a conversation regarding the propriety of taking historical objects out of their native countries. Looting, the way Theo and I saw it.”

“Yes, I have heard him express his views on the subject.”

“Is he in England again?” Walford asked. “I would quite like to see him.”

“No, I’m afraid he isn’t. It has been a while since we’ve heard from him. I’m not sure exactly where he is.”

Walford smiled, shaking his head in an admiring way. “He is one of a kind.”

Kyria wondered just how well Walford knew Theo. Was it possible that he knew anything about Kousoulous or the box that lay at home in their safe?

Surely, she thought, if he knew about it,

he would have mentioned it when she inquired about Ashcombe and his search for the reliquary. Or perhaps Theo would not have mentioned it to him if he was planning to ship the object out of the country; it sounded as if Lord Walford was very much opposed to such things. All in all, she thought, it would be better for her not to say anything to the man about it.

Smiling, she thanked him again for his time and trouble and turned away, looking for Rafe. Before she was able to locate him, however, she was besieged by several admirers looking for a dance with her, and she spent the next half hour dancing. She saw Rafe at a distance now and then, usually dancing with someone, and she could not deny the fact that seeing him with another woman in his arms sent a sharp stab of jealousy through her.

She told herself she was being ridiculous. She had no claim on Rafe, after all. She had known the man for only a few weeks. And even though his kisses had made her feel strangely weak in the knees, it didn't really mean anything. She did not intend to marry, and he . . . well, Kyria was sophisticated enough to realize that his kissing her a few times did not mean that he loved her. Nor did she love him, she reminded herself hastily.

She was so deep in thought regarding Rafe that she bade her last waltzing partner a rather distracted goodbye and walked right past one of her friends without seeing her until she heard her name being called loudly.

Kyria stopped and glanced around. "Alicia!" She felt a blush rising in her cheeks as she realized what she had done. "I am so sorry. My head was in the clouds."

She turned back to the plump, blond woman who had been one of her best friends when they made their debut together. Alicia Forquay had made an advantageous marriage and was now Lady Hargreaves, the proud mother of three rambunctious sons, as well as a leading society matron.

"Don't worry, I am not offended," her friend assured her. "But I want to introduce you to someone." She half turned toward the tall man beside her.

He was dark-haired and sharp-featured, and the gaze he turned on Kyria was bright and searching.

"Kyria, this is Prince Dmitri Rostokov. He is visiting from Russia and is a very good friend of Lord Buckley. Your Highness, this is Lady Kyria Moreland."

"My lady." He bowed with precision over her hand. "I have been most anxious to make your acquaintance." His English was fluent, though spoken with a distinct Russian accent.

"How do you do?" Kyria smiled politely at him.

"I am very well, thank you. I wished to speak to you about a certain matter . . ." He looked pointedly at Lady Hargreaves.

Alicia returned his gaze blankly for a moment, then her brows shot up and she said, "Oh. Well, I, um, I should go . . . um, somewhere."

Kyria turned her own surprised gaze back to the Russian. She wasn't sure if the prince was simply rude or arrogant or did not understand the language well, but it was unusual for Alicia to accept a dismissal so meekly, which made Kyria think that the Russian prince must be a very important person.

"I must speak to you on a matter of great importance," Rostokov told her.

Kyria felt a sinking sensation in the pit of her stomach. "Indeed?"

"Yes." He moved fractionally closer and lowered his voice. "I have been told that you have come into possession of a certain box."

Kyria gazed back at him levelly. "I am sorry. I am afraid I don't know what you —"

"Come, come, my lady. There is no point engaging in this charade. It is well-known in certain circles that Mr. Kousoulous brought this object to your house. Now you suddenly appear in London not long after your family removed to the country. It takes little thinking to surmise that your surprise visit concerns the reliquary." He paused, then went on, "I am personally interested in this box. I would like to acquire it from you."

"I am sorry. If I did indeed possess your reliquary, it would not be for sale," Kyria replied, and started to turn away.

"No, my lady, you do not understand. This matter is of great importance to me. I am willing to pay you a great deal of money."

Kyria countered, "Why is everyone so eager to get their hands on this thing?"

"It is, well, of historical value. You must understand. Lord Buckley tells me that your father is a collector of rare objects."

"My father is greatly interested in antiquities," Kyria conceded. "However, he does not normally travel to other countries and try to wheedle people's possessions from them."

"Wheedle? I do not know this word."

"Nor does he try to steal them."

"Steal!" The Russian's eyes widened, and he looked seriously affronted. "What do you mean?"

"I mean that this box seems to have aroused villainous instincts in some people."

"I have never stolen anything in my life!"

"Probably not, but I have no way of knowing who exactly is behind the attempted theft — actually, I am not sure *theft* is the appropriate word for breaking into one's house and threatening to harm one's family if one does not surrender the box."

"Someone has done this?" Rostokov asked, his eyes narrowing.

"Yes. Other people have also tried to buy the box from us, and the man who brought it to me was killed on our doorstep. You will pardon me if I am somewhat suspicious about anyone who is interested in this box."

"I am sorry," he said shortly. "I assure you that I have nothing to do with any murder or threat or theft. Is the box safe? Do you have it here in London?"

Kyria arched an eyebrow. "Do you honestly think I am going to tell you where the box is? *You* may be certain that you have not been engaged in any criminal activities, but I am not."

"Ask Lady Hargreaves. Her husband. Or Lord Buckley. They will vouch for my honor. I am a prince of Russia."

"In any case, sir, I have no intention of selling the box."

Prince Dmitri scowled. "You do not understand."

"No, *you* do not understand. I have refused your offer. I do not intend to sell the box. Now, if you will excuse me . . ."

Kyria started to turn away, but the prince grabbed her arm. "No! I cannot allow you to endanger the reliquary!"

"I beg your pardon!" Kyria looked pointedly down at the hand that so tightly gripped her arm.

He, too, looked at his hand, then released her arm and bowed a little. "Please accept my apologies. However, I must —"

"Having a little trouble here?"

"Rafe!" Kyria turned toward him with relief.

He gave her a quick grin, then turned toward the other man, his face suddenly hard and challenging. "You bothering this lady?"

"What? Don't be absurd." The prince glowered at him. "Please go away."

"Well, now, I don't think I can do that. The lady here doesn't seem to be enjoying your conversation all that much."

"It is none of your concern."

"You're wrong there," Rafe responded, taking a step closer to the Russian, his eyes boring into the man's.

The Russian drew himself up, his eyes glittering.

"You, sir, overstep yourself."

"And you, sir, are in danger of getting tossed out of here on your —"

"Gentlemen, please!" Kyria said sternly. She looked pointedly at Prince Dmitri. "You are attracting attention."

The prince cast a look around, hesitated, then took a step backward. "I am not through. I will speak to you again, my lady."

He turned and strode off through the crowd. Rafe turned to Kyria.

"What was that all about?" he asked.

"What do you think?" Kyria responded.

"The reliquary?" Rafe's brows soared up. He looked at the prince's retreating back.

"Yes. He offered to buy it from me."

"So . . . our friend Habib has a rival," Rafe commented.

"It would seem so."

"Well, this certainly makes things more

interesting. Do you suppose that he is the one who hired the intruders?"

"He says not, but I have no way of knowing. He fits the description that Sid gave us."

Rafe nodded thoughtfully. "He could have been the man at the tavern."

They looked at each other.

"I think I'm ready to leave," Kyria said.

"Did you get what you wanted?"

Kyria nodded. "And rather more."

Kyria had trouble sleeping that night. Her mind kept running over her meeting with the Russian and what he had said. She had felt sure that the Lebanese antiquities dealer had been behind the things that had happened at Broughton Park, but now she wondered. It could have been Prince Dmitri — or perhaps there were even others who wanted the box. Given what she and Rafe had discovered about it, she could understand why many people would want it. But for the same reason, it seemed even more important now that she not let go of it. If it was, as it seemed to be, a scrap of the original battle standard of Constantine inside the reliquary box, then it was a piece not only of great worth and age, but also one of enormous religious significance. Such a thing was virtually priceless, and it seemed wrong for it to be in the possession of a private collector. It should belong to . . . well, she was not sure where the box belonged, but it should not be locked in the vault of a single person, including herself.

With a sigh, she turned over and plumped up her pillow, then laid her head back down. She felt once again the same overwhelming urge to go look at the reliquary that had afflicted her before. She told herself it was foolish; she had, after all, looked at the box many times. It was pointless to take it out of her father's safe just to gaze at it for a while. Still, the longer she lay there, resisting the urge, the more she wanted to see it. It occurred to her that it was only practical to make sure that it was still inside the safe, that nothing had happened to it since they had been in London. There was, after all, the possibility that a talented thief could have crept into their house and opened the safe and spirited the box away without their being any the wiser.

Finally, she got up and slipped into her warm, velvet dressing gown and house slippers. She would not be able to sleep until she knew whether the reliquary was still safe, she reasoned.

She lit a candle and left her room, moving quietly along the long, dark hallway, then down the stairs to her father's study. There, she set the candle on his desk and made her way to the wall safe. It contained the family's most important papers, along with the more frequently worn pieces of her mother's jewelry. Most of the Morelands' gold and silver plate was kept in a much larger safe just off the butler's pantry, along with the oldest jewelry and other family heirlooms.

Kyria turned the combination lock of the safe and opened it, then reached in and pulled out the drawstring bag containing the reliquary. She took it over to the desk and set it down near the candle, then sat in the chair behind the desk and rested her chin on her hand, gazing at the black diamond that adorned the side. Gently she ran her finger over the stone. It somehow warmed her inside to look at it. It was enough to make her wonder if power could lie in certain objects, influencing people and events.

She shook her head at the fantasies into which she was straying. Firmly ignoring the part of her that wanted to keep the reliquary out and look at it longer, she put the box back into the safe. She closed the door and twirled the knob, then turned to get the candle. Just as she turned, a figure swiftly, silently edged around the door and into the room, a pistol in his outthrust hand.

"Hold it ri—"

Kyria jumped, a little shriek escaping her, and for a moment they stood, staring at each other, motionless, before Rafe dropped the pistol to his side.

"What in blue blazes are you doing?" he asked irritably. "I heard something down here, and I thought somebody had broken in to steal that infernal box."

Kyria let out a breath. Her heart was racing, and she pressed a hand to her chest as though to slow it. "You scared me. I thought *you* were sneaking in to steal it."

They looked at each other a moment longer, then broke into grins. Rafe pocketed his gun, shaking his head, and moved farther into the room.

"I'm sorry I frightened you," he said.

"Me, too." Kyria moved to meet him.

He looked down at her. Her hair was loose, curling over her shoulders in a fiery mass. He could just imagine the feel of the springy curls between his fingers. His gaze slipped lower. She wore a dressing gown, as concealing as any dress, certainly more so than the evening gown she had worn to-night. But there was an intimacy about seeing her in the soft, bedtime apparel that stirred his desire. He could not help but think that beneath the velvet robe, she wore nothing but a night rail. He could see the soft white cotton in the V between the lapels of the dressing gown, and his fingers itched to reach out and touch it.

Rafe tried to remember all the reasons that it was not a good idea for him to kiss Kyria. At the moment, none of them came to mind.

Kyria's heart was still racing. She realized that it was only partly because of her fright a few moments before. It was far too intimate, too casual, to be standing here with Rafe, wearing only her nightclothes. No matter how concealing her dressing gown was, she felt most vulnerable, without any of her usual social armor. Her eyes went to the tanned skin of his throat exposed by the open collar of his shirt. He wore no jacket, and his unbuttoned shirt had been pulled from his trousers and hung loosely over them. He had been about to go to bed, she thought, and the idea made heat curl through her abdomen.

Rafe's eyes drifted down her body, his face softening with desire, and her flesh tingled as if he had touched her. Her mouth was suddenly dry. Her thoughts were scattered and chaotic, and she could not bring them to their usual order.

The only thing she could think was how it would feel if he touched her. Her skin tightened in anticipation, and she took an unconscious step forward. As if he could read her mind, his hand came out and folded around her arm. His fingers slid upward, and she could feel their warmth through the velvet of her dressing gown. Kyria wished suddenly that nothing lay between his flesh and hers.

With a little sigh, she swayed forward, her hands going up to his chest. His chest seemed to sear her palms through the cloth of his shirt. Unconsciously, she dug her fingers into his shirt. Rafe made a noise deep in his throat, and his arms went around her, pulling her into him, his mouth coming down to take hers.

It was dangerous to feel this way, she knew, just as she knew that she should back away before it was too late, but she could not bring herself to move. She did not want to move, she knew. She did not want to be wise or safe or strong. All she wanted was Rafe.

14

Hunger flared between them, fiery and voracious. Kyria pressed herself into Rafe, amazed by how his body fit perfectly into hers, hardness into softness. His arms were like steel, holding her up, pulling her into him. She responded on a primitive level, reveling in his strength and power, realizing with some amazement that she wanted him now, hard and all at once, her body virtually trembling with desire.

She scarcely recognized herself as she clung to him, her lips and tongue meeting and matching his, her hands digging helplessly into his back. Kyria was suddenly, staggeringly, swept with passion. She had never felt like this, never even dreamed that she could feel like this. She shivered, hanging on to him as if he were the only stable thing in her world.

When at last he raised his lips from hers, she let out a little moan at the loss. He shuddered at her involuntary sound, his own desire burgeoning at her response. He kissed his way across her face to her jaw and down to the tender flesh of her neck. Her head fell back, exposing her throat to his ravaging mouth, and she panted, hot and eager, aching for a completion she wasn't even fully aware of. She moved against him and he groaned, digging his fingers into her buttocks, lifting her up and grinding her pelvis against the hard line of his manhood.

"Kyria . . . Kyria . . ." he muttered thickly.

The neckline of her night rail stopped the downward movement of his mouth, and he set her back on her feet, impatiently fumbling with the buttons of the garment, popping off a good number of them in his haste. Kyria scarcely noticed as she moved her hands restlessly over him, caressing his chest and shoulders and arms. She wanted to get beneath his shirt, to feel his skin under her fingers.

Rafe ran his hands beneath her dressing gown, pushing it back and off her shoulders. The sash at her waist unwound and fell loosely to her sides, letting the robe fall open. Kyria shrugged, moving her arms until the dressing gown slipped off her arms to puddle on the floor so that she was clad only in her white night rail. As chaste as its color, the garment revealed nothing, yet its soft folds clung to the voluptuous shape of her body, outlining hips and breasts in a way that made desire pound through Rafe's veins. His eager hands had unbuttoned the night rail halfway down her chest, and the two sides sagged apart, hinting at the dark valley between her swelling breasts.

He swallowed hard and reached out to lay his hand flat against the bared skin of her chest. For a long moment, they stared into each other's eyes, their breath coming harsh and rasping in their throats. Slowly, the passion swelling in them with each breath, each small brushing of his callused fingertips against her silken skin, he moved his hand across the hard plane of her upper chest and down over the curve of her breast. Kyria's eyes fluttered closed as his hand curved around the soft orb. She sagged a little, her legs going weak at the pleasure, and Rafe's other arm wound around her waist, pulling her side against his chest.

Gently, sweetly, with a slow touch that was at once pure pleasure and pure agony, his fingers caressed her breasts, stroking and teasing the nipples into hard points. An ache started deep within her abdomen, growing and throbbing. Kyria's head lolled against Rafe's chest, and her breath caught on a sob as his fingers tweaked her nipple, vaulting her desire upward into a new, almost unbearable plane.

Kyria had thought she could not want him more, but she discovered how wrong she had been as his hand took her ever more deeply into the dark, pulsing heart of her passion. His hand drifted lower, sliding off her breasts and onto the flat plain of her stomach. Kyria's fingers went to the remaining buttons, opening them rapidly down the front of her nightgown until they ended below her waist. She sucked in a breath as his hand smoothed down over her abdomen, seeking the nest of curls at the apex of her legs.

She had never imagined such a thing — nor the liquid heat that welled in her at his touch. She moved restlessly, a small moan escaping her. All her being was centered on his touch.

Then he bent his head and began to nuzzle her breast, his lips and tongue moving lazily over her soft skin. And all the while his fingers continued to work their magic, finding and separating the silken folds of her womanhood, opening her to him. Kyria buried her face against his chest, stifling the cry of pleasure. Her fingers dug into his skin as heat engulfed her.

"Rafe . . . please." She rubbed her cheek against his chest, then sank her teeth into the cloth of his shirt as the pleasure intensified. Her legs were trembling, and her entire body seemed on fire. She felt as if she might explode from pleasure, and at the same time frustration tore at her, teasing her that she would never reach the satisfaction she sought.

Her voice was low and husky with desire as she murmured, "Take me. Please."

He groaned and lifted his head. His eyes were glittering with passion. "I can't. Kyria . . . it would be wrong to . . . to take advantage of —"

Kyria's eyes flashed and she raised her head, her mouth seeking his. He moaned as she kissed him deeply, hungrily. She smiled against his mouth as she felt his flesh throbbing against her, hard and hungry, searching for release.

She pulled back, staring challengingly up into his eyes. "Do you think I am some weak creature who must be protected from herself?"

"No. But you don't know . . . you are untouched and . . . I cannot dishonor you."

"Do you want me?" she asked.

"You know I do. Sweet heaven, woman, you're killing me." His voice was harsh and rasping.

"Then show me."

Kyria thrust her hands into his hair and pulled his head down again for a kiss. His arms wrapped tightly around her and he squeezed her against him as if their bodies could melt into one another. Blood pounded in his head. He could not remember when he had ever wanted a woman as he wanted Kyria now.

When at last he raised his head, he mumbled thickly, "I'll show you. All right . . . I'll show you."

He grasped her nightgown and yanked it down over her arms. It fell to the floor around her feet. He stood for a moment, his eyes drinking her in, then he dropped slowly onto his knees, his hands skimming down her body as he went. His hands reached around to her buttocks and took firm hold, pulling her hips forward.

"Rafe!" Astonishment laced Kyria's voice. "What are you doing?"

He merely smiled up at her in answer, a lazy, wicked smile that lanced through her like a white-hot shaft of desire. His fingers kneaded her buttocks and moved caressingly over her hips and legs. Then he moved forward, and his lips and tongue began to work magic on her flesh.

Kyria's knees buckled with surprise and the onslaught of intense pleasure, but his arms steadied her and held her up. She moaned, her fingers digging into his hair, scarcely able to believe what he was doing to her. His tongue was like a wild thing, darting, caressing, lashing, rhythmically stroking, and all the while his hands roamed her legs and hips, teasing and caressing, parting her legs to give him greater access to her.

She groaned, her breath coming in gasps, her legs shaking. She felt as if she might fly apart under the exquisite, agonizing pleasure of his ministrations. She could not think, could barely breathe, as desire built in her until it was a great, pulsing, tangled ball. Release remained tantalizingly out of her reach, as Rafe's mouth worked delicately on her, nudging her gently to greater and greater heights of pleasure, then backing off just at the last moment, only to return an instant later to drive her even higher.

Kyria panted his name. His tongue stroked and teased, then flickered over her, shooting her to yet a new height of sensation. The knot inside her tightened and grew until it seemed that she could not stand it anymore. And then, suddenly, pleasure exploded within her, so hot and hard and intense that she cried out at the wonder of it, and her entire body rocked.

Slowly she sank to the floor, Rafe's arms supporting her. He pulled her close to him, cradling her, as she drifted in a haze of pleasure, too stunned to speak. He wrapped her dressing gown around her and picked her up, carrying her upstairs. Kyria cuddled closer to him, letting out a little sigh of pleasure.

Rafe carried Kyria into her room and set her down on the bed, pulling the covers over her. Kyria smiled up at him, her face so soft and glowing that all he wanted to do was climb into bed and make love to her all over again, finding his own shattering release. Instead, he dropped a kiss on her bare shoulder, then tucked the covers in around her.

"Rafe . . ."

"Shh."

"But I . . . you . . ." A faint frown marred her forehead.

He smiled and bent down to her, burying his face in her hair. "Don't worry. It was my pleasure," he murmured, then straightened and left the room.

* * *

When Kyria drifted awake the next morning, she snuggled deeper into her bed, clinging to the sweet contentment that permeated her body. Her eyes flew open as she remembered the reason for her happiness, and a blush heated her cheeks.

For a moment, she tried to convince herself that it had been a dream — a very sensual, highly charged dream, to be sure — but a quick peek beneath her covers assured her that it had been no dream. She was stark naked. Her night rail was wadded up in a ball on top of the covers, and beside it lay her dressing gown.

Rafe had put her to bed. Rafe had . . .

She covered her face with her hands and sank back against the sheets. How was she ever to face him again? She simply could not, she thought. She would have to send him a note and ask him to leave and . . . But even as she thought it, she knew that she would not. However embarrassed she might be, the last thing she wanted was to separate herself from Rafe. Truth be known, what she wanted was for the same thing to happen again — and more — and soon.

A small, secretive smile curved her lips as she lay thinking about her experience the night before. After a moment, she sat up and swung her feet off the bed. She stretched luxuriously. Never before had she been so aware of her body; never before had she felt so fully, wondrously alive.

Kyria hummed as she pulled her nightgown on over her head and padded over to the bellpull to ring for her maid. She had no idea what was going to happen now, but she'd never been one to shrink from the unknown. Whatever was to come, she was eager to discover it.

Seeing Rafe again turned out to be easier than she had thought, aided by the lively presence of the twins. They were all three in the breakfast room when she entered, arguing animatedly over, as best as Kyria could tell, whether a diamondback rattlesnake was deadlier than a cobra.

"The cobra's venom is much more toxic than a rattlesnake's," Alex was saying as Kyria entered, buttering his toast methodically as he spoke.

Con, on the other hand, laid down a slapdash swipe of butter on his piece of bread and dipped it in the pile of marmalade on his plate. "But the rattlesnake is far more aggressive, and it also produces a much larger amount of venom. Hello, Kyria." He saluted her with his piece of toast before folding it in two and cramming it into his mouth.

"Hello, Con. Alex." Her gaze went to Rafe, her heart suddenly skittering in her chest. "Rafe."

He stood up politely, his mouth curving up in a slow, sensuous smile that made Kyria blush and go a little weak in the knees. "Good morning, Kyria." His blue eyes were knowing and warm, and Kyria found that his gaze made her feel not so much embarrassed as eager to be alone with him again.

He looked away from her to the boys and reached down to give each of them a poke in the arm. "What are you doing sitting there? A gentleman stands whenever a lady enters the room."

"Oh, right."

"Sorry."

The boys jumped up, and Rafe came around to pull out Kyria's chair. His hand grazed her shoulder in a subtle caress as she sat, then he moved away, saying in a matter-of-fact voice, "Anyway, what does it matter, boys? Dead is dead."

"Exactly!" Con cried gleefully. "You can't kill a man twice. So the rattlesnake is just as deadly, and if it's more likely to attack than to run, then *it* is more dangerous."

"But it still is not as poisonous," Alex protested. "Therefore it is less deadly."

Kyria glanced at the footmen beside the buffet. Denby, accustomed to the twins' conversation, merely looked tired. The other man, a newer addition to the household, looked a trifle green.

"Con. Alex. I scarcely think that this is appropriate conversation for the breakfast table. You aren't in the schoolroom, you know."

"Ah, Kyria. There's nobody here but us!" Con argued.

"*I* am here," Kyria said. "Am I nobody?"

"But you aren't going to get all girly about snakes," Alex insisted.

"Still, I think it would be better if you confined your herpetological discussions to a time and place other than where people are eating. It will make you much more pleasant dining companions."

The boys grimaced, but subsided, contenting themselves with shoveling an amazing amount of food into their respective mouths.

"What's on our schedule today?" Rafe asked.

His tone was so ordinary that Kyria found she could answer without even a blush — although she did have a little trouble meeting his eyes. "I am hoping that Lord Walford will contact Mr. Ashcombe today so that we will be able to talk to him. And —"

She was interrupted by the sound of voices outside, and a moment later, the butler appeared in the doorway of the breakfast room, his face etched with disapproval. "Mr. Quick is here, my lady, and insists on speaking to you. I informed him that this was an inappropriate time to call, but he —"

"Show him in," Kyria said quickly, cutting off the rest of the butler's speech.

Tom, who had obviously followed Phipps down the hall and was hanging about just outside the door, stuck his head in and grinned. "My lady."

"Come in, Tom. I trust you will join us for breakfast."

"That sounds just the thing, ma'am." He gave them an all-encompassing grin and set to filling up his plate from the sideboard.

"What happened? What did you find out?" Con asked.

"Let the man have a chance to eat," Kyria admonished her brother, although she was as eager to know as he was. She could not help but think that his arrival this early meant that he had found out something about Mr. Habib.

Fortunately, Tom was quick to demolish his plate of eggs and kidneys. Then, taking a healthy swig of coffee, he patted his lips and turned to the rest of them and began his story.

"Well," he said, "at first I was thinking that I wasn't going to get anything done. Habib stayed in that inn the whole rest of the day. A couple of men went in to see him. I couldn't get close enough to hear what was said, but they was dark like him and wearing those robes that look like they're running around in their night rails with a big sash around their middles, and they had turbans on their heads, but not those fancy ones you see sometimes. More plain like. And they kept bowing to Habib, so to my way of thinking, they're probably working for him."

"No doubt."

"I thought about following them when they left, but I thought I better stick with him. He ate supper there and all, and I was beginning to think that I'd wasted my time, when finally, around midnight, he comes strolling out the front door. He took a cab, and I was afraid I might lose him, but luckily I managed to catch one, too. He led us into Cheapside and —"

"Cheapside!" Rafe exclaimed, and shot a look at Kyria. The Blue Bull tavern was in Cheapside.

"Right. I thought maybe he was going to that tavern you talked about. But he got off at some other place. It looked more like a warehouse, but it didn't have a sign. A real plain sort of place, and I was puzzled what he was doing there. I was hoping maybe he'd come to meet somebody, so I got up close to the building and sneaked open the door a bit — and then this fellow opens the door and lets me in. It's another one of them Eastern fellows, with the turban and robe and all. I looked around, and I'll tell you, I've never seen anything like it in me life. At first I couldn't figure out what it was, all full of smoke and people lounging around on cushions and these mats and rugs. Strangest of all, they were smoking these funny pipes. Then I figured it out — your friend Habib had gone to an opium den." He stopped and looked at them triumphantly.

There was a long silence. Whatever they had thought he might find out, it had not been this. Kyria glanced at Rafe, and he shrugged. She looked back at Tom.

Not surprisingly, it was Con who spoke first. "An opium den! What did it look like? What were they doing? Did you smoke some?"

"No!" Tom looked somewhat affronted. "And you shouldn't be talking about such things."

"Mother says that knowledge is power," Alex informed him gravely.

"I am not entirely sure that she would want you to have this much power," Kyria responded dryly.

"Do you think he went there because he's an opium addict?" Rafe asked. "Or was he meeting someone?"

"I don't know." Tom looked chagrined. "I lost him. When I first went in, I was a little taken aback, you see, and for a minute I just stood there gawking. Then there was this fellow trying to lead me to a cushion and set me up with a pipe. So I sort of followed him, looking around all the time, and I finally caught sight of Habib at the back. So when the fellow sat me down and went off — I guess to get me something to smoke — I got up and went over to where I'd spied Habib, but by the time I got there, he was gone. There were curtains, though, leading somewhere, so I started through them, but then this other fellow came over, squawking and waving at me not to go back there. He made such a fuss I couldn't get away with doing anything after that, so I left."

He sighed. "I'm sorry. I mucked it all up something proper."

"Nonsense. You did fine. I'm sure anyone would have done the same," Kyria said. "And now we know something more about Habib."

"We just need to find out if he went there to smoke an opium pipe or to tell his partner or employer about our visit yesterday," Rafe added. "I think I'll go back there tonight. Tom?"

"Sure," Tom said quickly. "I'll be glad to take you there."

"Should we dress up as Arabs, do you think?" Kyria asked.

"Oh, there were plenty of English folks there, as well," Tom assured her, even as Rafe turned to her, his brows vaulting upward incredulously.

"Kyria, you can't be serious. You cannot possibly go."

"I cannot?" she countered, her voice turning dangerously silken. "And who, may I ask, is going to stop me?"

Rafe winced at his poor choice of words. "I didn't mean you weren't *allowed*. I meant, it wouldn't be *possible*. A woman in a place like that . . . Even if there are English people, I am sure there aren't women."

"Except for the dancing girls," Tom said.

"Dancing girls?" Now *that* had possibilities, Kyria thought. "What sort of dancing girls?"

"Well, uh —" Tom began to blush and look distinctly uncomfortable "— you know, the sort of Eastern ones, with the coins on their belts and the bells and they, you know, sort of writhe about . . ." He stumbled to a halt.

"No," Rafe said abruptly. "Kyria . . ."

"Yes?" Kyria crossed her arms and gazed back at him stubbornly.

"It takes years of training," he told her flatly. "And you would have to dye your hair black and color your skin, and your eyes would still be green. There isn't a chance."

"All right," she conceded. "I won't go as a dancing girl. But I could go as a man."

"Kyria . . ." Rafe groaned.

"No. It will be perfectly all right. Before, when we went to the tavern, you were right. A stripling youth would have been terribly suspicious and out of place. But in an opium den . . . if there are Englishmen there, I am sure there must be some upper-class, poetical types who frequent the place. I can get away with that."

"Your hair."

"She can cut it," Con volunteered. "I'll help you, Kyria."

"No!" Rafe looked horrified, his gaze going to Kyria's flame-colored tresses.

"Perhaps it would be better if I did dress up as an Arab," Kyria mused. "I could wear one of those long, headdress things — what do you call it?"

"A *kaffiyeh?*" Alex offered.

"Exactly. With that and a floor-length robe, nothing would show but my hands and face, and I could dye them somehow. Alex, what was it you were telling me about dying your skin using nut oil?"

"Oh, sure —" her brother began eagerly.

"No, wait." Rafe held up a hand. "Please. No trying to pass for someone whose language you cannot even speak."

"I suppose," Kyria said, giving up the idea with a sigh. "I shall just have to be a young English gentleman — one frightfully steeped in wickedness despite my youth. I'll put my hair up under a hat. I am sure I can find some old suit of Reed's or Theo's when they were young that will fit me well enough."

"We'll help you," Alex volunteered, jumping off his chair.

"Sure," Con agreed, adding, "It would really be keen if we could go along."

"I am certain there are no children in

opium dens," Rafe put in firmly.

"Oh, all right," Con agreed, clearly not expecting to win the argument.

They made arrangements to meet Tom that evening, and Kyria and the twins went up to the attic to see what they could find to make a suitable costume.

When they had gone, Rafe rested his head on his hands with a groan. "She will be the death of me."

Tom reached over and patted his arm sympathetically. "Don't worry, guv'nor. You can't keep 'em from doing what they want. None of the Morelands, even the women. No, I should say, especially the women. Lady Olivia, who is as sweet as they come, does just exactly as she pleases. You can't change 'em."

"No, I realize that. I don't even want to. Her spirit is one of the things I admire most about her. It's just . . . damn, it gets harder every time she exposes herself to danger."

"You're doing fine," Tom told him with a grin. "Most gentlemen couldn't have lasted a week in Lady Kyria's company."

"It's a good thing I'm not a gentleman, then, isn't it?" Rafe replied.

Later that morning, after Kyria and the

twins had emerged triumphantly from the attic with a set of clothes that they hailed as "just the thing," she was surprised to have the butler announce the arrival of Lord Walford.

Hastily, she brushed the last traces of dust from the attic off her dress and gave a quick glance in the mirror to make sure her hair was in order, then went downstairs to the small, blue drawing room. Walford was already seated in one of the chairs, and he stood up with a smile when Kyria entered the room.

"Lady Kyria, I hope you will forgive this intrusion," he said, taking the hand she extended and, in a courtly gesture, elegantly bowing to press his lips to it. "I realize it is a trifle early for making calls, but I trust you will be pleased at what I have come to tell you. I spoke with Nelson Ashcombe a few minutes ago, and he will be happy to receive you this afternoon at three o'clock. I hope that will fit in with your schedule."

"Yes, of course. Thank you so much for arranging it," Kyria told him, smiling. "It was very kind of you to speak to him so quickly."

"I could scarcely let pass an opportunity to do a favor for such a beautiful woman as yourself," he responded, and returned her smile.

"I am in your debt."

"Then I must think of some way you can repay me. Perhaps one evening you would honor me by allowing me to escort you to the theater. I understand there is a charming comedy . . . ."

"Oh . . ." Kyria hesitated, surprised and feeling unaccustomedly awkward. She was used to receiving invitations from men, and she imagined that at some prior time she would have accepted his escort without even thinking. He was a handsome man and quite eligible, and she suspected that, given his extensive travels, he would make an entertaining companion.

But now, everything was different. Now, there was Rafe. And she knew that she had no interest in even flirting with another man.

"I am sorry," he said quickly. "I have presumed too much."

"Oh, no. I am just, well, that is, there is . . . actually, it is not a good time for me. My younger brothers are here with me, and I, ah, have some business to take care of. So I am not really accepting many social engagements."

She could feel a blush rising in her cheeks, and it irritated her. It was rare that she was so socially inept.

"Of course," Walford replied smoothly.

"I perfectly understand."

Kyria felt sure that he did not, as she had not explained herself well, but she was grateful to him for the pretense.

"Perhaps . . ." he began, then hesitated.

"Yes?" Kyria asked encouragingly.

"I was thinking that if you wanted, I would be happy to escort you to Mr. Ashcombe's this afternoon. He can sometimes be a trifle . . . well, intimidating."

Before Kyria could speak, a voice from the door drawled, "That's all right, sir. I've found that Lady Kyria can usually stand up for herself."

Both Walford and Kyria turned, startled, to see Rafe lounging in the doorway, his shoulder against the doorjamb.

"If he does scare her," Rafe continued, his mouth curved into a smile more wolfish than friendly, his eyes devoid of their usual sparkle, "I think that I can take care of her."

"Ah. I see." There was a wealth of comprehension in Walford's words. "I did not realize that Lady Kyria already had an escort."

"Lord Walford," Kyria said quickly, "allow me to present Mr. McIntyre."

"Yes, of course," Walford said politely, stepping forward to shake Rafe's hand.

"My cousin was so pleased to have you attend her rout. She could speak of little else. Welcome to England. I hope you are enjoying your stay."

"Yes, very much."

Walford did not linger after that and soon took his leave.

Kyria turned to Rafe with a grimace. "What possessed you to be so rude? Lord Walford has gotten Mr. Ashcombe to meet with us, which was quite nice of him."

"I don't like the fellow," Rafe replied shortly.

Kyria let out a small noise of irritation. "I can't imagine why. He has been nothing but polite. He had no obligation to pressure Mr. Ashcombe into seeing us."

"Little wonder why he did it," Rafe retorted.

Kyria quirked an eyebrow. "Exactly what are you implying?"

"The man's interested in you," he shot back, frowning. "Not, of course, that every other man I meet isn't also apparently attracted to you. I had to elbow my way through the crowd to get close to you last night."

He's jealous! Kyria was accustomed to seeing jealousy in men, but she had not before encountered it with Rafe. In general, she found men's jealousy rather tiresome, but here and now, with Rafe, she could not help but feel a little spurt of happiness. It was, she thought, rather cute, and she had to bring her hand up to her mouth to cover her smile.

He caught himself and grimaced. "Oh, the hell with it."

Rafe started to turn and leave, but at that moment, the butler appeared, looking deeply unhappy. He paused in the doorway and intoned, "You have another visitor, my lady."

It was clear what Phipps thought of the number of callers arriving at inappropriately early times.

Kyria looked at him blankly, surprised. "Who?"

"A Mr. Brulatour," the butler sniffed, "a French gentleman."

"French?" Kyria glanced at Rafe, who raised his shoulders in an eloquent shrug. "All right, Phipps. Show Mr. Brulatour in."

The butler retreated and a few moments later showed an impeccably dressed man into the room. Of average height, he had dark hair with a bit of a wave in it, oiled into submission. He had a prominent nose, with small dark eyes above and a thin-lipped mouth below, separated by a narrow black mustache.

"My lady." He bowed extravagantly. "Monsieur Alain Brulatour, at your service. Eet ees a pleasure to meet you. I 'ad 'eard you were beautiful, but words cannot begin to do you justice."

"How do you do, Monsieur Brulatour?" Kyria answered carefully. In her peripheral vision, she could see Rafe rolling his eyes, and she had to press her lips firmly together before she was able to continue. "May I ask what brings you to our house today?"

"I 'ave come, my lady, to relieve you of a great burden."

"Indeed?"

"Yes." He beamed broadly at her, revealing a row of rather crooked teeth, and finished, "I 'ave come to purchase ze reliquary box."

15

It was all Kyria could do not to groan. Finally, she said dryly, "How very kind of you."

"You jest, yes, I see," the Frenchman said in a jolly tone. " 'Owever, you will see. Eet ees true. Zere is a curse on 'ooever possesses ze box."

"A curse." A smile tugged at the corners of Rafe's mouth. "That's awful convenient, don't you think?"

"You may mock," Brulatour continued without rancor, "but eet ees true. Ze box ees cursed; 'ooever takes eet from eets 'ome ees cursed."

"I did not take it," Kyria pointed out reasonably.

"Ah, but you received eet. Eet ees ze same. As regards ze curse . . ." He paused, then said significantly, "You saw what 'appened to ze man 'oo brought eet to you, no?"

"Is that a threat?" Rafe asked, straightening.

"Oh, no, *mais non!*" Brulatour exclaimed, waving his hands in an exculpatory gesture.

"Ees no threat. Ees merely ze truth. 'E died, and before eem ze man 'oo sold eet to 'eem died." He shook his head, clucking disparagingly. "And so on, back to ze one 'oo stole eet. Ze box ees cursed."

"Then why precisely are you willing to run the risk of owning it?" Kyria asked.

"Ah, well you might ask!" Brulatour spoke with great cheer. "Eet ees because I 'ave promised to restore eet to ze church, where eet belongs."

He was, he was happy to explain, a most religious man, one who realized that all of the many blessings he had received during his career as owner of a munitions factory were, in point of fact, due to his deep religious convictions. Upon purchasing the reliquary, he would, he explained, install it with great pomp and ceremony in the Cathedral of Nantes.

So carried away was he with his vision for the reliquary that he appeared not even to notice that Kyria had not yet agreed to sell it to him. Finally, Rafe had to take him by the elbow and haul him out of his seat, saying, "Mister, the lady isn't interested in selling the box, so I think it's time for you to go."

Brulatour, however, was undeterred. "My card, my lady," he told her, whipping out a gold card case and extracting a calling card. "I 'ave written on eet zee 'otel where I am staying. Eef you change your mind . . ."

"I will let you know," Kyria assured him, and Rafe hustled the man out the door, turning him over to the butler in the hallway.

Rafe came back into the drawing room and sat on the sofa Monsieur Brulatour had just vacated. "How many of these fellows are there?" he asked in amazement.

"I don't know. I can scarcely believe it." Kyria popped up out of her chair and began to pace the room. "How does everyone know I have it? It is as though it has been posted somewhere."

Rafe shook his head. "I don't know. They all seem to have better information that we do. I'd like to find out where that thing actually came from and why the hell this Kousoulous fellow had it."

"And what Theo has to do with it, if anything. I know he would never be involved in anything illegal. I am surprised that he was even willing to send the box out of the country, especially if he had any idea of its historical significance."

"Maybe he figured it was a way to keep it safe," Rafe reasoned. "He probably didn't count on these folks following it all the way to England."

Kyria sighed. "It's absurd. Jennings seemed to think no one believed in it. Yet here are a multitude of people chasing after it."

"Well, maybe collectors and such believe in it. He just said that scholars don't — except, of course, for Ashcombe."

"Which, I must say, makes me more eager than ever to interview him," Kyria replied.

Three hours later she got her wish, as she and Rafe were shown by the same surly maid into Nelson Ashcombe's study. As they entered, a man rose from his seat behind his desk, the expression on his face wary.

He was tall and slender, with a gaunt, ascetic face. His hair, once blond, was swept through with white now; he wore it a trifle long and brushed back from his face, giving him a faintly leonine look emphasized by the pale golden color of his eyes.

"My lady," he said politely, and shook the hand Kyria offered him, but there was a distinct coolness in his tone that told Kyria that he was none too pleased to be talking to them.

"Mr. Ashcombe. It is an honor to meet you. My father was friends with the late Lord Walford, and he spoke highly of you."

Ashcombe inclined his head rather regally and said, "His lordship was an excellent gentleman. I was sorry to see him go."

Kyria introduced Rafe, then said, "I appreciate your agreeing to see us."

Ashcombe gave a faint shrug and replied, "I am always happy to speak to friends of Lord Walford." His carefully schooled face gave no hint of his real feelings.

"The reason I want to talk to you is this." Kyria saw no sense in leading up to the subject gradually. She wanted to get Ashcombe's immediate and unprepared reaction to the reliquary.

She opened the drawstring bag and pulled out the box, setting it down on the desk in front of the archaeologist.

Ashcombe shot a perfunctory glance at the reliquary. Then his gaze sharpened, and he stared, his face paling. He reached out a tentative hand and touched the box.

"It cannot . . ." He looked up at Kyria, stunned. "Do you know what this is?"

"We were hoping you could confirm it. Dr. Jennings told us that it looked like a reliquary of legend."

"The Reliquary of the Holy Standard," Ashcombe breathed. "I can scarcely believe . . ."

His golden eyes glittered, and he picked up the box, peering closely at the black diamond. "Have you opened it?"

"We could not at first, but one of my brothers figured out the trick of it." The archaeologist's eyes were so much that of a starving man facing a banquet that Kyria could not help but take the wires out of her reticule and use them as Con had shown her. There was a click, and she was able to open the lid, showing Ashcombe the faded cloth inside.

"My God." He stared at the reliquary for a long moment, and Kyria thought she saw the glint of tears in his eyes. "I didn't think . . . I had given up." He looked up at Kyria again. "Thank you, my lady."

Kyria closed the box and put it back into the bag, holding it securely in her lap. "We were hoping you could tell us a little more about the reliquary."

"I was unable to find it. I . . ." He stopped and collected himself, then continued in a more professorial manner, "I presume that Jennings told you the story of the banner and the reliquary."

Kyria nodded. "Yes, although we had not at that time discovered the latch to the box, so all he saw was the outside."

"It is enough. The Heart of Night — the black, uncut diamond on the front — is ample evidence that it is the Reliquary of the Holy Standard." He looked at Kyria intently. "Where did you get it?"

"That is the problem. It was brought to us, and we really don't know where it was found or how it came to be in my brother's hands. The man who delivered it to us, um, died without telling us anything about it. That is why we came to you. We were hoping that you could tell us where it came from and how . . ."

Ashcombe shook his head reluctantly. "I wish I could. I excavated in three different places, each of which I thought might be the site. You see, through my research, I came to believe that the reliquary was not a legend, but had actually existed. I came across a manuscript written by an Italian monk in the fourteenth century, which described the flight of the holy men entrusted with the reliquary into the barren mountains of eastern Turkey. Through my contacts in the area, I learned that the three sites, high in the eastern cliffs, were possibilities. It is a desolate area, difficult to make one's way through, a perfect place to hide." He sighed. "However, they came to nothing. Either my information was wrong, or I was simply unable to find the right spot. There are other accounts, not entirely reliable, that the monks might have fled even into the southern part of what we now call Russia."

"Russia?" Kyria glanced at Rafe and saw mirrored there the same interest that had been piqued in her. "Really?"

Ashcombe nodded. "It is certainly a possibility. Russia, after all, followed the Eastern Orthodox religion, the same one that was centered originally in Byzantium, and it lies close to Turkey. It would not be at all unlikely for the holy brothers to seek refuge among them, especially after the invasion of the Ottoman Turks and their conversion of the entire area to Islam. However, I have never found any reliable evidence that says so."

"You called the diamond by a name," Rafe said.

"Yes. The Heart of Night. It is also known as the Star of the Underworld. It is far older than the reliquary, you see, a sacred stone taken from an ancient temple. At some point, hundreds and hundreds of years later, it fell into Christian hands, and they, recognizing the mystic qualities of the stone, attached it to a religious artifact of their own."

They were all silent for a moment. Then Kyria asked, "Have you heard any rumors of the reliquary surfacing? In Turkey, perhaps?"

Ashcombe shook his head. "No. I have been in England for the past year. It is different when I am on a dig. Then I would hear all the rumors of the area. But here . . . no, I have heard nothing." He paused. "So you know nothing of its history or how it came to be in your possession?"

"Beyond the fact that it was brought to us by a man who was murdered almost on our very doorstep. His name was Kousoulous. Have you heard of him?"

Ashcombe frowned. "An antiquities dealer?"

"Yes. In Istanbul."

"I may have. I am not sure. I do not really buy or sell artifacts. My interest lies in excavating them."

"We have been told that it was stolen — but everyone seems rather vague on exactly how or from where."

The archaeologist shrugged. "Typical. I know of no excavation that has turned up the reliquary. But it is possible that someone stumbled upon the remains of the refuge where the holy brothers took the reliquary. This person who happened on it could have simply taken whatever artifacts he found and sold them to a dealer — or, more likely, to some middleman, who then sold them to a dealer. It could even have wound up in an Istanbul bazaar without anyone involved even knowing exactly what they had on their hands. Most people would not. At best they might recognize it as a Byzantine reliquary."

"So someone could have seen it there, recognized it and bought it," Kyria mused.

"Or he could have bought it, not knowing what it was, just thinking that it was a lovely work of art and that you would like the stone, Kyria, and so he sent it to you," Rafe said.

"Who?" Ashcombe asked, looking puzzled. "Who are you talking about?"

"Whoever sent the box to Lady Kyria," Rafe replied. "We never learned who sent it or why."

Ashcombe nodded. "It could have happened that way, yes."

"But there were others who did know what it was, who saw it at some point in all this, and they pursued the man who carried it," Kyria theorized. She looked at Ashcombe. "Do you know a French collector by the name of Brulatour? Or a Russian, Prince Dmitri Rostokov?"

Ashcombe thought for a moment, then

shook his head. "No, I am afraid not. As I told you, I have few dealings with collectors and such. They are collectors, I assume?"

Rafe nodded. "Tell me, Mr. Ashcombe, in your opinion, how valuable is this reliquary?"

"Valuable?" Ashcombe turned his pale eyes to Rafe. "Why, it is priceless. How could one put a price on such a piece of history? I imagine that there are those who would pay almost anything to possess it."

"Would they murder for it?" Rafe asked.

Ashcombe shrugged, seemingly unsurprised by Rafe's question. "My dear sir, there are men who will murder for a few shillings, let alone something like this. You are talking about a finding of vast significance to collectors, museums, churches, nations." He gave Kyria a stern look. "You had best take care of it, young woman."

"I will, sir. I promise you."

Rafe was quiet on the way home, his thoughts obviously elsewhere. After they had returned the wrapped reliquary to its hiding place in the safe, he said, "I've been thinking . . . perhaps we ought to put that thing someplace safer."

Kyria looked at him. "What do you mean?"

"I mean, there seem to be a lot of people in this town who know or suspect we have the box with us. I have a few of the footmen up keeping watch at night, and I've tried to keep an eye on it. But someone could break in here, despite that."

"They would have to get into the safe," Kyria pointed out.

"Yes," Rafe agreed, adding, "And do you think that if it came down to it, with a man holding a gun to Con's or Alex's head, that you wouldn't give them the combination?"

Kyria sighed. "Yes. If I could not get out of it, I would. But where do you suggest we put it?"

"A bank?"

"Still, if someone put a gun to Con's or Alex's head, I would go to the bank to retrieve it."

"It would give us more time and complications to use against the thief, though."

"Yes, no doubt you are right." Kyria realized that she hated to let the box go, even if it was only to the bank. "We should get the twins back to Broughton Park. Perhaps Denby would be able to take them." She brightened. "Or Reed. Reed must return soon, and then perhaps he will be able to return to the Park with Con and Alex."

Rafe nodded.

"Even better," Kyria went on, a gleam in

her eye, "maybe tonight at the opium den, we will find the man we are looking for and put a stop to what he's doing."

Rafe grinned. "Darlin', I like the way you think."

They left the house a little before midnight. Kyria had dressed as she planned in old clothes Theo had worn when he was not quite sixteen and had not yet grown to his full height. The trousers were a gray tweed, cut a little full and thereby concealing the very feminine swell of her hips. The combination of shirt, waistcoat and jacket effectively hid her breasts, but Kyria decided to wrap binding around her breasts to flatten them out, just to make sure. Her hair was the hardest part, for it was not only long and thick, but also curly, so that it was a great mass to stuff beneath a hat. Moreover, she was afraid that it would look odd for a man to wear his hat all the time he was indoors, and if she removed the hat, her piled-up hair would be revealed.

However, Joan, with her usual skill, was able to braid most of Kyria's hair into a single, thick braid, which she then wound flat against her head and pinned securely, covering it with shorter hair around

Kyria's face. It was not the most attractive style, but it would pass a cursory look if Kyria had to remove her bowler hat. She smoothed all of it over with pomade, which had the added benefit of darkening the distinctive red of Kyria's hair.

"What do you think?" Kyria asked Rafe when she descended the stairs to join him in the foyer. She turned around and plopped the hat on her head. "Will I pass for a boy?"

Rafe's eyes darkened in a way that made Kyria's abdomen tighten. He took a step closer to her, and his voice dropped. "Do you think I would get arrested for kissing a boy?"

Kyria smiled, heat snaking through her, as she looked up into his eyes. "I don't know. Why don't you try it?"

His hands went to her waist, and he lowered his head toward hers. She stretched up toward him invitingly.

The doorknocker thudded loudly just then, and the two of them sprang apart. Rafe grimaced and opened the door, waving off the footman who was hurrying into the foyer. Tom Quick stood on the doorstep.

Quick grinned. "I can see you haven't got the hang of being a gentleman yet.

Don't you know you aren't supposed to open a door?"

Rafe shrugged. "Bad habit. You know how Americans are."

Quick looked on past Rafe to Kyria, and his brows shot up as he let out a surprised whistle. "Well, look at you! I wouldn't have known you, and that's a fact."

"But would you think I am a man?"

"One of them tiresome artistic types, maybe," Tom allowed.

"I think a mustache would help," Kyria mused. "I wish I had one of those stage mustaches. Do you suppose if we went by a theater . . . ?"

"No time," Rafe said, taking her by the elbow. "Besides, it would just make you more noticeable. What we want, if you'll remember, is for you to blend in."

He reached up and settled her hat at a better angle on her head. "Try to keep your face in shadow."

They took the carriage, and as they drove through the dark streets of London, Tom told them about his further investigations. "I found out a few things today after I talked to you. I checked with some of me former acquaintances . . ."

"Of the criminal variety?" Kyria asked.

Tom shrugged. "Some are still in the

trade. Others are just, well, folks that would know about such things," he replied vaguely. "Nobody seemed to know much about this particular shop. Only one or two even knew about opium dens at all. Gin's cheaper and easier for them that ain't got money."

"Who goes to such places, then?" Kyria asked.

"Well, with the Englishmen and Americans and such, it's mostly either sailors who picked up the habit on their travels, or it's ones here who got some money and like to try something new and thrilling. Daring types. Some artists and writers and such who think it makes 'em creative, like."

"I see."

"What puzzled me, though, was the way it looked. I'd heard about opium dens, and, well, it was different from what I'd heard. Turns out there's two types. More common is the Chinese shop."

"The opium comes from China?" Rafe asked.

"No," Kyria said. "China actually imports it from India. That's what the Opium Wars were all about. It was scandalous, really. China was trying to shut down its importing of opium because of the damage to its citizens, and it was the British who wanted to keep them from doing so because it damaged our trade!"

Tom nodded. "Seems the opium comes in from India and Turkey and places. The way the Chinese folks smoke it is they take the opium and put it into this pipe that looks pretty much like a regular pipe, except with a really long stem, like. They smoke it straight and it's stronger. That's the sort of opium den where the Chinese and most others go. But there's another kind, the Turkish kind, and that's the sort I saw last night. There, it seems, they mix it with tobacco and smoke it in their water pipes."

"What are those?" Kyria asked.

"These sort of jugs that they put water in, and then there's this long tube that comes out of it, with a mouthpiece on the end, and that's what you smoke from. *Hookahs,* they call them, too. It's the way they smoke tobacco and other drugs. It's not as strong because they mix the opium with tobacco, see? And most who favor those dens are Arabs and Turks and such."

"Lebanese, like our friend Mr. Habib," Rafe added.

"So . . . another connection to Istanbul," Kyria mused.

"Yeah — or just the place Habib would

naturally go to if he's an addict."

When they reached the warehouse where the opium den was located, they had the coachman drive past it and stop a block away before they disembarked. The carriage lumbered off down a side street to wait for them, and the three of them walked back to the nondescript warehouse.

Tom pushed open the door, nodding to the man who stepped forward to greet them. Kyria kept behind Rafe in an attempt to show as little of her face as possible, but she glanced all around her interestedly. The term opium den conjured up in her mind a vision of sinful, exotic surroundings. She had envisioned dark red velvet sofas and low, flickering lights, gauzy curtains and enormous plush cushions on Persian-carpeted floors.

The reality was disappointingly stark. The floor was bare, old wood, scarred and pitted, and there was no red velvet or exotic lights anywhere in evidence. Ordinary kerosene lamps lighted the room rather dimly, and the drab walls were unadorned by any sort of hangings, gauzy or otherwise. Cushions and mats were scattered around the room, most of them occupied, and among the seating arrangements were low tables on which sat water pipes of various shapes and sizes. Men lay and sat beside these tables, puffing at the pipes and paying little attention to anything. In an area off to one side, one of the girls Tom had mentioned danced for a group of men, and Kyria's eyes widened a little at her skimpy attire of filmy trousers hung low on her hips and a short blouse that left her entire stomach area exposed. As she danced, bells tinkled at her wrists and ankles and waist.

The man who had greeted them went on to offer them all the pleasures of the place, but Rafe shook his head, saying, "I just want to look around a bit first. Visiting, you see. I'm from the States. I've never seen one of these places before."

"Very good, very good," the man said, smiling and bobbing his head. "You look. Anything you want."

Rafe, Kyria and Tom strolled through the room, the doorman trailing alongside them, still smiling and dipping his head obsequiously until finally Rafe stopped him with a sharp word. They looked carefully all around them as they walked. The customers were largely Middle Eastern in appearance, many of them clad in traditional robes and turbans, or *kaffiyehs,* some of them in Western suits. But there were a number of Englishmen, as well, and Kyria realized with a start of recognition that a man standing near a beaded-glass curtain at the rear of the room was the third son of Lord Herringford.

There was, disappointingly, no sign of Habib or either of the collectors who had shown interest in the box.

Kyria looked back at Lord Herringford's son and saw him nod to the man with whom he had been chatting and slip through the curtain of beads. Kyria poked Rafe in the back.

"Look," she hissed in his ear. "Someone went back there."

Rafe nodded and wound his way casually through the room until he was near the beaded curtain.

"Don't look back," he whispered to the others. "Be natural."

Kyria, concentrating on keeping her stride long and manly while at the same time unobtrusively scanning the room, decided it was hard enough just to keep from craning her neck behind her to see whether the doorman was watching them without having to think about what looked natural.

They paused in front of the beaded curtain, and as Rafe turned to Kyria, Tom slipped through the curtain into the back.

Kyria realized then that she and Rafe blocked the smaller man from the view of the rest of the room.

"Go on and stroll a little ways over there," Rafe murmured. "Then come back to meet me."

Kyria did as he told her, walking away from him and pretending interest in something on the low table in front of her. A man lay on a mat beside it, asleep, the long tube and mouthpiece of the water pipe dangling beside him. She turned and walked back. Rafe had walked farther away, and she sauntered over to join him.

She wondered what they were doing and why they had not joined Tom, but she kept her mouth shut, knowing that it would be disastrous for anyone to hear her voice. Rafe walked back through the room, moving without seeming haste. The doorman was watching them, and a frown appeared on his face. He glanced around, then looked back at Kyria and Rafe.

When they drew near, Rafe would have passed him, but the man planted himself directly in their path, saying, "Where is other?"

"What? Other what?" Rafe replied, looking puzzled.

"Other man. Other man."

"Oh, that chap. He stopped to visit someone he knew," Rafe said, gesturing vaguely behind them. "Very interesting place you have here."

He started around the man to the door.

"You like? You buy?" the doorman said, distracted from the matter of Tom's presence by Rafe's leaving. "Do not go. I give you good price, good price. First time offer," he said, grinning, in the tone of something learned by rote.

Rafe smiled pleasantly, waving him off as he walked away, Kyria in his wake. "It's not what I expected, you see. Not the sort of place I was told about. I think it must be a Chinese place we want."

"No. Chinese not the best way. Best opium in the world comes from Turkey!" the man said, opening his arms grandly. "Turkish way of smoking is the best way. You see. I show you. Give you first pipe free."

The man pursued them out into the street, earnestly selling the admirable points of his method of opium intake, but Rafe merely shook his head good-naturedly and walked on. After trailing them halfway down the block, the doorman finally gave up and trudged back to the warehouse, grumbling under his breath.

"What are we doing?" Kyria whispered, once the doorman was gone.

Rafe glanced back to make sure that the man was out of sight, then picked up his pace. "We're looking for an alleyway beside this building. Tom told me there was one. He's going to try to find a back door and open it for us, and we are going to inspect the back rooms of this place. I figured we might be able to hide Tom's slipping in, but if all three of us went back there, they'd be bound to come charging after us. This way, with any luck, we'll get in the back way and they'll not know it."

They came upon the alleyway and stopped, peering down it doubtfully. It was narrow, barely wide enough for two people to walk abreast, and enveloped in stygian darkness. They started down the alley cautiously.

As they walked, their eyes grew more accustomed to the dark, and they realized that there were a few dimly lit windows opening into the alley, though all were covered with curtains. A door opened not far ahead of them, a rectangle of light revealing Tom Quick, who was looking up and down the alley. They hurried to join him inside and shut the door behind them.

"There're a bunch of little rooms back here," Tom told them, speaking in a whisper. "I've looked into most of 'em. They're either empty or just have some bloke or two in 'em smoking away."

"Private rooms for their more important customers," Rafe said. "It makes sense. Any offices?"

"No." Tom nodded his head toward a plain staircase behind them. "But I haven't been upstairs yet."

"Let's try it. We might get lucky and find Habib," Rafe said, starting toward the stairs.

"Or whoever he was meeting." Kyria followed Rafe up the stairs, adding, "If, of course, he was meeting someone."

"And if we would recognize that person if we saw him," Rafe stuck in.

Kyria sighed. It didn't seem likely that they were going to meet with any success. Still, they had to try; it was the only lead they had.

At the top of the stairs, they found a hallway lined with doors on either side, all closed. They moved along the corridor, opening the doors as they went and peering inside. The first two rooms Kyria tried were empty, though obviously set up for a customer, with a narrow cot and a low table containing a water pipe.

In the third room, Kyria found a man

seated on the bed, leaning back against the wall, shoes off and collar opened, puffing on the pipe. It was Lord Herringford's son, whom she had seen earlier downstairs. He looked at her with a sort of languid disdain.

"Here, what are you doing barging in like that?" he asked, his tongue tripping a little over his words.

Kyria just smiled and shook her head, backing out the door. His eyes narrowed and he leaned forward a little. "I say, do I know you?"

"No," Kyria answered in as low and gruff a voice as she could manage.

Tom popped his head in beside her, saying cheerfully, "Sorry, mate," and they closed the door.

"Someone you know?" Rafe murmured.

"Not well," Kyria whispered back. "It's nothing significant, just a little surprising. His father is rather important in the government."

They turned down another hall, which ended in a set of stairs. They opened the first door, which seemed to be a storeroom of some sort, with stacks of black material on shelves, along with more pipes and several boxes. Rafe started toward the boxes.

At that moment, a large man coming out

of one of the rooms farther down the hall spotted Kyria and Tom standing at the storeroom door, and his brows rushed together.

" 'Ere!" he called, starting toward them purposefully. "Wot the devil are you doing? Nobody's allowed back 'ere without one of us!"

"Don't get yourself all in a pucker," Tom said cheerfully, starting toward him as Rafe quickly stepped back out of the room. "We're lookin' for a room, like."

"The devil you say! You're up 'ere lookin' for sommat to steal!" He reached out for Tom, who jumped back away from his grasp.

Faster than any of them could see, Rafe's gun was in his hand and pointed at the man. The man stopped, his eyes on the pistol.

"Let's go," Rafe said quietly, jerking his head back in the direction they had come. Kyria and Tom turned and walked down the hall with Rafe following them, walking backward, holding the large man at bay.

The man edged after him, but Rafe gave a warning twitch of his gun. "Stay right there. If I see your face around this corner, I'm firing. Got it?"

The other man nodded, his jaw set and his eyes blazing with fury. Rafe hurried behind Kyria and Tom, half-turned so that he could see back down the length of the hall. When he got to the stairs, he faced forward and ran down the stairs after the other two.

As he reached the last step, he heard their opponent letting out a bellow, "Thieves! 'Elp! Thieves!"

Tom and Kyria were waiting at the bottom of the stairs for Rafe, and as he appeared, Tom flung open the door. The last thing they saw before they slammed the door shut behind them was a door opening at the other end of the hall and a turbaned man charging out.

The darkness in the narrow alleyway slowed them down, but when they reached the street, they broke into a run. Unfortunately, to reach their carriage, they had to pass by the front door of the den, and before they could reach it, several men, including the large man who had stopped them in the hall, came storming out.

The sight of Rafe's gun pointed at them made them check. They started to walk around the group of men, but suddenly a rock came whistling through the air behind them and slammed into Rafe's shoulder, sending the gun flying from his hand. The gun went off as it hit the pavement, knocking a chunk of brick out of the building.

The men charged at them. Rafe threw himself in front of Kyria, shouting, "Run!"

"And leave you?" Kyria said with scorn, crouching down to pull the derringer from her boot.

She came up firing just as a man leaped at her, and he fell back with a shriek, clutching his shoulder. Rafe knocked one man out with a quick uppercut to the jaw, but another smaller man rushed in from behind swinging a knife and slashed out. Rafe spun quickly to the side to avoid the blade, but it managed to slice through his jacket sleeve, cutting his arm. He closed in quickly and grappled with the man, his hands clenched around the smaller man's wrist.

Tom, meanwhile, was slugging it out with the man who had discovered them in the hallway. The other man was larger by far, but Tom was light on his feet and could dodge in and out, escaping the man's swinging blows and landing a few punches of his own. Kyria's small gun held only one bullet, and before she could dig another out of her pocket and reload, another man was on her. All she could do was swing her arm as hard as she could into the side of her assailant's head, the small gun still resting in the palm of her hand.

But then the group of men who had

emerged from the door behind them were also upon them, and they were hopelessly outnumbered. A blow from behind knocked Kyria to the ground, sending her hat rolling and her hair tumbling free. Out of the corner of her eye, she saw Tom get knocked to the ground. Rafe gripped her wrist with one steely hand, yanked her to her feet and shoved her behind him, then lashed out at her assailant with the knife he had taken from its owner.

He swung wide, keeping their enemies at bay. Kyria fumbled a bullet from her pocket and into her gun. She raised it, and for a moment they were able to hold off their attackers, standing back to back, weapons at ready. But it was clear that their advantage would not last long; they were greatly outnumbered, at least six or seven men to their three, and there were more spilling out the front door. Tom, struggling to his feet, was blasted again by a blow from the large man's fist, and he collapsed.

Kyria screamed at the top of her lungs to their coachman, hoping the sound would carry to him, and waved her gun back and forth, threatening the men edging closer to them. In a moment, she knew, their enemies would rush them, and it would be all over.

16

Out of the shadows came a loud cry as several white-robed men came running out of the darkness, shouting in an unknown language. They carried stout sticks, and when they reached the startled combatants, they laid about them with their cudgels, knocking out several of the men Rafe and Kyria were fighting before their hapless victims even knew what was on them.

Rafe tucked the knife in his pocket and jumped into the fray with his fists, a weapon he was much more accustomed to using. Kyria, still holding her gun to keep the enemy at bay, skirted over to where Tom lay on the ground and reached down with her free hand to help him up. Tom grasped her hand and stood up somewhat dazedly.

They heard the clatter of horses' hooves on the bricklined street, and Kyria glanced down the block to see the Moreland carriage charging toward them. At the sight of the four-horse equipage, the combatants scrambled to get out of the way. The coachman hauled back on the reins at the last moment and the horses stopped, shaking their heads and snorting. The coachman wrapped the reins around one hand to hold the steeds and grabbed his long whip with the other.

He stood up, roaring, "Dare ye attack a Moreland?"

He brought down his whip with a mighty crack, catching three of the men from the opium den with it. It was the last straw. The enemy broke, running back into the building.

"Quick! Into the carriage. They may come back with reinforcements," Rafe said, running over to pick up his gun.

Kyria opened the door and helped Tom inside. She turned to the white-robed men who had helped them, motioning them toward the carriage. "Come. You had better get away from here, too, you know."

The men hesitated. Then one of them, apparently the leader, nodded to the others. He held out his hand in a courtly way to help Kyria up into the vehicle, then climbed in after her. The others scrambled up into the carriage, two of them hopping onto the back of the vehicle and the other two wedging themselves onto the seat with the coachman. Rafe, gun in hand and watching the front door of the opium den, was the last to climb in. The carriage took off, its pace more sedate because of the heavy load.

"Are you all right?" Rafe looked at Kyria with concern.

"Yes. What about you?" She reached over to touch his arm where the jacket was ripped and stained red with blood.

"Just a scratch," he replied, peeling back the edges of the jacket and shirt to look at the long red streak across his arm. "It's the blasted place where he hit me with that rock that hurts." Rafe moved his shoulder, grimacing.

They glanced at Tom inquiringly, and he gave them a nod, rubbing his hands over his face. "That big brute packed quite a wallop, I'll tell you." His jaw tightened. "I'd like to get another crack at him."

"You and me both," Rafe said grimly. He looked at the man sitting beside Tom.

His hair was dark blond and worn rather long. His face was thin and narrow, devoid of facial hair, and dominated by a pair of piercing blue eyes. He was dressed in a robe of a coarse white material, with a hood hanging down the back. Over the robe hung a white linen surplice, wide-necked and open at the sides, and embroidered on the chest in purple was a symbol that looked like the letter *P* superimposed over the letter *X*. A rope was tied around the waist over both the robe and surplice. Still in his hand was the knobby, stout stick.

Kyria's eyes were drawn to the symbol. It was, she felt almost certain, the Chi-Rho monogram that was said to have adorned the banner Constantine's troops carried.

"Thank you for helping us," Rafe said to the man. "Haven't I seen you before?"

The man's gaze flickered to Kyria and quickly away. Finally he said in a heavily accented voice, "We have been with you."

"*With* us?" Kyria repeated. She glanced at Rafe.

"I think they've been following us," Rafe told her. "Once or twice I've noticed someone in white . . ."

"Why?" Kyria asked the man. "Who are you?"

He appeared to think for a moment before he looked at her, carefully keeping his eyes on her face rather than on her mannishly dressed body. "I am Brother Jozef. I am . . . we are the Keepers of the Holy Standard."

The other three stared at him.

Finally Kyria said, "Do you mean to tell me . . ."

He gave a ponderous nod. "Centuries ago, our order was entrusted with the task of taking the Reliquary of the Holy Standard to a safe place and protecting it with our lives and honor. We retreated deeper and deeper as the years passed and the Ottoman Empire grew, swallowing all that had once been Byzantium. We kept to the true religion and kept safe that which we had sworn to protect with our lives."

"But surely you would have died out long ago," Rafe protested.

"We are holy men, sworn to chastity and obedience," Brother Jozef went on. "As the brothers began to die, they realized that they must bring others into their fold. They did so, journeying out every ten years to bring in new novitiates, so that the task was handed down year after year. The brotherhood has dwindled over time, of course, but it never completely died out. We are sworn to protect the sacred reliquary, and so we have done —" his face darkened and he looked away "— until a year ago."

"What happened?" Kyria asked gently when he did not speak for a few moments.

He straightened his shoulders. "One of us was chosen unwisely. He was impure of heart. Corruptible. Evil men, using the snare of a woman, lured him into stealing the reliquary. One morning we woke up, and we could feel that the sacred reliquary was gone. We went to the sanctuary and found that we were right. Our brother was gone, as well. We set out after those evil men, but they moved swiftly. We, as is traditional among our brotherhood, travel by foot. We were unable to catch them, and the Reliquary of the Holy Standard disappeared."

"I'm very sorry," Kyria said, touched by the man's forlorn expression.

"I have been entrusted with the task of recovering the reliquary. Without the Holy Standard, all the years, all the sacrifices, will have been for nothing." He looked straight into Kyria's eyes, his own blue gaze lit with the flame of fanaticism. "It is ours, my lady. We must bring it back to its rightful place. It is our duty, our desire. Next to it, our lives are worth nothing."

Kyria blinked, somewhat taken aback by the man's passionate statement. What was he saying, that they would take it from her by force?

The monk paused, drawing a calming breath, and went on, "My brothers and I have followed the trail of the holy reliquary, for wherever such evil men go, murder and mayhem follow. The box has been stolen from the thieves, sold and stolen again, until it wound up in the markets of Constantinople — Istanbul, as the heretics named it. There we learned that a man had bought it from one who did not fully realize what a treasure he had. And this man, this dealer, brought it here to England. To your house. We have followed the reliquary. It calls to us."

Kyria decided not to even pursue this last strange statement. She asked, "Why did Mr. Kousoulous bring it to me?"

"I do not know. No one does. I know only that you now hold our reliquary. That is why we have followed you to this place tonight — to protect you. We cannot allow any harm to come to the Holy Standard while it is in your care." He leaned forward, gazing earnestly into Kyria's eyes. "My lady, I beg you to return the reliquary to us. It is our sacred duty to look after the Holy Standard. We *must* have it. We must return it to its home. Please, return the reliquary to us."

There was a long moment of silence in the carriage after he stopped talking. Finally Rafe released a breath and said, "That's a good story, sir. The only problem is — how do we know that it's true? Just about anybody could dress up in a white robe and call himself a Keeper of the Holy Standard. You are asking Lady Kyria to just hand over to you a very valuable item."

"You accuse me of lying?" The man turned to Rafe, his eyes burning a hole in him. "I am a man of God. I have given my life to Him. I would not sully my name or His with a falsehood. How am I to prove to you that I am who I say? I have with me the order given to me by the head of our order, Brother Teodor, entrusting me with the task of bringing back the sacred relic. But I doubt that will convince a man such as yourself, who sees a liar in a man of God."

"Such an order would be pretty easy to write out," Rafe said.

Kyria shot him a quelling glance and turned to Brother Jozef, saying soothingly, "Of course, we do not think you are lying. It is just that we have to be very careful. You see, I don't know you or anything about you except what you have said. There are others who seek the reliquary, too, and all have pressed their claims with me. Some have even been willing to kill a man to try to obtain it. Certainly they would not stop at deceit. So you can see that I must be very careful. We recognize that the reliquary is a very important object, a sacred one, even. And for that reason, I must be even more vigilant about taking care of it."

The monk's burning gaze held Kyria's for a long moment. "I sense that you are a good woman, my lady, that you understand the powerful responsibility that possessing the Reliquary of the Holy Standard places on one. But you must see that it does not belong to you. It is not yours to keep."

"For whatever reason, sir, this box has been entrusted to me. I cannot shirk from that responsibility. I have to think very carefully before I decide what to do with it."

"The Reliquary of the Holy Standard is ours," Brother Jozef insisted. "We must have it back."

Rafe straightened, his hand going to the gun inside his jacket. "Are you threatening Lady Kyria?"

Beside the monk, Tom Quick, too, stiffened, and he turned toward the man, watching him carefully.

Jozef shot Rafe a disdainful glance. "I do not threaten. I am a man of God. I have told you. But the reliquary is ours, and we will have it." He turned back to Kyria. "You have seen what has happened to those who have taken the Holy Standard. Death and destruction have followed them. The reliquary belongs at home."

"I will think about it," Kyria assured him. "Very carefully. I promise you."

He looked at her for a long time, then gave a brusque nod of his head. "Very well, my lady. We will give you time to think. Then we shall talk again."

Having said his piece, the man sank once again into silence. They continued in that way until they reached Broughton House. The carriage pulled up in front and stopped. Brother Jozef jumped nimbly down, and Kyria and the others climbed out of the carriage. By the time they closed the carriage door and turned, Brother Jozef and his companions had melted away into the night.

Kyria looked all around them, and a shiver took her. She was glad when Rafe curled his arm around her shoulders and hugged her to him.

"Well," he said lightly, "this has been quite a night's work."

Tom was still a trifle wobbly on his feet and was glad to accept the offer of a cold compress for his jaw and a bed to sleep in. Kyria sent a maid for bandages and ointments, then propelled Rafe, protesting, up to his room.

She shrugged out of her jacket and tossed it aside. "I must say, there are some things I rather like about this mode of dress."

Rafe cast her a look, one eyebrow going up wickedly. "I must say, there are some things I rather admire about it, too. For one thing, I had not realized quite how long your legs are."

"Don't be impertinent," Kyria teased back, feeling a little giddy in the aftermath of all the excitement and danger. For a moment back there, she had thought she was about to die. It was difficult, therefore, not to want to simply fling herself on the bed and shriek out her relief.

Instead, she undid the cuffs of her shirt and rolled them up, then unbuttoned the collar and pulled off the constricting tie. "However, I do not understand how you can stand these collars and ties. They are the most ghastly nuisances."

Rafe chuckled and started to pull off his own jacket. Kyria noticed the involuntary wince he made as he slipped it off his arm.

"I can see that you are hurt more than 'just a scratch,' " she scolded, coming over to him. "Here, let me see."

"It's nothing really."

"Don't be nonsensical. Let me help

you." Kyria unfastened his cuff links and laid them aside. Her hair fell forward around her face and shoulders, and the scent of her teased his nostrils.

He could not help but think what a delightfully enticing picture she presented in the men's trousers, her hair tousled and wildly curling, spilling invitingly all around her shoulders. Just the sight of her stirred his senses — admittedly not a difficult task, considering the fact that all of his senses had been exquisitely attuned to her ever since the evening before. Unfulfilled passion had simmered in him all day long, and the excitement of this evening had left him relieved and surging with life, not a state conducive to quelling his desire. What he wanted most to do now was to take Kyria in his arms and kiss her, but he knew exactly where that would lead. It was not the kind of thing a man of honor did.

But it was damn difficult to retain any sense of honor when she was bending over his arm, unfastening his clothes.

Rafe stepped back quickly. "It's all right. I can do it."

Kyria raised her hands in a conciliatory gesture and moved away. Having two older brothers, she was well accustomed to the male's prickly demeanor when wounded.

She turned and saw the butler, tray in hand, hovering at the opened door. She felt a blush rising in her cheeks, although she told herself it was foolish; she and Rafe had not been doing anything untoward.

"Come in, Phipps," she said crisply.

"My lady." The butler crossed to where they stood and set his tray on the dresser. "Mr. McIntyre. I took the liberty, sir, of bringing a decanter of brandy, as well as the bandages."

"Phipps, you are a man in a million."

"Thank you, sir." He turned to Kyria. "Do you need my help, my lady?"

"No. I think I can handle it. Mr. McIntyre assures me his wound is nothing but a scratch. You may go on to bed, and tell Joan to retire, as well. I can manage easily enough by myself tonight."

"Very good." Phipps glanced at Kyria's manner of dress, but made no comment. He had worked in the Morelands' employ for too long to be disconcerted by anything they did. "Good night, my lady. Sir."

He bowed and left the room. Rafe poured a dollop of brandy into each of the small balloon glasses on the tray and handed one of them to Kyria.

"Here. I think this will help both of us a great deal."

Kyria had rarely drunk anything stronger than an occasional glass of wine, but this evening she did not hesitate to take the glass and down a healthy swig of it. She could not suppress a little gasp as it burned its way down her throat, but the burst of warmth in her stomach soothed her still-jittering nerves.

She took another sip, then let out a sigh and sank into a chair. "Well, it was quite an evening, wasn't it?"

"Yes." Rafe took another swallow of brandy and leaned back against the dresser, his legs stretched out in front of him. "And to think that I always assumed England was dull."

"It usually is not quite this lively," Kyria admitted. She sighed. "I had hoped we would answer some questions tonight. But if anything, it seems we've only added more questions."

"We still don't know who was behind Sid and Dixon's invasion of your house," Rafe said. "Or why Mr. Kousoulous decided to bring the box to you. However, if this Keeper fellow is to be believed, we at least know where the reliquary has been all these years and how it came into Kousoulous's hands."

"But how did all these people know he

had it? And that he was bringing it to me?" Kyria pondered.

"Well, in the part of the world where it was stolen, rumors have probably been swirling from the moment it disappeared. It is no surprise that Habib had heard about it, and he and other dealers may have written to collectors such as your Russian and French friends, hoping to make a sale if they could manage to get their hands on it."

"I suppose so." Kyria downed the rest of her brandy, grimacing.

Rafe smiled a little at the face she made, then said soberly, "Unfortunately, Brother Jozef's tale also gives us another candidate for the person behind Kousoulous's murder and the invasion of your house."

"The Keepers?" Kyria looked at him in shock. "You think the Keepers might have done it? But they saved us tonight."

"I am sure it would not help their cause any for us to fall into the hands of someone else who wants the reliquary," Rafe said. "That would be ample reason to help us out."

"That may be. But they belong to a religious order. Surely they would not condone murder and threats!"

"I hope not. However, I cannot overlook

the fact that they are desperate to recover the reliquary. Losing it is a stain on their history, a blot on the good name of their order."

"Still, it is hard for me to imagine their doing something wicked in order to recover a holy symbol."

"It is more than a symbol to them," Rafe countered. "It is their very reason for being, the thing to which they and countless others before them devoted their lives. They are zealots, Kyria, and sometimes zealots are willing to sacrifice everything to achieve the goal of their fanaticism."

His face darkened, and he levered his body away from the dresser. "Believe me, I have had experience with people with causes, and they usually leave a swath of destruction in their wake."

Kyria heard the pain that laced his voice, and she rose from her seat, saying, "Rafe?"

He turned to face her. "I had a cause. I was certain I was absolutely right, just as all of us were. I went into battle believing I was fighting a holy war."

"But you were. Your cause was just!" Kyria exclaimed.

"Is war ever just?" Rafe countered, and his face was drawn with remembered pain. "You know what I realized after a while?

Those men on the other side, the ones I was shooting at, the ones shooting at me . . . well, the funny thing was that they believed they were right, too."

"You were fighting to free men from slavery."

"Yeah, and the other side was fighting for their homes. Who wouldn't fight if an army invaded his land, saying, 'You have to do what we tell you'?"

"But, Rafe —" Kyria frowned, troubled "— are you saying that you don't believe that you were right? That you were justified?"

"I was right. Of course I was right to want to end slavery. If I had to choose today, I would do the same thing. But I wouldn't be so sure of myself and my righteousness that I would charge in, guns blazing. War would be my last recourse, not my first."

He turned away, and his voice became low. "A great deal of the war was fought back and forth across Virginia." He looked at her, and his blue eyes were bitter. "Can you imagine what it was like to have war waged for four long years over the land that was your home? It was devastating. When I went back after the war was over . . . my uncle's house, the place where I grew up, was in ruins. My aunt and her daughters were living in what had been the overseer's cottage. My uncle, the man who took us in, who raised me and sent me to college, had died of pneumonia. My cousins, the boys and girls I grew up with . . . Annie was left a widow and Tyler had died at Gettysburg. Hank lost an arm and an eye at Chancellorsville. Susannah's husband survived, but he wasn't the same man. They moved west to Texas. Our other cousin, James, went with them. There was nothing for them there anymore, just as there was nothing for me. The girl I had loved, the one who gave me back my ring the day I said I was signing up with the Union army, had married someone else and had his baby, and he had died, too. She was only twenty-three the last time I saw her, but she looked forty. There was nothing but bitterness in her face."

"Oh, Rafe." Kyria's eyes filled with tears and she reached out a hand to him. "I am so sorry."

"I'm a dead man to them," Rafe said tightly. "After I started making money, I tried to send them some, and they refused it. My aunt sent a note saying she couldn't take blood money. I tried going back there this year, but . . ." He shrugged. "I don't have a home."

Kyria went to him, wrapping her arms around him and leaning her head against his chest. Her tears soaked his shirt. "I'm sorry. I'm sorry."

His arms went around her convulsively, and he bent his head to rest it on hers. She felt his lips brush her hair. She stroked his back soothingly. A quiver of desire ran through her as she touched him, and she felt ashamed that she felt such a thing at such a moment, when he needed comfort.

"You aren't to blame for what happened to them," she murmured, releasing her hold on him and stepping back a little to look up into his face.

"No," he agreed hoarsely. His hand cupped her cheek briefly, then fell away and turned aside. "I did what I thought was right. They did what they thought was right. A whole country did that. And everyone was too stubborn, too convinced of their own rectitude, to do anything but go to war over it."

He moved to where the brandy sat and poured himself another drink. "It's over. There's nothing to be done now." He took a sip and turned back to her. "But I know one thing — zealots can be very dangerous men. They are far too prone to think that the end justifies the means."

"All right." Kyria wished that she could make him feel better, that she could bring him comfort and peace. But she could tell that he was finished with the subject. In the way of men, he was probably embarrassed that he had revealed as much as he had. So she smiled and said only, "I promise that I shall be suspicious of the Keepers. Still, I can't help but think that perhaps they have the best right to the reliquary."

Rafe nodded. "I know."

"I just wish I knew whether Theo had anything to do with it. I can't imagine why else Mr. Kousoulous would have brought the reliquary to Broughton Park. I hate to do anything until I have talked to Theo."

"The Keepers have waited this long," Rafe pointed out. "I'd say they can wait a little longer. You'll get a letter from Theo or he'll show up."

Kyria frowned, admitting for the first time the trouble that had been rattling around in the back of her mind for some days now, "Unless he can't. Unless something happened to Theo, too."

"No." Rafe set down his glass and crossed to her, taking her arms. "Don't think that way. There's no reason to think that anything has happened to your brother."

"I hope you're right."

"Of course I am."

Considering the conversation they had just had and Rafe's questions about his own self-sureness, both of them had to laugh.

"All right. There you are. Despite it all, I can't escape it," he said lightly. "I am destined, clearly, to be positive I know it all."

"Let's just see how right you are about your arm, then," Kyria responded. She turned and went to close the door. "You take off your shirt and let me look at your wound."

Rafe unbuttoned the front of his shirt, and as he tried to free his injured arm, his face contorted with pain.

"Here, let me help." Kyria crossed the room quickly and grasped the end of the sleeve on the uninjured arm, pulling it down as he pulled out his arm.

She tossed the shirt back, and his chest was exposed, browned by the sun and firmly padded with muscle. She caught her breath, hoping he could not sense how desire had twisted through her at the sight of him. She remembered the feel of his back beneath her hands only moments earlier, and the way her insides had tightened.

Kyria purposely kept her eyes on Rafe's

injured arm as she began to pull down that sleeve. She did not want him to see in her face the way she responded to the sight of his naked body. She reminded herself that she was supposed to be tending to his wound, not thinking about his bare chest and the fact that she wanted to move her hands all over him as he had done to her the night before.

His sleeve stuck to his arm where the blood had dried on it. She tugged gently, but it did not move, so Kyria wet a cloth from the pitcher on the washstand and pressed it gently against his arm. As she stood there, holding the cloth to him, she glanced up into his face, and the look of raw hunger she saw there stopped the breath in her throat.

She quickly glanced away, swallowing hard. Her heart was galloping in her chest. She could not help but think of the way he had looked at her the night before, with the same deep hunger. Kyria had never felt anything like what she had experienced with him last night. From the moment it had happened, she had been wanting to experience it again — and more. *Why did he stop when he did?* She had tried to tell herself that it was because, being a gentleman, he had not wanted to take advantage of her. But she had not been able to expel from her mind the thought that perhaps he had not felt the same desperate intensity that she had. What if she had not pleased him?

Kyria set the wet cloth aside and pulled gently at the sleeve again. It came loose this time, and she slipped his shirt the rest of the way off and tossed it onto the nearby chair. She picked up the cloth again and rewet it, using it to clean the long red wound across his upper arm where the knife had sliced him.

She realized that he was right; the wound did not appear to be very deep or serious as she cleared the blood away from it. Up higher on his arm, where the rock had struck him, was a large bruise, and she suspected that area would be stiff and sore tomorrow, perhaps even more so than the cut.

Rafe looked down at Kyria as she worked over him. Her head was bent; her hair brushed his arm now and then as she moved, as light as butterfly wings and soft as silk. Her hair fell into her face and she flicked it back over her shoulder, and the ends swept across his bare chest. Desire sizzled through him, hot and immediate.

He felt as if something inside him, some

hard, brittle thing, had loosened earlier when she slipped her arms around him to comfort him. He had never spoken of the war to anyone, even Stephen, had never expressed the heartache that had lain inside him all those years. He had chosen his path and had accepted the consequences, and he had thought that he would never reveal it to anyone. Then somehow, with Kyria, it had just slipped out, and when it had, something within him had softened. He felt more vulnerable, and curiously, the feeling did not really bother him.

He felt, too, as if his willpower had drained out of him with the rest of it. He knew that he should step away, should put Kyria aside before he did something he regretted. But his thoughts went no further; he did not move. It seemed all he could do to hold himself still and not pull her to him and bury her mouth under his.

"Maybe . . ." His voice came out hoarse, and he had to clear his throat before he spoke again. "Maybe you ought to dab some of that brandy on it. I've found liquor works wonders for healing."

"Really?" Kyria tilted up her head.

He felt as if he could drown in those huge green eyes. There were tiny golden flecks, he saw, encircling her pupils.

Kyria's mouth was dry, and it took an effort of will to move away and pour a bit of brandy onto the cloth. She pressed it softly against his wound, wincing as he sucked in his breath sharply.

"I'm sorry," she murmured, and then, surprising herself almost as much as him, Kyria bent and brushed her lips over his arm just below the scratch. His flesh was warm and tasted faintly of salt, and his skin quivered beneath her lips.

Kyria raised her head and looked up into his face again. Rafe was unmoving, his skin taut over his bones, but his chest rose and fell rapidly, and color blazed high on his cheekbones. Kyria gazed at him for a long moment, then slowly, deliberately, went up on tiptoe and laid her lips gently against the deepening bruise on his shoulder.

Rafe sucked in his breath, and his hands went automatically to her waist. His fingers curled, catching the waistband of her trousers, then tightened convulsively.

"Kyria . . ." His breath grazed her cheek and sent a shiver through her. "Kyria . . ."

He leaned forward, burying his face in her mass of curling hair, and his hands slid down, curving over her hips, separated from his touch by only the material of the trousers. His hands moved over her rounded bottom, desire rocketing through him with every caress.

Kyria's hands went up to his chest, sliding over him experimentally, searching out the lines and curves of him, the hard ridge of bone and the firm padding of muscle, the tightening nubs of his nipples, and the light sprinkling of curling, coarse hair, narrowing into a line downward to his navel.

Rafe shuddered as she touched him, and a moan escaped his lips. He knew that he should not let this go any further, but he could not make himself move, could not speak.

She ran her fingers down his back, exploring the central valley of his spine and the rise of muscle on either side. She touched the bony outcropping of his collarbone and the tender flesh of his throat above it, her hand curving around his neck to slide up into his hair.

Daring more, Kyria pressed her lips to the warm skin of his chest and was rewarded by the quick hiss of his breath, the involuntary trembling of his flesh. He plunged his hands into her hair as her lips roamed his chest and stomach. She let her tongue slip out to taste his skin as he had done to her yesterday, and she delighted in the feel of his manhood hardening against her in response. Remembering how his hands had caressed her skin and his mouth and tongue had teased her nipples to an engorged sensitivity, she did the same to him.

The way he felt, the way he tasted, excited Kyria, and she could not hold back little sounds of pleasure as she explored his body. Rafe was almost as aroused by the noises she made as he was by the touch of her mouth and hands. Desire coiled within him, tightening with every brush of her fingertips, every flick of her tongue. When her mouth closed around the flat button of one of his nipples, he groaned, stunned by the pleasure that radiated through him.

He had to kiss her, had to taste her. His hands on either side of her head, he turned her face up, and his mouth swooped down to claim hers. Passion exploded within them, shaking them both with its power. Rafe's arms lifted Kyria up into him, grinding her against his heated, eager body. Kyria responded with a wantonness she had never realized existed in her before, wrapping her long legs around his waist.

A shudder of pure animal desire ran through him at her movement, and he locked his arms around her, clamping her to him as his mouth devoured hers. The very center of her heat was pressed against him, tantalizing him through the layers of clothing between them. He turned, making his way blindly across his room to the bed, still kissing her greedily.

They fell onto the bed, hands and mouths searching. Heat seemed to sizzle over their skin as they kissed and caressed, the desire within them building to an almost unbearable heat.

At last he pulled away from her and stood looking down at her. She gazed back at him, her mouth full and reddened from his kisses, her hair spread around her like a fan of fire.

"You are beautiful," he murmured huskily, and his fingers went to the buttons of her waistcoat. "I want to see all of you."

Kyria smiled at him, making no move to stop his fingers from their work. She wanted him to look at her, wanted to watch his face as his eyes roamed her body.

He unbuttoned the waistcoat, then the buttons beneath it that fastened her shirt. Hooking his thumbs beneath the side of her shirt, he pushed both garments aside, then down off her arms. His face tightened as he took in the bindings she had wrapped around her breasts to hide them, and he untied the tapes, lifting her with an arm under her waist and pulling the wrappings away.

Tossing them aside, he stroked his fingers gently over the red streaks the bindings had left on her skin. " 'Tis a crime to hurt such beauty," he whispered and bent to press his lips gently against the marks. "Promise me you will not do so again."

He reached down to pull off her boots and then her socks, his hands gliding over her legs beneath the trousers. His hands moved to the waistband of her trousers, unbuttoning them and sliding them smoothly over her hips and off her legs, quickly following them with the thin cotton pantalets she wore beneath.

Kyria lay naked before him, and his eyes feasted on her loveliness, his pulse hammering in his head. Kyria, a little amazed at her own lack of shame, lifted her arms above her head and stretched sinuously. Rafe's eyes darkened as he watched her, and quickly he toed off his shoes, his hands going to the waistband of his own trousers.

He divested himself of his garments, and Kyria raised her arms to him, her eyes glowing, her mouth softly beckoning. With a small, final sigh of surrender, he stretched out beside Kyria and began to make love to her.

Rafe's mouth roamed her breasts and stomach, teasing and exploring. He played havoc with her senses, stoking the passion within her until Kyria felt as if she might scream with pleasure. She dug her fingers into his back, panting with desire.

He parted her legs, his fingers slipping down into the moist, heated center of her. Kyria ached for him, an emptiness inside her that she knew only he could fill. She opened her legs farther, and her hands roamed restlessly up and down his back, urging him on.

At last he moved between her legs and thrust slowly, deeply inside her. Kyria stifled a groan against his shoulder, the sharp twinge of pain quickly replaced by a deep satisfaction as he filled her. He began to move within her, pulling slowly back, then sinking deep again, and Kyria wrapped her arms and legs around him. Her senses whirling, she moved with him, every new sensation driving her desire higher.

She let out a sob, feeling as if she might explode. Suddenly, the tension within her broke, sending strong waves of pleasure radiating through her. Kyria shook under the force of it, a cry escaping her lips, and at her movement, Rafe shuddered, too, a deep groan issuing from his throat.

They clung together, riding out the blinding storm of passion. They collapsed, spent and panting, and Rafe rolled onto his back, his arm around her, pulling her close. Kyria rested her head against his chest, letting herself drift, replete and content in a way she had never imagined existed.

So this, she thought, was love. Smiling to herself, Kyria drifted into sleep.

17

The next morning, Kyria awoke alone late and did not go down to breakfast, but had only toast and tea brought up to her on a tray. Humming to herself, she bathed and dressed, then went downstairs. She heard the sound of masculine voices talking, and she frowned, puzzled, then followed the sound of them to the library. There she found Rafe and Reed in conversation.

"Reed!" she cried, rushing to him with a smile. "When did you get in?"

"Just this morning. I took the early train back from Liverpool." He stood up to hug her. Then he stepped back, saying, "Rafe here has been telling what you two have been doing."

"What?" Startled, Kyria's eyes flew to Rafe's face.

"I was telling your brother why we brought the reliquary to London."

"Oh! Oh, of course." Of course he had not told Reed anything about what had happened between them personally! A blush rose on Kyria's cheeks. She must learn to control her reactions better, she thought fiercely, or Reed would begin to suspect something.

Rafe smiled at her, his eyes lingering on her face. Reed looked from his sister to the American, and his eyes narrowed shrewdly.

"Have you shown Reed the standard?" Kyria asked Rafe, eager to distract her brother.

"Not yet. You are much better than I at wielding those wires of Con's."

Kyria ran off to fetch the reliquary and returned a few moments later. She showed Reed Con's method of unlocking the box, then opened it to let him see the fragile cloth. Reed was as awestruck as everyone else had been.

"That's amazing," he said, sitting back as Kyria closed the box. "It seems impossible."

"I know," Kyria agreed. "Even more astonishing, apparently the rest of the legend is true, too. It seems there really is a group of men who have devoted their lives to keeping the box safe — passing it down through generations. The Keepers of the Holy Standard, they call themselves."

"You have met them?"

Kyria nodded. "They rescued us last night."

"*Rescued* you?" Reed's eyebrows vaulted

upward. "What do you mean, rescued?"

"We were surrounded and outnumbered," Kyria explained. "I thought we were doomed, but then the Keepers came running in out of nowhere and started fighting off our attackers."

"Who attacked you? Why?"

"We're not sure why," Kyria told him carefully so as not to alarm him. "I think we weren't supposed to be where we were."

"Or it might have been someone who wants the box, I suppose," Rafe put in.

"This Habib fellow?" Reed asked.

"Possibly. But he doesn't fit the description of the man who paid Sid and Dixon to break into Broughton Park and try to steal it," Kyria reasoned aloud. "We think Mr. Habib might have a partner. We tried to catch him at the Blue Bull, but he got away."

"What? Who tried to catch him?" Reed asked.

"Why, Rafe and I."

"At a tavern?" Reed stared. "*You* were in a tavern?"

Kyria nodded cheerfully. "Yes, on the docks. It was quite an interesting experience. I dressed up as an old hag."

Reed was rendered momentarily speechless.

"But we still don't know who he was, because he got away that night," Kyria went on. "We don't know if he and Habib are somehow acting together or if he is an entirely separate party. I mean, he could be the Frenchman or the Russian prince."

"Who the devil are the Frenchman and the Russian prince?"

"They have both approached me since we've been in London, offering to purchase the reliquary."

"Good God, how many people are after this thing?" Reed exclaimed.

"We know of three, well, four, if you count the Keepers," Kyria told him. "But we don't know if the man at the tavern is one of these people that we know about, or if he is someone else altogether. That's why we set Tom on Habib to follow him and see if he could catch him meeting with someone. So Tom followed him, and that is why we went to the opium den last night, to see if —"

"Opium den!" Reed exploded, rising to his feet. "You went to an opium den?"

"Yes. That is where we were attacked, and the Keepers came to rescue us."

"Good God, McIntyre!" Reed exclaimed again, turning toward him indignantly. "You call this keeping my sister safe?"

"No one has to keep me safe!" Kyria protested. "I can look after myself." She swung on Rafe, who had opened his mouth to respond to Reed, and shook her finger at him. "Don't you dare apologize for not stopping me from going. We all know that I —"

"Do exactly as you please," Reed finished her sentence with a groan. "I know. I know. I shouldn't get angry with McIntyre, poor chap. I should pity him for having to try to reason with you."

As Kyria opened her mouth again, her eyes flashing, Reed raised his hands in a conciliatory gesture. "No, no, don't start breathing fire. I abjectly apologize. I know you are a grown woman and fully capable of taking care of yourself. However, I don't think I can take any more of your adventures just now. I'm going to visit the twins."

Rafe grinned. "I don't think those two will be much of a relief for your nerves."

"You're probably right," Reed acknowledged. "But at least it will be an entirely different set of worries."

After luncheon, Kyria was in the sitting room conferring with the housekeeper when she became aware of a high, thin wail. Frowning, she looked at the housekeeper, then toward the open door. Suddenly she realized that the sound was from one of the twins, screaming for help. She jumped up and ran down the hall toward the back of the house, nearly running into Reed coming out of his office. Behind them came the pounding of more running feet.

As Kyria and Reed reached the back hallway, Con rushed out of the conservatory door. He saw them and sagged against the wall, struggling to catch his breath, his small chest heaving.

He was a terrible sight — his pants torn and muddied, leaves in his hair and caught on his jacket, his hair damp with sweat and sticking out every which way, his face scratched and bleeding, his cheeks flushed from exertion. A fierce red mark splotched his forehead just above his eyebrow.

"Con!" Kyria and Reed rushed to him, just as Rafe ran up to join them.

"Al . . . Alex!" Con panted, pulling back as Kyria reached out to take him in her arms. "You gotta . . ."

"Alex?" Kyria asked. "Something happened to Alex?"

"Where is he?" Reed put in.

In answer, Con turned and started off at

a run back through the conservatory. Kyria, Reed and Rafe pelted after him. Con ran out onto the terrace and down the steps into the garden, racing along the paths into the informal parklike area beyond.

Although the grounds of Broughton House were small compared to those at their country home, they were large for a house in London, containing almost a city block of trees and grass inside the walls of the estate. Con led them toward the back of the grounds. There, close to the high east wall, beneath a large tree, lay the sprawled still body of Denby, the footman Kyria had set to look after the boys. Alex was nowhere in sight.

The fear that had been growing in Kyria with every step now blazed into full-blown terror. "Alex!" she shouted. "Alex!"

"He's gone!" Con panted, dropping to his knees beside Denby. "They . . . they got him!" He pointed vaguely toward the stone wall.

As Kyria knelt beside Denby, Rafe and Reed ran to the wall. Jumping, they grabbed the top and pulled themselves up to look over, then returned to where Kyria knelt beside the footman, her handkerchief pressed to his temple.

"He's been hit on the head," she told

them. "He's bleeding and unconscious, but I don't see any other wounds. I don't think he was shot or stabbed."

"They hit him," Con panted out. Though his face was pale, the bright red mark standing out sharply, he was regaining his breath, and he managed to add, "With a big stick."

"Who are they?" Reed asked.

Con shook his head. "I don't know! There were three of them. They came over the wall. Alex and I were over there." He turned to point at a spot a short distance away. "We . . . we saw them. We didn't know what they were doing. They just climbed over. Denby was watching us, and he didn't see them at first. Then he turned, and one of them hit him hard, like this." Con demonstrated. "They came after us. So Alex and I ran." Con stopped, tears starting in his eyes.

"Good lad," Reed said encouragingly. "You did exactly right."

"But they caught Alex?" Rafe asked.

Con nodded. "Me, too, but when they were climbing back over the wall, they didn't have hold of me good enough — Alex and I were kicking and hitting and trying to get away, you see — and anyway, at the top of the wall, I pulled away real hard, and he dropped me. So I came to get you."

At this point, Denby groaned and opened his eyes. His eyes wavered around, and he squeezed them shut again, moaning, "Ow, me head."

"Stay still," Kyria told him. "You'll be all right."

She looked up at Rafe, who was standing with one hand comfortingly on Con's shoulder. Her gaze was filled with fear and pleading.

"Don't worry," Rafe said quietly. "We'll get him back."

"That's right," Reed agreed. He glanced over to where several of the servants, who had trailed out of the house after them, now stood silently, watching. "Phipps, get Denby inside and make him comfortable." He turned back to Kyria and Con. "Con, you stay with your sister. I'm going out front and see what I can find out."

He looked at Rafe, who gave him a nod and came around to join him. Con looked anxiously after the two of them. "I can help them."

"No!" Kyria exclaimed, then added more softly. "Please don't, Con. I need your help with Denby."

The servants carried the injured

footman into the house, Con and Kyria following. They laid him down on the couch in the housekeeper's sitting room, and Kyria cleaned and bandaged his head. After she cleaned away the blood, she found that the wound was not as bad as it had looked, the skin merely broken over a rapidly rising knot.

"Do you remember what happened, Denby?" she asked.

"I . . . I'm not sure. The boys were playing, and then . . . I think, was there a noise? I started to turn around and . . ." He sighed. "I don't remember anything else."

"He didn't see them, or at least not much," Con said. "He turned around just as they were on him."

"I'm sorry, my lady," Denby said. "What happened? Where's Master Alex?"

"We're not sure. He seems . . . he seems to have been taken." Kyria struggled to clamp down on the terror rising within her.

Who had taken him? Where had they gone? What was going to happen to him?

Con slipped his hand into hers and squeezed, and Kyria looked down at him, smiling and blinking back the tears that flooded her eyes. "We'll get him back," she said firmly, returning the squeeze.

She and Con left the footman in the care of the housekeeper and started toward the front of the house. They met Rafe and Reed coming back in the front door.

"Did you find anything?" she asked eagerly. "Did anybody see where they took him?"

"The only person who saw anything was a street sweeper at the intersection," Reed told her. "He said there was a carriage standing outside the wall all day. He had noticed it because it didn't move. Then he saw a fellow climb over the fence out of our grounds and go to the carriage, then two men got out of the carriage, and they all climbed back over the wall. Naturally, he thought this odd, so he continued to watch, and the next thing he saw was the men coming back over the wall, carrying two boys, but one of the boys fell back inside. They carried the other one, kicking and screaming, into the carriage and drove off. At least he could tell us the direction the carriage went."

Kyria felt deathly cold. "Oh, poor Alex! Who could have done this? Why?"

"I don't know who," Rafe said, "but I think it's a safe bet that the why is to get hold of that reliquary."

"I agree." Reed nodded. "Given everything that's been going on, I think it has to be related. I directed the footmen to talk to everyone they can find in the direction the carriage went. I've sent for Tom Quick to help in that hunt. Maybe we can find someone who saw where the carriage turned or . . ." Reed stopped and sighed, then turned to Con. "Let's go sit down, and I want you to tell me again everything that happened. Try to remember every single thing."

Con nodded. When the four of them were seated in Reed's office, Con once again told of the men climbing over the wall and knocking out the footman, then chasing and capturing the twins and hauling them over the wall.

"Did you get a look at any of their faces?" Kyria asked. "Could you recognize any of them again?"

Con shook his head. "They wore masks over their faces. You know, like you wear to a costume ball."

"Half masks?" Kyria asked.

He nodded. "All black. I saw the bottom part of their faces, but . . ."

"No, I realize. You wouldn't be able to recognize them," Reed said. "Was there no scar, no oddity about a mouth or nose?"

Con thought for a moment, then reluctantly shook his head. "Nothing I remember, and they were all dressed in black."

"Did they say anything?" Rafe asked.

"Yes!" Con brightened. "The one who dropped me said something. It sounded like an oath — the way his voice sounded, I mean. But I couldn't understand what he said. And one of the other men said something to him. Several words. But I couldn't understand them, either. I think it was a foreign language. It didn't sound familiar at all."

"Would you have known if it was French?" Kyria asked.

"It wasn't French. I'm pretty sure of that. Or German. We've studied both those languages."

"You think it's Habib?" Kyria looked over at Rafe.

He shrugged. "Could be. I certainly think we should have a talk with the man. But it could have been the man who escaped us, the one at the tavern. He was apparently foreign, too. And of course, the men the other night —"

"Oh!" Con exclaimed. "There was something else. I just remembered it!"

"What?"

"The chap who picked me up had a medallion on a gold chain around his neck. It was under his shirt, but when he was climbing over the wall and trying to hold on to me, it fell outside his shirt, and I saw it. It was gold and round and it had this, I don't know, a kind of symbol or something engraved on it."

"What kind of symbol?" Reed asked eagerly.

"I don't know. I'd never seen it before." Con paused. "I could try to draw it."

"Good." Reed whipped out a piece of paper and a pencil and handed them to the boy.

Con bent over the paper, drawing, his tongue clamped between his teeth in concentration. He scratched out his drawing and started again. Finally he stopped and held it up for the others to see. They bent forward to look at the drawing.

Inside the circle, two lines ran parallel, curving up and together and bending to the right at the top, joining in a swirl. Kyria stared at the drawing, the blood draining out of her face.

"Oh, my God!" she whispered. "I've seen that. I drew it!"

There was a moment of stunned silence, then Reed and Rafe began to talk at once.

"What? What are you talking about?"
"What does it mean?"
"I don't know what it means. It's just . . . something I drew. I was sketching a design for a necklace." She paused, thinking. "Well, actually, I think I may have started drawing this design first, and then I made it into a necklace. I don't know what it means, if anything. I'd never seen it before that. Wait. I'll show you."

Kyria left the office and darted up the back stairs to her room, returning a few minutes later with her drawing pad. She opened the pad and set the sketch of the necklace down on the desk beside Con's drawing.

"That's it!" Con said excitedly, jabbing his finger at Kyria's drawing. "That is exactly what the medallion looked like."

"See, I drew it down here first, just the symbol, and I liked the design. Then I got the idea of putting it on metal squares and linking them into a necklace."

"This is too much coincidence," Reed said. "You can't have just happened to think of exactly the same design that is on the kidnapper's medallion. You must have seen it somewhere."

Kyria shrugged. "Perhaps. But I don't know where. I have no memory of ever seeing it before I drew it. It was an idea that popped into my head one day."

"Maybe you saw it someplace that we have been the past few days," Rafe suggested, "and you just didn't notice it enough to remember. Like at Ashcombe's place. It has that look of something ancient, don't you think? Where else have we been? Here, of course, and the Blue Bull tavern. I wouldn't think there was anything like that there. The opium den . . ."

"No, no, it couldn't have been any of those places," Kyria protested. "I drew it before we came here. I drew it at Broughton Park, not long before we left. I had been looking at the reliquary, and then I went back up to my room. I was just sitting there, daydreaming, and suddenly this design flashed into my mind. So if I saw it, it must have been at Broughton Park."

"It looks like the kind of things Papa has," Con commented, tracing the whorled design with his forefinger. "Perhaps you saw it on one of his pots or bracelets or something."

"Perhaps," Kyria conceded. "But it doesn't seem exactly Greek or Roman."

"Byzantine, then," Rafe suggested. "Especially if you had just been looking at the reliquary. It triggered some memory in you of Byzantine art."

"Or the Near East," Reed put in. "It reminds me a little of that silver belt Theo sent you that time, the one with the tiny bells hanging off it."

"The harem-dancer belt?" Kyria tilted her head. "Yes. It's not the same design, but there is a sort of Levantine flavor to it."

"You probably saw it in some book or other of the duke's," Rafe said. "But which one? And primarily, what does that mean about the men who are wearing it?"

"No, wait," Kyria said. "Were *all* of them wearing it or just the man who had Con? Because if it was only him, then it could just be some personal decoration, and he wears it because he thinks it's attractive. But if all of them are wearing it, then it would seem to denote some sort of club or order . . ."

"Like the Keepers of the Holy Standard?" Rafe asked.

"Yes," Kyria said, "I suppose so. But this doesn't seem like something they would do. After all, they rescued us last night. Why would they turn around and try to harm us? They presented their case to me, and I told them that I would think very carefully about it. I am rather inclined to return the box to them."

"Yes, but they don't know that," Rafe pointed out.

"All right, then," Reed said. "Shall we start with them? These Keepers?"

"If we knew where they were," Rafe said. "Unfortunately, they just seem to pop up now and again. We don't know where they are located."

"I'm not at all sure that finding the Keepers would help," Kyria argued. "I don't think they are the ones who kidnapped Alex. That symbol doesn't look like a religious one. Wouldn't it be more likely that they would have a medallion with the Chi-Rho emblem on it rather than this? That was what was on the front of Brother Jozef's garb last night."

Rafe shrugged. "You're probably right. As for Alex's kidnappers being foreign, that does not give us much direction, either. This whole affair is crowded with foreigners — the Lebanese dealer, the Frenchman, the Russian, even the man who originally brought the reliquary to you. Then there's the man who hired Sid and Dixon, and we have no idea whether he is the Frenchman, the Russian or someone else altogether."

"Well, we can't just sit here. We have to

start somewhere," Reed said pragmatically.

At that moment, there was a knock on the door, and one of the parlor maids came in. "There's a letter here, my lord. My lady." She looked from Reed to Kyria. "A boy just delivered it. It has no address on it, and when I asked who it was for, he said he didn't know. They just told him to deliver it to this house."

" 'They?' " Reed repeated, rising. "Who exactly is 'they'?"

"I don't know, sir. I made the boy wait here, in case you wanted to talk to him — I mean, what with all that's going on."

"Quite right. You were smart to do so." Reed took the letter and ripped it open, his eyes running quickly down the page. "You were right, McIntyre. They want the reliquary."

"What does it say, Reed?" Kyria asked anxiously. "Don't keep us in suspense."

"Sorry." Reed began to read the letter aloud. " 'We have the boy.' Obviously they wrote this before they actually accomplished the deed — they have written 'boys' and then crossed out the 's.' 'We will give him to you in exchange for the box. Tomorrow. We will send you time and place.' " His jaw tightened. "Damn! They intend to keep him all night!"

"Poor Alex! He will be so frightened!" Kyria said, sucking in her breath in a sob.

Rafe wrapped an arm around her, pulling her against him comfortingly. "Don't worry, darlin'. We'll get him back."

"We certainly will," Reed agreed grimly. "Bring the messenger in here, Milly."

She bobbed a curtsy and appeared a few minutes later with a street urchin in tow. The boy's face was pale beneath his dirt, and he looked as if he would have run if it had not been for the firm grip Milly and another maid had on his arms.

"I din't do nothin'," were the first words out of the boy's mouth as soon as the maids let him go and stepped back out of the door.

"Don't worry. I'm not going to accuse you of anything," Reed told him calmly. "I just want to hear about the person who gave you this message to deliver here."

"I din't know 'im or nothin.' 'E just give me a couple o' coppers and told me to bring it 'ere. 'E din't say nothin' about yer grabbing me and all."

"Yes, well, I don't intend to harm you." Reed fished a half crown out of his pocket and held it up in front of the boy. "In fact, I plan to give you this if you will think very hard and tell me everything you can about the man who gave you the message."

The boy's eyes widened. "All right. I'll tell you everythin'. Uh, 'e was shorter than you, like. Regular lookin', I guess."

"Was he foreign?" Reed asked.

The boy looked surprised. "No. 'E sounded like you. You know, upper crust, like."

"Really?" Reed cast a glance at Rafe and Kyria. "What color hair and eyes did he have, do you remember? What sort of complexion?"

The boy shrugged. "Regular. Not dark or nothin'. Brown 'air, I thinks. 'Is eyes . . ." The boy seemed to cast back in his mind, then said, "I don't know. Sorry. I didn't notice 'em much."

"How was he dressed?"

"Like a gentleman. Like you or 'im." He looked toward Rafe. "Dark-gray sort o' jacket, it was, and trousers the same. White shirt. Bowler 'at."

"So, a well-spoken, well-dressed English sort of chap," Reed summed up.

The boy nodded. Reed cast a look at Rafe and Kyria, both of whom shook their heads. They could think of nothing else to ask. Reed gave the lad the coin and sent him on his way.

"All right," Reed said. "So now, what do we know?"

"That at least one of the kidnappers is English," Kyria began, "and apparently dresses and talks like a gentleman. And the others, or some of the others, are foreign. We know of at least four people or groups who want the reliquary — the Keepers, Prince Dmitri, Monsieur Brulatour and Mr. Habib."

"What about Ashcombe?" Rafe asked. "I don't know that you can discount him."

"But he is an archaeologist!" Kyria looked shocked.

"That doesn't exempt him from greed," Rafe pointed out. "He has been looking for the reliquary for years. I would think that it would mean a great deal to him to be able to show it to his colleagues. To prove that it existed."

Kyria thought for a moment. "All right. Say we ignore the fact that he is world-renowned and has a spotless reputation as a scholar and archaeologist, and we suppose that he is overcome by greed and the desire to prove that he was correct. The fact of the matter is that if he gets the reliquary by criminal means such as extorting it from us by kidnapping a child, then he can never show the reliquary to any of his colleagues or anyone else. If he does, we — and everyone else — will know that he is a criminal."

"That's true." Reed nodded. "Besides, with an archaeologist, it is extremely important to prove where it came from. All he can trace it back to is us. We have no proof of what it is or where it came from."

"So, except for admiring it, he really could not do anything with it," Rafe said. He gave a nod of his head. "I would agree that he is the least likely of any of the possible suspects. Although I cannot entirely dismiss him, either. However, I think that we should go talk to him about the meaning of that symbol on the medallion. The medallion seems to me the best clue we have, and Ashcombe is the only scholar we have at hand. We are more likely to find out what it means from him than from trying to sift through the books in the library here hoping to spot it."

Kyria nodded. "I agree, we need to talk to him about that. What about the others? Do you think we should confront Habib or any of the collectors?"

"What are we going to say — did you have Alex kidnapped?" Reed asked. "No one is going to admit to it. It would be better to have them followed, don't you think?"

"We already have Tom Quick on Habib."

"Do we know where the other two collectors reside?" Reed asked.

"Yes. They both gave me their cards," Kyria replied.

"What about this other chap?" Reed asked. "The English gentleman who gave the boy the message to deliver."

"I have no idea who he is. One of the men who attacked us last night was English, but he was quite large and did not dress like a gentleman."

"He could even have been a decoy," Rafe suggested. "Habib or whoever might have hired him to give the message to the boy, knowing that we would be likely to question the lad."

"Or the man from the tavern. He could have been English. For all we know, he could have assumed an accent to fool Sid," Kyria suggested in turn.

"Well, we can't do anything about him since we have no idea who he is. I think we'll have to start with these Brulatour and Dmitri fellows."

"What about Walford?" Rafe asked.

"Who?" Reed asked, confused.

"Lord Walford," Kyria told him. "The young Lord Walford." She turned to Rafe. "But why would he have anything to do with it? He is the only one who isn't interested in it."

"And doesn't that strike you as odd?" Rafe asked. "After all, it's his archaeologist who's been looking for the blasted thing for years. Wouldn't that indicate that he wants it, too? Yet he said nothing to you."

Kyria grimaced. "You just have a prejudice against Lord Walford. Why would he have helped us? He got Ashcombe to see us. And he didn't seem to believe that the box really existed. I suspect it was more his father who had been interested in it, and Walford just let Ashcombe continue because of that."

Rafe shrugged, and Reed said, "We'll put somebody on him, too, just in case."

Kyria went upstairs to get the cards Brulatour and Prince Dmitri had given her. When she returned, she found Phipps, the butler, in the office, talking excitedly to Rafe and Reed.

"They found someone who saw the carriage some distance east of here," Rafe told her.

"Really?" Kyria's spirits lifted a little.

"Yes, my lady." Phipps beamed at her. "One of the footmen questioned a hansom driver who said that he saw a carriage moving along at a rather great rate of speed — faster than was safe, he thought, which made him pay attention to it. He happened to be following it east, he said, and at one point he saw a young lad pop his head out of the carriage, then get pulled back in. He didn't think anything of it until we came along asking questions, except that the occupants of the carriage were rather careless, moving at that pace and allowing a boy to stick his head that far out the window."

"Alex?" Kyria cried. "Trying to escape?"

"We can only hope," Reed responded. "I'm going with the driver to the last place where he saw the carriage, and from there Phipps and the footmen and I are going to start looking about for anyone else who might have seen Alex or the carriage." He took the two calling cards from her. "I'll put our barrister on these two and Walford — he can use his law clerks. Kyria, you and McIntyre go to visit the archaeologist. He'll be more likely to talk to you since you've talked to him before. We'll meet back here later."

"But what about me?" Con cried, jumping up from his chair. "I want to help find Alex! I can't just sit here waiting."

Reed frowned, looking at the anxiety on his younger brother's face. After a moment, he smiled faintly and said, "All right. You come with me. You can help us ask questions — you're good at that. Besides, we won't have to describe Alex to everyone. We'll just ask if they've seen a boy who looks like you."

Con gave a shout of joy. "Thanks, Reed. You're the best."

Reed looked over at Kyria. "All set? We'd better get started. It is getting to be late in the afternoon."

Kyria nodded, trying not to think of poor Alex alone tonight with his kidnappers. Rafe moved up beside her and slipped his hand into hers, linking their fingers and squeezing her hand reassuringly.

"Don't worry," he murmured. "We'll get him back."

Minutes later, they were in the carriage headed for Nelson Ashcombe's house. Kyria's hand still lay in Rafe's. She was grateful for the bit of comfort. She supposed she should have insisted that they split up, that she could go to Ashcombe's alone and let Rafe do something more important, like follow one of the collectors. However, she could not bring herself to do that. She needed him beside her now, and she refused even to think about how dangerous it was to her self-reliant life to need a man this much.

It was after four o'clock when they reached Ashcombe's house. The winter day would be drawing to a close before long. Kyria tried not to think about how difficult it would be for Reed and the others to question people on the street after darkness fell. With every minute that passed, it grew more and more unlikely that anyone who had seen the carriage would still be out and about.

They were met at the door by the same uncooperative maid, who informed them that the master was "resting." She started to close the door, but Rafe braced his arm against it and shoved hard, opening the door wide and sending the girl staggering back, surprised.

" 'Ere, now!" she exclaimed. "You cain't just barge in 'ere like that!"

"I just did," Rafe replied shortly. "Where's Ashcombe?"

The maid cast a quick, revealing glance up the stairs, then said, " 'E's not receivin' now. Best be yer come back tomorrow."

"He will receive us." Rafe took Kyria's hand and led her up the stairs, the maid hurrying along behind them, screeching and waving her hands ineffectually. "Which door?"

"No! Yer can't!"

Rafe charged down the hall, throwing open every door as he went until finally he found Nelson Ashcombe. The man was reclining on a chaise lounge in his bedroom, a familiar-looking pipe on the small table beside him. The air was sweet and stifling.

Kyria and Rafe stopped, staring at the scene in front of them. They turned to each other, their eyes mirroring the possibilities that had just opened up in front of them. Nelson Ashcombe was an opium addict.

18

Ashcombe looked up at them vaguely.

"I'm sorry, Mr. Ashcombe," the maid cried, rushing into the room behind them. "I told them you wasn't receivin' visitors. They just pushed their way in!"

"It's all right, um . . ."

"Celia, sir."

"Yes, of course, Celia." Ashcombe looked at Kyria. "My lady. Was I . . . expecting you?"

"No. I am sorry to disturb you, Mr. Ashcombe," Kyria began politely. It seemed even more important now that they talk to the man. "But you see, I need information from you."

"And what is that?" He smiled benignly at her, leaning back in his chair.

"We need your mind, sir," Rafe said urgently, coming forward and moving the table with the pipe aside. He turned to Kyria. "I think he's just begun smoking it." He looked on past her to the maid. "Make him some coffee and bring it to him in his study."

" 'Ere, now!" Celia said in protest.

Ashcombe waved a weak hand at her. "There, now, better do it, girl. Mr. McIntyre has already found out our little secret, and I can tell that he is the sort who won't go away until he has gotten what he came for." The archaeologist sighed and swung his feet off the seat, sitting up. "Go ahead, I'm capable of talking to you. You are right — I had only started. And the Turkish way of smoking is not as strong as the Chinese. Much more civilized, don't you think? If you will just give me a little help up . . ."

Rafe put his hand under the other man's arm and lifted him from the chair. Ashcombe wobbled out of the room and down the stairs, clutching the handrail on one side, with Rafe on his other side, poised to catch him if he stumbled. Which he did only once, then strolled languidly into his study and sank into his chair behind the desk.

"Now," he said, "tell me. What is it you want? Something about the reliquary?"

"I'm not sure," Kyria replied. She reached into her reticule and removed her drawing of the necklace and the symbol. Unfolding it, she laid it out on the desk in front of Ashcombe.

"Ah," he said, smiling and nodding. "Yes. Inanna."

"What?"

"Inanna." He pointed to the symbol. "The knot of Inanna. And this is what, a necklace? Bracelet? I don't believe I've ever seen this one before. What book did you copy it from?"

"I didn't copy it. This is something I drew."

"Really? Ah. Seems you captured the style of the period very well. It is quite similar to some of the jewelry recovered in Mesopotamia."

He looked at their blank faces and said, "The knot of Inanna was a symbol often used to represent the goddess Inanna in ancient Mesopotamia. It was carved in her temples, on jewelry." He paused, then went on, "You remember the other day when I told you that the black diamond on the Reliquary of the Holy Standard was a mystical object from an ancient religion, one that the Byzantines then appropriated as their own religious artifact?"

Kyria and Rafe nodded.

"Well, legend has it that the black diamond originally belonged to the goddess Inanna. Her religion thrived in the Mesopotamian region and the Levant. She was the Goddess of the Earth, very important, and she had many worshipers. Among her titles were the Grandmother of God, the Queen of Heaven and Goddess of the Evening Star. She was the goddess of fertility and also of war. Temples dedicated to her have been uncovered at Uruk in Sumeria. She was known by many names — Nana, Inanna, Hathar. The Hittites called her Inaras, the Syrians Astarte, the Babylonians, Ishtar. But it was the same goddess, the same story."

"What is the story?" Kyria asked, intrigued.

"Oh, it is a common enough one in myths — the story of rebirth and regeneration. Similar to the Greco-Roman myths of Persephone and her mother — and also with certain aspects of the story of Orpheus, I suppose. The idea is that her lover, the great king/god, died, and to get him back, she died herself and went down into the underworld, adorned in her favourite jewelry of lapis lazuli. She stayed in the underworld for three days — you note the popular mystical number — and then she returned, alive. And according to the myth, she brought with her out of the underworld a powerful and beautiful stone — the black diamond named the Heart of Night — and it was placed in her crown in the temple."

A shiver ran down Kyria's spine. The archaeologist's words brought to her mind the dreams she had had of being in a dark place built of stone and lit only by torches and a brazier. There had been something in one dream about a crown, hadn't there? She remembered the heaviness of the bracelets on her arms, as well as something weighing down her head.

No, she told herself, that was ridiculous. She had not dreamed about a temple. The dreams had been vague in the extreme, and she could not really remember them well, only the general feeling of dread and anticipation. There was nothing in them that pointed to a temple; it was just that for some odd reason she had happened to remember them as Ashcombe spoke.

But why was that? she could not help but wonder.

Ashcombe was going on, talking about the worship of the ancient goddess. "The temples were staffed, of course, by priestesses. Powerful women of their time — the people's contact with the Earth Mother. There were festivals for the goddess held in the spring, the season of rebirth. Fertility rites to ensure the growth of crops. For example, in one ceremony, the goddess, who was viewed as both a fertility figure and as a sacred virgin — an interesting dichotomy, don't you think? — would each year renew her virginity and become the bride of the sacred king, thereby making him immortal. It was all a very potent mixture of fertility and rejuvenation, ensuring the king's status as a superior being and also giving the people faith that their crops would grow, that spring would always follow winter.

"The worship of the goddess faded away with the passing of these civilizations and the rise of monotheism. Of course, there were still pockets of people who kept up the ancient religions and maintained their devotion to the goddess. But eventually, as I said, the magnificent black diamond found its way into the hands of the Byzantine Church, and it was chosen to adorn one of their most sacred relics. Interesting, is it not, that it was still conceived as having, even by the Christian religious hierarchy, a sort of mystical power?"

"Yes, very interesting," Kyria murmured. Even more interesting was the fact that she had drawn this symbol of the goddess moments after staring at the box containing the diamond.

"Let me see . . ." Ashcombe rose and

strolled over to one of his bookshelves, looking through the shelves until he found the book he wanted.

Opening it on his desk, he flipped through the pages until he came to a drawing. "Here. This is a drawing of some of the pieces found at the excavation of Uruk."

Rafe and Kyria leaned closer to look at the drawings. One was a pen-and-ink sketch of several broken bits of jewelry, and beside it was another sketch of how the artist imagined the necklace must have looked when it was new and complete. Like Kyria's necklace, it was squares of gold, linked together, and on each small square was engraved a symbol much like the one both Kyria and Con had drawn. Ashcombe turned the page, showing them another plate, this one of a drawing of two earrings, each a rectangle of gold on which was etched a stylized image of a woman. From the bottom of the rectangle dangled little irregular beads.

"This is very typical of the jewelry given to Inanna or worn by her priestesses and followers," Ashcombe told them. "We are not sure which it was. This image, made out of lapis lazuli, the stone favored by the goddess, and carnelian, is of the goddess herself. In this representation, she is seen as the Queen of Heaven, one of her many appellations. The gentle, beautiful lady — unlike the representations of the later, more warlike tribes, in which she is pictured as the goddess of war. These things dangling from the earrings represent pomegranates, the fruit that she carried out of the underworld."

Kyria stared at the drawings, a chill running through her. She had never seen these things before, yet the irregular shape of the beads was almost precisely what she had drawn beneath the squares of her necklace. And the symbol, the knot, was as similar to what she had drawn as Con was to Alex.

How could she have drawn so accurately something she had never seen? Never even heard of before?

"Mr. Ashcombe." Rafe moved closer to the desk, his eyes intent on the other man. "Have you seen this symbol here? Recently? Say, on a medallion?"

Ashcombe blinked. "A medallion?"

"Yes. It is gold and round and hangs on a chain around the neck, and on the medallion is an engraving of this knot of Inanna."

"I . . . uh, no." Ashcombe looked around vaguely. "I can't recall having seen such a medallion." He returned to his chair and sat.

"It's very important," Kyria told him. "My little brother's safety may depend on it. Please think hard."

"Your brother? I don't understand." Ashcombe's eyes skittered away from her and over the room.

"Someone has kidnapped him, someone wearing a medallion with the knot engraved on it. I am afraid he will come to harm. Please, if you know anything about such a medallion — or the person who might be wearing it . . ."

The older man shook his head, more firmly this time. "No. No. I don't know who . . . It's a terrible thing, to steal a child."

"Yes, it is," Rafe agreed. "I needn't tell you that Lady Kyria is very worried about him. We are all very worried. He is only ten, you see."

"Surely they would not hurt him." Ashcombe looked troubled.

"Who? Who is it you think wouldn't hurt him?" Rafe pressed gently.

"Oh. Um, whoever kidnapped him, I mean. I'm terribly sorry, but you must excuse me now. I am very tired, you see. I was just about to, um, retire."

Kyria glanced pointedly at the clock atop a set of shelves. It was not yet five o'clock. Ashcombe saw her gaze and had the good grace to look a trifle embarrassed.

"I am sorry," he repeated, standing, and there was little they could do but leave.

"He was lying. I'm sure of it," Kyria said as she sat down in the carriage. "And he is an opium addict."

Rafe nodded. "Yes, it makes one wonder, doesn't it, if he is acquainted with the place we went last night." He leaned out toward the coachman and said, "Go down to the corner and turn right, go to the end of that block, then come back and stop at the corner."

He sat down, closing the door, and the coachman did as he instructed. When the coach pulled to a stop, Kyria turned to Rafe.

"What are you planning? Are we going to watch his house?"

"Like you, I think he was lying," Rafe said. "At the end, anyway, after we asked him about the medallion. I don't know exactly what he knows — I don't think he knows anything about the kidnapping. That seemed to disturb him. But I think he's seen the medallion before. He may even know who wears it. But I thought we might get more out of him by watching his house and seeing if he leaves, then following him. If he is upset enough about the idea of Alex being kidnapped, then he might just go to the person he knows has the medallion."

Kyria's stomach tightened in excitement, and she lifted the corner of the curtain to look out the window. "Do you think he will notice us?"

"I am hoping if he watched us leave or set that maid to watching us that our turning the corner and disappearing from sight would have been enough. I don't think they would wait to see if the carriage reappears at the corner. And this carriage is plain, not the one with the crest."

"What if he doesn't do anything?" Kyria went on anxiously. "I'm not sure he would be able to. He was clearly drugged."

"Yes, but I think he had not smoked very much by the time we interrupted him. While we were talking to him, he seemed to grow more alert."

"I only hope he is alarmed enough that he doesn't decide to go up and finish his pipe."

It was only a few moments later when the front door of Ashcombe's house opened, and the man himself emerged.

Not even glancing in the direction of their carriage, Ashcombe turned and began to walk the other way. Rafe leaned out and gave the coachman instructions, and after a moment, their carriage pulled out and started down the street after the archaeologist. Two blocks over, Ashcombe hailed a passing hansom and climbed in. The cab set off, the Moreland carriage following at a discreet distance.

"Back to Cheapside, it looks like," Kyria said, peeking out the side curtain.

Rafe nodded. "This is starting to look very familiar."

Kyria leaned across him to look out his window, and his arm curled around her, steadying her. For an instant, she wanted nothing so much as to simply lean against him and give way to the tears and anxiety that hammered inside her.

As if he knew what she was thinking, his arm tightened around her and he bent to brush his lips over her forehead. "It will be all right," he murmured. "We'll find him."

Kyria swallowed her tears, muttering thickly, "I know. I just wish . . . oh, why didn't I send them back home earlier? I should just have sent Denby with them and not waited for Jenkins. None of this would have happened!"

"Don't fret over what might have been. You didn't know what would happen. You couldn't have. Besides, has anyone ever been able to keep the twins out of trouble?"

Kyria smiled weakly. "No. I suppose not. Still, I feel responsible."

"It's the bastards who did it who are responsible. And trust me, they will pay for it."

Kyria looked at his face, cold and implacable in the dim light, and she had no doubt that he would follow through on his words. She kissed him lightly on the cheek. It was all she could do not to tell him of the love swelling in her heart at that moment. It wasn't the time or the place for the words, though, and she was not even sure that he would want to hear them at any time.

So she contented herself with whispering, "Thank you."

He smiled at her, his face softening, and he started to speak, but at that moment his eye was caught by something outside the window. He turned to look.

"Well, well, well," he said, satisfaction in his voice. "Looks like we're back."

Kyria's gaze followed his. "The opium den! It *is* involved. Do you think he's going to meet Habib?" Another thought struck her. "Do you think Alex may be held prisoner here?"

"If we're lucky," Rafe said as the carriage eased to a stop. "At the very least, we are going to see who our friend Ashcombe talks to. And *that* person may lead us to Alex." He paused, watching. "He's gone inside." Taking Kyria's hand, Rafe opened the carriage door. "Come on, darlin'."

Alex opened his eyes slowly and found himself staring at a brown-brick wall. He blinked, disoriented. His head hurt, and he had no idea where he was.

It was cold and he was lying on a narrow bed, a cot, really, with only a thin mattress of some sort, not nearly as soft as the down mattress in his own bed. It was then that he remembered the masked men in black clambering over the garden wall and hitting Denby on the head, then seizing Con and him and climbing back over the wall. He had struggled and screamed, but his captor had placed his hand over Alex's mouth and tossed him into the carriage, and the three men had climbed in after him. He had managed to slip out of his captor's grasp another time after the carriage had gone some distance. He had stuck his head out of the window and yelled before they had yanked him back in. That was the last thing he remembered, that and his head cracking hard against the carriage wall as his captor threw him to the side.

The blow must have knocked him out, he reasoned, as he had no memory of the rest of the trip. He wondered where he was. How long had he been asleep?

He began to sit up, and for a moment the world spun sickeningly. After a time everything righted itself, and he moved again, more slowly this time, gradually sitting up. He looked around the room, moving his head in the same slow, gingerly way.

There wasn't much to see. Besides the small bed, there was nothing in the room but a wooden stool and a pot. The room itself was small, one wall of brown brick and the others of cheap-looking wood. The floor was wooden, also, old and pockmarked. High on the brick wall was one small window, through which came the only light in the room.

It must still be daytime, Alex reasoned, *for there to be light outside, but not bright enough for it to be midday. It must be late afternoon.*

Alex shivered. It was cool in the room;

there was no fire. He wished he were home again. He wished Con were here. Things were always easier with Con around. He knew he wouldn't have felt so afraid.

He turned toward the door and lay back down on his side, curling up. His head hurt and so did his shoulder where it had slammed into the carriage door. His stomach growled. He was sure it was past teatime, and he thought with longing of Cook's tea cakes. Tears filled his eyes. A drop trembled on the end of his lashes, then plopped onto the bare mattress.

This was not, he thought, a very fun adventure at all.

He lay for a moment that way, thinking of Con and his home. Of Kyria and Reed and Rafe. His chest ached, thinking how much he missed them, how far away from him they were.

But thinking of them roused his spirits. They would come for him, he knew. Con would have run inside the house to tell them — Alex experienced a moment of bitter regret that he had not been able to get away from their captors as Con had — and they would have set out after him. But how would they find him? How would they know where he was?

He sat up again, thinking, the ache in his

head and his shoulder unnoticed now. He did not know why those men had taken him. He had heard of people being kidnapped and held for ransom, and he could only assume that that was what had happened. It was all, he suspected, related to that box. Reed and Kyria would, of course, pay them to get him back, even if it meant giving up the box. But something might happen; something could go wrong. Anyway, it seemed unfair that they should have to give up the box or pay just to get him back. And though his family would search for him, they might not be able to find him. Clearly, he thought, he could not just sit around bemoaning his fate, waiting for the others to rescue him. It was up to him to do something himself.

He cast his eyes around the room again. There was still nothing hopeful or prepossessing about it. He got up from the bed, crossed to the door and turned the knob. It would not open, which didn't surprise him. There was a keyhole above the knob, and he bent to look through it. He could see only a dark hallway beyond the door, even more poorly lit than the room he was in. He turned back and faced his room. The only exit beside the sturdy, locked door was the high window on the brick wall.

He walked over to it. It was too high for him to see through, even if he jumped. Nor was the window set in enough for him to get any purchase and pull himself up. He looked down at the stool and the bed and decided that the bed was higher, so he dragged and pushed the bed against the wall beneath the window and stood on it.

Now he could see out the window — at least as much as the window allowed. The window frame had been painted apparently rather vigorously, for a great deal of the paint had slopped over onto the windowpanes. The rest of the glass was so grimy that he could see very little through it, only the vague suggestion of other buildings outlined by the pale glow of the setting sun. He reached up and tried to push open the window, but it wouldn't budge. He spotted the window lock, and tried it, too, but he could not get it to move. He suspected that both window and lock were painted shut.

He sat down on the bed, trying to think what to do. He wished he had one of Rafe's guns — that little one he had given Kyria would be wonderful. He would call and call, and someone would surely come, and then he would pull the gun on him and force him to let him out . . .

Alex sighed and sat down on the bed. It was no use thinking about the gun; he didn't have it and that was that. He tried to think what Theo would do, or Rafe, if either of them was in the same situation. What was it Theo had told him and Con? *If you're stranded somewhere, you have to make do with what you have.*

He stuck his hands into his pockets and pulled out everything in them, making a little pile on the bed. There was a piece of string and three interesting pebbles he had picked up in the garden today, the stub of a pencil, his jackknife and one of Uncle Bellard's little lead soldiers that he had found lying in one of the hallways.

He studied his pile. It didn't look like a very helpful lot. He picked up the small knife and unfolded it. The blade was only a couple of inches long. He thought about how he could conceal it behind his back and then lure someone in — surely there must be somebody here besides himself — and then he could plunge the knife into that person and make his escape.

Looking at the small knife, he had to wonder if it would actually go in deep enough to do any damage. He had the feeling it might just snap off. It wasn't terribly sharp, either.

Finally, he stood up, climbed onto the bed and applied his knife to the lock of the window, scraping at the paint. After what seemed like an inordinately long time and a great deal of tugging — and one broken fingernail — he managed to force the lock open. The window, however, still would not open. The paint no doubt, and he set to work chipping away at the paint all around the edge of the window.

There was the sound of feet in the hallway outside, and Alex quickly dropped to a sitting position on the bed. Nerves jangled in his stomach when he heard the rattle of a key in the lock. A moment later, the door opened.

One of his kidnappers stood in the open doorway, masked and dressed in a black robe. A gold medallion hung around his neck. Involuntarily, Alex swallowed and scooted back a little. The man carried a tray. On it was set a bowl and a spoon and a hunk of bread. He set the tray down on the floor and pointed at it.

"Eat." He turned and started to leave.

"No, wait!" Alex hopped off the bed and hurried toward him. "Don't go yet!" He tried to peer around the man into the hall. Were there any others with him? "I . . . um, I need a light. Light. See?" He pointed toward the small window, through which increasingly less light shone.

The man looked blankly at him, then at the window. He shook his head.

"A candle. That's all. Please? Couldn't I have a candle?" Alex went on. "It will be dark soon."

The man continued to look blank, then finally shrugged and left the room. Alex heard the ominous click of the lock.

He sat down on the stool and picked up the bowl and spoon. He poked at the meat and vegetables in the bowl of soup. It looked none too appetizing, but he was quite hungry. He wondered if they had drugged it.

Eventually hunger won out, and Alex dug into the soup. It was not the best he'd ever eaten, but at least it was filling, and he didn't feel any ill effects, at least so far. He gulped the food down as quickly as he could, then climbed back onto the bed to work on the window. He feared the light would not last much longer.

He chipped away at the paint around the frame of the window as high as he could reach, pausing now and again to try to shove the window up. Finally, to his astonishment, the window let out a crack and moved. He renewed his efforts, and slowly, creakingly, the window inched up.

Through the open window he could see the tops of a few buildings and the sky, deepening into purple now, but little else. He needed to be higher to see out of it properly.

He jumped down and picked up the stool, placing it on the bed below the window, then stepped shakily onto it, holding on to the window for balance. He was high enough now that he could stick his head out the window.

It wasn't a pleasant sight. He was in the midst of a number of buildings of similar height and color. Below his window, the building ran straight down three stories to the narrow street below. Alex sucked in his breath, feeling faintly sick as he looked down. There was no hope of escaping through this window.

He began to pull his head back into the room, and as he did so, he noticed that farther along the building, no more than a few yards away, the building jutted out below his floor, so that beneath those windows lay the roof of the lower part of the building. If he had been in a room down the hall, he would have been able to climb out of his window and jump down onto the roof below.

He wished fiercely that he had been placed in a different room. He looked across the jut-out of the roof and saw that it came up to another building of the same height. It looked as if only a foot or so separated the two buildings. Alex knew that he could jump that easily. There would be an opening from that roof into that building, wouldn't there? He would be able to go down the stairs of that building and out the door. Or there might be a fire escape running down the side of the building.

It seemed bitterly unfair that they had put him in this room, instead of one farther down the hall.

Alex eased back through the window and shut it. He returned the stool to the floor and sat down on it to think. If only he could get his captors to let him out of this room, perhaps he could run down the hall and into one of the rooms where the roof abutted. He knew that he could not outrun a man all the way down the stairs to the first floor, especially since he had no idea where the stairs or the door were. But surely, if he took them by surprise, he could get past them to one of the other rooms. And if he locked the door behind him, it would give him time to get out the window and across to the other building. It seemed to him an eminently reasonable plan. And wouldn't Kyria and Reed and Rafe be surprised to see him?

Alex allowed himself to bask for a moment in the imagined glory of his homecoming. Then he set himself to thinking about how to get out of his room and into the hallway. He would have to do it soon, as dusk was falling.

He went over to the door and began to pound on it, using both his fists. "Hello! Come here! Open up!"

A voice outside yelled something in a language Alex did not understand. He continued to shout and pound. Finally, the key rattled in the lock again, and the door opened. The same man who had brought him his food stepped in, frowning.

"No!" he roared. "Silence!"

Alex noticed that the key was in the lock, hanging from a string. Did all the doors open and lock with a single key? Alex looked as agitated as he could, saying, "Please . . . I have to, you know, use the facilities."

The man stared at him blankly, and Alex tried his best to pantomime his needs. The man glared at him, but this time with some understanding.

"There," he growled, pointing to the pot in the corner.

"No!" Alex exclaimed. "I can't! You don't understand! I cannot! Please!" His voice grew higher and louder with each word, and he screwed his face up, wondering if he could manage to make himself cry. Con had done such a good job of whining and carrying on the day the men invaded their house, it seemed to him that he should be able to, as well. He began to wail, covering his face with his hands to hide the lack of tears.

Then he remembered one of his many cousins, a pudgy blond girl who had thrown a tantrum when denied another tea cake. This, he thought, would be a perfect time to emulate her.

"I won't!" he screeched. "I won't! I want to go home!"

He then flung himself onto the floor and began to drum his hands and feet on it, shrieking and crying and making as much noise as he possibly could. The man backed out of the room quickly and closed the door. With disappointment, Alex heard the key turn in the lock.

Alex drew breath and redoubled his efforts, screaming and pounding on the door. After a long time, he heard voices in the hall again. Pleased, Alex grew even louder in his sobs and wails.

"Bloody hell!" he heard a voice say, and the door opened again.

A different man stood in the doorway. He, too, was dressed in the black robe, with the same gold medallion dangling from his neck, and he wore a black mask on the upper half of his face. But this man had fair skin, and the hair on top of his head was strawberry blond.

"What the devil do you want!" he snapped. "Here! Stop making that infernal noise! What do you want?"

"I have to go!" Alex wailed. This man was standing outside the room, holding the door open, and Alex could see past him. The other guard, the one who had entered the room before, stood behind him, leaning against the wall on the other side of the hallway. The key dangled loosely on its string from his hand.

"Well, use that." The man gestured at the pot.

"I can't! I just can't!"

"Do you think you're at home in your castle?" the man asked derisively. "Do you think there's indoor plumbing here?"

"I don't care! I don't care! I won't stay in the same room with it! I can't. I want to go home! I can't stay here any longer! I want to go home!"

Alex found that he was actually rather enjoying his tantrum, which at home would have gotten him sent straight to his room with the admonition to not come out until he was ready to apologize and had written a five-hundred word paper on why he should control his anger. Jumping up and down in a paroxysm of childish rage, Alex moved closer and closer to the Englishman, who edged back, his face contorting at the assault on his eardrums. Alex finished his tirade by kicking the man in the shin as hard as he could.

The Englishman let out a high shriek of his own and clutched at his shin, hopping about. Behind him the other guard began to laugh, quickly covering his mouth with one hand. At that moment, Alex lunged forward, grabbing the key from the man's lax fingers and pelted off down the hall.

"Blast! Well, don't just stand there, you fool! Get him!"

Belatedly the other guard started running after him. But by that time Alex had passed several doors and was sure that he was far enough along to be in the section where the building jutted out. He opened a door, relieved to find that it was not locked and darted in, slamming the door shut after him. Quickly he put the key in the lock and twisted it, letting out a laugh of relief and happiness when the key turned the lock.

Whirling around, he scanned the room. There were some crates in this room and a wooden chair. He grabbed the chair and put it under the doorknob, hoping that that would delay them a little even if they managed to unlock the door.

The knob rattled and the door trembled in its frame as the guard shook it, letting loose angry words in the same unknown language. The Englishman must have joined him, for Alex heard him say, "Well, go get another key, you bloody fool. There must be one down in the office."

Alex did not wait to hear any more. He ran to the window and began to work on its lock. This one was not painted over, fortunately, but it still took him three tries and another broken fingernail to get it undone, and then several more strenuous attempts, fueled by fear, to shove the window up. He stuck his head out. It was dark now, but the moon and stars and a few street lamps provided enough light to see the expanse of the roof a few feet below him and, not far away, the other building.

Drawing a breath, Alex swung his leg over the sill and wriggled around until his legs were completely out of the window. He had to force himself to let go. The fall wasn't far, and he landed on his feet. He turned and made his way across the roof, moving slowly in the dim light. He reached the edge of the roof and saw that the next building was more than a foot away, at least two. He knew he could easily jump that far, but this high, in the dark, the gap looked huge. He moved back, thinking that he would have to do a running jump if he hoped to make it.

His heart pounded madly in his chest. He could do it, he told himself. He frequently jumped the brook at home, and it was wider than this. Still, his stomach jittered with nerves.

Behind him there was a roar, then a crash. *They had gotten into the room.* Alex took off and launched himself at the other building.

19

Kyria started toward the front door of the opium den, through which Nelson Ashcombe had entered, but Rafe took her hand and held her back.

"This time, let's start with the back door."

"What if it's locked?"

He shrugged. "We'll improvise."

They took the narrow passageway that led between the opium den and the windowless brick wall of the building next to it. It was dark, with only a little light straying in from the street and the covered windows of the building that housed the opium den. Kyria tried not to think about what she might be stepping in as she lifted her skirts above her ankles and followed Rafe. They reached the vague outline of the back door, and Rafe turned the knob. It did not surprise either of them that it was locked.

"Stay right here," Rafe whispered, and moved down a few feet to a window. It was dark, and Rafe leaned close for a minute, listening. Then he pulled a pistol from the depths of his coat and rapped the handle sharply on the glass, breaking it. Carefully, he reached inside and turned the lock, then pushed the window up. Motioning to Kyria to stay where she was, he slipped over the windowsill and disappeared into the dark room.

Kyria waited in a fever of impatience until the back door opened and Rafe reappeared. Letting out a breath she didn't realize she had been holding, Kyria joined him inside. Rafe silently jerked his head toward the staircase, and she nodded, following him over to the stairs and up.

They tiptoed along the hallway above, pausing outside doors, listening for the sound of voices. A few flickering sconces lit the hallway dimly and cast odd shadows as they passed. Kyria had noticed the first time they searched the opium den that light was not something seemingly favored by the patrons. The uncertain light and wavering shadows reminded her of something, she wasn't sure what. She shivered, remembering what it was — the flickering torchlight in her dreams.

There were murmuring voices in one or two rooms, and once they heard a man's soft laughter, but they moved on, suspecting that it was not what they were searching for.

They were approaching another door when they heard an explosive voice issuing from within. ". . . the devil are you playing at!"

They stopped and glanced at each other, then crept closer, putting their ears to the door. They heard the murmur of another man's voice, the tones soothing and calm.

Then came the first man's voice again, at first low, then louder as he apparently turned back toward the door. ". . . just a boy. How can you expose a child to danger?"

Rafe and Kyria looked at each other again. She was sure the voice was Ashcombe's and just as sure that they were talking about Alexander. But who was the other man? She strained her ears trying to distinguish his words.

She heard a murmur, then the words "a fool," followed by more murmuring, ending with "will happen."

"You hope so," Ashcombe replied, then must have moved to the other side of the room for the rest of what he said was undecipherable.

There was the sound of feet on the stairs, and Rafe and Kyria sprang back, alarmed. Quickly, they darted across the hall, and Rafe opened the nearest door. They slipped inside, easing the door shut behind them, and turned to see a young man reclining on his elbow on a narrow bed across the room. There was a small table beside him, and on it the usual water pipe and matches, as well as a few small ornate boxes. The sweet smell of opium and tobacco hung in the air.

Kyria's stared at the young man, her heart slamming in her chest, certain the man was about to yell for help. To her surprise, he just smiled sweetly and breathed, "Ah, a goddess. Or are you a muse, come to visit me?"

Kyria shook her head and held her finger to her lips for silence.

"Ah," the young man said, nodding as if he understood. "The muse is silent. It is ever so, isn't it?"

He pulled again on his water pipe, and it burbled almost musically. Kyria looked back at Rafe. He had opened the door a sliver and had his eye to the crack. She heard steps in the hallway and then the opening and closing of the door opposite.

Rafe eased the door to and leaned closer to Kyria, whispering in her ear, "One man just entered. He was dressed in black, with a cloak flung over his shoulder and carrying a mask. And there was a gold medallion hanging around his neck."

Kyria's eyes widened, and she clutched Rafe's arm. "Alex? Did he have Alex?"

He shook his head, then added softly, "I doubt they would bring him here — too many people about. But I wonder if the man might not be coming from or be on his way to wherever they're keeping Alex."

He opened the door a fraction again and looked out. They waited an agonizingly long time. Kyria was afraid the occupant of the room might at any moment start talking to them again — or worse, decide to take offense at their invading his room and call for someone to evict them.

When the door across the hall opened again, she jumped at the cracking sound. Her fingers dug into her palms as she waited, tautly listening to the man's footsteps as he moved down the hallway toward the stairs. Then Rafe looked at her, and she nodded. He opened the door and peered out, then slipped out of the room, Kyria right behind him.

"Farewell, fair muse," said the man in the room as they eased the door closed behind them.

They hurried down the hallway, paused,

looked down the staircase, then moved silently down it and out the back door. At the end of the narrow alleyway, they saw the dark-robed figure silhouetted eerily for an instant against the faint light of the street. Then he turned left and disappeared from sight.

Rafe and Kyria hurried after him, stopping when they reached the street and carefully peering around the corner of the building. They saw their quarry striding down the street in the distance, and they set out after him on foot.

They kept a good distance behind him, staying in the shadows cast by the building walls. The area through which the robed man walked was much the same as where the opium den was located, dark and squalid, consisting primarily of stark warehouses and shipping offices, and as he came closer to the docks of Cheapside, cheap taverns and seamen's hotels began to appear. Now and then noise and light spilled out of a tavern as the door opened and closed.

One such door opened in front of Rafe and Kyria, and a number of men and a woman staggered out, laughing. For a moment they blocked their view of the cloaked man. Rafe and Kyria hurried around the group and found that the street ahead of them was empty. Their quarry had disappeared.

"Did he see us? Do you think he tried to lose us?" Kyria asked as they broke into a trot.

"I don't know. It could have been sheer bad luck, too."

They reached the spot where they had last seen the man and proceeded more slowly, looking carefully around them. Rafe was very aware of the fact that if the man had spotted them, he might have just stepped into a darkened doorway in order to attack them.

They reached the cross street and turned to look up and down it, searching for a glimpse of the cloaked and hooded man. They saw no one.

"No!" Kyria cried softly. "We have to find him!"

Her eyes filled with tears. She had been so hopeful that the man would lead them to Alex! It seemed unbearably cruel that they had lost him now.

Rafe cursed under his breath. "Even if he didn't lead us to Alex, I figured I could grab him and make him tell me what they'd done with him."

"What are we going to do now?"

Rafe shrugged, looking again all around them. "Just take a guess which way he went, I suppose."

Kyria turned to look up the narrow side street and spotted a dark carriage rolling down the street toward them at a fast pace.

"Rafe . . ."

"I see it." Rafe took her arm and whisked her up the street, looking for a deep doorway.

The carriage behind them picked up speed. A dark figure stuck his head out the window. Rafe jumped into the nearest doorway, pushing Kyria in before him, then whirled to stand in front of her, guns at the ready.

The driver pulled up the horses, and the carriage clattered to a stop beside them. "McIntyre! Where's Kyria?"

Rafe relaxed as he recognized Reed, and he stepped out of the doorway. Kyria ran around him and up to the carriage.

"What are you doing? You scared me half to death!" Kyria scolded. "How did you know we were here?"

"I didn't," Reed said. "I just happened to see you. Get in. We are trying to find where Alex is hidden."

"We?"

Reed opened the door, and Rafe and

Kyria climbed into the carriage. Next to Reed sat Con, and across the seat from them was one of the white-robed Keepers of the Holy Standard.

Kyria slipped into the seat next to Con and quietly took his hand in hers. His fingers curled around hers tightly.

Rafe took a seat across from her, beside the Keeper, and said mildly, "All right. What happened?"

"We lost the trail, couldn't find anyone else who had seen the carriage," Reed said. "So we went back home, and Brother Philip was there."

He gestured toward the Keeper, and the monk nodded gravely to them. He was a young man with thick, curling, black hair and huge, dark eyes, in which burned some emotion, though Rafe was unsure whether it was religious fervor or simply the excitement of the hunt.

"It seems," Reed went on, "that Brother Philip has been watching our house the last few days, working in shifts with some of the others. He happened to see Alex abducted this afternoon, and since there was only one of him and three of the kidnappers, he wisely decided not to try to fight the men, but to follow the carriage. He lost it somewhere around here close to the docks. So he came back to the house to tell us, and we have been driving around, hoping to see something that will give us a clue where Alex is." He paused, then added, "What are you two doing here?"

The carriage started up again as Rafe told them his story. Reed and Brother Philip looked out the window, searching for anything that would help them. Kyria and Rafe pushed aside the curtains on the other side of the carriage and joined them in the search.

As they rode, Rafe told them how he and Kyria had followed the archaeologist to the opium den and from there had pursued a black-clad figure wearing a gold medallion.

"Alex must be around here somewhere!" Reed burst out. "It isn't just coincidence that we both found our way to this spot. They must be keeping him somewhere near."

"Yes, but where? How are we to find him?" Kyria asked. "How can we know which of all these buildings he is in? It seems impossible."

The carriage turned right at the next corner, the coachman turning in ever-widening circles as he had been all the time they had been near the docks. Rafe stiffened and looked more closely down the street ahead of them.

"What's that? Something is happening down there."

Everyone crowded to the windows on that side. In the next block they could see that several men had run into the street and were looking up at the top of a building as if searching for something. The occupants of the carriage turned their eyes upward, too, and there they saw a flash of movement in the dark. Reed thumped the roof of the carriage twice, and the coach jumped forward.

They pounded down the street toward the knot of men. Kyria, her eyes glued to the roof of the building, gasped as she made out a small figure running across it, then jumping across the gap onto the next building.

"Alex! Oh, my God, it must be Alex!"

Alex landed on the next building and fell, rolling across the flat roof, filled with relief to find himself on the sturdy surface of the roof, instead of falling down the narrow shaft between the buildings. Behind him, his pursuers were clambering out of the window and running across the roof after him.

Alex jumped to his feet and took off

across the roof, running over to the other side. He stopped when he came to the short parapet. It was a good four feet from this roof to the next one, a space he didn't dare risk. He turned and looked behind him. The black-clad men were jumping across the gap and pounding toward him. He turned and ran toward the front of the building. He could see several men on the street below, gesturing and talking. A carriage was rattling down the street toward them. The men in the street ran toward the door of the building on which he now stood and tried to open the door, but it would not budge.

Alex turned and started running back to the side he had just left, looking for a fire escape. But there were three men on the roof with him now, all closing in on him. He turned and ran back the way he had originally come, once more throwing himself over the gap and onto the roof of the building he had just escaped. As he landed, he heard the sweetest sound he had ever heard.

It was the voices of his brothers and sister, all crying, "Alex! Alex! Hang on!"

He could see the top of the fire escape on this building, and he ran along the roof toward it. He had just reached it and was about to swing his leg around onto it when hands grabbed him roughly from behind and snatched him back.

Kyria and the others tumbled out of the carriage and rushed toward the crowd of men. Rafe pulled his pistols from his coat as he ran and fired over the men's heads, sending most of them running, then charged in the front door of the building. Brother Philip began to lay about him with his thick, wooden staff, quickly taking out another two ruffians. Reed, armed with only his fists, was doing a good job of taking care of the two who remained. Kyria ran for the metal staircase that went up the side of the building. The passageway between the two buildings was narrow, but she slipped through it easily and pulled down the bottom section of the fire escape, then started charging up the metal stairs toward the roof, where her little brother was now struggling in the grip of his captors. Constantine was right on her heels.

By the time Kyria and Con reached the roof, a man was dragging Alex inside through the window. The boy was still squirming and kicking and screaming — at least until his captor doubled up his fist and slammed it into the side of his head. Alex went limp.

Kyria let out an unholy shriek and ran across the roof, not so much climbing through the window as diving through it straight into the back of the man carrying Alex. All of them went tumbling to the floor, with Con jumping in on top.

Rafe, running up the stairs inside the building, heard Kyria's high-pitched scream, and he took the last flight of stairs as if shot from a cannon. He met two of the black-clad kidnappers at the top of the stairs and took out one with a well-placed foot behind his knees that sent him crumpling to the stairs and then tumbling down them. The other one swung at Rafe's head, and Rafe blocked the swing with his left arm, turning the pistol in his right hand around and bringing the butt of it down sharply on the man's head. He slumped to the floor and Rafe stepped over him, then ran down the hallway toward the sounds of fighting.

What met his eyes — and Reed's, as he charged into the room a moment later — was the sight of a large man rolling across the floor, desperately trying to fight off the flying fists and feet of a redheaded woman and a boy. He was screaming, more in fear, Rafe thought, than in pain, but Kyria silenced that finally by grabbing his hair with both hands and banging his head sharply against the floor.

"All right, all right, that's enough," Reed said, moving in as she started to rap the man's head against the wood a second time. "I think you've stopped him."

Kyria looked up and saw her brother and, beside him, Rafe, who was grinning down at her, his blue eyes electric with the excitement of battle. "Alex!" she cried suddenly, remembering the reason for her rage.

She scrabbled across the floor to where he lay, still and silent. Tears flooded her eyes as she slipped her arms under him and lifted his head and shoulders, holding him to her. She cradled him against her chest, saying his name and smoothing his hair back from his forehead.

"What happened?" Reed asked, kneeling beside them.

"Is he all right?" Con cried, squirming between them. "Alex? Can you hear me?"

"That brute struck him!" Kyria told them hotly, her anger flaring anew at the thought of it. She bent and kissed his forehead. "He's breathing." She looked up anxiously at the others. "Do you think he'll be all right?"

"We'll take him home," Reed told her,

"and send for the doctor."

"We have to go!" Rafe said urgently. "They're coming."

He swung out into the hallway, leveling his pistols. "Stop right there!"

Three of the black-clad men were charging toward them from the stairs. The masks had fallen off two of them, and the third one's dangled foolishly from one ear. Rafe was not sure whether or not any of them spoke English, but apparently the guns in his hands were something they could all understand, for they came to an abrupt halt and gazed at him warily.

"We are leaving now," Rafe went on, "so I want you to move back." He motioned with his guns, and the men obediently backed away.

Behind him, Reed came out into the hallway, carrying Alex in his arms, Con and Kyria beside him. Rafe started forward, and the black-clad men fell back even farther.

There was the sound of feet pounding on the stairs, and a moment later, the dark head of Brother Philip came into view. He stopped at the sight of the tableau before him. "Ah! I see you have them."

"Are there any more out in the street?" Rafe asked.

"No. They have all fled. They took the man I knocked out with them. I would have pursued them, but I feared you might need my help."

"I do. I think I saw a key back there, lying beside that fellow whose head Kyria was cracking."

The monk's eyes widened a little at this statement, but he said nothing.

Reed spoke up. "Yes, there was a key."

"All right. Good. I'm going to put these fellows in that room behind them." He spoke to the men, motioning again with a pistol. "You all go into that room. That's right."

The men backed into the room, and Rafe closed the door. "Now, Brother Philip, you get that key and I will lock them up. Then you go with Reed and the others down to the carriage."

The monk nodded and bounded away to fetch the key. Kyria, Con and Reed, still carrying Alex, started slowly down the stairs. Brother Philip returned and handed Rafe the key, then ran down the stairs to join the others, his staff at the ready just in case some of their enemies had found the courage to return.

Rafe tried the key in the door and found that it fit. With a smile, he turned the key.

"So long, fellows. Don't worry, we'll send someone to get you out. What is it you call them here? Oh, yeah, 'peelers,' isn't it?"

He caught up to the others on the stairs and passed them to go out the front door first and make sure that no one was waiting for them. The dark street was deserted except for their carriage, the coachman standing anxiously at the horses' heads.

The coachman let out a gusty sigh of relief and climbed back to his seat, urging the horses forward to meet them. Rafe climbed into the carriage and took Alex from Reed, the others piling in behind them. Brother Philip, to give them more room, joined the coachman.

As the carriage rolled forward, Alex stirred and muttered something incomprehensible. In another moment, his eyelids fluttered open. They soon focused on his sister.

"Kyria! I knew I heard you. And Reed. Where's Con?"

"I'm here! I'm right here," Con cried. "You're all right! I knew you would be!"

"Are you kidding?" Rafe said, leaning over to ruffle Con's hair. "It'd take a lot more than these fellas to do in either one of you."

* * *

Rafe trotted down the front stairs the following morning, his mind on the task before him. They had returned to Broughton House late the night before, and after Reed had sent for the police and a doctor, they had spent a good deal of time looking over Alex and seeing that he was fed and put to bed.

The doctor had pronounced Alex fit, despite the bump on his head, and had advised a day or two of rest for the boy, advice, he acknowledged with a sigh, that was unlikely to be followed. He had, after all, been the Morelands' doctor for many years. The police had left and returned sometime later with the disheartening news that the miscreants had all fled the warehouse by the time they arrived. They had assured Reed that they would investigate the matter thoroughly, including visiting the opium den, but it was clear that they found the Morelands' explanation preposterous and were likely going to go through the motions solely because of the family's prominence.

Everyone had finally retired, Rafe kissing Kyria's hand and leaving her and Reed to put the twins to bed, then going down the hall to his own room. He spent a lonely and rather wakeful remainder of the night alone in his bed, thinking.

By morning, he had decided on a course of action, and so planned to leave the house early to conduct a little private business.

As he reached the bottom step, he was startled to see the front door open and a large, rather odd-looking individual step inside. The stranger was tall and broad-shouldered and dressed in a lightweight white suit at odds with the chilly November weather. He wore no hat on his thick, black, shoulder-length hair, and his bronzed face was half-covered by a bushy black beard and mustache.

"Who the hell are you?" Rafe demanded, striding forward.

"Who the devil are you?" replied the intruder in a crisp British accent, dropping the valise he carried in one hand and balling up his hands into fists in readiness.

At that moment Rafe's question was answered by a shriek from Kyria on the stairs above him. "Theo!"

20

Kyria raced down the stairs past Rafe and threw herself into the large man's arms. He hugged her close, laughing.

"Well, it's good to see I haven't been forgotten," Theo said, planting a kiss on Kyria's forehead. "My God, girl, you get more beautiful every time I see you. I suppose half the hearts in London are still at your feet."

"Don't be silly." Kyria's face was wreathed in smiles. "It is so wonderful to see you. We were all hoping you would be here for Olivia's wedding."

"I was, too," Theo said ruefully. "But I ran into some problems, and I'm a few weeks late. I'm sorry."

His arm around Kyria's waist, Theo's eyes went beyond her to Rafe, his expression curious and faintly wary.

"Oh!" Kyria exclaimed. "Theo, you must meet Rafe."

She took Theo's hand, pulling him over to Rafe. "Theo, this is Rafe McIntyre. He is, um, a friend of Stephen St. Leger. He came for the wedding and has been . . . well, it's a terribly long story, but he has been helping us ever since. Rafe, this is my eldest brother, Theodosius, Lord Raine."

The two men shook hands, silently taking each other's measure. They were interrupted by a tornado in the form of the twins, who came bounding down the stairs, shrieking their brother's name, and launched themselves at him. Theo staggered back under the onslaught, but it was clear from the broad smile that creased his face that he did not mind it.

"Theo." Reed's greeting was quieter as he descended the stairs, but his grin was broad, and he maneuvered around the bouncing twins to shake his brother's hand heartily.

"What is this?" Reed teased, giving Theo's beard a tug. "Have you gone native?"

Theo's teeth shone whitely between the curling black beard and mustache, and his bright blue eyes twinkled. "Just got out of the outback and then jumped a ship straightaway to get to Olivia's wedding. Storm set us back, though, blew us off course, and I lost most of my luggage. Why else do you think I'm freezing in this summer suit?"

Kyria urged them all into the sitting room and rang for tea and food for Theo.

"I'm so sorry you didn't make it for the wedding," she told her brother. "It was lovely, and Olivia was ecstatic. They'll be on their honeymoon for a month in Europe. Please say you will stay until they get back so that you can see them."

"Of course I will. Got to give them their present, after all — Olivia will be happy to know I managed to save it, even if I did lose my clothes," Theo said cheerfully.

"So the box wasn't a wedding present," Kyria said. "I thought surely it was not. But was it you who sent it, Theo? I know you have barely gotten home and I hate to plague you with questions, but there has been the most enormous mess over that box, and I just have to know —"

"Know what?" Theo looked at her blankly. "What box? What are you talking about?"

"The reliquary," Reed told him. "Are you telling us that you didn't send it to Kyria?"

"What's a reliquary?" Theo asked.

"You didn't send it?" Kyria cried. "Then who did? And why?"

"I'll show you the thing," Reed said in answer to his brother's question, and went to get the box from the safe in the study.

While he was gone, the twins proceeded to pelt their eldest brother with their versions of the story about the box.

"It's a religious thing," Con told him, "and I was the one who figured out how to open it."

"And they kidnapped me 'cause they wanted it," Alex stuck in. "But I got away, and then Rafe and Reed and Kyria came and got me —"

"Me, too!" Con said indignantly.

"And Con. He's the one who told everybody about the men grabbing me."

"They grabbed us both, but I got away."

Theo looked at Kyria in confusion. "What are they talking about? Alex was kidnapped?"

Kyria nodded and shushed the boys. "Let me tell him the whole thing."

By the time she finished, Theo's jaw was hanging open in astonishment. "Are you having me on?" he asked suspiciously.

Kyria laughed. "No. I promise you. I know it's all terribly bizarre, but that is what happened."

"Here," Reed said, coming into the room and setting the box down in front of his brother. "See for yourself."

His large hands moving carefully, Theo

removed the reliquary from the drawstring bag. He sucked in his breath in admiration. "It's magnificent! No wonder everyone wants it. Look at this jewel — is that a black diamond? It's huge!"

Kyria nodded. "It's called the Heart of Night. The box opens. Show him, Con."

Con proceeded to do so, and Theo looked even more awestruck at the sight of the ancient scrap of cloth. He closed the box and returned it to the bag, then handed it to Reed, saying, "But why was it sent to you, Kyria?"

"We thought you had done it. The man who delivered it was named Leonides Kousoulous, or so we think. That is the name that was on his calling card, and —"

"Kousoulous! But I know him." Theo frowned, saying, "That must have been what he was talking about! Oh, my God — you said he died?"

"Yes. I'm sorry. We thought you had sent him, but then when you didn't know about the reliquary, I assumed you didn't know him, either."

"How did you say it happened?"

"Someone stabbed him," Rafe explained. "I saw it happen, but I was too far away to get there in time to catch the culprit. We carried him inside, but he was too badly wounded to survive."

Theo put his head on his hand, looking stricken. "He must have been bringing it to me. Bloody hell! If only I had made it in time . . ."

"What do you mean?" Reed asked. "Why did he ask for Kyria?"

Theo shook his head. "I don't — Oh! He probably was saying *kyrie*. He was Greek. He always called me *Lord* Moreland. Kyrie Moreland. I didn't bother to explain the titles, and *kyrie* means *lord* in Greek."

"You said he talked to you about the box?" Rafe prodded.

"He wrote me." Theo sighed and rubbed his face with his hands. "I got a letter from him right before I left Australia. He was being very secretive, talking about some object without ever really saying what it was. He wrote that he needed my advice. He said he had bought something and had later learned that it was even more valuable than he had thought. He and I had talked many times about artifacts and what should be done with them. We agreed that they shouldn't be looted and sent all over the world to wealthy private collectors." He looked at Kyria. "I'm sorry. Father knows how I feel about that."

Kyria nodded encouragingly. "I know.

That is one reason that we were so puzzled, thinking that you had sent it."

"I could hardly make heads or tails of what he was talking about, he was so blasted mysterious — and his handwriting looked as if he'd done it in the dark. He kept bringing up faith and God, and I hadn't the least notion what he was upset about. If I hadn't known him and trusted him, I would have dismissed his letter as a lunatic's ravings. Anyway, he wanted me to come to Istanbul and talk to him. Alternatively, he said he would meet me somewhere, anywhere I chose. So I cabled him back, telling him I had to return to England and that I would meet him here in London. But then my ship was delayed, and I didn't make it back in time."

"He came here, but the servants didn't know what he was talking about," Kyria said. "They thought he was saying Kyria Moreland, too, and they told him we had all gone to Broughton Park for the wedding."

Theo nodded. "He was not proficient in English. We usually conversed in French." He sighed. "Poor chap."

"Well then," Kyria said, "the reliquary belongs to you. It was you he was bringing it to." She was aware of a curious reluctance to turn over the reliquary, even to her brother.

"Me?" Theo shook his head. "Oh, no, it's not mine. It was Kousoulous's. He was just asking my advice. He gave it to you."

"No, we just *thought* that was what he was doing."

"It is as much yours as anyone's," Theo insisted. "You are the one who has been dealing with it. You should make the decision of what to do with it." He paused, then added curiously, "What *are* you going to do with it?"

"I don't know. I hadn't made any decision because I was waiting to hear from you. I thought you had sent it for a reason. Now that I know why he brought it here . . . well, it obviously doesn't belong to any of us. And I certainly have no intention of selling it to that dealer or one of the collectors."

"What about a museum?" Reed asked.

"There is the Imperial Ottoman Museum in Istanbul," Theo suggested.

"Yes. But I can't help but think that the Keepers have the best claim to it," Kyria mused. "Their order was entrusted its care, and they have cared for it for hundreds and hundreds of years."

"That's true," Rafe agreed. "And I think that they have amply demonstrated that they were not the ones who killed Mr. Kousoulous or invaded your house."

"They certainly helped us yesterday," Reed agreed. "And they saved you two the other night."

"It seems a shame to hide it from sight," Theo said.

"I don't know. Perhaps that would be the best thing in the larger sense — to protect it, to restore it to the holy order that has looked after it for centuries, rather than making it an object of display in a museum." Kyria shrugged.

"Well, whatever you think is best, Kyria," Theo said. "I trust your instincts."

Kyria smiled at him. "I'm not sure *I* do." She was quite aware of feeling again that curious reluctance to give up the reliquary.

She was still feeling it some hours later as she sat in the study, the reliquary sitting in her lap, her hand resting lightly on it. The others had all gone — the twins to their studies, Rafe out on some personal business matter, and her older brothers, once Reed's valet had shaved Theo and cut off an excess of hair, off to their club to while away their time with a few drinks and masculine company.

Kyria had puttered around for a while, starting and stopping a number of tasks, her mind not on any of them. She had thought about Rafe and wondered what pressing personal business had sent him off this afternoon. It seemed odd that he should suddenly decide that he needed to work on some business matter when he had been in the city for some time now and had not made the slightest move to do any business. She could not help but wonder if he was considering an imminent departure.

There was no reason, she told herself, to think that he was planning to leave other than that was precisely what everyone said men did if one was unwise enough to let a man "have his way" with one. Rafe was different, she knew. He had not set out to seduce her. He had, in fact, tried to play the honorable role. It wronged him to think that he would just leave now.

But he had not said he loved her.

Of course, Kyria thought, she had not said the words, either, but she knew that she felt them. She would not have gone to his bed, otherwise, no matter how carried away she had been with passion. She wanted to think that Rafe would not have done so, either, but every time she told herself that, her insecurities rose up to scoff at her.

To get her mind off Rafe, she had decided to think about the problem of the reliquary, instead. That problem, she found, was no more easily resolved. The box should go back to the Keepers, she thought. She could not help but believe that their story was genuine. But she was too honest to ignore the fact that she hated to give it up.

Finally, she had gone to the study and taken the reliquary out of the safe again. She held it in her lap, her thumb unconsciously caressing the black stone. The Heart of Night . . .

It seemed such an apt name. Lyrical and romantic, an appropriate jewel for a goddess. She thought about the worship of the goddess that Nelson Ashcombe had described to them. The world had once had a number of goddess cults, she knew; after all, the themes of harvest and rebirth were similar to the Druidic religion that had thrived in England in ancient times. Odd, how ancient religion had centered on the female . . .

"Fascinating, isn't it?" A man's voice spoke from the doorway of the study.

Kyria jumped, almost knocking the reliquary from her lap, and she whirled around to look at the doorway, her hands clamping around the box. "Oh!" She let out a shaky little laugh of relief. "Lord Walford. You startled me."

"I am sorry." He smiled at her and advanced into the room. "I hope you will excuse me for dropping in on you like this."

Kyria rose and set the box down on the small table beside her. "Of course. You are quite welcome here."

However, she thought, she intended to have a talk with Phipps about the servants' letting a visitor just walk in without announcing him first. She supposed they, too, must be excited by Theo's arrival, but still . . .

"Shall we repair to the drawing room?" she suggested, gesturing toward the door. "If you will excuse me, I will just put this away, and then I will join you."

"Oh, please, don't put it away." Walford stopped, looked abashed. "I am sorry. You must think me terribly presumptuous. But if that is the Reliquary of the Holy Standard you have there, I would very much like to look at it. Ashcombe told me about it. I have never seen the man so excited."

"Oh. Of course." Kyria picked up the box and held it out to him. She felt a bit uneasy about showing it to anyone, but after all, Walford had done them a favor by insisting that the archaeologist speak to them. Without Ashcombe, they would probably not have been able to rescue Alex the night before.

"Exquisite," Walford said, taking the reliquary in his hand and gazing reverently at it. "The Star of the Underworld," he breathed.

"What? Oh, yes, that is one of the names that Ashcombe said the diamond was called. I did not realize that you were interested in such things as the reliquary. I thought it was more your father's subject."

"Oh, I'm not interested in the reliquary," he said carelessly, handing the box back to her. Kyria turned away and began to rewrap the box and return it to the drawstring bag.

"It is the diamond that I desire," Walford went on behind her.

Kyria turned, suddenly uneasy. She found herself staring into the end of a revolver. The air rushed out of her lungs.

"You," she said at last. "It was you —"

"I have had the devil of a time getting it," Walford said conversationally. "I realized finally that I had to stop relying on subordinates and take the matter into my own hands. So —" he motioned with the pistol "— please walk out the door in front of me. I am putting my gun into my pocket, but I will still be able to shoot you if you decide to refuse."

Kyria walked out into the hall on legs that were suddenly wooden. How could Walford possibly hope to get away with taking the reliquary? She had seen him; she would simply go to the police and — It was then that it struck her. *He is making me walk out in front of him because he is planning on taking me with him! That way I will not be able to tell everyone what happened.* Her blood ran cold as she realized that the only way he could permanently keep her from revealing his identity was to kill her.

She stopped in the hallway. "No," she said firmly. "I won't go. Just take the thing and leave."

"My dear Lady Kyria, I cannot possibly do that. You must see that it is impossible. If you refuse to go, I will have to shoot you, and then all the servants will come running, and I will have to shoot them, as well. Unless you want to have their blood on your conscience, I suggest that you start walking."

Numbly, Kyria did as he said. The man was mad, she thought. He sounded perfectly reasonable, but his words were stark, staring mad!

She walked on, hoping that a maid or footman would see them and then tell Rafe and her brothers what had happened. Where were all the servants, anyway?

They made it to the front door without attracting anyone's notice, and Kyria was both relieved and terrified. Once they stepped outside, she realized that the servants were no longer in danger, so drawing a breath, she let out a piercing scream.

Walford, cursing, grabbed her around the waist and picked her up, carrying her to the dark, plain carriage that stood in front of their house. Kyria kicked and screamed and tried to hit him with the box. But it did no good. The man atop the carriage jumped down and opened the door for Walford, then grabbed the bag from her and tossed it in onto the seat. Together the two men grasped Kyria's arms and started shoving her into the carriage, as well, despite her struggles.

There was a flash of white, and Kyria realized that someone was running toward them, shouting. It was one of the Keepers! Hope surged in her, but Walford pointed his gun and fired, and the monk went down, blood staining his white robe.

"No!" Kyria screamed, and suddenly the world went dark as Walford punched her in the side of the head, then threw her into the carriage.

Rafe was humming beneath his breath as he alighted from the hansom and started up the steps to Broughton House. He was rather surprised that no footman opened the door at his approach, as was customary.

He had just entered the house when a wild-eyed footman came hurrying toward him. "Mr. McIntyre! Thank heavens!"

"What?" Alarm rose up in Rafe. "What is it? Where's Kyria?"

"That's just it, sir!" The footman looked close to tears. "She's been taken!"

For an instant Rafe could say nothing, could not even move. Then he sprang forward, grabbing the servant by the front of his jacket. "What the hell are you talking about? What happened?"

Fortunately for the footman, who went pop-eyed and started jabbering incoherently, Phipps came hurrying in, saying, "Mr. McIntyre!"

Rafe abandoned his unsatisfactory prey and turned to the other man. "Where's Kyria?"

"She has been abducted, sir." The butler retained his preternatural calm, although the level of his disturbance was evident in the beads of sweat that had formed at his hairline. "We thought she was leaving with a friend. Milly saw them walking out the front door, and she said that the man did not have hold of her and Lady Kyria did not seem to be forced. But there was quite a commotion after they stepped outside, and a man — I believe you call them Keepers, sir — was shot."

"Shot! Is he dead?"

"No, sir, merely wounded. The doctor is with him right now, but he insists on speaking with you. He will not let the doctor give him chloroform until he has spoken with you."

"Where is he?"

"Right this way, sir." The butler led him quickly toward the smaller formal dining room.

A gaggle of servants stood outside in the hall, obviously upset, and with them were the twins, white-faced and abnormally silent. When they saw Rafe, they ran to him.

"You've got to do something! They've taken Kyria!"

"I know. Phipps told me. Let me talk to the Keeper and find out what happened." Rafe put a hand on each boy's shoulder and gave a reassuring squeeze. "Hold fast."

The twins nodded, looking calmer. Rafe went past them into the dining room. The doctor was standing beside the long mahogany table, looking both worried and irritated, and before him on the table lay a whiterobed monk.

"Sir!" The Keeper saw Rafe and let out a relieved cry.

"Tell me what happened," Rafe said, going to his side and taking the hand the man held out to him. He was little more than a lad. His face was deathly white, and one side and sleeve of his robe were stained grimly with blood. "Did you see who took Kyria?"

"Yes, but I did not know him. He was . . . tall . . . dark hair." The man winced at a sudden pain, his words coming out in gasps. "She screamed. She was fighting. He threw her . . . in the carriage. I ran to them. He shot me."

"Can you tell me anything about the carriage? Was there anything distinctive about it?"

"Plain." The young man squeezed Rafe's hand harder, looking up earnestly into his face. "The reliquary. He was carrying a bag. I think the reliquary was in it. I could sense it. It called to me."

Rafe remembered Brother Jozef's similar

statement about the sacred object. Whatever feelings the monk might have about the reliquary, Rafe felt sure that he was right: the reliquary would be with them. It was, after all, what the man had come for.

"You did well," Rafe told the Keeper, giving his hand a squeeze. "I will take care of it now. Let the doctor get to work on you."

The young man nodded, closing his eyes in relief, and his hand slipped out of Rafe's grasp. Rafe turned and left the room. The twins, as well as all the servants, were waiting anxiously for him.

Rafe shook his head. "He doesn't know who the man was. Did only Milly see him?"

It appeared that she had been the only one. She came forward, her face tear-splotched, and told him that she had not recognized the man. "I'm so sorry, sir! I never thought there was anything wrong! She didn't act afraid."

"She wouldn't," Rafe said. "I imagine the fellow had a gun on her — you just couldn't see it."

"Do you think they took her to the place where I was?" Alex asked.

"I think it's unlikely, since we know about the building. I suppose it will have to be checked out, though. Phipps . . ."

He turned toward the butler, and at that moment, the front door flew open with a crash and there was the sound of running feet. "Phipps!"

A moment later Reed and Theo appeared at the end of the hall and hurried toward them.

"What the devil's going on?" Reed shouted, his face etched with worry.

"What did Phipps's message mean, 'Kyria's in trouble'?" Theo said.

"She has been kidnapped," Rafe replied, and told them the story. "The Keeper thinks they have the box, too, and I feel sure he's right."

"But if he has the box, why did he take Kyria, as well?" Reed asked.

Rafe looked grim. "Because she could identify him."

Theo's tanned face paled. "You mean, then, he would . . ."

". . . see to it that she *can't* identify him, I would imagine," Rafe finished for him. "We have to find her as soon as possible."

"Good God! Where do we start?"

Alex once again brought up the warehouse where he had been taken, but Reed, too, dismissed it as unlikely. "I can't imagine they would go back there, and the police found nothing that seemed to connect the place to anything."

"What about this opium den?" Theo asked.

Rafe nodded. "That's a better place to go, I think, although since we have already confronted them there, I wouldn't think they would take her there, either. I want to talk to Ashcombe again. He clearly knew something. When we followed him to the den, we could hear him arguing with someone about Alex's abduction. So he knows, if not the man behind all this, at least someone higher up in the organization. And just as clearly, he felt uneasy about kidnapping a child. He would have to be just as uncertain about the possibility of their murdering someone. I can break him, I'm certain of it."

Given the look on Rafe's face, no one was inclined to argue.

"Ashcombe?" Theo asked, looking puzzled. He had not heard all the details of the events of the previous night. "Are you talking about the archaeologist?"

"Yes. He is involved somehow." Rafe's face cleared. "Say, you can use your influence with Walford. If he confronts Ashcombe, the man will —"

"Lord Walford?" Theo frowned. "The old man? What are you talking about? I don't have —"

"No, his son," Reed explained impatiently. "The old man died a year or two ago, and his son came into the title." He looked back to Rafe. "But why would Theo have any influence with the man?"

"Because they are friends." At the blank looks on the other two men's faces, Rafe went on, "Lord Walford told Kyria that you and he had become friends when you were both in Turkey or somewhere."

"Good heavens, no!" Theo said. "Gerard is a rum one — I've never heard anything good about him. There were a number of unsavory rumors about him going around the English community in Turkey."

Rafe looked at him for a moment, his face hardening. "He *is* involved in it! Dammit to hell! How could I have been so stupid? I dismissed my suspicions about him because I thought it was merely jealousy."

"Walford? You think it's Walford behind this?" Reed asked.

"I don't know. But I think he may very well be involved in it. His archaeologist certainly is. Ashcombe has been searching for that box for years. Maybe he was doing it for his employer. Or maybe the two of them share the mania."

"Let's go talk to Ashcombe," Reed said. "We'll catch a cab. We haven't time to bring around the carriage."

For once, the twins did not protest when told they could not accompany them, and moments later, the three men were rolling down the street in a hansom. They were well armed, Rafe and Theo with a brace of pistols each and Reed with a shotgun. Theo also took the added precaution of concealing a scabbard with a rather large knife in the side of his boot, a souvenir, apparently, of his trip up the Amazon some years earlier.

At Ashcombe's house, Rafe did not even wait for the maid's protestations, but shoved open the door as soon as she opened it and marched inside, Reed and Theo following him. The maid's mouth dropped open as she took in the men, all obviously armed. Raising her hand, she pointed down the hallway at her employer's study.

Ashcombe was at his desk, and he jumped up, startled, when the door slammed open and Rafe barged in.

"Good Lord! What are you . . ." He straightened, squaring his shoulders, and went on, "What is the meaning of this intrusion?"

"I want the truth, Ashcombe, and I want it now." Rafe strode over to the man and wrapped his hand around the lapels of his jacket, twisting and jerking the man forward.

"I . . . I don't know what you mean."

"Who abducted Alex yesterday? Who were you talking to in that opium den? Who the hell is behind all this?"

Ashcombe gaped at Rafe, then began to sputter. Rafe gave him a single hard shake.

"Don't even try to lie. I will have the truth from you if I have to peel your skin off strip by strip to get it. He has taken the box *and* Kyria." Another shake. "What the hell is going on?"

"He . . . . he took Lady Kyria?" Ashcombe looked dismayed, and he glanced around vaguely. "Oh, my God. My God, I told him . . ."

"Who?" Reed barked. "Is it Walford?"

Ashcombe nodded. "He has gone mad! I told him he would go too far . . ."

Rafe released him, and the older man staggered back a little. He cast a look around at the three implacable faces, then sighed and began to talk. "Gerard was wild when he was young. He got into serious trouble here, and his father barely managed to buy his way out of it. Lord Walford sent him off to one of my digs, hoping it would straighten the boy out. It didn't. He didn't care for archaeology. All he cared about was himself — and pleasure. He . . . he got involved in the opium trade in Turkey. And he made a great deal of money."

He paused, then went on, "He came to me several years ago. He wanted me to find the Reliquary of the Holy Standard for him. Of course I had heard of it, but I had always dismissed it as a legend. He insisted that I change the direction of my studies, that I devote myself to finding it. Naturally, I told him that I would not — I answered only to his father. But he . . . he knew about my weakness, you see." Ashcombe cast a glance at Rafe.

"Your opium addiction," Rafe supplied.

Ashcombe nodded. "Yes, I was injured on a dig many years ago, and I was given opium for the pain. I came to depend on it, crave it, and it is easy enough to come by there. Gerard knew about it, you see, and he threatened to reveal it to my father. And he . . . he kept me supplied with it, even when I was in England. When he returned here to take the title, he set up that place, the one in Cheapside."

"So he owns the opium den," Reed said.

"And he wants the reliquary," Theo added.

Ashcombe nodded. "Yes, well, it isn't really the reliquary he wants. It's the Heart of Night."

"The what?" Theo asked.

"The black diamond," Rafe said. "He's only after the diamond? But why?"

"Because it is an object of great mysticism. Part of the religion of the goddess Inanna. When he was in the Middle East, he came to believe in the goddess. He feels that it was Inanna who helped him into the opium trade, who vanquished his enemies and enabled him to become the wealthy, powerful man that he is."

"He's insane!" Reed exclaimed.

Ashcombe nodded unhappily. "Yes. I am afraid that he is. He has become more and more determined to find that diamond over the last few years. Frankly, I wasn't sure that either it or the reliquary existed except in his mind — until you and Lady Kyria showed it to me here. Lord Walford is sick. He . . . well, as I told you, he was a wild young man, and he contracted syphilis long ago in his youth. He is already showing signs of the mania. He knows that he is unwell, that he will die. But he believes that the Heart of the Night can cure his illness."

"What?"

"I told you, the disease has affected his mind. He believes that the diamond and the goddess will give him immortality. He has started a group of worshipers. Some are men who worked for him in the Levant. Others are Englishmen, susceptible young gentlemen with too little to do and not much sense. They hold meetings and worship the goddess. Lord Walford wants to have a ceremony — the sort of thing I told you about the other day, Mr. McIntyre."

"That explains why he took the box, but what about Kyria?" Theo asked. "Why the devil did he take our sister?"

"Is he so far gone that he plans to kill her?" Reed added anxiously.

Ashcombe's gaze skittered around, and he started to speak, then paused, then cleared his throat. "He plans, I think, to reenact the ancient ceremony where the king, ah, couples with the goddess in the form of a priestess. The king, ah, becomes a god, immortal, and the goddess is reborn."

The three men stared at him, shocked. Finally Rafe said through bloodless lips,

"You are saying he means to use her in the ceremony, to *rape* her."

"And precisely how will she be reborn?" Theo asked him grimly.

"Well, in some of the cultures, it was merely a . . . a symbolic thing. The couple retired and, um . . . But in others, the king took the ceremonial knife and after the, ah, intercourse, the priestess, a virgin, of course, was, um . . . slain."

21

Kyria slowly returned to consciousness. Her head was pounding, and she had no idea where she was or why she was there. She closed her eyes and lay still for a moment, and gradually she began to remember the day. *Theo returned home late this morning, and then sometime this afternoon, he and Reed . . .*

Her eyes flew open as she remembered Lord Walford coming into the study unannounced. He had seized the reliquary at gunpoint and forced her to come along, too. She remembered walking to the front door, then out . . . After that, there was nothing.

Clearly, she thought, he succeeded in abducting her. Why else would she be in this strange room? She tried to sit up, and it was then that she realized that she was bound, hand and foot. It was not rope, but a soft, silken cord that did not abrade her skin. Her bound feet and hands were each tied to one of the posts of the bed, and she effectively could not move.

And she was not wearing her own

clothes. A shiver ran through her as she gazed down at her body. She was dressed in a white garment resembling something she might have seen on a piece of her father's pottery. A gold clasp fastened one shoulder, leaving a sweep of train that would fall down her back if she stood, and around her waist was a golden cord. Her hair had been taken down, and it fell in curls around her shoulders.

It made Kyria's skin crawl to think of someone changing her clothes while she was unconscious. Worse, she wondered if it had been Walford who had done it.

The door opened, and she tensed. Lord Walford entered. Kyria saw that he, too, was wearing a long, tuniclike costume, white, like hers, but with a purple train fastened at the shoulders with clips and trailing down his back. A gold belt went around his waist, and on it was fastened a scabbard with a jewel-encrusted hilt sticking out. His feet were clad in gold sandals.

It looked to Kyria as if they were dressed for a costume ball.

Walford smiled. "Ah, my goddess, you are awake now. I am glad. It is growing time for the ceremony. We eagerly await you."

Kyria stared at him dumbly. The man sounded quite mad.

"Please, do not be angry with me," he went on in an apologetic tone. "I am sorry that I had to hurt you. I would not have harmed you for the world, but there was no time to explain to you, to make you understand. I assure you, you have been treated with the utmost respect, as befits you."

"Respect?" Kyria asked, dismayed that her voice came out in a rusty croak. She looked down expressively at her clothes.

"Of course. Do not worry. It was not I who put on these garments. One of your handmaidens helped to dress you. You must, of course, be properly attired for the ceremony."

"Ceremony?" Kyria repeated. "What are you . . . ? I don't understand."

"No, neither did I, at first." He came closer to her, his eyes blazing with eager delight. "The goddess does not reveal all of her plan to us mortals until the time is right. But when you received the Heart of Night, I knew that it was meant to be. I saw for the first time the true wonder of Her plan, the breadth of Her wisdom."

The goddess? Kyria simply looked at her captor, thunderstruck. *Is he talking about the goddess Inanna that Ashcombe had told us about?*

"I knew she would give me immortality. I knew the sacred stone would heal me. But I did not understand until you appeared that I must conduct the entire ceremony. The warrior king must come to his goddess. And you — you are the very embodiment of the goddess, pure beauty and fire. It is you who must carry the dark jewel that Inanna brought forth from the depths of the underworld. You who must bring immortality to your mortal lover and be yourself reborn."

Kyria's mind was spinning. The man was clearly mad — and quite terrifying. She could not get around the fact that he sounded as if he intended to mate with her in the sort of ancient ceremony that Ashcombe had described to them. Everything within her quailed at the thought. *Oh, Rafe, where are you? Where are Reed and Theo? Do you have any idea where I am or what has happened?*

"No. Please, I know you think that this is what is meant, but I am quite sure that it is not," she said. "You have the box, you have the Heart of Night. You don't need me."

"Oh, no, my goddess. You test me. But I know now what must happen. I will not swerve from it. The time has come. Your worshipers await you."

He turned with a grand gesture and clapped his hands. Four men trooped into the room. They were dressed in hooded black robes. They wore no masks, and Kyria realized with a thrill of fear that they were not worrying about her identifying them. They knew that she would not leave this place alive.

The men came forward, and one of them bent to untie the cords that bound her feet to the bedpost. As soon as the knot came loose from the post, Kyria whipped back her legs and lashed upward, using the whole force of her body to crack the man in the face with her feet. His head snapped back, and he stumbled backward, falling and crashing into a chair. Kyria hopped off the bed, but her hands were still tied to posts and she could not move. In frustration she yanked at her rope.

"Bloody hell!" she exclaimed, using one of Theo's favorite oaths.

"Well, go get her," Walford said pettishly, waving the other men forward. He turned to Kyria. "You have no need to fight. You are going to be honored."

Kyria looked at the other men. "You dare to touch me!" she shouted at them.

She flung her hair back with a toss of her head, straightening as best she could while still attached to the bed, trying for as haughty a look as she could manage. "The goddess will smite you for laying a hand on her high priestess! You will die a violent and horrible death, for Inanna allows no harm to come to her handmaidens!"

She thought it was a pretty good speech, and it seemed to work on the men, for they hesitated and looked from her to Walford.

"Oh, for pity's sake!" Walford snapped irritably. "She is lying to you. The goddess wants us to conduct the ceremony. You know that. Take her downstairs." He quirked an eyebrow. "What, is this something you Englishmen haven't the courage to do? Do I have to call the bloody Turks?"

His remark seemed to decide the men, for they came forward, though they moved warily as they reached past Kyria and unfastened the other ropes from the bedposts.

"Then you are Englishmen?" Kyria gasped. She could see that, indeed, their hands and their faces inside the hoods were fair-skinned. Somehow this kicked her fear into an even greater anger. "Englishmen, and you would do this to a woman?"

They dragged her out from the bed a little, one man on either side of her, firmly grasping her arms. As they held her, Kyria immediately kicked out at the third man and then twisted, trying to kick the two who held her. It was difficult, however, to land much of any blow, as she had to kick sideways, and the men immediately began to drag her forward through the door, so that she had to use her feet to walk.

She did not cease struggling as they dragged her out the door after Walford, the other two men falling in behind them, one of them still cupping his sore jaw. Nor did she stop the steady stream of verbal condemnation she rained down on them, denigrating their ancestors, their courage, their strength and their masculinity.

The small procession made its way down a set of back stairs, coming out into a room, then going down and down a circular staircase for what seemed an eternity to Kyria. They came out at last onto a landing, which opened out onto a vast room. Kyria drew in a sharp breath.

The room was enormous, at least two stories tall, the ceiling supported by huge stone pillars. Around the gray-stone walls were sconces that held torches, casting an eerie, flickering light. Dozens of men in black robes stood in a ring around a raised dais in the center of the room. A block of dark marble lay in the middle of the dais, and on either end of it were low braziers. Both were lit, and thick smoke curled up from them, strongly aromatic.

Kyria remembered her dreams — the dark stone walls and the flickering torchlight, the braziers. She remembered, too, the fear that built inside her to the point of terror. *Did I dream this moment, foreseeing the future? Or was I remembering something, instead, some moment from thousands of years past?* Kyria shivered, the hair on the back of her neck prickling in a fear more primitive than the dread of what waited before her now.

Walford paused at the edge of the wide staircase leading down to the floor below, and all heads in the room turned toward him. When he had everyone's attention, he started down the stairs, Kyria and her guards right behind him. When they reached the bottom, two of the black-robed figures came forward, carrying cushions on which rested two golden circlets. Behind them marched another man, this one holding in his hands the Reliquary of the Holy Standard, turned so that the black diamond on the front of it faced upward.

The men knelt before Walford, and he held out his hands over their heads as if in blessing. Then he reached down and took the smaller of the two crowns and turned to Kyria. She saw that it was a simple golden band, the front of which rose into the Knot of Inanna. Gravely Walford set it onto her head. Turning, he picked up the matching crown and set it on his own head. Then, taking the reliquary, he held the box up in the same manner as the other man had and walked to the altar. They moved in a slow, measured tread, Kyria continuing to struggle even as she schemed to get out of this some way. She had to fight and delay them, to give Rafe time to find her. She realized with a cold stab of fear that it might be that he and her brothers would not be able to find her at all. In that case, her only hope was herself.

She looked at the dozens of men around her, their faces avid inside their hoods. It was a daunting prospect.

They reached the dais, and Walford set the reliquary down on the altar, then turned to Kyria. A ring on one end of the altar held a set of chains, manacles attached to the ends. The men beside Kyria held her arms tightly, pinning her in place, and Walford proceeded to place the manacles around her wrists. She saw that the chains were long enough for her to lie on the altar. The thought of what awaited her there made her stomach turn.

She closed her eyes, willing herself not to give in to her fear, but to remain calm and clearheaded. She needed to think, to take advantage of whatever opportunity might show itself. So she forced herself to stand calmly, facing Walford. She did not even try to kick out at her guards, for she was afraid that they might bind her ankles again, and she wanted them unbound if she ever managed to get the chance to run.

Kyria coughed. The smoke from the braziers was almost overwhelming, and she wondered whether the fire might have some sort of drug in it that intoxicated everyone in the room. She swallowed hard and made herself focus on Walford. She could not afford to fall into lassitude.

"We do not need this Christian box," Walford said with a sneer and, wrapping his fingers around the black diamond, tried to pull it away.

The stone remained firmly attached to the front of the reliquary. He tugged and tugged, his face growing red and the cords in his neck standing out, but still the stone stayed on the reliquary. His eyes flared with anger, and he muttered a curse.

Taking the box in his hand, he brought it down hard on the marble altar to break it. It remained intact. Again and again he crashed the reliquary onto the table, but it did not break. The scene would have been quite comical, Kyria thought, had it not been for the red haze of madness that rose in Walford's eyes.

Finally, panting in his rage, he whipped out the large ceremonial knife from its scabbard at his waist and stabbed at the sides of the stone, trying to pry it out or carve it from the box. The box remained impervious. Walford let out a shriek of rage and flung the reliquary onto the stone floor. It bounced and rolled off the small stage onto the floor below.

There it lay, the stone still very much attached.

Walford stood for a moment, glaring at it, but at last he pulled the tattered edges of his dignity about him and gestured at one of the black-clad figures to get the box. The man did so, handing it up to Walford. Kyria caught a glimpse of the man's rapt face, his mouth slightly open, his face slack and his eyes blank. Kyria suspected that Walford had made sure that all the men here had had a great deal more drugs than just whatever was smoking in the braziers.

Walford took the box and set it on the altar. He put his hands on the box, turned his face upward, and began to chant in a singsong voice:

Come to us, oh, Goddess.
Come to us, your humble servants.
Oh, Inanna, the beautiful,
    the magnificent . . .
Queen of Heaven, Queen of Night.
Come to us . . .

Ashcombe led Rafe and Kyria's brothers to Walford's mansion. It was, he told them, the place the man was most likely to have taken Kyria.

"It is the ancestral home," he told them, "a stone fortress, built after the Great Fire. It is no longer in a fashionable part of town, and the family more or less abandoned it. His father and mother lived in a more modern place in Mayfair. But when Gerard returned to take the title, he decided to refurbish the old place. He has modernized a small portion of it to live in and conduct his affairs." Ashcombe made a small moue of distaste, adding, "His father would be devastated if he had any idea how his son turned out."

He seemed lost in reverie for a moment, but then he went on. "The most significant change was the renovation of the cellars beneath the house. Gerard has turned them into one large empty room, where he has placed a marble altar. It is here that he conducts his worship of the goddess."

"You have been there? You've seen it?" Rafe looked hopeful.

Ashcombe nodded. "He wanted me to join his group of worshipers." He grimaced. "I found it appalling, and to call what they do 'worshiping,' I suspect, is largely inaccurate. God knows what all they do down there — smoke opium and drink and cavort with prostitutes, I imagine, and pretend it's all some sort of religion."

"Why aren't you there, then, for this ceremony?" Reed asked.

"I refused to join. I told him I was too old for such nonsense. As he was still avidly searching for the reliquary at the time, I think he needed me too much to force me to do it against my will. Besides, he probably decided I would just throw a damper on the proceedings."

"But you can get us into that room," Rafe said.

Ashcombe nodded. "Oh, yes, at least, I

know where it is. One goes in a side door. There will probably be a guard or two."

"We'll take care of them," Theo assured him grimly.

The estate was indeed in a run-down area close to the Thames, an area that had been fashionable hundreds of years before. Stone walls surrounded the house, with tall iron gates barring the drive. There was no one standing guard, but Rafe quickly climbed the gates and opened them to let in the others. They left them open and instructed the hansom cabdriver to wait on the street. A gold sovereign and the promise of more to come ensured his compliance.

They hurried down the driveway, moving as fast as they could without leaving Ashcombe behind. The square, stone house loomed up in front of them, dark and foreboding. There were no lights burning in any of the windows. Ashcombe went around to the side, where a tower jutted out. A black-robed guard stood outside the tower, leaning back against the wall, arms crossed.

Rafe grasped Ashcombe's arm, halting him, and glanced at the other two men. They nodded to him, and the four men spread out and began to creep closer to the guard. The guard did not see any of them until they were almost upon him. He glanced to the side and saw Theo, and he let out a cry, yanking a knife from a scabbard at his waist. But before he could lunge at Theo, Rafe brought down the butt end of his pistol on the back of his head, and the man crumpled to the ground.

Quickly they stripped him of his weapon, robe and a ring of keys, then tied his hands and feet together using the ascots Theo and Rafe wore. Rafe donned the robe and unlocked the door to the tower. Inside was a round room, empty except for another guard, who stood at an inner door. He turned questioningly toward Rafe when he entered. Rafe crossed the floor in two quick strides and felled him with a swift blow to the jaw. The others came in behind him. They used Ashcombe's and Reed's neckties this time to bind the man, then unlocked the inner door. A dark, narrow staircase wound down in a spiral before them.

"The room is at the bottom of the stairs," Ashcombe whispered.

"All right, let's go," Rafe said. "Ashcombe, you can stay here or go, whichever you wish."

The man's face firmed. "I am with you."

"Good, then. Come on."

They went down the stairs, moving as quickly as they could along the dimly lit staircase. After a time, they began to hear the faint murmur of voices. The sound grew steadily louder until at last they emerged onto a large landing. They stared down at the vast room before them in amazement.

Its very size was awe-inspiring, but what riveted their attention was the dais in the center of the cellar room. On it stood a dark altar, and at one end of it was Kyria, chains linking her hands to the marble slab. Her hair was down, with a simple gold band around it like a tiara. She wore a white robe, and in the flickering torchlight, she looked like a figure straight off of an ancient vase. Beside her stood Lord Walford, wearing a white tunic with a purple train. A narrow gold circlet sat on his head, matching Kyria's. His hands were closed over something, and he was chanting.

Hear us, oh, Goddess.
Mother of Heaven.
Mother of Earth.
Hear the cries of your children
Who wait here in the dark for you.
Hear us and come.

Rafe and the others looked at each other, swept with relief that Kyria was alive and seemingly unharmed, but at the same time wondering exactly how they were going to set her free. They were greatly outnumbered, at least twenty to four by Rafe's reckoning, and he wasn't sure exactly how much help the older, opium-addicted Ashcombe would be to them in a fight.

They were, of course, well armed, with at least twenty-four shots between him and Theo without their having to reload. However, because of Walford's close proximity to Kyria, the shotgun Reed carried was effectively useless, and Rafe was reluctant even to use the pistols, given the ease with which a stray bullet could hit Kyria.

He leaned closer to Theo and Reed and murmured, "Look, I'm a pretty good shot. I figure I can hit one or two on the edge of the crowd, farthest from Kyria, and that'll send them into a panic. Then we can charge down the stairs and —"

Rafe stiffened, hearing the scrape of feet on stone behind them. He whirled around, as did the other men, and went down into a crouch, pistols up and aimed at the opening to the staircase. There were more muffled noises, and a white-robed figure emerged quietly onto the landing.

The Keepers! Rafe sagged in relief and lowered his guns as the four remaining Keepers filed silently out of the staircase, sticks in hand. Bringing up the rear of the group was the Russian Prince, Dmitri Rostokov, dressed in formal attire with some sort of sash across his chest and a long-barreled pistol in his hand.

Theo glanced at his brother questioningly, and Reed nodded, gripping his arm and leaning close to whisper, "These are the Keepers of the Holy Standard. They'll help us. I don't know who that other chap is."

"Don't ask." Rafe moved silently over to Brother Jozef, who looked as surprised to see Rafe's group as they were to see his. Rafe glanced toward the Russian, but decided to follow his own advice. Whatever reason had brought the prince with the monks, this was no time for questions.

"The reliquary has called to us," Brother Jozef whispered to Rafe. "Great harm confronts it, and we have felt this. So we have come."

Rafe saw no reason to dispute whatever strange homing instinct had drawn the Keepers. "Good," he said. "Now we are nine." He drew the other men over to witness the bizarre scene below them.

Kyria watched Walford as he continued to call down the goddess. His face was rapt, his eyes wild. Suddenly he turned and grabbed Kyria's hands, forcing them onto the diamond, his own hands on top of hers holding them down.

Sacred Goddess, hear me.
Come to us in all your glory.
Come now to the sacred marriage bed.
In light do you walk. At your
    appearance do we rejoice.
Honeyed are your lips. Your mouth
    gives life.
Come to me, oh glorious Goddess.
Come to this sacred couch and all
    your myriad charms reveal.
Your humble servant, I call on you.
Come and restore all life.
Bring to me your divine and
    unending power.
Let me join with you and reign forever.
Bathe me in your sacred blood.
    Give to me your unending life.

Kyria gripped the reliquary, the huge diamond digging into her palm. She closed her eyes as an idea came to her.

"Oh, sacred Goddess!" she cried. "Glorious Inanna."

Beside her, Walford's voice stumbled to a halt, and he turned to look at her. Maybe, Kyria thought, she could catch him off guard and crack him in the head with the box. She struggled to remember all the things she had heard Walford and Ashcombe say about Inanna.

"Mother of Heaven!" she shouted, standing tall and straight and flinging back her head. She opened her eyes and looked intently up at the top of the far columns. "Mother of Earth! Pay heed to me. Thy daughter calls you. Come to me and endow me with thy strength."

Kyria could sense that she had the attention of everyone in the room. Walford was staring at her, and his hands fell slowly away from Kyria's on the box. Kyria curled her fingers more tightly around the diamond. It felt strangely warm against her palm.

"Come to thy handmaiden's aid, oh, Mother of the Gods!"

Warmth seemed to flow from the diamond into her hand and up into her arms, and Kyria was aware of a tremendous surge of power. She felt faintly dizzy as words rushed up from her throat, pouring out of her in a hoarse voice quite unlike her own.

Sovereign Goddess, come to me in
my hour of need.
Goddess of Love. Goddess of War.
Lady of the nether abyss.
You brought life out of the darkness.
Power out of weakness.
Now give me thy power.

The diamond seemed to throb in her hand. Her fingers curling around the large stone, Kyria lifted her hand and the diamond came away easily. It glowed with a strange, dark light, red pulsing in its depths and shining through her fingers, the glow permeating her palm so that it shone deep red, as if her blood had turned to fire.

Walford took a step back, staring at Kyria, his jaw falling open in awe.

"Mother of all the heavens, help me now," Kyria cried, raising her hand. "Destroyer of the wicked, help me now!"

With a final, primal shriek, she threw herself at Walford, bringing her hand down and slamming the magnificent stone with all her force into Walford's forehead.

He staggered back and fell to the floor with a crash. And at that moment, all hell broke loose.

Wild cries came from above them, and shots rang out. Kyria dived to the floor, crawling up against the end of the altar, seeking its shelter, as a gang of men erupted down the staircase, screaming.

They plowed into the group of worshipers, already demoralized by Kyria's performance and the sudden loss of their leader. Confused and slowed by drugs, the men barely put up any resistance as Rafe, Kyria's brothers and the Keepers laid about them with fists, sticks and the butts of their guns.

The fight was over in a few minutes, and Rafe shoved his way through to the dais. He bent solicitously over Kyria, who was crouched on the floor, leaning weakly against the cool marble of the altar.

"Kyria. Kyria, my love?" He reached out and gently brushed his hand over her hair. "Are you all right?"

Kyria looked up at him. She felt suddenly weak, and she started to tremble uncontrollably. "Rafe! Oh, Rafe!"

She flung herself into his arms, tears pouring from her eyes. "Oh, Rafe, hold me! Don't leave me."

"Never," Rafe promised solemnly, his arms tightening around her. "Never."

"I doubt we'll ever know the whole story," Reed said, standing beside the fireplace, his arm stretched across the mantel.

"No, probably not," Theo agreed.

They both looked over at their sister, who was curled up on the sofa, Rafe by her side, his hand in hers. Kyria had been unusually quiet since Rafe had unfastened her manacles and carried her from Walford's house last night.

Rafe had taken Kyria straight up to her room and put her to bed, telling her brothers that he would spend the night with her, his eyes daring them to deny him. They had agreed without a murmur, and after a few minutes of holding the twins to her, Kyria had lain down, and Rafe had closed the door, shutting out the rest of the world.

Reed and Theo had taken care of the rest of it, sending for the police and leading them to Walford's mansion to show them Walford's trussed-up followers, as well as Walford himself. He, it seemed, had died in a freakish manner, his forehead, right between his eyes, crushed. The police could not imagine what had hit him with such force at precisely the right spot to kill him.

The Moreland brothers had merely shrugged and said they had no idea.

The Keepers had just visited Kyria and

the others at Broughton House, once again bringing along the Russian prince. They had left the house with the sacred reliquary, but the huge black stone they had insisted that Kyria keep, saying only, "It belongs with you, madam."

"I was surprised to find that Prince Dmitri was actually helping the Keepers," Kyria commented.

"Yes. He explained it to me last night after the fight," Reed said. "The Keepers moved onto his lands a long time ago when they moved farther northward to escape the Islamic Ottoman Empire. His family has been their protectors ever since. He took the loss of the reliquary hard."

"His family's honor and all that," Theo added.

"What about Habib and the Frenchman?" Rafe asked.

Reed shrugged. "The peelers have questioned them both. Habib finally cracked and admitted that it was he who tracked down Kousoulous all the way from Turkey and killed him at Broughton Park. He had been working for Walford for several years, his primary task being to find the reliquary. He admitted Walford's entire scheme to get the box, including hiring those men to invade our house. Apparently, Walford decided that hired help were too untrustworthy and incompetent, so he got his own men to kidnap Alex. I suspect when they track down the ownership of that warehouse, it will turn out to belong to Walford."

"But Brulatour, oddly enough, turned out to be just a collector of ancient objects," Reed went on. "He is apparently a nouveau-riche French industrialist who spends all his spare time snapping up as many valuable artifacts as he can."

"Just the sort of fellow I despise," Theo said, glowering. "He only wants to acquire objects for his own glory. No interest at all in preserving a people's history and culture."

"But how did he even know about the reliquary?" Kyria asked.

"Apparently Habib in some unguarded moment told another dealer why he was going to England, and this chap sent word to Brulatour. Monsieur Brulatour arrived and spoke to Habib, who decided to tell him you had the reliquary in return for several thousand francs. Habib's only god, I believe, is Mammon." Reed shrugged.

Reed looked at Theo, then at Kyria. He shifted uncomfortably from foot to foot. "How, uh . . . are you feeling all right, Kyria?"

Kyria favored him with a small smile.

"Yes. I am. I just, I don't know, feel a little dazed. When I think about what I did and said last night . . . it was so strange. It feels almost as if it were a dream."

"You gave me cold chills," Rafe said, smiling.

"When you held up that diamond and starting calling on the goddess . . ." He gave an exaggerated shiver. "I hope to never get you angry."

Kyria grimaced.

"What are you going to do with that diamond, Kyria?" Theo asked curiously.

She reached into her pocket and pulled out the stone. She rubbed her thumb over it. "I have been thinking about that. It's beautiful, but I don't think it's meant to be kept in a safe. You know where I thought it would fit best?"

"Where?"

"That clearing in the woods near Broughton Park, the one with the stones?"

"Ah." The others nodded, thinking of the secluded grove with its silent, eerie grouping of stones.

"It seems the sort of place where the goddess belongs. One of the stones has a deep hollow, and I think I will put it right in there."

"I think you're right." Rafe leaned closer

to her and planted a kiss on her forehead.

"Kyria!"

They all looked up as Con and Alex pelted into the room.

"Are you all right?" Alex asked.

"Reed said we had to be quiet around you," Con said. "Is that true?"

Kyria smiled and pulled her brothers close for a hug. "No. But you have to let me give you an extra hug and not wriggle away."

"Ah, Kyria . . ." they chorused, blushing.

They stayed for a few minutes, showing Kyria the interesting things they had picked up in the garden this morning, and then Theo and Reed shooed them out.

"I think it's time we let Kyria have a little of that rest and quiet," Reed said, firmly guiding his younger brothers out the door.

Theo, with a grin and a wink at Kyria and Rafe, followed. For the first time today, Rafe and Kyria were alone.

Kyria looked down at her hands. She still felt tired from the events of the previous night. But that was not the only reason she had been so quiet.

Rafe had held her in his arms all through the night, and it had been glorious. She had felt safe and secure and warm, and she knew that she never wanted it to stop. She loved Rafe, and she wanted to spend the rest of her life with him. She understood now why people married. She could not imagine anything more wonderful than spending the rest of her life with Rafe.

But Rafe had never spoken a word of love to her. No matter how tightly he had held her, no matter how sweetly he had kissed her, he had not said he loved her or wanted to marry her. She knew he had enjoyed the passion between them, but surely that was not enough to keep him.

Their adventure was over. He had no more reason to stay. Soon he would set out on his tour of Europe again, and then she would lose him. The thought filled Kyria with sadness.

Rafe stood up and walked away from her, then turned and walked back. "Uh, Kyria . . . I, um, I had something I wanted to talk to you about."

Kyria's heart felt like lead in her chest. *He is going to tell me he is leaving!* She could not raise her eyes to him, and she was afraid that she would start to cry.

"All right," she said, struggling to keep the tears from her voice.

"You know, when I came to England, I was meaning to travel all around Europe.

And the thing is, I think it would be better with someone to guide me. You know, someone sophisticated. So what I was thinking was that, well, maybe you'd like to do that with me."

"What?" His words were so far from what she had expected that Kyria raised her head and stared at him. *Is he asking me to be his mistress?* The idea pierced her heart.

"We'd have to delay it, of course, for a few more months. I know you would want a bang-up wedding. But then, the trip would make a nice honeymoon."

"Honeymoon!" Kyria gaped, barely able to believe her ears. "Honeymoon! Are you . . . are you asking me . . ."

"Ah, hell, Kyria, I'm no good at this," Rafe said candidly. He plunged his hand into his pocket and brought out a box.

Walking back to her, he sank down on one knee in front of her, opened the box and held it out to her. Kyria's hand flew to her lips as she stared at the large, sparkling emerald ring.

"A ring! You bought me a ring!"

"Yeah. That's where I was yesterday afternoon. I know I should ask your father's permission and all that, but I figured I better ask you first or you'd have my hide.

So I went to find you a ring. I wanted one that would suit you. I know a lot of women prefer diamonds, but this looked like you to me. You see, it's almost exactly the color of your eyes."

"It's beautiful," Kyria said in a shaky voice, tears starting in her eyes.

"Oh, here, now, don't cry," Rafe exclaimed, and brought her hand to his lips to kiss. "If you don't want to marry me, just say so. I know your family might not approve, since I'm an American with no title. But there is all that silver — I can support you. And nobody could love you more than I. Before I met you, I didn't think I could love anyone or anything again. The war killed something in me. I had no heart, no home. Then you dropped into my life, literally. And I knew then that you are my heart. Wherever you are is my home. I love you, Kyria."

"Oh, Rafe! Rafe! I didn't know you loved me! You never said so. I thought you were going to tell me you were leaving."

"Leaving!" Rafe stared at her, then laughed. "No, I'm not going anywhere. Even if you turn me down, I'll just stick around and keep on trying. That's the way I am." He paused, then prodded gently, "Well, *will* you marry me?"

"Yes!" Kyria beamed. "Of course I'll marry you. I love you desperately."

"You don't need to do it desperately." Rafe grinned and stood up, pulling Kyria up into his arms. "Just do it forever."

"I will. Forever."

AUTHOR'S NOTE

For those of you who like to separate fact from fiction:

The Emperor Constantine, his vision, the battle standard, the battles between him and the other emperors, and his tolerance for the early Christian Church can all be found in history books, although I have presented them here in a much-shortened and compressed version. Sadly, the sacking of Constantinople and the plunder of its churches' treasures by the Western knights during the Fourth Crusade is also true. The worship of a powerful goddess, variously named Inanna, Astarte, Ishtar, etc., flourished in ancient Mesopotamia and the surrounding areas, and the tale of her descent into the underworld and rebirth were, in some form, part of that worship.

However, the reliquary of this book and its contents, the black diamond known as the Heart of Night, the Keepers, the twisted version of the ceremony performed herein, as well as all the characters and events in this book, are entirely figments of my imagination and, as they say, bear no resemblance to any actual person or persons, living or dead.

Candace Camp

ABOUT THE AUTHOR

CANDACE CAMP is the bestselling author of over forty contemporary and historical novels. She grew up in Texas in a newspaper family, which explains her love of writing, but she earned a law degree and practiced law before making the decision to write full-time. She has received several writing awards, including the *Romantic Times* Lifetime Achievement Award for Western Romances.

The employees of Thorndike Press hope you have enjoyed this Large Print book. All our Thorndike and Wheeler Large Print titles are designed for easy reading, and all our books are made to last. Other Thorndike Press Large Print books are available at your library, through selected bookstores, or directly from us.

For information about titles, please call:

(800) 223-1244

or visit our Web site at:

www.gale.com/thorndike
www.gale.com/wheeler

To share your comments, please write:

Publisher
Thorndike Press
295 Kennedy Memorial Drive
Waterville, ME 04901